**"Are you saying you were in the cave during the rescue?" Marina asked Varden.**

His expression became solemn; she fancied he looked almost reverent. "In the embrace of Gaia. Yes, I was there. She was reaching out to you. Could you feel it?" His voice was a low rumble.

Marina didn't reply. Her moments of commune with Gaia had been private and sacred, and the fact that Varden had felt the same… perhaps even was attuned to her personal, electric connection to Mother Earth…unsettled her.

He seemed to understand, and it disconcerted her even more when he said, "Much as I despise admitting it, Mariska Aleksandrov, you are instrumental to the Skaladeskas and their—our—connection to Gaia. To protecting her. You are the heir, after all."

His steady gaze caught and held her eyes, and for a moment, Marina felt the shimmer of connection with Varden. It was the same energy she felt when she was in Lev's presence, or when she was close to Gaia, recognizing Her power and life.

"Lev needs you to stay alive," Varden went on, his voice hardly more than a low rumble. "And you must understand that you're in danger. Not only from Hedron, but also from him." He flicked his eyes from hers to the space behind Marina, toward Bruce.

# Other Books by Colleen Gleason

## The Gardella Vampire Hunters

### Victoria
*The Rest Falls Away*
*Rises the Night*
*The Bleeding Dusk*
*When Twilight Burns*
*As Shadows Fade*

### Macey/Max Denton
*Roaring Midnight*
*Raging Dawn*
*Roaring Shadows*
*Raging Winter*
*Roaring Dawn*

---

## The Draculia Vampires
*Dark Rogue: The Vampire Voss*
*Dark Saint: The Vampire Dimitri*
*Dark Vixen: The Vampire Narcise*
*Vampire at Sea: Tales from the Draculia Vampires*

---

## Wicks Hollow Series

Ghost Story Romance & Mystery
*Sinister Summer*
*Sinister Secrets*
*Sinister Shadows*
*Sinister Sanctuary*
*Sinister Stage*
*Sinister Lang Syne*

## Stoker & Holmes Books

(for ages 12-adult)
*The Clockwork Scarab*
*The Spiritglass Charade*
*The Chess Queen Enigma*
*The Carnelian Crow*
*The Zeppelin Deception*

## The Castle Garden Series
*Lavender Vows*
*A Whisper of Rosemary*
*Sanctuary of Roses*
*A Lily on the Heath*

## The Envy Chronicles
*Beyond the Night*
*Embrace the Night*
*Abandon the Night*
*Night Beckons*
*Night Forbidden*
*Night Resurrected*
*Tempted by the Night* (only available to newsletter subscribers; sign up here: http://cgbks.com/news)

## The Lincoln's White House Mystery Series
(writing as C. M. Gleason)
*Murder in the Lincoln White House*
*Murder in the Oval Library*
*Murder at the Capitol*

## The Marina Alexander Adventure Novels
(writing as C. M. Gleason)
*Siberian Treasure*
*Amazon Roulette*
*Sanskrit Cipher*

## The Phyllida Bright Mysteries
(writing as Colleen Cambridge)
*Murder at Mallowan Hall* (Oct 2021)

# SANSKRIT CIPHER

## A MARINA ALEXANDER ADVENTURE

### C. M. GLEASON

*Sanskrit Cipher: A Marina Alexander Adventure*

Copyright © 2021 by Colleen Gleason

All rights reserved. No part of this publication may be used
or reproduced or transmitted in any manner whatsoever, electronically, in print, or
otherwise, without the prior written permission of Colleen Gleason, except in the
case of brief quotations embodied in critical articles and reviews.

PUBLISHER'S NOTE: This is a work of fiction. Names, characters, places, and incidents either are the product of the author's imagination or are used fictitiously. Any
resemblance to actual persons, living or dead, business establishments, events, or locales
is entirely coincidental.

Cover and interior design: The Killion Group, Inc.

*To Gary March, D.O.:*
*for all of your ideas, brainstorming, expertise, and,*
*most importantly, angst over the bees—thank you*
*from the bottom of my heart.*

*And to Patricia Denke, PhD:*
*for your entomological expertise and enthusiasm*
*(not to mention your love for Eli), as well as the loan*
*of your name—I couldn't have done it without you.*

# PRELUDE

*Two thousand years ago*
*In the shadow of the Himalayas*

The sun had just begun to rise. The mists from the staggering mountains looming above the village still curled, steaming, from the ground. The world was frosted with a chill gray cast, but the pale pink that was barely glowing from beyond the far edge of the world indicated that the gods had blessed the Earth by allowing another sunrise.

It was an auspicious beginning to the annual hunt for precious and sacred honey.

Timbal, who'd been born twelve summers ago, was the youngest of the hunters. He fairly danced with impatience as his grandfather Bhulat murmured a prayer of thanks for a day dawning clear and still. Timbal knew it was important to thank the gods for their favor, but he wanted them to be on their way!

Bhulat, the patriarch of a family blessed with the task of foraging for honey, was leading his last hunt today. He would be turning over the role to his son, Khlari, who was Timbal's father.

Someday, Timbal himself would be leading the group. He fairly burst with pride thinking of the day he and *his* sons and grandsons would be sent off into the misty morning by their village. The entire village relied on Timbal's family to bring back the sweet and succulent golden liquid that was used for many purposes.

Today was his first hunt, and he would begin the first task of taking on his family's tradition by shouldering the heavy coil of the rope ladder. Father had warned him it would be heavy and that he could pass it off to the next youngest when he tired, but Timbal was determined not to ask for help during the half-day's journey. No other first-time member had succeeded in carrying the heavy coil the entire distance, and he intended to become a legendary honey hunter from the start.

The ladder was no light burden, for it weighed nearly as much as Timbal's younger sister. And each hunt required a new ladder to be woven from fresh bamboo fibers and reed. Thus, it took many months to create. During its construction, the materials were intertwined with prayers, incantations, and protections. When completed, the ladder was long enough to cross the entire village three times.

Since he had been five summers of age, Timbal had assisted his family members with the weaving, each time waiting impatiently for his chance to go with the men.

At last the day had come.

As the entire village came out to bid the hunters farewell, Timbal straightened his shoulders and adopted a serious expression. He would have reached for the rope ladder and hoisted it to his shoulder, but his father laid a hand on him and shook his head. *Not yet.*

Timbal hid his frustration. He would manage it. The ladder wasn't so very heavy that he couldn't stand and hold it for the moments of the blessing, then continue on their way.

A pointed look from his mother had Timbal turning his attention to the *paju*, one of the village's two shamans. The elder bestowed protections on the hunters, their rope ladder, and the live chicken they would sacrifice just before the hunt itself.

And then, *finally*, they were off.

The hunters' path was strewn with rocks, boulders, and tufts of grass determined to grow in such intolerant soil. Timbal strode along in bare feet, unconcerned by the rough terrain and enthusiastic about the task ahead. Neither his roomy tunic, woven from wool and hemp, nor the trousers that ended above his ankle did much to protect him from the chill air here in the foothills of the Great Mountains.

By the time the sun had risen above the horizon and was near the tops of the lowest trees, Timbal began to wonder how much further they must walk. The coil of rope seemed to grow heavier with every step, and though he shifted it from shoulder to shoulder, the ache never seemed to dissipate even when the burden changed. Its rough hemp and bamboo abraded the skin of his neck and the top of his shoulder.

"Allow Arhat to carry the ladder for a time, my son," his father said after they stopped for a brief rest and to drink.

But Timbal refused, lifting the ladder back to his shoulder with renewed determination.

Yet, as the journey wore on and the sun grew higher and warmer, his steps lagged. He began to focus only on putting one foot in front of the other, over and over again. He was dimly aware of conversation, singing, and the random cluck of the chicken tucked under Father's arm, but he was far too out of breath to join in any of the camaraderie.

He would finish this.

He would do it.

And then, perhaps, he'd be the youngest man ever to climb the ladder in the quest for honey.

At last, Grandfather called a halt to the expedition in a clearing at the base of a sheer cliff. Timbal, who was suddenly elated because he'd managed to carry their ladder the entire way, was relieved to slide the heavy coil from his shoulder and let it collapse on the ground. He glanced at his father, who'd been watching him with solemn eyes. A brief nod and small smile indicated Khlari's approval.

"Timbal." He looked over as his grandfather pointed. "There. Do you see?"

Timbal's eyes widened as he beheld the massive bee nests attached to the side of the cliff. Each one was as tall as a man, and as wide as two of them. The large, flat golden nests glimmered with the life of the busy, moving bees, creating a shimmering relief against the harshness of the rock wall on which they were built.

The only other beehive Timbal had ever seen was so small that a man could carry it. It had been a clay-made hive in the shape of a large urn, its mud base strengthened with reeds and grasses. This special hive had been borne on the back of a traveling holy man who'd visited their village some summers ago.

A shout yanked Timbal's attention to the awesome glittering bee nests above him. He helped his uncles and father unpack their meager belongings and arrange them in a small camp. But all the while, he had to peek at what his grandfather was doing.

Bhulat had crouched near a large, flat stone the size of ten men's hands and mixed up a thick paste of millet until it was the consistency of mortar. Then, with his practiced, gnarled fingers, he modeled the paste into the figure of one of the mountain spirits, or *pari*.

By the time he finished the crude sculpture, the hunters had organized their camp and Khlari had started a small fire. The five gathered around as Bhulat placed his *pari* figure on the large stone.

Then, speaking the prayers and chants he'd been saying for over forty years—ones he'd learned from his father, who'd learned from his father before him, and the ones Timbal would someday learn—Grandfather Bhulat sprinkled the hunters' offerings onto the stone: millet, rice, sheep's wool, fragrant twigs, and a bundle of sage and juniper.

At the proper moment, Khlari offered his father a cone of thin bark wrapped around a stick and then set ablaze. Grandfather took the torch and set the bundle of herbs and twigs on fire, offering a final chant as it crackled merrily and released a pungent scent into the air.

The chicken met its end on the same altar table, executed as a sacrifice to the mountain spirit in hopes that he would spare their lives during the dangerous task ahead of them. The head was presented to Bhulat, and he sprinkled its blood over the offerings.

As Timbal helped prepare their dinner of chicken and rice, he looked up at the sheer, looming cliff that rose above their camp. Now he understood why the ladder must be so long, and so heavy, and he burst with pride that he, and he alone, had carried it the whole distance.

Before he'd seen the mountainside, Timbal had imagined himself dangling from the rope, high above the ground, calmly and expertly doing the work that today would fall to his father and eldest uncle. He'd pictured himself lowering down a rope like the first king, Gnak'ri-bstan-po, had done on his descent to Earth from heaven. But now that he was faced with the mountain's mind-boggling height and the unrelenting starkness of its stony cliff face that seemed to glare down at them, Timbal was secretly relieved he wouldn't be the one taking the risk.

Not yet.

Maybe next year.

At last his grandfather said, "Start the fires."

Timbal's pulse leapt. *Now* it began: the sacred, dangerous hunt for honey.

Three large pyres rose from along the base of the cliff. The older, dry wood had been placed on the bottom of each pile where the fire was lit, and the top covered with newer branches and some damp leaves and grass to make the blaze smoky.

"Watch," said Grandfather Bhulat, curling his fingers around Timbal's arm as they looked up. "The bees—do you see? They are afraid their nests will be burned. So what do they do?"

Timbal knew the answer to that. "They eat."

"They stuff themselves full—as we do in preparation for a long journey—so they can travel far to safety without tiring. And that is good for us, why?"

"Because...because if they are full, they are slow. And the smoke confuses them. So maybe they won't be bothered to sting."

Bhulat gave a rare smile. "You have been listening. And now we begin, Timbal. Watch your father."

Before he began the dangerous ascent, Timbal's father turned to the effigy of the mountain spirit and knelt before it, bowing his head as he asked for permission from the *pari* to climb the mountain, and for safe passage. Then he picked up the rope ladder, and he and his brother Viri began to climb the mountain.

Instead of attempting to make their way up the sheer face of the cliff where the bees' nests clung, they took a different path on a gentler side of the mountain—still rocky and difficult, but more accessible than the choppy vertical rise. Viri carried the long bamboo poles called tangos, along with a satchel of other equipment.

While Timbal and two of his uncles stoked the fires on the ground and opened up the broad baskets made from reeds, they watched the pair climb the cliff like the goats many of their villagers tended: quickly, and with great agility. The thick smoke from the three fires rose, already bothering the bees, but the climbers were too far to the south of the cliff face for it to clog their eyes and noses yet.

Once Khlari reached the crest of the cliff, he tied the long ladder to the most stable tree then threw the rope over the cliff. The ladder was so long that it fell more than halfway down the side of the mountain—but still ended much higher than any man would care to jump or fall. Timbal realized he was holding his hands in tight fists as he watched his father check the knots on the ladder.

Timbal could hardly see through the thick smoke, and his eyes stung as he peered at the activity above as his father took the pair of long tangos from Viri. Timbal was so intent on watching that he nearly jumped out of his skin when one of his uncles shouted and tossed one end of a large honey basket to him.

Gripping the handle and holding his side of the basket wide open, Timbal hardly breathed as his father climbed down the swaying ladder while managing the long bamboo tangos and a torch in one hand.

With the smoke from below billowing around him, the flames from the torch dangerously near his ladder, and the threatened bees beginning to realize there was more danger afoot, Khlari and his descent made Timbal wonder if that was how the gods and shamans felt when they climbed down the *dmu-t'ag*—the ladder stretching from heaven to Earth—into the dark, dangerous underworld.

But his father had been doing this since before Timbal was born. He knew just how to safely balance the tangos and torch, and how to avert his face from the brunt of the smoke and worst of the bees as he made his way from rung to rung. After what seemed like forever, he reached the height of the first nest. Because the nest clung to the cliff face, and the ladder fell straight down away from the stony surface, Khlari needed to use the bamboo poles in order to reach and attack his prize.

"Here," shouted Timbal's basket partner, and they moved so they were in position beneath the nest.

Through all of this activity, Bhulat sat in front of the millet effigy of the *pari*, praying while keeping one eye on the work his family was doing. Somehow, that gave Timbal comfort while he watched, breathless, as his father balanced on the ladder.

Khlari's feet, hardly visible from the ground because of the smoke, were hooked around the sides of the ladder, and an arm was laced through one of the rungs. He tucked the handle of the torch into a loop in one of the sides of the ladder above him, adjusting it so the flames weren't close enough to set the bamboo weave on fire. Then he needed both hands to maneuver the tangos, using them like two long chopsticks to push, prod, and pull the lower part of the nest free from its moorings.

Timbal knew this bottom part of the nest was where the immature bees lived—and this larvae was delicious. The wax therein would be rendered and used for candles as well as sculpting effigies and other religious images, but the hunters and their families would enjoy the delicacy of the young bees as a reward for the dangers they faced in obtaining the honey and wax.

The bees might have been full and slow from their unexpected feasting, but they were still displeased by the disruption to their nest. Though many of them had flown to safety from the smoke, others remained, and Timbal could hear the angry buzz and whirr as the large bees swarmed around the hunter threatening their home. Each insect was nearly the length of the first two segments of his finger, and they stung without hesitation. Timbal had seen his father and the others after they returned from previous trips: swollen in the hands and face from all the stings.

Now the torch came into play, and Timbal watched, holding his breath, as Khlari pulled the flaming bundle free from its moorings and brought it close to the bottom of what remained of the nest. While the close proximity of the smoke choked the insects, the sounds of their agitation filled the air as they rose from the nest.

As the bees vacated their home in a dark swarm, more of the dark golden honeycombs were revealed, and Khlari used the tangos to pummel and pull on the larger part of the nest. Timbal's mouth watered at the thought of the sweet, reddish syrup and the crunchy combs he would soon be tasting.

A great shout went up as Khlari detached the nest from its last bit of mooring, and Timbal and his partner scrambled into place below just as it fell.

*Thwump!*

The satisfying sound of the nest slumping into the huge basket brought with it a surprisingly strong jolt to Timbal's arms, and another shout of triumph from the honey hunters. It was one thing, Timbal knew, for the nest to be safely extricated—but it was just as important for the great mass to be captured before it crashed to the ground and broke into pieces, spilling all of its precious honey into the dirt.

Khlari detached three more nests in this same manner—bottom, larvae-laden portion first, then upper, honey-drenched section—before climbing back up and giving Viri a turn with the ladder, torch, and tangos. In all, they corrupted five nests from their positions clinging to the stony wall. Three huge baskets were filled, and one nest dashed against the side of the cliff and shattered as it tumbled down.

Though it was mostly a loss, the destroyed nest also yielded a few hand-sized pieces for the hunters to eat. Grandfather Bhulat, pleased with the take from this springtime trip and that neither of his men on the ladder had been injured other than a multitude of stings, took the first piece of the tender, lower part of the nest and bit into the sweet larvae with a satisfying crunch.

His wrinkled face creased with pleasure as he tasted the sweetness that Timbal knew could be found nowhere else. Soon, Timbal would eat as well and, for the first time, feel the effects of this springtime harvest of honey: a loose, pleasant hallucinogenic state that would stay with them as he and the others celebrated late into the night.

The take was large enough that Timbal's family would sell enough to feed them and part of the village for many moons. They would render the wax and sell that too. A small portion of the special red honey would be blessed and given to the shamans in order to assist them with their magic dreams and visions.

And, most important of all, they would put offerings of honey and some of the bee larvae in three beautiful pots, sealed and closed. These would be offered to the mountain spirit who'd given them safe passage and a good harvest.

Finally, Grandfather would place the last and most important offering in the sacred cave near their village.

The cave was the place where the holy man known as Saint Issa, who traveled from a very distant country with his own small hive of bees on his back, had slept when their village was infected by a great illness. Issa was obviously surrounded by the *pari's* blessing when he reclined there that night, for the next morning, he had come forth from the cave and healed the village of its plague.

Timbal had been five winters when Issa visited, and he remembered being ill with the fever and how nothing would soothe him until the cool, calming hand of the gentle saint had touched his brow…and how the heat and pain had evaporated at his touch.

Saint Issa had left soon after, carrying the rounded hive made from pottery on his back, but the villagers never forgot him. Bhulat and some of the other elders had marked the cave in which Issa slept with the same symbol carved on the holy man's beehive.

Nothing like that plague had ever come to the village again, and each spring and autumn, the bee hunters went on their quest—not only for the riches of the honey, but also to make a sweet offering to the mountain spirit who'd sent Issa to save them.

# PRELUDE II

*April 1897*
*Paris*

It was a miserable, desperately miserable, spring day. The sky was a dull gray, the air nipped with uncharacteristic venom, and the clouds wept constantly—as if to bemoan a less than perfect April in the City of Light.

And yet Nicolas Notovitch had no real complaints. Paris, in any weather, was a far better place to be than the stark Peter and Paul Fortress in St. Petersburg, where he'd unwillingly spent half a year in a cell. And Paris was an entirely different world altogether from the wild remoteness of Siberia, from where he'd been allowed to return in March.

Still, despite the fourteen months he'd spent exiled in Siberia, Nicolas was huddled in his greatcoat as if it were a blizzard assaulting him and not some recalcitrant spring day. He watched his feet in order to dodge puddles of water and piles of horse crap, alternating with glancing up and over his shoulder and listening for the jingle of bridles or the clomp of horseshoes.

He'd been unable to hail a *fiacre* due to the ill-tempered weather, and thus he was relegated to being on foot as he returned from Île de Citie after a very unsettling appointment at the city morgue. Ducking against the splatter of rain, which followed him though he changed direction, Nicolas crossed the street and turned onto the Champs-Élysées.

The broad avenue, capped at one end by the Arc de Triomphe,

boasted the magnificent, indulgent homes of Paris's wealthiest. Constructed of characteristic creamy blocks or, in some cases, of gray stone, a single mansion could sprawl over an entire block, decorated with twisting iron grates for balcony or portico.

Nicolas was, as always, struck by how very different these *maisons* were from the mean and simple brick house of his youth as a Jew in Russia—and how they were almost otherworldly in comparison to the huts, caves, and block-built structures he'd experienced when living with the Buddhist monks in Tibet and Nepal.

Yet Nicolas wasn't bitter about the vast wealth and carelessness demonstrated by the very rich. After all, he himself had risen well above the mean little house in which he'd been raised. And despite the difficulties (if one could call being imprisoned, then exiled to Siberia a mere difficulty) related to his recent book, it was still making him hundreds of francs a week and an even tidier sum of dollars, thanks to his American publisher.

Nicolas might have been utterly complacent about being back in his favorite city but for the lingering unpleasantness of the meeting at the morgue.

For most Parisians, a visit to the city morgue was a social event, akin to a tourist attraction. Located in the shadow of Notre Dame, adjacent to La Sûreté where the officers *de la paix* and homicide inspectors worked, the morgue opened its doors to the public every day of the week. A steady stream of people—pairs or trios of men brandishing walking sticks and hats, clusters of chattering women in fine dress, even entire families in more drab clothing—flowed in one door and out the other.

Inside the morgue's main entrance was the display area, where unidentified bodies that might have been pulled from la Seine, discovered in an alley of Monmartre, or encountered beneath a pile of leaves or refuge beneath a bridge were arranged on tables in hopes that some bystander would identify the unfortunate soul.

Shrouded to cover all but face, shoulders, and arms, the corpses—cleaned up, but in various states of decay—were accompanied by whatever clothing or possessions had been found with them. These pathetic items—sagging coats, empty dresses, battered shoes; in some cases horribly small ones—hung above the slabs on which their respective owners were displayed.

Nicolas himself had gone through those doors when, only a few years ago, a wooden trunk had been on display in relation to the celebrated murder case against Gabrielle Bompard.

A body—that of a Parisian bailiff named Gouffé—and the trunk had been discovered twenty miles from Paris. Because of the publicity over the case, the authorities had decided to display the trunk in hopes that someone could identify it—then hopefully lead to the murderer.

Tens of thousands of people viewed the infamous wooden chest, and the display had been such a popular attraction that palm-sized souvenir copies of the trunk were sold on the *quai* across from the morgue next to the Pont Notre-Dame.

Until today, that was the only time Nicolas had been to the morgue. He'd seen enough death and destruction during his life, not to mention while traveling through India and the Orient.

But it was his journey into the Himalayas that had truly altered his life—changed him from a brash, obnoxious young man to a more careful, thoughtful one.

He knew the truth.

He knew what he'd seen, what he'd been told, what he'd discovered in the shadow of the Himalayas in Tibet—and he'd be damned if anyone would make him forget about it, even if they decried his book. Especially since he had proof—carefully hidden behind a poster in his rooms.

Certainly, Nicolas must be less vociferous about what he knew, now that the Catholic Church had had its say by sending the Third Section—the Russian secret police here in Paris—after him.

And so the appointment at the morgue…it had greatly unsettled him.

When he descended to the basement of the building in the company of two officers—one from la Sûreté and one from the Third Section—Nicolas feared he was about to be arrested again. Or worse.

Instead, the two officials brought him to a laboratory where an American pathologist was doing the postmortem on a man—a man who'd obviously been murdered by a slit to the throat.

Actually, it wasn't a slit, Nicolas realized once he understood he wasn't being arrested and was able to calm his nerves. It was a cut in the shape of a Y that went up from the bottom of the man's breastbone and veed out toward the shoulders. He shivered deep inside.

"Make it quick," said the American, ignoring even a basic, polite "bonjour" first. The pathologist stepped over a massive dog that lay sprawled and snoring on the middle of his laboratory floor. "Death was from a bullet to the back of the head. Damned obvious."

Only then did Nicolas look closely enough at the corpse to see the circular wound at one temple where the bullet must have exited.

"Do you recognize this man, M. Notovitch?" asked Auchaud, the officer from la Sûreté.

"I'm sorry to say I don't, inspector."

Why had the Russian secret police and the Parisian authorities brought him here to identify a dead man?

His question was answered when the inspector handed him a small brown quarto. "This was found in his pocket."

Nicolas took the copy of his own controversial and bestselling book, lifting his brows and offering a quiet smile. "But, monsieur, it is impossible for me to know everyone who is in possession of *La vie inconnue de Jésus*—"

"Look inside if you please, monsieur."

When Nicolas flipped open the book, he saw that his name and the address of his new apartment had been written inside—the apartment he had let since his return, only three weeks ago. And below it was some small, rustic doodle. A bird...no, perhaps an insect. It appeared to have a rudimentary set of wings.

A bee.

Shaken, Nicolas closed the book. So this must be a recent purchase. Or, at least, a recent notation. A little quiver of nerves shot through him. Not many people knew he was returned, and even fewer knew where he lived.

And even fewer would know the meaning of the tiny doodle.

"No, inspector, I still do not know this man." He handed back the quarto with a steady hand.

"It appears he may have been interested in contacting you, at least," said the agent from the Third Section, speaking for the first time. Watching him closely. "About your book."

Nicolas merely bowed his head in acknowledgment, but said nothing more. Now his pulse had increased and his mouth dried. Would his answer be enough, or would they arrest him again?

"Very well then, monsieur," said Auchaud.

To his utter shock and wild relief, Nicolas was allowed to leave the morgue. And so he did, with hurried steps up from the basement laboratory before they changed their mind.

After that, he could have waited on the *quai* to try to hail a *fiacre*, but the meeting had so disturbed him that he needed to put as much distance between it and himself, and so he walked. And now he had turned off the Champs-Élysées and onto Avenue Carnot, being within three blocks of his rented rooms.

Why had they called him in for this? Was la Sûreté simply trying to identify the man, and the Russian had been there because of Nicolas's past troubles? Could it be that simple?

Or was it a veiled—or perhaps not-so-veiled—threat that he'd best remain silent about his book; that he'd best cease promoting the *truth*?

Had the man's body had been nothing but an excuse to make the threat? For there was no proof the book had actually been in the dead man's possession; it could have been planted in his pocket—

"M. Notovitch?"

Jolted from his thoughts, Nicolas turned to the voice, his knees weak with fear. At the sudden movement, a slew of collected raindrops slid off the edge of his hat's brim. He saw two men approaching; one had been the man who hailed him.

Neither were of the Russian secret police, but nor did they look Parisian.

Stunned, he realized the two men must be from Tibet. It would have been immediately obvious had he not been so certain that Rachkovsky's officers had come after him, for the two men standing there in front of Ste Ferdinand wore Western-style greatcoats…but the saffron robes of their religion were obvious, flowing from beneath the coats' woolen hems. And he could see no glimpse of hair from beneath their bowler hats. Their faces were also clean-shaven.

"Yes, I am he," Nicolas replied. He was intrigued but no longer apprehensive. The Buddhists were nonviolent, and the ones he'd met during his travels—most of them—were kind and friendly.

"We require a word with you, please," said the one who'd originally spoken. Now Nicolas could hear the accent thickening his French. The speaker was older and slighter than the other, and his mahogany skin was crisscrossed with wrinkles. A square emerald winked from his ring as he made a gesture toward the street that would take them to Nicolas's apartment. "In private."

"Of course."

He mulled over the appearance of a Buddhist monk and his companion in the middle of Paris, but had no qualms about leading the men into his rooms.

"Please, make yourselves—"

Nicolas didn't get the words out before the younger man shoved him across the threshold. Before Nicolas could react, his assailant closed the door sharply. Now he stood in front of it, arms crossed over his middle. The hem of his robe fluttered below the greatcoat he still wore.

All of a sudden, Nicolas's comfortable room became much smaller. When he looked at the older man who'd hailed him on the street, he saw that he held a pistol.

"M. Notovitch, if you would take a seat there." The monk removed his hat and the greatcoat, revealing a shaved head and flowing robes. Nicolas hardly paid attention, for the gun barrel glinted wickedly and the green stone on the heavy ring the Buddhist wore shone dully in the dreary light. "We have much to discuss."

Nicolas sank into the chair and resisted the urge to stroke his beard nervously. "Who are you?"

"I come from His Holiness at Hemis."

Hemis. That was the monastery in Tibet where Nicolas had made his earth-shattering discovery. His Holiness was the lama there, who'd spent much time with Nicolas.

"My blessed greetings to His Holiness," Nicolas began, trying to regain control of the meeting that had somehow overtaken his personal rooms and put him in danger. "I—"

"I bear a message," continued the old monk, moving closer with his pistol still trained on Nicolas.

Now that the emerald ring was directly in front of Nicolas's eyes, the scent of incense clinging to the man wafted to his nostrils. It was a scent Nicolas had experienced many times during his journey in the Himalayas and throughout India. Nam chala.

"Heed his message well, or your body will be the next one found with a bullet hole in the back of its skull."

Nicolas blinked and a cold sweat broke out over his body. Whatever happened to the Buddhist tenet of nonviolence?

"What is the message?" he managed to ask—and then he noticed the engraving on the large emerald directly in front of his eyes.

It looked like a bird...or an insect. And, God help him, did it resemble the rough drawing beneath the notation of his name and address inside his book? Or was terror blinding him? He blinked, trying to focus, to think—

*Not a coincidence.*

*That body with my book was not a coincidence.*

*The monks here, not a coincidence.*

A shaft of cold anxiety pierced him.

"Forget everything about Hemis," said the monk. The pistol was suddenly pointed directly at Nicolas's forehead, just above the space between his eyes. "Renounce what you have written, and forget it all. None of it existed—it was all a lie. None of that tale you spread will ever be seen nor heard of again from anyone of the West. If you persist..." He didn't finish the words, merely moved the gun so the barrel kissed Nicolas's clammy skin.

He closed his eyes and waited.

Of course they would kill him now. There was no sense in giving him the warning, but then leaving him to do as he might.

He closed his fingers tightly over the arms of his chair and prayed, prepared to meet God.

But then, a small shift in the air, a slight waft of nam chala, alerted him to movement.

When he at last had the courage to open his eyes, the monks had gone.

And, to his great relief, the painting that hung in front of his hid-ey-hole remained undisturbed.

They hadn't found his papers.

But now Nicolas knew what he must do with them.

The truth must be protected. He had to send his papers, and the *proof*, somewhere safe. To someone who believed in him, but who was safe from the Russians and their Parisian cohorts.

And he knew just the person.

# PROLOGUE

A llen Schleuter was a well-groomed yet undeniably homely forty-five-year-old. He had sparse hair that waffled in color between corn-chip yellow and gingerroot, and it was a sad sort of frizz that had neither body nor shine. His nose was broad and misshapen. His skin was light with an underlying gray cast, and age spots and so-called beauty marks dotted his face in the most unfortunate locations. His eyes were too small for his face, but they were intensely blue and sharp with intelligence. His chin was weak and his lips thin and narrow.

Nonetheless, Schleuter's lack of physical attractiveness had done nothing to dampen his professional success. For the last fifteen years, he'd held high management or executive-level positions in four different companies—each move being a higher step up the chain. Ironically, one of his most successful stints had been EVP of product development at a beauty and skin care company.

Schleuter was savvy, strategic, and intelligent, and most of all, he had vision and charisma. All of these attributes had brought him success upon success, and whenever he'd been ready to move to a new position, there'd been more than a handful of corporations ready to talk.

His landing as CEO at EcoDraft | HydroPure only three years ago had been the high point of his career thus far. And now he was about to take the next step, propelling the company he ran into the next phase…a phase that would cause profits to skyrocket, market share to explode, and, most certainly and in short order, result in an IPO that would make him almost as rich as Jeff Bezos.

All because of an article he'd read while stranded on a plane with a laptop he'd dropped just before boarding and, to top it off, with no Wi-Fi on the flight. The computer was toast, and without Wi-Fi, he couldn't even use his phone. That left him with little to do but flip through the flight magazines one of the attendants brought him, because it was a short trip that offered no in-flight entertainment.

And it was then he'd happened upon a benign article about glacier ice melt.

Even today, after twenty months of secret maneuvering, careful negotiation, and a lot of under-the-radar scientific testing, he was still keeping a lid on the most important move he'd ever make in his career. He was going to take this company to the stratosphere, but only three people knew of his plans. And of those three, one was his wife.

One of the other two, Hedron Burik, was going to be in the room when Schleuter announced his plans to the rest of the executive staff at EcoDraft.

His admin buzzed through on the intercom: "Mr. Schleuter, Mr. Burik has arrived. The rest of them are in the conference room."

"Thank you, Hailey."

He smiled to himself, checked the mirror to ensure that his wispy frizzle of hair was as flat as he could make it, and tightened his five-hundred-dollar tie. *Let's do this.*

"Good afternoon, everyone," Schleuter said as he and Burik strode into the conference room.

The seven members of his executive team were seated around the long table, all facing the screen where he would eventually show them the numbers and the potential explosion of growth they could expect with the new product that was going to blow their minds.

But he wasn't going to begin with a slide presentation, because he'd dared not put any of the strategies and information in writing anywhere. Having been a corporate spy himself (that had been the launch pad that moved him from director of product development at Helmsley Corp to vice president of operations at Wherring Industries), he knew that the best way to keep secrets was to keep them in one place: inside his brain.

The numbers, once he showed them to his team, would mean nothing without the background and backdrop of his brilliant idea.

He smiled expansively at everyone, taking note of the curiosity about his companion. Instead of introducing him, however, Schleuter said, "Everyone comfortable? Have something to drink? There's coffee, tea, soda… Please, help yourselves. This is going to be intense."

There was a low-key nervous chuckle among the executives, as if they weren't sure whether to believe him or not, and since Schleuter hadn't told them the purpose of the meeting or even its topic, he could understand their trepidation.

Good. That meant they'd be listening closely…and what he told them would be a pleasant surprise.

Once everyone was settled again, their seven pairs of eyes trained expectantly on him, Schleuter began to speak. He took his time, wanting to paint the picture and bring them along with him.

"Do you all remember when I first started here at EcoDraft and I dropped my laptop? Broke the damned thing just before I got on the plane from Cleveland to New York." He smiled as he looked around the room. "Ron, I know I gave you an earful about it, didn't I?"

His executive VP of legal affairs chuckled, nodding. "As I recall, you blamed yourself for your ham hands about three minutes, then went on to bitch about the airline not having Wi-Fi on that particular flight. About thirty minutes later, I finally escaped and went into a meeting about a potential lawsuit—and I considered myself lucky."

The others in the room chuckled—a little less nervously this time.

"Well, as it turns out, that very frustrating moment was the impetus for some extremely exciting information I'm going to share with you today. Because while I was stuck on that damned puddle-jumper, I had only a few magazines to look through. And one of them was a *National Geographic* that had an article about glacier melt."

Schleuter smiled, watching the way his audience reacted to this news. Glacier melt equaled water, and EcoDraft was, of course, a beverage company.

Cynthia Belcher, his chief marketing officer, tilted her head sharply, her eyes narrowing with interest.

Bradley Wisniewski, the EVP of operations, sat up straight and stopped fiddling with the stylus for his tablet.

Warren Ott, director of logistics, put down his coffee cup.

And so on.

"Did you know that the melting glaciers have a number of interesting characteristics?" Schleuter went on, spinning his tale like a bedtime story. "Not only are they melting faster due to climate change, but they are also revealing some very interesting things. Yes, I know, everyone is interested in what's being exposed in the Arctic by the melting glaciers—the electronics companies are all salivating at gaining control of the land up there so they can mine for the rare earth metals required to manufacture our tablets and phones and computers..." He made his smile a little crafty, a little condescending. "But we're not an electronics company, so we're not going to be in that battle. I'll leave that to Elon Musk and his ilk."

Jon Parker, the product development VP, relaxed a little, and Schleuter smiled at him. "No, you have nothing to worry about, Jon—we're not going to expand into making digital watches or gadgets or anything like that."

Again, the members around the table laughed lightly. Some of them glanced at Hedron Burik again, and Schleuter smiled to himself. He could see the curiosity growing in their eyes, and he was close to reeling them in.

"No, we're going stick with what makes us who we are now—the number one *premier* bottled-water company in the world. The Evians, the Fijis...all the rest of them might have a larger market share in the high-end bottled-water market—right now, anyway—but we're about to blow them away." Schleuter didn't spare even a moment of thought to the ridiculousness of their collective pitch—"the high-end bottled-water market." The very concept was ludicrous—how was water, a plentiful natural resource, ever "high-end" in First World countries?

Yet EcoDraft had that special flair, that sense of elan, that element of style that made it worth spending five U.S. dollars for a twelve-ounce *plastic* bottle.

A plastic bottle that, EcoDraft | HydroPure claimed, was made from fully recycled material *and* was compostable. Another ludicrous assertion, but, by Jove, it worked. The eco-sensitive and greenies all bought EcoDraft compostable bottled water in droves.

And that was why Schleuter no longer flinched internally when he talked about the high-end bottled-water market. Because the public would buy anything you wanted them to—as long as you sold it to them.

"Along with the accelerated glacier melt in the Arctic exposing landmass or ocean floor that will be prime real estate for mining rare earth metals like terbium and cerium, there are also other interesting consequences of the melt.

"For example, there have been instances of fossils and other archae-ological finds, such as burial and home sites. Fascinating for those who have interest in anthropology, which doesn't include EcoDraft *except* relative to how man acts, reacts, and lives his—or her—daily life…so we can better learn how to appeal to the buy, buy, buy gene!"

Another little patter of laughter.

"A quite interesting outcome of the rapidity of glacier melt is that there are also new—or perhaps one should say *old*—bacteria being revealed and released by the melt. Bacteria that are unique and unknown to science because they've been trapped within the glacier and inert or otherwise inaccessible for millennia.

"With all of this in mind, imagine what these melting glaciers might reveal that could change our world…change the way we live… change the way we *age*." Schleuter knew his eyes were sparkling by now, and he saw the same spark of interest beginning to flare in that of his team. "It could change our *health*—for the worse, if these bac-teria are dangerous—or, more interestingly, change our health for the *better*. To improve it."

He removed the piece of paper that had been blocking the light of the projector, instantly revealing the image of his brainchild.

The words on the slide said: *GlacierDraft HealthH20*

The container was gorgeous—stylized almost like a bottle of Wil-lett's—or like the djinni's bottle in *I Dream of Jeannie*, which Schleuter remembered fondly from after-school viewing as a child. Made from plastic (compostable, of course, as all EcoDraft water bottles purported to be, and oftentimes actually *were*) of a clear, faintly aqua blue, the bottom third bulged out like a flat turnip bulb while the neck stood straight up, tapering slightly toward the top. But what made the packaging so stunning was the texture of the plastic itself: the bulbous bottom had divots in a pattern that made the bottle look like cut crystal glass, while the neck was striated up and down. There were slender rings around it that separated the two different textures, adding a tastefully decorative element to an already stunning package with a sort of Far Eastern look to it.

Schleuter waited while the others in the room took in the image and all of its detail. Even Jon Parker, who managed all elements of product packaging, hadn't previously seen the image, although one of his staff had designed it without knowing what it was for.

"It's a stunning package. But that's going to be ridiculous to produce—and stocking it on the shelves will be a nightmare. The base is too big and the grocers won't allow that much shelf space," said Warren. "For bottled water?" He scoffed, shaking his head. "So what's the pitch, Allen?"

Schleuter had been waiting for this. He was surprised they hadn't put it together yet, even with the way he'd built the narrative. Although Cynthia was smiling a little—she probably got it. She had the most vision of anyone on the executive team, which was why she was so good at her job.

"I'm pleased to announce that EcoDraft is about to finalize a contract with the government of a small region near the Pangong mountains in what's called Little Tibet to bottle the water sluicing from the melting Tazhnev Glacier. *Exclusively* bottle the water, I mean to say," he went on, well aware of the dramatics of his presentation.

Princeton Fairmont, the CFO, wasn't convinced. "All right, so we're going to sell glacier melt as drinking water...so what? That's been done countless times over. Springs, glaciers, whatever you want to call the source...that's old news. Even if we put it in a bottle like that, no one's going to pay whatever it's going to cost for us to produce that. The economies of scale will destroy us—we'd have to sell it for ten U.S. dollars a sixteen-ounce bottle to make any money."

"Oh, but this water is special, Prince," Allen said. "Remember what I said about the melting glaciers revealing unknown bacteria? Well, this particular meltwater has a colloidal compound in it that not only contains a unique type of electrolyte that is beneficial to humans, but also collagen enhancing—a natural, *vegan* collagen support! The greenies will love that!—as well as additional antibacterial minerals like copper and silver. All in trace amounts, of course, so as not to be of a concern for the FDA. And it all occurs *naturally*. And we are going to have the exclusive rights to bottle and sell this *miracle* water. The cleanest, purest, healthiest, most age-defying water in the world."

The room was silent as the members of his team digested this information.

He glanced at Burik, who was watching with a satisfied smile. If it hadn't been for him and his connections, Allen wouldn't be here making this announcement.

Then the questions came like the pounding of hail in a storm—or like the ones he knew he'd be facing at the future press announcement.

"Is it safe?" was the first one. From Ron, the lawyer, of course.

"Absolutely. Even in large quantities. The makeup of these inorganic colloids in the water is balanced and safe to ingest in high quantities—high quantities *meaning*," he went on before the question could be asked, "up to twenty ounces a day, every day, indefinitely."

"And this unique electrolyte…what exactly is it supposed to do—and what claims are we going to make?" asked Ron, obviously with his legal hat still firmly in place.

"Brings extra oxygen to the blood while assisting with detoxifying the organs. It's like a flush, if you will, a—"

"Like a douche for the entire body," said Warren. Everyone laughed, and Schleuter was pleased to see that they were on his side.

He was gratified that they were—as a whole, as a body, as a team—on his side in this concept. Intrigued, curious, and, he saw, greedy.

That was precisely what he was hoping for.

"The vegan collagen support…that's going to be huge," said Cynthia. "When can I get a sample?" She preened exaggeratedly.

Again, the room erupted with laughter, and Schleuter replied smoothly, "Not that you need to worry about that, Cyn, but I'll make sure you get a generous supply delivered to your office. Then you can try it out for yourself and report back on the skin glow and firming, hair growth, and energy. Oh, yes, I know the benefits of collagen. You're not the only person who wants to protect her youthful beauty." He indicated his homely self, knowing that would cause another round of laughter. And it did.

"In all seriousness, folks, let me just say that we are about to embark on an entirely new take on the bottled-water market. We're going to bring to the market a way to improve health and vitality—*naturally* and, more importantly, *exclusively*—in the most basic, wholesome way." Schleuter smirked. "And people are going to pay for it. They're going to pay for this *fountain of youth* elixir. Hence the high-end packaging."

Warren said, "I notice it has a sort of Oriental look to it—"

"Not Oriental," Cynthia said. "Don't use that word. It's very outdated and not PC. We say Asian or—in this case, it looks almost like it was inspired by Hindu or even Muslim art?" She looked at Allen with a raised brow.

"Indeed."

"We'll have to take care not to be accused of cultural appropriation," she went on, but she was making notes on her tablet's attached keypad with the clickety-click of her long pink nails.

"No worries there," Allen told her. "The glacier melt is being collected in the mountains that border northern India, Nepal, and Tibet. Ladakh, India, is the name of the region—also known as Little Tibet."

"Oh, great—we're going to have to deal with the Chinese, then," said Ron.

"Our contract is with the lieutenant governor of one of the regions of India, so China is not involved."

"Yet," Ron said cynically. "They've always got their noses in everything over there related to Tibet and Nepal. It'll only be a matter of time—"

"We've kept this under the radar for over a year now," Schleuter said. "And one of the most important elements of our contract with the government official is the complete and utter secrecy of the agreement. The source of our special elixir— I like that term; maybe we should make that part of the marketing campaign? Or even the product name? Can you work up some ideas, Cyn?"

"Already on it. I like trying for a play on 'fountain of youth,' too," she said. "Because 'elixir' might sound too...magical or witchy-like. Or, you know, medievally alchemical. Or even juvenile, like Harry Potter."

Schleuter nodded. "You'll figure it out. I leave that in your capable hands. As I was saying—of paramount importance to our agreement and the launch of this product is the complete and utter secrecy of the arrangement. We cannot allow anyone to learn of the source of our special elixir—for obvious reasons—and at the same time, the entity with whom we're making the contract is likewise intent on secrecy. It would cause great political upheaval in the region—as well as with their own people, who rely on the glacial ice melt for their own farming and ranching—should anyone learn of the diversion of that water stream. Therefore, I will not, at this time, divulge the precise location of our source. And even after the contracts have been executed, that information will be confidential and on a need-to-know basis."

He looked around the room and saw agreeable nods, lights of interest, and the blank-eyed look of mental calculations and estimations. Good. Just as he'd expected.

"Would you all like to try the water?" he said, beaming. Without waiting for the positive reactions—of course they all wanted to taste the miracle water—he buzzed the intercom to the anteroom. "Hailey, bring in the glass pitchers—the cut glass ones on the side table there."

He watched with delight as his executive team poured, examined, tasted, and swished as if they were sampling a fine vintage of wine.

Jon put his glass down. "It tastes different," he said. "It really does—I admit, I wasn't expecting much of anything, but this is really... It's different."

Cynthia nodded. "Agreed. It's very crisp and clean, with the slightest metallic hint—but in a pleasing way. And I even get a little floral on the back end. Anyone else?"

"Definitely a little earthy—that's the metallic part, I think," said Princeton. "And yes, a hint of sweetness, even—and there's a sort of different *body* to it. You know? It's…difficult to explain, but it's lighter without being effervescent?"

"Oh, yes, you've noticed one of my favorite elements of the water—it has microscopic bubbles in it which gives it that effervescentness—is that a word, Cyn?—without being bubbly or giving you added gas." Schleuter lifted his own glass and admired the way the light filtered through it, spreading through the unique makeup of the water in a subtle kaleidoscope of color. "The first time I tasted this, I knew it was something different. I knew it would blow the market wide open." He raised the glass to his team, but it was Burik to whom he gave a brief nod. Thanks to the man who would make his career. "Cheers."

Warren Ott folded his arms across his middle and settled back in his chair. "All right, Schleuter…you've done the pitch. You've sold us all on it. And I'm on board—I really am. I think it's going to work. But now you're going to tell us this is really just from some natural spring in Montana or somewhere like that, right?"

Schleuter put down his glass. His entire demeanor changed. "No. Oh, no, not at all, Warren. Everything I've told you about this water—its source, its makeup, its benefits—is completely true. Take it back to the lab and have it analyzed. You'll see.

"No, I might be motivated by the almighty dollar—as you all are—but I'm not a liar. I'm not selling snake oil here. This is real. And that's why it's going to be insane…and that's why we have to keep a lid on it."

# ONE

I n a well-appointed office with heavy oak furniture and well-cushioned chairs sat a distinguished man of fifty-seven.

Dressed in the unrelieved black of his vocation, the man was clean-shaven, with his silver-black hair worn cropped short and close to his skull. He possessed long, slender fingers with a single ring on the left hand: a signet with a large, square emerald into which was carved a bee. The symbol was hardly noticeable unless one examined the stone closely; however, it served as a constant reminder to its bearer.

The rug on the polished walnut floor was subdued in color and design, hand-woven in Morocco, and thick and easy on the feet. The long black armoire of polished wood opposite the window was invisible unless he opened one of its six doors with a complicated remote control he kept at his desk. Tucked behind the armoire's doors were a small refrigerator, an impressively stocked liquor cabinet, a swing-out kitchenette counter with a complicated espresso machine and microwave oven, utilitarian file cabinets, and a large television. Another discreet door led to a private lavatory adjacent to the office.

Despite being surrounded by this luxury, the man was agitated and ill at ease. It was all he could do to keep from pacing the wide expanse of his personal office space. Instead, he sat at his massive desk and looked down at the crucifix he gripped, hoping for some bolt-of-lightning answer or shock of guidance to come from it.

He brooded and churned in a space with far more luxury than he should ever have acquired—for the man formerly known as Theodore Villiani had taken vows of poverty, chastity, and obedience more than forty years ago. Over the decades, Cardinal Villiani had kept the last two of his priestly vows…though he'd ridden the line on obedience more than once because the Vatican didn't always see things the way they (the collective "they"; not including himself) should. So he'd learned over the decades that it was better to ask for forgiveness than permission.

After all, wasn't that one of the tenets of the church? Ask for forgiveness, and it would be granted.

However, of his three vows, the poverty element had always been beyond his capacity. A man needed his comforts if he was to sacrifice the other pleasures of life in order to serve the masses—as well as serve *at* Masses.

After all, when a man spent the majority of his time listening to the worst of vile sins, placating hurt, shocked, or grieving parents, spouses, and children—and generally being required to act like a rock during the most traumatic and painful times of human experience— one needed a sanctuary of one's own in order to relax.

Thus: the expensive antique furnishings, the large plate-glass window overlooking the age-old city and offering glimpses of rolling hills and mountains beyond. The liquor cabinet with twenty-year scotch, vintage madeira, and three-figure Euro bottles of Chianti. The private chef, the housekeeping staff including two gardeners, the personal assistant, and the embossed letterhead decorated with the Vatican coat of arms.

There were also the brass and gold fixtures in his residential lavatory, complete with toilet, bidet, and dual-head shower—not to mention a separate room for the hot tub with large windows overlooking a small ridge of mountains. And an estate-sized bed draped with royal-purple brocade curtains that, true to the one vow he'd never broken, remained a vessel for one, and one only.

He'd worked hard for this position, for his possessions, and for his comfort.

He'd grieved with widows and prayed with parents; he'd baptized dying children and fat, squirming, crying ones.

He'd married men and women who had no business committing to each other for life on Earth, and those who, he felt certain, would make a happy life together.

He'd visited war-torn countries and devastated landscapes after earthquakes, tsunamis, fires, and other destruction.

He'd been there in his calm, easy, peaceful capacity, spouting the prayers and placations in which he still believed, still trusted.

He'd been there as Christ had been: listening, supporting, guiding, healing.

And he'd risen from among the chattel, made his way up the ladder from such mundane tasks to his current one where, still beloved by many, lauded by his peers, he now was able to cloister himself in wealth and comfort in a more scholarly exploit here at the Vatican Apostolic Archive—where all the secrets of the church were kept in a repository.

But *this*…now…

His throat tightened with fear, and his belly—empty due to his regular Friday fast—churned with bile.

This news could destroy all of it: all of his life, his work, this beauty and comfort that surrounded him—and the church herself.

He looked down at the information he'd been given. The Buddhist lama had been very specific.

*Patricia Denke, an American student who'd been studying in Ladakh, India.*

Villiani could hardly believe it. Was it possible the Catholic Church could be destroyed by a woman?

Villiani looked down at the crucifix, placing a reverent kiss upon the peaceful face inscribed on it, and reached for the telephone. He pressed a single key that would make the connection.

For not only did Theodore Villiani have at his disposal a personal chef and housekeeping staff…he also had certain other resources at his fingertips.

This was yet another case where he would ask for forgiveness instead of permission, for the entire church was at stake.

But he would attend to it himself. There was no need to bother anyone else with the news.

The call connected and a familiar voice answered almost immediately—a testament to Villiani's influence.

"Rastinoff," Villiani said without preamble. "I need to see you *now*."

# TWO

F ar from the well-appointed office of the man who'd taken vows of poverty, chastity, and obedience and prayed while holding a figure-laden cross was another man, communing with the deity to whom he'd dedicated *his* life.

Unlike the other, who prayed with fervent despair and was lean and strong, this man was frail, with only the barest wisps of white hair straggling over his scalp. His arms and legs were sinewy with muscles still ropy and tough at his advanced age. His feet, bare so as to feel the heartbeat of Earth beneath them, were long and white and currently folded into a cradle position.

A drum the size of a large plate sat in the bowl of his lap, still reverberating gently from the last thrum of beat. The image of an elk—one he'd scratched on the stretched skin decades earlier—decorated the drum. The drum's handle spanned across the open side of the instrument and was fashioned in the shape of a woman with outstretched arms. Her head and feet were attached to the top and bottom of the drum frame, and her arms touched the sides. Her hair was long and wild, carved lovingly from the piece of Siberian elm that formed her figure. Curling within and at the end of each tendril of hair were flowers, animals, insects, leaves—even stones and mountains. Her feet and hands grew into roots and branches that grasped the edges of the frame.

Despite decades of being held and carried, the figure was still as perfect as it had been the day she was carved. Her details had not been smoothed or obliterated by the touch of calloused hands and strong fingers.

The elderly man's name was Lev. He was well over a century old, having been birthed by Mother Earth, or Gaia—or, at least, somehow protected by Her—during the great and terrifying upheaval in Tunguska, Siberia, in 1908.

When the fires that raged and scored the earth on June 30, leaving trees blackened and skeletal, settled and died at last, the ground was left bare of all but ash and smoldering coals. Wildlife disappeared. Everything green or living was incinerated for miles around.

The only sign of life in that devastated world was the wail of an infant—alone, naked, and miraculously untouched by the explosion that had lit northern Siberia and was seen from twenty miles away.

The infant bore the mark of the Skaladeska people, yet none from the mountain tribe claimed or recognized him. Nonetheless, Lev was taken in and protected. And because of the mystery of his origins, he was raised to be the revered leader of the unknown tribe hidden in the far reaches of Taymyria in Siberia.

Today, far from the elegant, luxurious man-made office of Theodore Villiani, Lev had settled in his own worship space, the only cathedral he'd ever known: within the embrace of Gaia.

He sat in the center of a ring of trees so old and large they created a dappled, rippling canopy over him. His hands, palms flat, fingers wide, sank into the lush green grass on either side of his body. The vibrations of his drum still hummed through his limbs, centered in the core of his body. He'd only just opened his eyes, returning from his journey to the Lower World and the spirit animals and teachers who'd spoken to him there. Now he merely sat in the embrace of Earth, contemplating on what he'd learned.

Here, now, he was one with Gaia, the living, breathing entity the Out-Worlders called Earth. He sensed Her despair and Her pain, and he felt Her determination to survive thrumming through his own body.

It was that determination, that strength he felt pulsing through the grass and dirt beneath him. He closed his eyes and felt her with every part of his being.

*Gaia is one with us all.* He silently recited words from the holy Skaladeska text he'd absorbed and lived by for more than a hundred years. *And all living creatures are one with Her. And if there be a species of this Earth that threatens the whole, it shall be expelled.*

A shiver lifted the sparse hair on his arms, and he opened his eyes. *And if there be a species of this Earth that threatens the whole, it shall be expelled.*

Humankind was such a species.

Lev had come to believe and understand that. Gaia's pain and suffering was due to the atrocities committed by Lev's fellow man—their carelessness and greed, the rape and pillage, the wanton destruction of the very entity that gave them life and sustenance.

He was called by Gaia, he and his family—Roman, Mariska, and the others of their clan: Hedron, Varden, even Stegnora, an Out-Worlder—to help their Earth protect Herself and recover.

Today during his journey to the Lower World, Lev had spoken to elk, his first spirit animal. Elk had shown him a beautiful flowing river coming from snowy mountains that Lev recognized as Siberian. The river glittered with all colors of the rainbow, as if every gemstone of every possible hue had been strewn into the riverbed and now tumbled and tossed with the rush of water.

It was powerful water, and its spirit churned and sparkled and danced in her cloak of living, celebrating rainbow gems. As water spirit frolicked and swirled, bee approached, flitting and darting from flower to flower.

*Protect.*

Elk's command settled into Lev's conscious during the journey.

*Protect. That which is sacred is threatened.*

Bee, ethereal and delicate, danced in front of Lev, her fuzzy body glittering magenta-gold in the strange light of Lower World. Her gossamer wings shone with a hint of pink. A glow of white light surrounded her entire being as she buzzed and spiraled and swooped around him.

*That which is sacred is threatened. Thus you are threatened. Protect that which is sacred. Protect yourself. Protect Gaia.*

Now, back in reality, Lev sat within Gaia's embrace: the roots and trunk of a tree, moss surrounding him, grass beneath his hands. He felt solid and real, connected to the ground—so different from the weightlessness he often felt while journeying.

And yet the words from elk reverberated through his thoughts as strongly as if the spirit animal stood there speaking once more.

*That which is sacred is threatened. You are threatened. Protect that which is sacred.*

He understood little of what had been told him, but that was no strange thing. Often he came back to the world and had to live to understand what his guides, teachers, spirit animals meant for him to understand.

But he did know whatever the threat was, it was not only to Gaia this time, but to him as well.

# THREE

J ill Fetzer sneezed. Again.

Automatically pushing her glasses back into position, she reached for the box of tissues she'd placed on the long worktable among the stacks of papers and banker's boxes. Being an historian who had an allergy to dust wasn't the greatest combination, but between toting her ever-present box of tissues and a daily dose of antihistamine, Jill had learned to come prepared when she was digging around in old boxes.

Normally, the old boxes she dug around in were in the special collections at places like the Newberry Library, or the Regenstein at the University of Chicago, or even the Library of Congress. But this weekend's project was something far less esoteric than what she was used to poring over as a well-published and tenured professor at Northwestern.

As she crumpled the used tissue and tossed it with the others into a small bin, Jill sighed and surveyed the results of what could only be called a pet project. Or a labor of love—one for her beloved maternal grandmother.

"Well, who else would be better suited for the task than our very own history expert?" Grandma Donovan had asked in a quavery voice.

The unsteadiness in her voice was belied by the glint in her gray eyes and the firm grip of her cool, wrinkled fingers around Jill's hand.

Grandma Donny was pushing eighty-five, and she had both a will and a spine stronger than steel.

And that was how Jill got saddled with going through all of her great-grandfather's old boxes, which had been tucked away in the attic of Grandma Donny's house for decades. Now that the elderly woman had moved into what she'd termed "adult summer camp"—a senior community that included all levels of assisted living, not to mention every activity under the sun—everything in her home had to be pared and trimmed down, sold or saved, trashed or donated as necessary so the house could be sold.

Not that Jill minded in the least, truly. After all, she loved history so much she'd made it her life's work—and what history was more interesting than her own family's, which had lived in Chicago or its surrounding areas for over a century?

Who knew what she might find in these old boxes?

Sure, she, like everyone in her profession, fantasized about being an *Antiques Roadshow* success—like the man who'd bought an old picture from an antiques shop for the frame and ended up finding an original, signed copy of the U.S. Constitution mounted to the back of it—but that was pure fantasy.

What would be more likely, her scholarly mind told her—but still firmly in the realm of fantasy—would be if she ran across something like when the Gwen John paintings had unexpectedly been discovered among Arthur Symons' papers at Princeton. Something like *that* was possible.

But mostly, Jill figured she'd find things like old correspondence belonging to her great-great-grandmother Alexina, a Frenchwoman who'd married Grandma Donny's grandfather, and perhaps some vintage clothing and photographs related to the Chicago Donovans. And yet another reason for her capitulation to the request from her grandmother, she admitted privately, was because of Jill's reclaiming of her surname professionally after her divorce. After years of being Dr. Fetzer-Traft, she was now simply, and happily, Dr. Fetzer.

Jill sneezed again, and this time she had to blink rapidly because her eyes had begun to water. That meant it was time to call it a day; her antihistamine and box of tissues could only stand up to the dust mites and musty particles for so long. It was late Saturday night, anyway—the only time she could justify spending on this project—and she probably had something she wanted to watch on Hulu. It would take her forty minutes to get to her townhouse in Libertyville, and she could pick up carry-out on the way.

She was just closing the box—a tattered, musty banker's box that looked at least fifty years old—when she noticed a package within.

It was addressed to Mrs. Alexina Donovan, in care of Rand McNally & Company.

Rand McNally? Had her great-great-grandmother worked for the publishing company? Considering the fact that Alexina had come from France, it was quite an interesting question.

Jill forgot her itchy eyes and sneezes and pulled out the package. Rand McNally & Company was of course known for publishing the world atlas, along with railroad guides, maps, Handy-Guides to various cities, and other nonfiction books since the late nineteenth century. It had been a Chicago-based business for nearly a century before moving to the suburb of Skokie—and then back into the city again in the late 1980s.

Women's history was always of particular interest to Jill, for obvious reasons, and the idea that her grandmother had been employed in some professional capacity in what had to have been around the turn of the nineteenth century fascinated her. There could be a paper topic here, she thought gleefully, examining the package. *Might not be as exciting as an original painting, but it could be something compelling nonetheless.*

The stamps were in French and so was one of the postmarks. Maybe from a family member, left back in Paris? Ignoring the tickle in her nose that portended another sneeze, she pushed up her slipping glasses and shined her mobile phone's flashlight on the fading ink.

The postmarks were hand-stamped, and she identified one for Paris—which appeared to be the originating location—and another for New York City. Years weren't added to many postmarks or cancellation marks until the turn of the nineteenth century, and as the ones on this package were missing the year, she felt another skip of her pulse. *Before 1900 probably, but later than the mid-1800s.*

She was mildly disappointed to see that the ink of the sender's name had bled away and wasn't legible. The last few letters of the name looked like *itch*, and the initial of the first name might have been an N or an M. Hmm. That sounded Russian, so it probably wasn't a family member.

Careful not to destroy the wrappings, which, as far as she could tell, hadn't ever been opened, Jill snipped the worn string that criss-crossed the bundle, knowing that it had likely spent a month or more in transit from Paris to Chicago. And to never be opened? What sort of work had Alexina done for Rand McNally? And if she didn't work for them, why would someone send her a package there?

Jill pulled the crisp brown paper away, setting the wrappings aside to behold her treasure: a wooden container, about the size of a cigar box. In fact, it *was* a cigar box—and its cover instantly dated it as the mid-to-late 1890s Art Nouveau style of Belle-Époque Paris.

*My God, is this a Mucha?* She paused to admire the beautiful illustration of a woman on the front. The intricate, pale pastels—particularly peach, melon, and sage—and painstaking, undulating detail of flowers, swirls, and long hair that coiled like macaroni were definitely the hallmarks of Alphonse Mucha's distinctive *fin de siècle* style. And when she saw his name on the printed image, Jill gasped with pleasure. If nothing else, she was holding a beautiful, wonderfully preserved antique box that belonged in a museum.

The container opened easily. Jill set the top aside and surveyed the contents. A letter, addressed to Alexina Donovan with the notation *Privée* on the outside of the envelope. Three thick packets of papers, each folded into squares, and possibly ten pages each. The papers were aged and brittle, and she carefully spread the first packet open. Handwritten in fading ink in French.

Good thing she had a decent handle on the language. It was difficult enough trying to read old, spiky writing; it would be nearly impossible if she didn't know the language.

Resisting the urge to skim at least the first pages, Jill set the papers aside and turned her attention to the last item, which was nestled on the bottom among some wads of cotton batting: a cloth-wrapped bundle that was about the size and weight of a teacup.

When she took it out, Jill had the impression of an item very old and fragile; there was something about the way it felt in her hands— solid and substantial, like metal or stone—and the way it smelled, the way it had been so carefully packaged.

Yet, despite her burning curiosity, she forced herself to set the small bundle next to her on the table, then looked inside the cigar box to see if there was anything else tucked down in the cotton batting.

She found a small cork cube, unpainted, unadorned other than a blob of wax on one end. She couldn't imagine what it was for—it wasn't the right shape or size for a wine bottle—but she put it aside. When she pulled out the musty wadding, she unraveled it gently over the box and something fell out of it. A very small glass vial with a dead insect tucked inside. Jill wondered how a bee— Or was it a fly? Maybe a moth? No, she decided as she gave it good look, it was a bee.

How did a bee get caught up in the wadding and packaged inside this box—with all the other contents that had been put together so carefully?

*Was* it actually a bee? Jill frowned as she looked at it, not quite certain why it mattered so much, why it had snagged her interest. It was just an old bug.

But it had been caught in there for over a century, she realized. Sometime before 1900, this poor little insect had been trapped inside the cigar box and left in there to die during his trans-Atlantic voyage.

Interestingly enough, the creature wasn't damaged or crushed, as one might expect an insect to be in a box that had been shipped all the way from Paris.

She'd never seen one that looked like this (not that she was an expert on bugs by any stretch). Her first instinct might be correct: the creature was sort of fuzzy, like a bee, and it had stripes on its body. But the colors weren't gold and black. Instead, the stripes were black and a sort of reddish-pink-gold. It was the size of a housefly, smaller than most honeybees she could think of. Maybe there were different species of bees in Paris.

Jill tipped the cigar box so the winged insect fell out, and when it tumbled into her palm, she realized there was a pin stuck through its abdomen. *Ah.* That was what the small block of wood was for, and maybe the glass vial: the bee, or whatever type of insect it was, had been mounted on the cube by the little pin stuck through it, like a specimen in a lab, and then protected by the glass vial, which made a sort of top over it. There was a bit of wax on the vial that must have been a stopper to keep the chunk of cork in place and sealed. She suspected the whole glass container had been wrapped up in the batting to protect it. Amazing that it had traveled so far and that the insect was still intact.

The situation was fascinating and a little startling. What was so special about this insect that it had been packaged up and sent overseas to her great-grandmother, along with—whatever was in this other bundle?

She set the bee gently on top of the batting and turned her attention to the cloth-wrapped item. The fabric was an unexceptional contemporary linen weave, undyed, unadorned. No stitching or embroidery. A thick string tied it around the weighty, solid object, and once again Jill cut the bindings carefully. She'd saved this part for last, hoping there would be some significant revelation when she opened it, that she'd immediately know whether she had a find, or a *find*.

Carefully unrolling its wrappings, she let it sit on the desk in front of her. The object was revealed to be a small, simple clay pot, roughly three inches across and five inches tall. A lid made from the same material fit tightly and was sealed closed with a substance like wax all around its seam. She couldn't determine the original color of the clay, for now it was gray-brown with the wear of centuries. It didn't have any sort of glaze on it like more modern stoneware, nor was it painted or decorated with beads or other pieces of pottery. Fashioned from clay and some grasses or reeds for added strength, the pot put her in mind of a small medicinal or even perfume container. If anything was inside, it made no sound when she gently shook the jar.

There were etchings on the jar—if she had to guess, she'd say it was text and not merely decorative markings. Definitely not French. Nor was it Germanic or Latin… Asian, perhaps, or Middle Eastern.

Crude lettering aside, this unpainted, rough in texture, and crudely formed jar made Jill think *ancient*. Her fingers trembled a little as reality sank in. This pot was far older than a century or two.

What it was or where it had come from, she couldn't guess. Well, she *could*—and her mind was already jumping to wild possibilities—but she was an historian. A scientist. She would take this step by step.

But oh…she was *excited*.

Jill reached for the letter marked *Privée,* hoping this, at least, would be legible and easy to read. Before she left tonight, she wanted an idea of who'd sent this package with its curious contents and why.

Carefully, she used a letter opener to slit through the age-brittle envelope. The paper inside crackled alarmingly as she eased it out of its enclosure. The one-page letter, addressed to Mrs. Alexina Loranger Donovan, was also written in French, and in very hurried, scrawling penmanship. Ink blots, smudges, and streaks abounded. It would take significant work to parse the characters and words from the messy paragraphs before she could begin to translate them. Nonetheless, she scanned it, looking for anything that jumped out at her—proper names or places, dates, anything.

Only the date and place from which it was sent—Paris, 20 April, 1897 (she'd been right in dating it by the postmarks)—along with the addressee and sender's names were legible to her.

*All right, then,* Jill thought, removing her glasses to rub watery, weary eyes. Despite her enthusiasm, it was late and her vision was blurring. And if she was going to make her yoga class at five thirty, she had to get going.

*Tomorrow, when I can actually see clearly, I'll start on this letter.*

She couldn't wait to find out why someone named Nicolas Notovitch had shipped a *bee* and an ancient medicine jar to her great-grandmother—all the way from Paris to Chicago.

# FOUR

Tina Janeski hesitated outside Dr. Sanchez's office door. Her palms were a little sweaty and her stomach slightly queasy, but in a good sort of way.

She was only a lowly undergraduate student who was working as an admin during the summer semester, but like most of the female students in the entomology department—and some of the male ones too—she was half in love with Eli Sanchez. Well, as much as she could be from a distance, anyway.

Even Patty Denke, the tall, willowy blonde who had plenty of her own admirers, admitted Sanchez had that certain something-something that attracted people like flies—or bees.

Oh, God, it was just *horrible* about Patty!

And that was why Tina was more than a little nervous. She'd had Dr. Sanchez for one lecture, but had never met him one on one. And now, here she was, about to deliver some pretty bad news to him about one of his best grad students.

This was not the way she wanted to get on his radar, so to speak. But it had to be done.

She knocked and, when his answering response told her to come in, opened the door. And there he was.

To Tina, thirty-seven-year-old Eli Sanchez didn't look anything like a world-renowned entomologist who specialized in beetles—Coleop-teroids, she corrected herself—and bees. Apis.

He reminded her of a musician in a reggae band, with his light brown skin, deep-hooded black-brown eyes, and long, lanky body. When she first started at UIUC, he'd had shoulder-length dreadlocks that he usually wore in a ponytail, but he'd since cut them off. His dark hair, which had silver threads in it, had grown back thick and wiry—not quite an Afro, not merely curly—and just long enough to pull it into a very short tail.

A Chinese letter was inked just behind his left ear; she'd looked it up and learned it was the symbol for peace. A goatee that was considering going gray obscured most of his mouth, but when he smiled, he revealed handsome white teeth.

It was difficult to get into one of Dr. Sanchez's classes because he did a lot of fieldwork, and therefore didn't teach as much as he used to. And Tina knew that Sanchez had even been called in by the FBI for help on a few cases—one of which was about potentially deadly insects from the Amazon that had been part of some sort of possible terrorist threat. He'd even been on television—NatGeo for one. That obviously just made him even more interesting.

As Tina walked in, Sanchez looked up from the thick sandwich he'd been eating. She eyed it warily, but there weren't any insect legs or wings protruding from between the bread slices. It looked like normal ham and cheese, dripping with some sort of sauce.

She'd never forget the first lunch of her sophomore year when she saw him sitting at a table in the most popular dining hall near the entomology school. He had a plate filled with insects—later she learned they were mopane worms—and was enthusiastically crunching on them and offering them to anyone who wanted to try. It was almost enough to put her off her crush on him.

"What can I do for you?" As usual, the professor was wearing a t-shirt, jeans, and Birkenstocks beneath an open white lab coat. Today, his shirt read "Spider-Man," but it was nothing like the Marvel logo. Instead, there was the silhouette of what looked like a mad scientist splashed on the front of a psychedelic spiral with arachnids dangling from his fingertips.

"Hi, Dr. Sanchez, sorry to bother you. I'm Tina Janeski, one of the summer interns—uh, admins working in the office here for the summer," she said, then mentally kicked herself because she sounded like a repetitive, babbling idiot. And her cheeks felt hot, which meant she was blushing. "I—uh. I just took a phone call that I need to tell you about."

"All right." More sauce oozed out when he set the sandwich down. "Go ahead."

"Well, um, Patricia Denke is— She died. She's dead. They're—uh—sending her notes and papers back here to you."

The professor stared at her for a moment, and Tina hoped against hope he wasn't going to freak out or burst into tears or anything. As far as she was aware, he and his graduate student hadn't had anything romantic going on, but who knew for sure? After all, who could work so closely with him and *not* want to jump his bones?

"Say that again," he told her, his face blank with shock.

"Patty Denke's dead. She died—"

"That's what I thought you said." He closed his eyes briefly, made a gesture with his right hand (the sign of the cross?) then muttered something that could have been a prayer. Finally, he looked back up. "When? How?"

"I-I don't know. It was her parents who called, her father." Tina fumbled through what little she knew. "Sounded like it was just a few days ago? Maybe a week?"

"She was still in India, then." Though he appeared shocked, he didn't seem completely devastated, which gave Tina a little bit of hope. "That's just terrible." To her surprise, he bowed his head and his lips moved soundlessly, briefly. Then he looked up at her again. "I'm so sorry to hear that. What a loss—to the department, and to the rest of us. Patty is—was—well, she was a great woman. Smart. Did her parents say what happened?"

"Um…no. Not really." With all of his dark-eyed attention focused on her, Tina felt like her brains were leaking out of her ears. She pulled herself together. "But yes, she was still in India. That's what Mr. Denke said. They—her parents—are sending all of her stuff to you; all of her papers and everything that came back with her—I mean, related to her work here, I guess." Tina wondered what Patty had been doing in India. She'd been way up near the Himalayas, next to Nepal, which sounded wonderfully exotic and, at the same time, a little frightening. "Wonder what she was doing over there."

"Working on her dissertation project," Dr. Sanchez replied, surprising her with the prompt answer. "Titled—let me see if I remember it…uh…'Biochemical Analysis of Rhododendron honeys, with special emphasis on "deli bal" from Turkey, India, Nepal, and Inner Mongolia…and'…uh, let me think…oh, right, 'and Behavioral Differences Between and Among Hives During Mad Honey Season.' But in her last message, she said she might change it to something along the lines of… 'A Novel Species of Apis Bee from the Himalayan Mountains.'" His smile was a little crooked. Sad.

"Right," Tina said, trying to look intelligent. What the hell was mad honey season?

"What about arrangements?" he asked.

"Arrangements?"

"Funeral, memorial service? Did Mr. Denke tell you anything about that?"

"Um, no. I-I didn't ask."

"Well, she's from Cincinnati, so I suppose it'll be there," he said, half to himself. "Did they leave a number? I'll call and find out."

"I can do that," Tina said eagerly. It would give her an excuse to talk to him again. "I'll call them back and find out, and let you know all the details."

"Thank you. As soon as you get a date, let me know, because I'll have to clear my schedule."

"You're—you're going to go? To Cincinnati? For the funeral?"

"Yes, of course I'm going to go. And there may be others who want to go as well. Can you send an announcement with the info when you get it? To the entire department, please."

"Yes, certainly. I'll want to attend as well." Tina was already imagining riding in a car with Dr. Sanchez, just the two of them, all the way to Cincinnati.

How long of a drive was that? She couldn't wait to find out.

# FIVE

*Cleveland, Ohio*
*July 8, Tuesday morning*

Randy Ritter zipped up his windproof jacket and flipped its hood over his head, ducking against the unexpected rain dashing from the sky. A distant rumble of thunder had him hunching down a little more and frowning at the dark sky south of here.

*Gonna be driving right into that,* he thought, walking out of the warehouse to where his tractor and its loaded-up trailer were waiting in a row with five others.

Miserable day, and now he was thirty minutes late getting on the road because some asswipe had taken it upon himself to spray down the rigs waiting out here in the docks at Cargath Steel.

*Fat lotta good it does now, driving into a boomer like that.*

"Yo, Ritter, drive safe," called Nate, one of his trucker buddies, as he dashed out to his own rig, parked alongside Randy's. "Where's dispatch got ya headed?"

"Louisville, then down over to Nashville," Randy replied, scrunching down into the hood and collar of his jacket as the rain swept down harder. Stupid cleaning crew, putting him behind schedule. He wanted to get to Cincinnati before nine so he could sleep at his favorite truck stop—Bill Nodd was supposed to be there about that time on his way into Detroit—but with those roiling clouds and spears of lightning, along with the construction he'd been hearing about on I-71, it'd be a miracle if he got there before midnight.

"I'm off to Atlanta, then Mobile, then back up here. See ya on the flip side," said Nate as he closed the door of his tractor.

Randy was almost to his sleeper tractor when he felt something shift from off the front of him, then his next step was an ugly crunch.

*Shit. Crap. Damn.*

He bent in the middle of the sluicing rain to pick up what was left of his Aviator-style sunglasses that had been tucked into the pocket of his jacket. His Aviator-style *prescription* sunglasses.

Just freaking great.

He had another pair of sunglasses, but they weren't prescription, and so he'd have to wear his regular glasses stacked behind them.

Stupid truck-cleaning crew. Had he even *asked* them to wash his tractor? *No.* Had the truck even been dirty? *No.* Why the hell did anyone spray wash *under* the damned rig anyway? Who could see it under there?

Probably some newbie trying to make good with the warehouse boss or something.

Still swearing under his breath, Randy hoisted himself up into the seat of his rig, closing the door painted screaming red on the exterior with his own personal yellow and black logo on it. Ritter-*Goes*, he'd called it, and the image was a yellow greyhound with lightning-bolt eyes and four truck wheels for paws.

Randy had owned his own tractor ten years gone now. It was a sleeper with a roomy bed and a windshield that popped out so he could pull up to the bays at the truck stops and get electrical and heat or air conditioning pumped inside. He'd been leasing it and his driving expertise to GrayTech Logistics near Detroit for nearly as long. Most of the time, Randy only vaguely knew what was in the trailer he pulled behind—usually barrels filled with some sort of hazmat stuff like corrosive acid or gasoline or whatnot—and he cared even less to ask as long as he was paid for delivering the load.

He had a squeaky-clean driving record—which was why he was allowed to carry hazmat cargo for long hauls—and he got good wages that were always paid on time. And one of the guys in dispatch was a buddy of his, so he made sure Randy got some of the best hauls.

But now some asswipe who washed down all the rigs just before a frigging thunderstorm—and who caused him to step on his freaking four-hundred-dollar glasses—was going to make him miss dinner with Bill Nodd at the Tier 1 Truck Stop because Randy was gonna have to refuel then drive right through in order to keep his on-time going.

He hated missing dinner with Bill Nodd. They shot the shit and told trucker stories and sometimes argued about politics or the crappy state of the nation. Randy was a libertarian and Bill was just a plain old conservative, and once in a while, Jenny Bender—who was a bleeding-heart liberal and a lesbian to boot—joined them at their table. That was when the arguments got loud enough they usually collected a group of eager spectators—as if they thought Randy, Jenny, and Bill would come to blows.

Nope. Never happen. Because after dinner and a shower, the three of them would find a fourth and they'd happily play euchre or pinochle at one of the back tables till it got too late.

Good times.

Having gotten himself situated with his mega thermos of coffee (black and extra sweet), a bag of pork rinds and one of peanuts, and a freaking bottle of water (his wife was always bitching at Randy that he needed to drink more water, but that just made him need to stop and piss more often, and it sure as hell didn't keep him awake and alert), Randy started the engine.

That sound—the low growl of the massive steel machine below and around him—and the feel of the seat rumbling pleasantly under his butt was almost as good as sliding into bed after a long day. It felt like coming home. There was hardly any other place he'd rather be than sitting on the driver's seat that had been broken in to perfectly fit his ass and shoulders, with his grip on the wheel, his radio at hand, and the road in front of him.

Even if it was lined with lightning, thunder, and sheets of rain.

At least he wouldn't need his sunglasses.

# SIX

Faith United Methodist Church
Cincinnati, Ohio
July 8, Tuesday morning

**"I**'m sorry again about your daughter," Dr. Sanchez said, shaking the hand of a short, rotund man in a final farewell.

Tina watched from a prudent distance, trying to appear suitably sober and attentive—and not bored, which she totally was. It helped that the professor looked even hotter than usual in a dark suit and cobalt tie with tiny bees on it. His cocoa-bean hair was smoothed back in a neat tail, and he'd trimmed the goatee.

"She was one of my most creative and intelligent students," he said.

"Patty spoke very highly of you, Dr. Sanchez. She felt you were someone who gave her a chance, not because of the way she—uh, well—looked, but because of what she did. Thank you for that."

"What do you mean, how she looked? Did she have two noses or something?" the professor said with a short laugh, then patted the other man's arm as the laugh lines around his eyes disappeared. Tina eyed Sanchez's long fingers and knobby wrists. "She was a lovely woman, both inside and out. I'll miss her terribly."

Tina had already been caught off guard when one of the Denke family had asked her how she knew Patty, and she had to fumble through a coherent response. Considering the fact that she'd met the dead woman once, and that was at a department mixer for students who'd just declared for entomology, she didn't have much to say. It certainly wouldn't be appropriate to mention their entire conversation had been based around how difficult it was to get into Sanchez's classes because he was so popular.

But the awkward moment with a Denke cousin—or was it a sibling?—was worth it, because Tina had driven all the way from Champaign with Dr. Eli Sanchez *alone*. Apparently, no one else in the department was able to attend—or if they were, they came from a different direction, since it was summer and plenty of students were out on fieldwork.

She'd even offered to drive, once she got a look at Dr. Sanchez's aging Jeep Cherokee. Between the rust spots and the sagging bumper held in place by a bungee cord, plus the grating sound of the engine, his vehicle—which he called Juanita—didn't look like it would make it to the mall, let alone the four hours to Cincinnati.

"If you really don't mind driving," Sanchez had told her with a smile that made Tina's knees go weak. "Juanita's got to go in for an oil change and some work on the brakes. Plus, that will give me time to work on my laptop during the trip."

No, she didn't mind at all.

In fact, Tina was trying to figure out an excuse for stopping overnight somewhere, instead of making the drive to and from in one day. Or maybe if she had a nail in her tire…they'd get far enough away, then have to stop—

She jolted when she realized Dr. Sanchez and Mr. Denke were both looking at her expectantly. "I'm sorry?"

"It was so nice of you to come, Miss—umm…I'm so sorry I've forgotten your name." Mr. Denke looked lost and bewildered.

"Miss Janeski," Sanchez replied before Tina did, and she flushed with pleasure at the smile he gave her. "She's been amazing—even offered to drive so I could get some work done on the way. I wouldn't have missed this regardless," he said, just as Mrs. Denke came up.

Patty's mother appeared distraught. "I'm sorry to interrupt, Dr. Sanchez, but I've got to talk to my husband for a moment. Brett," she went on as if Sanchez and Tina weren't standing there, "I just got an update from Officer Tupperley. I can't believe he called me during our daughter's funeral service—I *know* I told him we were going to be busy. I don't want to call him back right now." Her voice wavered and her eyes were red, sending a wave of compassion over Tina.

From what she understood—for everyone had been talking about it—not only had the Denkes' daughter died in India, but their house had been broken into last night while they were at the funeral home visitation.

"Jilly, darling, please don't fret," said Mr. Denke, sliding an arm around his wife and tugging her close. She was a full head taller than he was, and as slender as he was round. Tina could see that Patty had gotten her looks from her mother. "He can wait. We'll talk to him after this is over."

"Yes, yes, of course," Mrs. Denke said, then looked up as if seeing Sanchez and Tina for the first time. "I'm so glad you can take Patty's p-papers and all of her s-stuff." Her eyes swam with tears. "I know if there's anything you can do with them, Eli—I hope you don't mind if I call you that; she always did and—and…" She stopped and swallowed.

"I certainly will," he replied gently. "It was nice of you to bring it all here for me."

"We weren't certain whether you'd be here last night at the visitation or today, so we just brought it all and left it here," Mr. Denke said, still looking lost. "She was pretty excited about something she found in India. Maybe it'll make sense to you." He shrugged. "I'm just an electrical engineer. I don't know anything about bugs."

"*Insects*," his wife said with a little laugh through her tears. She looked up at Sanchez. "It took Patty years to teach us to say insects instead of bugs. And to stop killing spiders and beetles that made their way inside the house. She wanted me to catch them instead. Even fruit flies!" She used a tissue to dab at her pink-tipped nose. "Did you get all of Patty's things? There was a computer tablet—I think it belonged to the university. And all of her notes, and who knows what else."

"Not yet. But we're going to leave now, so I can get it from the office and load it up," the professor replied.

Seizing on the moment, for Tina was long past ready to leave, she said, "I'll go grab the car and pull it around so you don't have to carry it far." She figured that might help facilitate getting them out the door in the next thirty minutes.

"Oh, thanks, Tina," he said. "I don't think there's all that much—just a box—"

"That's all right; I don't mind," she said quickly. "I'm so sorry again for your loss, Mr. and Mrs. Denke. Patty will be greatly missed."

And before they could stall things any longer, she turned and hurried off…but not so fast that she didn't give Dr. Sanchez ample time to admire her legs (shown to advantage in *killer* heels that were coming off the minute she got in the car) and the way her black skirt fit her butt.

"It was very kind of you two to come all the way from Champaign," Mr. Denke said, watching Tina walk away.

Eli didn't look; he was fully aware of the shape of the undergrad's legs and the way her clothes fit—she'd been painfully obvious that she wanted him to notice. And sure, Eli had a pulse, and he liked women, so, yes, he'd noticed her—in the same way he'd notice the shape of a plumose antenna or the facets of a pair of tabanid eyes. That is to say, objectively. He was fully aware of the effect he had on some of the undergrads in his department, even if he didn't exploit it.

That was why, for the first few days of every semester, he parked himself in the most popular dining hall and opened his plastic containers of mopane worms, crickets, and caterpillar pupae and crunched away. That usually put off most of the eager ones, especially when he offered samples to anyone who wanted to try them.

He rarely got any takers.

The Denkes thanked him again for making the drive and once more for being Patty's advisor, and then Mrs. Denke insisted on walking him to the office at the church where she'd put her daughter's things.

"I just don't understand how this could happen," she said, her voice raw with fresh tears. "One minute, Patty was fine—she Skyped with us a few days earlier, and said she thought she'd found something really exciting, and she couldn't wait to tell you about it—and the next thing, we get a phone call from the U.S. consulate that she's *dead*. It took over a week before they cleared her body and sent it back."

Eli let her talk and weep, and tried not to think about what Patty's body might have looked like when she was found after being crushed in a vehicular accident in the mountains of Ladakh. He didn't know the details of what happened, but it had been a closed-casket funeral for obvious reasons.

They were walking out of the church office, with Eli carrying an empty shipping box filled with Patty's papers and computer tablet, when he heard a sudden, ominous noise from outside.

"That sounded like an explosion," he said, hurrying toward the outside door—and the words were barely out of his mouth when people started running and shouting.

Still carrying the cardboard box, Eli shoved open the glass door and rushed outside.

"*Oh my God.*" The box slid to the ground, then he started off at a run.

He didn't get very far, for he was stopped by the raging heat from a rolling ball of fire...in exactly the place Tina Janeski's car had been.

# SEVEN

N ow, who the hell left this canister right in the middle of the damned warehouse?

Filbert Strung grumbled to himself as he bent to swoop up a white plastic container with an attached sprayer hose. It was probably big enough to hold at least two gallons of whatever was inside, and it looked like one of those things his wife used when she was spraying their garden to keep the rabbits away.

The milky beige stuff she used smelled like piss on steroids, and Filbert didn't like the way the stink lingered in the yard for hours after Karleen sprayed it around. One time he'd been helping and accidentally got some on his pants, and then he smelled like coyote piss—because that's what it was—for the rest of the day. Good thing it had been Saturday of a holiday weekend and he was off, for once.

The abandoned container sloshed a little when he picked it up, and somehow he grabbed the handle in such a way that he managed to spray himself all over his work boots and the front of his shirt and pants, because Murphy's law hated him and so did physics.

He cursed and glowered at the stuff—which didn't seem to be anything worse than water. At least it didn't smell like coyote piss or even anything at all except a little earthy.

The spray dampened the front of him from belt to boots, but he supposed it would dry. He hoped it wouldn't stain, because that would just be all he needed, Karleen griping at him about his new boots and the fancy leather belt she'd bought him for his birthday. Big-ass buckle on the front with his initials—no, it was a monogram, was what she called it. FSE—the middle initial was for his last name, which was weird in his mind, but she'd explained that was what a monogram was, and that was why the middle letter was bigger than the other ones. Anyway, he liked it, and thank Jesus that whatever he just sprayed all over himself was only water.

But who the hell left this here by the docks, anyway? He was sick and tired of picking up after the lazy sons of Bs that worked here at Cargath Steel. Trying to keep a safe workplace, and you got shit like this happening. Good thing it wasn't anything flammable or chemical or whatever—all of that hazmat stuff was in the barrels and canisters they'd loaded up.

What a bunch of clueless yahoos.

He was the foreman and he was in charge and yada yada, but he wasn't the guys' mothers, you know?

"Sandy!" he called when he saw one of the guys—who was actually a gal—walking across the far side of the warehouse.

"'Sup, boss?" she asked, veering around to head toward him.

She could make a direct beeline right now because the warehouse was mostly empty since all the drivers had left an hour or so ago. They'd loaded up a shit-ton of barrels of corrosive acid and other hazmat waste, but pretty soon there'd be another load coming in.

"You know who left this out? I'm sick and tired of puttin' away the guys' crap all the time," Filbert said, thrusting the canister toward her.

"Haven't got a clue, boss," she replied, putting her hands on her hips as if to prevent him from handing her the problematic canister. "Good thing nobody tripped over it," she added with a wry smile. "Or spilt it all over. Mighta broken your safety record. Hundred and twenty-two days and counting's pretty good."

"Damn right it is," he replied, unable to hold back his own smile. He liked Sandy. She didn't take any crap from anyone, even though she was one of only three women who worked at the warehouse at Cargath. "Wish I knew whose it was."

"Wasn't it the guy cleaning the trucks out there?" she said, a little frown line appearing between her eyes. "Ritter was bitching about not needing his truck cleaned and it making him late."

"Who was cleaning the trucks?" Filbert asked in astonishment. "We don't clean trucks here. We're not a flipping car wash. Next thing you know they'll be wanting their tractors *detailed*."

"That's what I thought, but there was a guy out there, spraying them down. Mighta been using that."

Filbert was very confused. "In the rain? Who was it?"

Sandy shrugged, lifting her hands from her hips to spread them, punctuating her response. "I don't pretend to know what goes on in the minds of men."

Filbert shook his head and, with a growl, flung the stupid plastic canister into the nearest trash can. Whoever was using it was going to be missing it now, weren't they? That was how he and Karleen raised their kids—you don't pick up after yourself, your stuff gets tossed in the trash. End of story.

It only had to happen once, when Matty's favorite video game console got left out for two days—after being told to put it away. Karleen whipped it up and into the garbage and marched the trash can down to the road where the garbage collectors were just up the block.

Goodbye, game console.

Matty was only nine, but he learned his lesson.

Too bad Filbert's adult employees hadn't had a mom like Karleen.

"I'm outta here," he called to Sandy, and jammed on his ball cap as he fished the keys out of his jacket pocket. "See ya tomorrow."

# EIGHT

*Mid-Ohio*
*July 8, Tuesday late afternoon*

"How long has he been missing?" asked Marina Alexander, her attention not on the grave-faced sheriff to whom she was speaking, but on the cave opening looming next to them.

From the looks of it, at least initially, she'd be able to stand upright inside, but she also knew that the cave turned into a labyrinth of narrow, twisting tunnels that burrowed down into the earth.

Named Turncoat Don after a Union soldier who hid inside for three days then escaped to the South and enlisted with the Confederate Army, the cave was such a dangerous warren of tunnels, waterfalls, and streams that the opening could only be accessed if you had the key to a metal door that had been fitted over the cave's entrance. Unfortunately, Benny James and four of his friends had obtained the key—by fair means or foul, Marina didn't know—and now he was somewhere lost in the maze deep within the earth.

"More than three hours," replied Sheriff Tanner, his wrinkled face settling into more lines of tension. "It's our good luck you and your dog—and your team—were here in the area and heard it on the scanner. Would've taken a coupla more hours to get another search and rescue team over here."

"We can't promise miracles," Marina replied, patting her waiting German Shepherd Dog on the head, "but Adele here has just finished her hundredth hour of SAR training, and she's raring to put it to use." She flashed a smile then tightened the chin strap that held her helmet firmly in place. "Bruce? Kylie? You with me?" she called to the other two members of her team.

They'd been sharing a ride back to Michigan from a caving expedition in Northern Kentucky—for fun and training for Adele instead of work—when Bruce heard the report on a police scanner app he listened to on his phone. Usually he paid attention to the scanner in order to avoid traffic slowdowns, but in this case, instead of a notification about an accident or construction, a bulletin had come out about a caver lost inside Turncoat Don and the call for help from the authorities.

"Always," said Bruce, brushing lightly against Marina as he patted Adele on the head. "She's such a beauty."

"She's young yet, but very eager. And super smart," Marina replied, thinking of her beloved Boris with a sharp pang. The German Shepherd was eleven now and just couldn't do what he used to when it came to search-and-rescue work. She'd had to leave him at home back in Ann Arbor, but before she left, she'd promised him they'd go on a mission together soon.

She would set it up so he'd have a challenging time, but not too challenging for his arthritic hips and fading hearing. Anything so he could get his tennis ball as a reward. Chomping on the rubbery sphere as he dared her to try to tug it away from him was his favorite thing in the world.

Blinking back a surprise sting of tears, Marina looked down at Adele. The dog's pretty, narrow face was upturned and her eyes were trained on her mistress as she waited not so patiently for something to do. Her eyebrows were dark and expressive over intense honey-brown eyes. She was Boris's great-great-grandniece, and the two had bonded well, although Boris definitely made certain Adele knew the pecking order. So to speak. Although Adele had a sharper, more elegant face than her older relative, Marina fancied she saw a lot of Boris in the two-year-old girl.

"Ready, Adele?" she asked, and the dog—who'd sat still and unmoved even during Bruce's attentions—alerted into a tight, quivering mass whose eyes went bright with anticipation as they locked on Marina.

"All right, let's do this." She led her team into the opening of the cave, then took the sock Mrs. James had given her and held it in front of Adele's nose. "Find Benny!"

The dog, who was equipped with a red harness boasting reflective strips and a small glow light on the back, bolted into action as if she'd just been released from a tight leash. Her nose bopped to and around the ground as she sniffed around in circles, then, once she caught Benny's scent, it moved up and around and back to the ground again in a familiar arrhythmic pattern as she picked up and followed the boy's scent.

Marina well knew how dogs' noses worked to find and filter through the stew of smells that constantly assaulted them. As each person moved through the environment, they threw off a cone of scent that left rafts of cells and bacteria wafting behind, imbued with their personal smell. Adele and other trailing dogs checked the ground and other surfaces where the rafts fell, as well as the air—where scent also hovered—as they followed the particular smell they were asked to track.

Marina stepped inside, turning on her headlamp, and was immediately embraced by the familiar cool, clammy scent of the earth's interior. She smelled sulfur, rust, and dampness. The walls of the cave were pale gray-brown, rough on the ceiling but smoother on the sides where, for centuries—perhaps even millennia—countless hands had touched the stone as humans (including Turncoat Don) made their way into and through the passage.

Adele started into the leftmost of three passages that led to the depths of the earth and the cave, and Marina followed her working dog.

Sheriff Tanner had provided them with maps, and as Bruce and Kylie trailed behind, the beams from their own headlamps bouncing around in the dark tunnel like spotlights at a furniture sale, Marina checked her map and discovered that this tunnel was known as Lefty's Cleft. Lefty's appeared to lead to a large cavern about a half-mile in that had a stream running through it, and about ten different tunnels branching off from the vast open area.

As always, Marina was happy to be inside the sharp, cold environment of the earth's passages, but she wouldn't be spending time admiring the variety of speleothems they'd likely encounter within. A young man's life was at stake. It was up to her and Adele and the rest of the team to do what they could to save him.

Fifteen-year-old Benny James and four of his friends had gone into the cave early that morning. They'd gotten separated, and he hadn't come out.

When Marina and her friends arrived, a group of four other teens had been sitting pale-faced and green around the gills next to the police car and ambulance with their parents standing around like sentries. Marina knew the teens were in a heap of trouble, even barring what happened with Benny, because somehow one of the boys had obtained the key to the cave door—which was only supposed to be given out to those who'd reached their majority and who signed a release. Which, obviously, none of them had done.

"Good girl, Adele. Find Benny," she said again as the dog paused to look back at her. Adele darted away at this encouragement, nose once again bouncing from the cave floor to the air, and along the flow-stones on the sides of the tunnel walls and back to the ground again.

"Sorry about the busman's holiday, guys," Marina said, taking advantage of the fact that she could still look over her shoulder before the tunnel became too close and tight to turn. At least she was still upright.

Kylie was just behind her, and Bruce's taller form loomed close behind the younger, very petite woman.

Marina had been working on SAR—search and rescue—missions with Bruce for years, and there was absolutely no one else she trusted more with her life, those of her dogs', and that of whomever they were on a mission to find, but she was a little apprehensive about their third companion.

Kylie was like Adele—young and eager—and she had far less experience than Marina and Bruce. But she was also small—barely five foot two and around a hundred pounds. Because of the nature of cave rescue, it was important for a well-rounded team to have a more petite member who could more easily crawl and maneuver through tight spaces—which was often where people got stuck.

Of course, someone Kylie's size wouldn't have the strength to force-fully extract someone who was stuck, but she could scout the area and offer initial assistance to the victim. If she couldn't help them get free, then she could offer water, first aid, or blankets to a victim, then move away for the larger, stronger members to do the brute work, using ropes, pulleys, and other extraction tools as necessary.

"No problem," Kylie replied cheerfully. "I'm really glad to be get-ting my feet wet this way."

Marina hoped the young woman didn't literally get her feet wet, which was a very real possibility in a cave known for gushing water flows.

"Whither thou goest and all that," Bruce said jovially in his deep voice, which echoed gently around them. His headlamp was tall enough that it beamed over Marina, its light joining with the stronger one shining from her helmet. "We're a team, aren't we?"

They were a team, Marina agreed, but not in all the ways Bruce wanted them to be—which was another reason she'd invited Kylie to join them on the trip. Bruce had separated from his wife almost a year ago, and their divorce was due to be final at any time. Marina wasn't certain what was going to happen after that, but she knew she wasn't interested in any sort of serious relationship with Bruce. Not now. And probably not for a long time, if ever.

Her feelings—or lack thereof—could cause a serious rift in their cohesive team. Before now, the wedding ring he'd worn had worked as a sort of barrier against anything more than professionalism. But now, things had a completely different feel.

Ahead, Adele gave a short, sharp bark, and Marina tucked the map inside her innermost pocket, trusting that Bruce would manage the navigation and mark their trail with small plastic flags so she could handle the dog.

The short yip was Adele's check-in, to make sure her handler was still with her—still playing the game of search and find.

"Good girl, Adele! Find Benny!" And then Marina cupped her hands around her mouth and called, "Benny! Benny James!"

Her shout echoed and bounced around them, but Marina didn't

hear any response. Still, Adele's testing bark indicated she'd found something that kept her on the trail.

The tunnel narrowed enough that Marina, who was five foot six and slender of shoulder, had to duck and twist to the side for a few steps as she followed in her dog's path. The tunnel tightened and widened in turn as it curved and bent, and Marina had to hold her breath, bend, turn, and edge gingerly in order to get through in places. "Cleft" was an appropriate name for this narrow, twisty passage of golden-brown rock.

She hoped Bruce would be able to make it through—though for a big man, he was surprisingly adept at maneuvering through tight places. He was six feet tall and nearly two hundred pounds of muscle—extremely helpful when it came to needing bulk and strength for a rescue, but not so much in tight channels like this one.

Yet, despite the inherent dangers of being in a cave—winding, narrow tunnels, unexpected water streams and flash floods, labyrinthine passages that all looked the same—Marina felt completely at home in this sort of embrace from the Earth.

There was so much beauty here, in the womb of Gaia. Color that ranged from crystal to rusty brown to bluish-gray to pale yellow. Texture that was soft and bubbly or spiky and stiletto-like, or rippling and draping in appearance—all formed from mineral deposits.

When she stilled and listened, removing a glove to put her bare hand on the walls or floor of these interior spaces, Marina swore she could feel the heartbeat of Mother Earth.

She'd always been drawn to the inside of the Earth, and she'd been a caver for many years before she learned about her family's heritage and the fact that her father and grandfather were the leaders of a small, secretive tribe that honored and worshipped Gaia. They were called the Skaladeskas and had lived in the Taymyria region of Siberia until five or six years ago.

It seemed Marina's attachment and love for being underground and within the depths of the Earth were obviously ingrained in her by her ancestors. It was as close as one could get to the entity—the living being most called Earth—that had, according to tradition, birthed her grandfather Lev.

*Gaia, I'm here.*

Marina said the words strongly in her mind as she pressed a bare hand against the bumpy, wet wall, pausing for a moment to allow the Earth's energy to vibrate gently into her palm. *I feel you.*

And she did: she felt the gentle, subtle, *living* tremor that was Gaia's response to her daughter's acknowledgement.

Adele barked in the distance.

"She's found something," Marina said, shoving her hand back into its protective glove as she picked up the pace—still careful, but with a little more speed. "Good girl, Adele!" she called.

"All right, I'll—" Whatever Bruce was about to say was cut off by a feminine *oof!* and a sharp cry of pain from Kylie, followed by a rattling thud.

She bumped into Marina from behind as she tumbled, and Kylie's headlamp clanged brutally against the stone. Its light instantly popped into darkness. "Ow," Kylie said, her voice tight. "That hurt."

"You all right, Kylie? Bruce?" Marina felt a little agitated as Adele continued to bark in the distance. The dog was trained to stay with the find until her handler arrived or commanded her otherwise, continuing to alert until help appeared. The urgent barking echoed through the cavern, adding a desperate layer to the situation.

"I'm good," Bruce said. "Looks like you went down pretty hard, Kylie."

"I think I turned my ankle," said the young woman, her voice thready with pain. "Stepped down wrong on a stone. Ouch. I felt a yucky sort of pop, so it might be a tendon or something."

"All right, we'll get you out of here," Marina said as the dog continued her alert barking in the distance. "Bruce, can you help her out? I've got to get to Adele."

"I think my lantern went out too," Kylie said. "I can't put any weight on my ankle. I'm sorry."

"I'll call back to the ground and let them know we've got a casualty and we need help," said Bruce, who already had the radio the sheriff had given him in his hand. "Kylie, you can lean on me and we can start to make our way back."

"I'm on my way to Adele," said Marina, adjusting her chin strap once more. Kylie's bump had knocked it a little askew. "Sounds like she's found Benny."

Bruce said sharply, "Just wait a few, Marina—I can go with you after we get Kylie out—"

"It's not far—I can hear Adele," she said, talking over him. "I'll be fine."

Yes, safe caving rules required no one going in alone—three people minimum must stay together all the time, unless one of them were injured—which: case in point. "Tanner and his team will be in here shortly to help you get her out. I need to see what Adele's found." And what condition Benny James was in.

"I can wait here by myself," said Kylie. "You can go on with Marina."

Marina looked at Bruce over the slumped girl's head. Their eyes met and he grimaced, but the message was there: he'd stay with the less experienced caver, who was more likely to have problems staying warm in the chill temperature. Marina would go on to find her dog.

"I'll be right behind you," he said firmly, holding her eyes with his. "As soon as I can. Be *careful.*"

# NINE

Randy Ritter jounced along in his rig. The highway rolled out in front of him like a silver-gray ribbon, curving then rising and falling then curving again.

The thunderstorm was more than thirty minutes behind him—it had been more bluster than anything else, he'd happily discovered—and there was even a chance he might make it to Tier 1 Truck Stop before ten p.m.

But until then, it was just Randy and the open road, filled with possibility and adventure, solitude and routine.

That was the reason he drove long hauls. He liked being alone with his thoughts, and when those weren't enough, he'd listen to the latest audiobook by Lee Child or David Baldacci. The stories gave him something to think about during the hours of endless road.

Like now, when he was heading west here in middle Ohio. Flat, yellow, and empty were the farm fields that rolled on by as he cruised along. Too bad the windows had to be closed so he could hear the audiobook story—which was about one of the badass men who saved the world every other week. It was ridiculous how often the nation, the world, even the solar system was at risk in those tales, but the thrillers and adventure stories held his interest during the long days.

Randy had thought more than once he should write a book like that. He had plenty of time to think up a plot with all these hours alone, trundling along. He'd come up with a few already, based on "what if" thoughts he'd had over the years.

What if a rig like his stopped to pick up a hitchhiker (not that Randy would ever do something like that) and the hitchhiker turned out to be a radioactive zombie?

What if a tractor was parked at a truck stop, and four days later a dead body was found in the sleeper section—and the corpse wasn't the driver?

What if a guy was hired to drive a load across the country and he was hijacked along the way—only to find out the load he was hauling was uranium? Or dead bodies? Or the president of the United States?

Or his body?

*That* would be a story.

He smiled to himself. He could give Baldacci or Rollins or Cussler a run for their money if he just had the time to sit down and write out the words. Maybe one of them would want to buy his idea and write it themselves. He scratched the sparse hair on his head and adjusted the visor overhead, for the sun was just about to that place where it shone directly between the bottom of the visor and the top of the horizon—right in his eyes.

And his mangled, four-hundred-dollar prescription sunglasses hung uselessly from the visor.

How did those glasses makers get away with charging so damned much money for a pair of specs? It was highway robbery, it was, and Randy and his wife didn't have eye insurance to help cover the costs.

He sure as hell wasn't looking forward to telling her that he'd stepped on his four-hundred-dollar sunglasses. Not at all.

Good thing he wasn't going to be home for another four days—had to finish this haul to Louisville, then pick up another and take that one to Nashville. That'd give him time to come up with a good story that didn't include his klutziness. Maybe Bill Nodd would have some ideas.

Randy chuckled as he drove along, then frowned as he felt a funny sort of shiver from below. Almost like a gentle rocking. Weird.

He eased up on the gas a little, but the strange shimmying of the tractor didn't lessen…if anything, it was getting worse.

Randy knew what it felt like when a tire blew. This definitely wasn't that sort of lopsided tugging—it was a deep…well, *shiver* was the only word he could think of.

No strange noises, though, and the engine seemed fine. He'd be able to hear if there was something haywire under the hood.

So he pressed on the accelerator again and jabbed his finger at the smartphone to start up the next chapter of the latest Sargent Blue thriller.

And on he rolled.

# TEN

Filbert barely got in the door at home before they were all over him.

"Dad! Look at what Stanley did to my *shoe!*" cried Matty, thrusting one of his trainers into Filbert's face.

"Daddy! You're home!" squealed six-year-old Rachel as she threw herself at him, wrapping her arms around his thigh.

Stanley barked and ran in circles and tried to look innocent next to the shoe that had definite puppy teeth marks all over it and a hole in the heel.

"You're home on time," said Karleen, looking at him from the stove, where she was stirring something that smelled really good. "That means you can eat dinner with the rest of us instead of having to heat up leftovers." She smiled. "That'll be nice."

"I can't wait," he said, examining the chewed-up trainer as he hiked up the waist of his pants—which were sagging alarmingly from the dog jumping on him.

"Matty, I thought we told you not to leave your shoes out where the dog— Yes, Stanley, I see you," Filbert said, reaching to pat the black lab who hadn't stopped writhing in excitement since his master had come through the door. "Matty, you can't leave your shoes out where Stanley can get them. And we just bought these! Did you see this, Karleen?"

He started toward her in the kitchen and felt his boot give away. He almost stepped out of it, but instead only stumbled, just catching himself.

"What the h—" He cut himself off just in time. Karleen had a very strict Swear Jar rule because of the kids, and he'd already put more than ten dollars in it this week because he was trying to fix a leaky pipe in the bathroom.

When he looked down, he saw that the buckle at the top of his work boot was missing, and so were the little metal hooks that he wound the laces around near the top.

"What the…?" He didn't remember catching his boot on anything, and certainly he would have felt whatever had been intense enough to tear a buckle and metal hooks out of their leather moorings.

"What is it, Fil?" Karleen asked, coming from the kitchen with a spoon dripping with what he thought looked like beef stroganoff. Mmm. It looked and smelled delicious. He couldn't wait.

"My boot," he said, hitching up his pants again as he lifted his foot to show her. "The buckle's gone, and so are the lace hooks."

"Did Stanley chew on your shoe too, Daddy?" asked Rachel, tugging on his pants.

He felt his chinos slip down alarmingly, and that was when he looked down to check his belt…and it was *gone*.

Or, more accurately, the buckle—the big metal buckle with his monogram on it—was not there.

"What the *hell*?"

"*Filbert!*" Karleen snapped, clapping her hands over Rachel's ears, heedless of the gravy dripping from the spoon. Stanley dove for the floor and began slurping up the drops, his tail thwacking Fil's leg enthusiastically. "That jar's going to be full enough for us to go to Hawaii at the rate—"

"My belt buckle is gone," he said, looking down at the leather belt, which was still in the loops on his chinos…but the buckle was missing. "It must have fallen off or something."

As soon as he said that, he regretted doing so.

It would have been much better if he'd just kept to himself the fact that he'd somehow lost his birthday gift after only a week. He'd find it soon enough—it had to be at the warehouse or in his car. He distinctly remembered buckling it when he used the john at the end of his afternoon coffee break.

"What do you mean, fallen off? Well, I hope you can find it, Filbert

Strung," Karleen said, heading back into the kitchen. "It cost almost as much as Matty's trainers, getting it all personalized and everything for you. What's it been, a week? Geez, Fil, this is why we can't have nice things!" She slammed her spoon down in the kitchen and went about putting the rest of dinner together with a bit more vim and vigor than usual.

"Daddy, we have lots of nice things, don't we?" asked Rachel, her brown eyes wide and worried as she pulled his pants down a little more. "Like our house, and Stanley, and my bed with the twinkle lights over it, and—"

"Yes, honey, we have lots of nice things." Filbert pulled up his pants, already thinking back over his day to determine when he might have lost the buckle.

"Then why did Mommy say—"

"Mommy's just a little annoyed right now. I'd better go in and help her set the table."

But first, he'd run upstairs and put on a different belt.

# ELEVEN

*Cincinnati, Ohio*
*July 8, late night*

A car bomb.
     In *Cincinnati.*
In the parking lot of a Methodist church.

Eli still couldn't wrap his head around what seemed utterly inconceivable: that one of his students had been killed—*murdered*—while attending the funeral of *another* of his students.

A sickening coincidence, and one that weighed heavily on him. After all, if Eli hadn't suggested Tina might attend Patty's funeral, she would still be home safely in Champaign.

It was his fault. Tina hadn't known Patty well enough to go to her funeral. Obviously she'd only come along because *he* was going. *Dammit.*

Eli got through the surreality of interviews with the authorities, explaining how he and Tina Janeski had driven from Illinois in her vehicle and how she'd gone outside to pull up the car, which had been parked at a far end of the lot in order to keep it shaded.

And it was only after several hours, when he'd finished answering countless questions about how well he knew Tina (hardly at all), whether he had any idea of someone who might want to harm her (of course not), and if he'd seen anything suspicious (nothing at all), that Eli realized *he'd* nearly been killed as well.

If he'd walked out with Tina instead of her offering to pull up the car to load the box, he'd be dead too.

Eli had had more than a few close calls in his lifetime of fieldwork, especially since he preferred the more adventurous locales like the Amazon and Indian jungles, but this was so…cold. Cold and lethal. So sudden.

So random and impersonal.

Deliberate.

Now, brooding in his hotel room in Cincinnati—it was far too late to drive back tonight, and he had to wait till morning to get a rental car anyway—Eli sipped tequila from one of the paper cups stocked with the in-room coffee maker.

His attention fell on the box from the Denkes. Besides the excellent bottle of Don Julio 1942, the box was the only thing he had brought into the room besides a carry-out bag with a burger. His laptop had been blown to kingdom come along with the young, naive, fresh-faced Tina.

*Jesus.*

He couldn't stop thinking about how one minute Tina had been there, and the next she was lost in a pile of mangled, smoking metal and flames. Just…gone.

She'd been fresh and enthusiastic, asking him about her plans for classes and future research projects. He hadn't known her before she delivered the news about Patty, but during the drive he'd learned several random facts—Tina loved IPAs, K-pop, and the Marvel Universe (Ant-Man being her favorite, of course)—and he found it impossible to believe that such a vibrant life had been snuffed out. All because she'd had a harmless crush on Eli.

Damn.

His insides swished and surged, and he considered whether it might be a good idea to ease off on the tequila. Then he lifted the paper cup and sipped.

Not tonight. Not after today. He deserved it.

He shook his head, blinking rapidly as he recalled the scene at the church. The poor Denkes had been inconsolable. Imagine, a terrorist attack—it had to be that, right?—on the grounds of your church during your daughter's funeral the day after your house got broken into.

The world was insane.

And Eli was far too wound up to sleep. He hadn't been able to eat the burger and fries he'd picked up when the cops drove him here. There sat the bag, untouched and adding a layer of grease and salt scent to the natural hotel-room smell. It seemed to grow stronger and heavier, making his stomach turn. He rose from the chair.

He had to get the smell out of the close, antiseptic room.

Tense and frustrated, Eli twisted the knob more viciously than necessary and yanked the door open, then stumbled back when he came face to face with a man who'd been standing—no, *crouching*—right in front of his door.

"What the—"

The man seemed as surprised as Eli, and he jolted up and back. Something fell from his hand with a soft thud, and Eli dropped his food bag, his pulse kicking up. He raised his hands, balanced on spread feet and soft knees, and prepared to defend or attack.

The other man took in the aggressive stance Eli had adopted, then turned and rushed off down the hallway.

"Hey!" Eli shouted, and nearly went after the man before he realized he'd be locked out of his room as soon as the door swung closed. *What in the hell?*

Wrong room?

If so, why did the man run away? Why didn't he apologize and explain?

Prickles lifted the hair on Eli's arms. Had the man been trying to get in to Eli's room?

His pulse still thudding, Eli kicked aside the greasy food bag and was just about to go back into his room when he noticed what the man had dropped.

A *syringe*. Eli's breath turned shallow as he bent to pick it up. On the floor nearby was a plastic hotel keycard and the Do Not Disturb sign he'd hung on the knob, and he gathered them up as well.

But it was the small needle and liquid-filled syringe that made his blood go cold.

*Something is really, really wrong here.*

He bolted the hotel room door behind him, but that was small relief, as he knew there were ways to get in through the security bolts. He considered calling the police, but he left his smartphone untouched. He was too damned tired of talking to them, and it was late, and he didn't want to talk anymore.

He just wanted to think.

Eli started to examine the syringe, then paused, realizing there might be fingerprints on it as well as on the keycard. His heart rate was still high, but his thoughts—thoughts swamped with a few shots of tequila—were clearing.

*What in the hell is going on here?*

First the car bomb, then a possible break-in in his room. Surely not a coincidence. But why? *Why?*

And then suddenly he remembered that the Denkes' house had been broken into last night. *What the—?*

Eli shook his head. "That's got to be a coincidence." He said it out loud and still didn't believe it.

Really? Three violent events within twenty-four hours, all related to…well, what? The Denkes didn't know Tina Janeski; no one in Cincinnati knew Tina.

But *Eli* had been with her. Riding with her.

And now someone had just tried to break into *his* hotel room. With a damned *syringe*.

What was the connection?

Eli looked around the shadowy room, unseeing, as his thoughts scrambled for something that made sense. And then his eyes lighted on the moonlit shipping box.

All at once, goosebumps rose over his entire body. Patty's notes? Was it possible?

What on earth could interest someone about an entomological expedition in India?

But the more he thought about it, the more it made sense.

If something was in Patty's notes that someone was trying to get at—but what?—they might have broken into the Denkes' house looking for them. But the Denkes had already put the papers in their car for Eli and driven to the funeral home, so there was nothing to find.

And the car bomb…if the papers had been in Tina's car, they would have been destroyed—along with Eli.

And tonight, here, the only thing anyone could want in this hotel room was the box of papers and—or—Eli.

His next thought had Eli surging to his feet with a sharp gasp.

What if Patty's death was related to all of this? What if *she'd* been *killed*?

No, no, no… That happened in Ladakh, India. Thousands of miles from here.

But she had told her parents she'd found something exciting. And she'd told him the same thing in her last status update—about a new species of Apis—when she mentioned changing her thesis project. *It might be a game-changer,* she'd said.

Could Patty Denke have been killed over something she found in Ladakh?

That was seriously crazy. *Seriously.* She'd been studying the effects of mad honey…and then she'd proposed changing to studying a particular Apis bee. She'd changed her thesis project while she was there.

Because she found something else?

Because she found something else.

And now she was dead.

Eli sank back onto the bed.

Why would that be a reason for someone to kill her, kill Tina, and try to destroy Patty's papers? He looked at the box filled with papers, notes, and whatever else had come back with Patty.

Seriously crazy.

But that was the only thing that made sense. And now Eli had to figure out why.

# TWELVE

*Western Ohio*

Randy was about four miles past Yatesville on I-71 when he realized something was definitely, really wrong.

The shimmying and swaying of his vehicle had become more pronounced, and even though the tires rolled on smoothly and the engine growled the way she always did, he could sense something was off.

He'd have to stop at the next opportunity, but he was in a stretch of pretty much nothing for the next ten miles or so.

Unfortunately for Randy Ritter, ten miles was too long to wait.

What had been an increasingly concerning shimmy-shiver suddenly turned into heavy swaying and bouncing, and then, all at once, everything below him gave way.

Randy had time to think a terrified *Holy sh*— before he was dumped onto the highway beneath his rig...beneath the sixteen wheels that subsequently rolled off in sixteen different directions as the tractor collapsed on top of him, its momentum flattening and spreading Randy's body as it screeched and slid across the concrete highway.

Filbert Strung was awakened just after midnight by his pager. He cursed and reached over in the dark to stop the tinny ring, already predisposed to read the riot act to whoever was disturbing him after one of the best evenings he'd had at home in a couple weeks.

Dinner with the family, story time with the kids, a little screen time with Karleen and Stanley, and then a little adult time with his wife. That last was a miracle, considering the misplacement of his belt buckle birthday gift, but he'd softened up his wife by getting Rachel in the tub and then putting the kids to bed while Karleen cleaned up the kitchen.

And now some loony was disturbing his night by calling him in the middle of a perfect sleep.

"What?" he barked quietly into the phone, expressing his annoyance while trying not to wake Karleen.

"Fil, we've got a big problem." Despite his grogginess, Fil recognized the voice of Herb Rutsinski, who was Cargath Steel's warehouse manager. "You need to come in right now."

"Right *now*? In the middle of the night? What the—"

"It's awful. Ritter and Maloney and Durowitz are—well, they're dead."

"Dead? What? How? All three of them?" Fil's feet were on the floor next to the bed, and he realized his voice had risen enough to cause Karleen to grumble at him to be quiet.

"Who's dead?" she said, suddenly sitting up, her eyes wide in the darkness.

"It's work, honey," he said as Rutsinski went on, "Three horrific accidents. I need you in here now, Fil. There's gonna be a whole lot of safety questions about everything, and our asses are gonna be in the fire if we don't have answers. Hurry and get in here."

Fil disconnected the phone and stared at it unseeingly for a minute. The bright light of the screen burned his eyes in the darkness, and he almost appreciated that visual shock, for it made him numb for a minute.

"What's going on?" Karleen turned on the bedside light, and the additional, softer illumination had him snapping out of his stupor.

"Three of our drivers—they all died in accidents today. I don't understand how..." He put the phone down and began to dig out clothes.

"Three of them? How horrible! Were they all in the same place?" she asked, confused. And rightly so.

"No. Not at all. They were all going in different directions. I just..."

don't understand how something like this could have happened. What're the chances of even one of them…?" He bumped into the dresser as he hopped on one leg while dragging on his pants. He didn't even want to think about what had happened to the hazmat cargo…

Oh man, oh man…

"Who called? What did he want? Surely you don't have anything to do with it?" Karleen sounded as grumpy as he felt, but there was a layer of worry in her voice.

"That was Mr. Rutsinski. It'll be fine—I'm sure it'll be fine."

Fil told himself that as he drove in the darkest part of night back to the warehouse. The company couldn't be liable for three different accidents that happened in different areas of the country. They didn't even own the tractors that had been pulling the loaded trailers…the trailers that were loaded with hazmat materials.

Fil shivered when he thought about the horrific messes that had potentially been made. Rutsinski hadn't given him any details about the crashes.

When he got to the warehouse, it was lit up like Christmastime. Rutsinski greeted him with worried eyes and a set face, and Filbert recognized the two gentlemen he was speaking to as biohazard specialists. Yeah, that made sense, since all the drivers had been transporting hazmat waste.

What a mess.

But, as he learned, the mess there at the warehouse was nothing compared to the bloody disaster that had taken the lives of three men that day.

"They all— The same thing happened to all of them?" Filbert scratched his head. "What exactly did happen?"

"No one's sure," said Rutsinski. "Only thing we know is Nate Durowitz called into dispatch complaining about how his rig was wobbly and shaking for no good reason, and wanted to know if anyone did anything underneath the tractor or anything. Do you know of anything?"

Filbert felt the heavy weight of the pair of biohazard officers' attention settle over him, and he really wished he'd taken the time to drive through a twenty-four-hour McDonald's and get a frigging coffee. It was too late—or early, depending how you looked at it—for him to be coherent without caffeine.

"No, of course not. We don't do any maintenance here," he said, softening his voice as he looked at the steely gazes of the two officers. They didn't look any happier about this middle-of-the-night crap than he did. "The tractors—you know, the part of the rig where the driver sits—are each independently owned and operated by the drivers, and they handle all of their own maintenance and repair work. All's they do is pull up to the trailer they're assigned to at the docks and leave it sitting there till the trailer's loaded."

He knew that was exactly the right answer—it was the honest one, thank goodness—when Rutsinski gave him a subtle nod.

"All right, then. Seems strange, though, that three of these tractors all crashed today after leaving here," replied one of the officers. His expression was filled with suspicion and maybe even accusation.

"What actually happened?" Filbert asked, his armpits going damp.

"Near's we can tell, the bottoms just dropped out of the tractors as they were driving along—seventy, eighty m-p-h," Rutsinski said grimly. "And then…well, you can imagine."

Filbert really wished he'd stopped for that frigging coffee, because that simply didn't make any sense. "The bottoms just dropped out? Of the rigs? How is that possible?"

It wasn't. It simply defied logic.

"All three of them? Ritter and Durowitz *and* Maloney? The same thing?" Fil did not like the way his stomach was pitching and churning and swaying.

"Isn't going to be a coincidence," the lead officer said. "Three all on the same day? Same way? Yeah, *no*."

An ugly shudder zipped up and down Filbert's spine as he broke out in a cold sweat. No, it probably wasn't a coincidence.

He just hoped it wasn't somehow going to be *his* ass that was held responsible for whatever caused this horrific *non*-coincidence.

# THIRTEEN

M arina heard the familiar crackle of the radio behind her as Bruce messaged back to the sheriff, and with the assurance that all was in hand, she went on ahead alone.

"Adele, good girl," she called over her dog's barking. "I'm coming. Benny! Benny James! Can you hear me?"

She moved swiftly and easily, but taking care so she didn't end up in the same condition as Kylie. The passage opened up a little, then twisted into a hairpin bend with a little crevice that jutted off to the side—and then, several paces later, she was in the large cave room known as the Cathedral that she'd seen on the map. She noticed pale yellow cave popcorn studding the flowstone on the wall next to her when she paused to get her bearings.

As Marina took in the area, the beam from her headlamp swung around, spotlighting a chandelier of cone-like stalactites, slender soda straws, and seemingly undulating ribbons. She looked up and saw that the space's roof was about twenty feet high in the center, and she caught a glimpse of a few shifting bats among the crusty formations.

Marina pulled out her flash and used it to cast a broader wave of light around the space. From the ground, stately columns, pointy cones, and wide towers that reminded her of wedding cakes had formed around a small lake that took up most of the floor of the cave room. The pool of black water was thirty feet in diameter, and there was barely enough dry ground to walk on around the edge. She didn't take the time to pull out the map to see whether the water depth was indicated, and since she didn't see Adele, that meant Benny *wasn't* in the water. *Whew.*

Marina was a strong swimmer, and she'd even rescued people—including the man she'd believed was her father—from dangerous water several times, but it was just slightly less than terrifying for her to be submerged. She'd nearly drowned when she was young, and always had to fight that memory and fear when she was in the water.

The nine other tunnels branching off from the large cave room had her pausing to listen for the direction of the barking. It was too difficult to tell exactly which passage it was coming from because of the way the sound bounced off the walls and echoed about.

"Adele, come," she called, breathing in the sharp, cold air. "Benny, I'm here! I'm coming!"

Marina heard a joyous, responsive bark, and then, moments later, Adele burst out of the fourth opening, which was at Marina's eleven o'clock. Because she was a dog and didn't feel the need to follow paths or dry land, Adele leapt into the water and ran directly to her mistress, bounding like a deer through the shallow underground lake.

At least this told Marina that the water was no higher than mid-calf, but she took the dry route—no sense in getting water in her boots unless she had to, for that would contribute to lowering her body temp. She carefully picked her way toward the tunnel from which Adele had come. "Find Benny," she said. "Adele, find Benny!" And then she called the boy's name again.

The passage Adele indicated was covered in flowstone that looked like large rust-colored bubbles oozing down the sides. This tunnel was slightly more easily navigated than the one where she'd left Bruce and Kylie, Marina noted gratefully. Wider but lower, and she had to duck for the entire way as she followed Adele—who'd bounded along ahead of her, excited that the game was afoot and that her mistress was about to reward her for the find.

"Benny! Benny James!" Marina called again, and finally heard not only Adele's nearby alert, but also by a very, very faint shout.

"Benny, I'm here. I'm here to help you," she called, knowing how important it was for a lost or injured person to hear those words. She repeated them over and over as she made her way to the place Adele indicated and discovered a pair of legs jutting up from an opening in the cave floor.

The teen was stuck upside down, past his hips, in a hole in the floor inside a tunnel barely five feet wide.

Mostly upright, the legs sagged, widespread. They were bent double at the knees, and Benny's booted feet dangled loosely about a foot above the cave floor. One of the feet twitched as she called Benny's name again.

"Benny, I'm right here," said Marina, pulling out the rope toy she used for Adele's reward after a find. "Can you hear me? Good girl, Adele," she said to the dog, petting her vigorously before offering her the rope toy.

Adele took one end and Marina held the other, playing a little game of tug in the cramped space as she continued to speak to Benny while doing her best to assess the situation. One of the first things one had to do in a cave rescue situation was check for hypothermia, but that would be difficult if not impossible, considering how the boy was trapped. A temp reading on his bare leg wouldn't be very helpful. "Benny, my name is Marina. Can you hear me?"

"Yeah," came a weak, exhausted voice. "I'm…stuck."

"I can see that." Marina was still tugging with Adele—it was the dog's reward, and she couldn't stint on it if she expected Adele to do the job in the future.

Normally after a find, she would step away and give her full attention to praising and rewarding Adele while the other members of her team worked with the victim, but right now she had to be both dog handler and rescue crew. She yanked the rope from Adele's mouth and tossed it a short distance back down the pitch-black tunnel so the dog could bound after it. "Are you hurt anywhere, Benny?"

"My arm got…stuck and I can't…push myself up." He was a little breathless, but she could hear the relief in his thick voice. "I want to get out of here." That came out a little stronger.

"We're going get you out of there, Benny, no problem," she said, noting how tight the cavern's floor hole was gripping him. He must have seen the opening in the ground and tried to crawl down and through, headfirst. She sighed. That was what cavers did—crawl into and through tight places—but experienced ones, unlike Benny, wouldn't be alone, and they would have a safer technique. At least he'd had the sense to wear boots.

"Do you feel cold?" she asked, sliding her hand beneath his jeans leg and sock. Not surprising: the skin there was cold to the touch.

"Not really," he replied. "I was, but now I'm not so much."

Marina grimaced. Not a good sign. She began to dig in her pack for the thin blanket and large plastic bags she carried as part of her first-aid kit. At the very least, she could remove the boots and wrap his legs and feet in the blanket, then the plastic, to help keep in whatever body heat she could. "Where are you stuck? Are your shoulders trapped too?"

"It's…tight…all around me except my h-head. And one of my a-arms. It's so dark—I want to get…out of here!"

As Marina shined her flashlight around the edges of where he was stuck, Adele returned with her rope toy, panting happily, and Marina tugged on the rope again while she examined the situation. If she could extract him right away, she wouldn't have to worry about warming him up until he was out.

She could see that he was trapped from just below the hips, and from the sounds of it, all through the torso. If he had no injuries, it should be possible to pull him out without further damage. She'd need Bruce for that, and maybe even some pulleys installed in the cave wall.

Marina paused to give her sweet, brave, smart Adele a good rubbing and loving, then she tugged on the rope toy a few more times before tossing it once more. That was all Adele wanted or needed for the amazing hard work she did: someone to play tug and fetch.

This time, when Adele returned, she settled down in the darkness behind her mistress and began to gnaw on the toy while Marina prepared a first—and hopefully only—attempt to extract the boy. With the help of her flashlight and headlamp, she was able to see just the tips of Benny's ice-white fingers wedged tightly between his right hip and the cavern wall.

"Benny, can you move your left hand?" she asked, maneuvering carefully in the close space to watch.

"It's s-stuck."

Okay, so that was his left hand crisscrossing over his abdomen and trapped by his hip. If she pulled on him, it should become unwedged and hopefully fall away, loosening the cave's grip at his hips. "What about your right hand? Is that one free?"

"I cut it on a rock and it hurts really bad. I tried pushing with it, but I'm too stuck." His voice was weak and tearful, and getting more slurred. "My head hurts...so bad. And my legs feel really funny too."

Marina nodded grimly to herself. Yes, they would. Her EMT training had taught her about all sorts of trauma, including that the human body was not meant to be suspended upside down for an extended amount of time. The heart wasn't used to working against gravity to pump blood into the legs—and, more importantly, away from the brain.

The situation wasn't good. Not only was he suffering from hypothermia and probably dehydration, but there were other more unique—and life-threatening—dangers in this case. A body could only survive upside down for so long before its systems began to fail. Blood would be leaking from capillaries and gathering up with other liquids in the teen's brain and other organs. Toxins would be building up inside as well.

Benny had been missing for more than three hours before they got there, and Marina had been underground on the search for at least another seventy minutes. Although she wasn't certain how much more time he'd have left before his body shut down, Marina knew it was a matter of hours. Not only that, but there was the chance of asphyxiation from the constant and traumatic constriction of the lungs.

She wrapped her arms around his thighs and tried to pull him out that way, but the ceiling of the tunnel was too low for her to stand upright and get good leverage. Next, she tried grasping him by the ankles while she was crouched low to the ground, pulling gently and smoothly...but he was simply wedged too tightly, and she wasn't strong enough to maneuver him free while working against the force of gravity. Bruce, if he were here, might be able to.

"I'm still here, Benny," she said, touching his leg so he'd know she hadn't left. It was time to call in help, and also to start trying to warm him up. "I'm going to remove your boots so I can warm you up a little, and I'm going to radio for more help. Your mom is outside waiting for you, and so is the sheriff and a bunch of other people who are going to help me get you out of there. I'll be right here the whole time."

He responded with a weak "Okay." The syllables were very slurred, and that was concerning.

Marina sat next to Adele and petted her happily panting dog while she radioed back to the surface and apprised them of the situation. She didn't need to specify how urgent it was to extract Benny James; the EMTs and paramedics standing by would understand.

From her brief conversation, she learned that Kylie had made it back out and was having her ankle seen to, and that Bruce was leading in a team of rescuers. That meant Marina might have to go back and meet the group so she could lead them to Benny.

"Benny, more help is on the way, all right?" she said as she removed his boots, but there was no response. She put a warm pack on each thigh, then began to wrap his legs and feet in the lightweight but insulating blanket. "Benny? Can you hear me?"

Still no response, and that had Marina's pulse kicking up higher. "Benny, can you hear me?" She jiggled his legs a little as she began to wrap a plastic garbage bag—to help hold in the heat even more—over the blanket, hoping to provoke a response. She heard a faint groan, and there was a slight tremor beneath her grip.

Was his body failing already?

"Benny? Benny, can you hear me?"

He groaned quietly. "Help me."

"I'm right here to help you, Benny." She needed to keep him talking so she could continue to assess and monitor his condition. "Can you tell me if you feel pain anywhere?"

"Yes." His voice was feeble, and it wheezed a little.

Not good.

She was already unlooping the strong nylon rope she had in her pack. "Benny, do you have any pets?" She knew he had a dog because his mother had brought the mutt, named Danger, with her.

"I don't think so... It looks green," he replied, slurring his words thickly.

"Benny, this is Marina. I'm going to get you out of there. Can you tell me about your dog?" Concern rose through her as she tied two lover's knots around Benny's ankles. "Benny?"

"I went there…last summer," he said. His voice was barely audible. "Snowmen."

This was bad. Marina braced the rope over her shoulder and began to pull, slowly and steadily, until his legs were straight and she felt resistance.

"Stick with me, Benny," she called, and put all her weight and muscle into pulling on the rope that was tied to his ankles. She felt a little give—just the barest of movements—before gravity and friction had their way and stopped Benny from popping out.

*Damn.*

"Benny," she said, keeping her voice easy and modulated even though she knew things were extremely urgent and growing direr by the minute. "I'd like to know about your dog. What's his name?"

There was no answer, and as fear galvanized her into further action, the radio crackled, interrupting her.

"Marina? We need guidance." It was Bruce's voice.

"He's starting to fail," she said, yanking open her pack again. "I need you here ASAP. I'm sending Adele." Then, looking at her dog, she said, "Go get help. Adele, get *help.*"

Her dog knew that command, which basically meant to go back the way she'd come, find a human, and bring him or her back. Adele also knew Bruce, and he knew her, so that would make things easier—although Adele had been trained to work with any handler as necessary when commanded to do so by Marina.

Meanwhile, Marina had pulled out the sharp knife she carried for a variety of tasks—in this case, to cut away the jeans or other clothing of a trapped victim. Every millimeter of extra space helped when trying to extract a trapped person—and denim jeans were notorious for thick, bulky seams—but the tightness of the cave's hold also made it a challenge to safely cut away the clothing without injuring the victim.

Now she had to partially undo the blanket and plastic she'd just wrapped him in, but there was no help for it. Something had to be done stat.

With the illuminating aid of her headlamp, Marina was able to see her way to cutting along one jeans leg all the way to its stone embrace. The opening of the cave was irregular, so there were a few places around Benny's waist where the stone didn't fit as tightly, while there were many more spots where he was wedged like an octagonal peg in a round hole. She found two areas where she could fit the knife blade, and, working in the cramped space of the tunnel, she cut through the heavy denim and up through the belt he wore.

That should help. It might just help enough.

She quickly replaced the knife in her pack, worried because although she'd kept talking to Benny, he hadn't responded with more than wheezing groan.

"All right, Benny, here we go… I'm going to get you out of here."

She hauled the rope that was still tied to his ankles over her shoulder and, bent slightly because of the low ceiling, began to pull steadily.

This time as she was pulling, she felt a little more movement as the denim and belt stayed in place and Benny's hips began to shift up and, hopefully, out.

*Come on, come* on, come on*!*

Marina was breathing heavily and her muscles were aching, but she kept pulling, grinding her hobnailed boots into the stone floor for purchase and taking step by tiny step as she was bent over. Her headlamp bumped against the ceiling and she inhaled dust and grit and damp air as she fought and fought…

She was just about at the end of her strength when she heard Adele and saw a hint of light bouncing in the darkness.

"Bruce!" Marina called. Her voice echoed wildly in the cavern, and Adele barked in response. "*Hurry.*"

Bruce was bent nearly double when he got to where she crouched next to Benny. They didn't need to speak; he immediately comprehended the situation. She had to send Adele back, telling her to *stay* so that the dog wasn't in the way. Bruce couldn't get past Marina in the dark, narrow tunnel, so he took the ends of the rope she'd been pulling and, with Marina kneeling next to Benny to help guide him out, Bruce settled into position.

He sat on the ground, facing Marina, his face shadowed and tense beneath the plastic brim of his helmet, legs spread as far as possible in the narrow space. He planted his boots against the sides of the cave and began to pull hand over hand.

She wrapped her arms around Benny's knees and, bending over, her back aching, thighs straining, jaw tight with tension, gently but firmly helped to work the boy's body within the embrace of the cavern walls. Little by little, tug, shift, pull, twist…

And, at last, *Benny moved.*

# FOURTEEN

When Benny James slid free, Marina barely caught herself before falling on her duff. Then she helped ease the teen up and onto the ground, hoping he was still breathing...still alive.

"He's out," Bruce called to the rest of the team, and she heard him shuffling back and out of the tunnel so one of the medics could take his place.

Marina was already checking the boy's pulse and was about to start CPR in the close space when Benny took a shuddering breath. Then he began to cough wildly, getting rid of hours of dust and grit that clogged his lungs and nasal passages. She offered him a bottle of water, drizzling it gently over his parched lips even as she scrabbled for the discarded blanket to wrap him in.

"Dr. Alexander, we'll take over now," said a medic whom she'd met briefly aboveground. "Thank you."

Grateful, Marina made her way out of the narrowest part of the passage so that the medics could get in to the patient.

"Thank goodness you showed up when you did," she said to Bruce once she got back out to the large lake-filled cavern. "We were losing him."

"I'd have been with you all the way if it weren't for Kylie," he said a little grimly. "She should have been watching where she was going."

"It's really Adele we need to thank," Marina said, sitting on a boulder so she could give some loving to her pup. Bruce handed her a bottle of water, which she took and gulped thankfully. Adele had already slurped up half the lake—or so it sounded, from the noises she was making—and was happily chasing rocks that Marina tossed in there for her.

"She's still got a lot of puppy in her," she said with a grin, looking up at Bruce.

"I can see that." He looked like he was about to say something else, but they heard the sounds of the medics coming back through with their burden. "I'd better take them back out."

She nodded. "Adele and I will be right behind you."

But Marina found she was in no hurry to leave. Now that the rescue had taken place and the urgency was past...and now that she was alone in the space, she wanted a moment to spend quietly inside Earth. Close to Gaia.

Adele seemed to sense her mistress's change in mood, and she came to lie at Marina's feet, panting quietly next to her.

Once the medics and Bruce had made their way past, Marina turned off her headlamp and Adele's glow light. She removed her gloves and drew in a settling breath of the chill, damp underground air. Then, surrounded by the blackest, most unrelieved darkness anyone could imagine, she pressed her hands to the cold stone surrounding her and closed her eyes. Subtle energy—a quiet heartbeat that melded gently with her own—thrummed from the damp cavern walls, heating her bare palms and finger pads and sending little frissons of sensation through her limbs.

Marina didn't think of herself as a religious person—at least, she hadn't until she learned about her family's history and tradition. And then her strong connection to the Earth began to make sense.

The Skaladeskas believed that the Earth was a single organism with countless interacting parts. Every living creature, every blade of grass, every layer of dirt, bark of tree, speck of pollen, microbe, fish, insect... everything about the planet was connected into one being that took and gave and worked together to create the single entity of Gaia.

That was a religion, a spirituality that Marina could comprehend— the sense that she and her race were simply one part of a remarkably complicated, stunningly beautiful, and awe-inspiring entity. And even if she didn't agree with the violent tactics adopted by the Skaladeskas, she did, at least, understand their motivation to protect Gaia.

And a large part of her—a part that she'd had to ignore and tuck away over the last few years—wanted to know more. She wanted to know Lev—her grandfather—better, wanted to understand his secrets and to learn how to connect with Gaia. And she also yearned for the opportunity to explore, unchecked, the secrets of the library belonging to Ivan the Terrible, which had been in her family's care for centuries.

But she'd resisted both of those temptations for fear of how far they could drag her from what was right to what was easy and prestigious.

And then there were two other even more unpredictable factors related to the Skaladeskas: her father, Roman, and Rue Varden. She trusted neither of those men with good reason, and yet she had strong, unwanted connections to them both.

She sighed, her fingers digging gently into Gaia as her living, breathing, warm dog panted next to her—another piece of the living organism Earth.

"Marina!" Bruce's voice echoed from far away.

She opened her eyes, and in the distance, she saw a very faint gray on one end of the unrelieved black that surrounded her.

Bruce sounded tense and concerned, and she felt a moment of guilt for causing his worry.

Marina reached up and flipped her headlamp back on, then donned her gloves while rising to her feet. "Here," she called just as she saw the soft beam of his light spilling from where Lefty's Cleft joined the Cathedral.

"Everything all right?" he asked as his sturdy figure came into view. "I thought you were going to be right behind us."

"Adele and I just wanted a moment here to enjoy the beauty of this space," she said.

"I hear you." Bruce looked around at the cave room, his headlamp sweeping like a spotlight. "There's a lot going on in here. Wow…look at those straw formations. They look just like the fringe on my old suede jacket."

Marina didn't know whether to believe him or not—did he really have a coat with a long fringe like that? She couldn't imagine him wearing one; he was much more of a cargo pants, work boots, and flannel sort of guy. "Thanks for your help with Benny," she said. "What did the medics say?"

"We got to him in time, thanks to you and Adele. Good chance he'll make a full recovery." Bruce smiled down at her, then offered his hand to pull her to her feet. "Shall we explore a little more or head out? You're probably hungry."

Marina chuckled a little. She was notorious for her traditional after-the-mission meal of medium-rare steak, loaded baked potato or scrambled eggs (or both), and red wine—no matter what time of day they finished. In fact, the first time she'd met Gabe McNeil of the CIA—a specialist who worked with intelligence on the Skaladeskas— she'd insisted he order that exact meal from room service at five in the morning while she showered after a particularly grueling rescue in the Alleghenies.

"I could eat," she said, and felt a little awkward when he didn't immediately release her hand after she stood. In fact, his fingers tightened a little around hers and he tugged a bit so she moved closer to him, their arms and hips brushing.

"If it hadn't been for Kylie, I'd have been with you when you found him. Might've gotten him out sooner. I hope there aren't any residual effects." When he looked down at her, the beam from his headlamp shined in her face, making her eyes water a little.

That was a good excuse for her to look away and slip her hand loose from his.

"I'm just glad we weren't too far into the cave before she did that," Marina said lightly as she bent a little to pet Adele. Giving her dog attention was always a good distraction from awkward moments with Bruce. She wondered if he'd picked up on that or not.

She also wondered if it was time for her to leave the team. "It would have been a lot more difficult to get her out, and more of a delay."

"She's going to have to learn to be more careful if she wants to get certified for SAR," he said. "First rule of caving: look in front of you. Second rule: look down."

Marina laughed a little and stood upright. "I'm sure no one's more annoyed about her accident than she is—missing out on the rescue and being injured as well."

Bruce gave a quiet snort, but only said, "She's young. She'll learn."

Marina released Adele to go on ahead of them, and she started back across the Cathedral toward Lefty's Cleft, but before she got there, her headlamp beamed onto something that glinted and gleamed. It was down inside one of the other passages that led out of the large, lake-filled room.

"What's this," she murmured more in wonder than as a question to be answered, for she could already see into the very narrow crevice. Its walls were striated with crystalline formations that ran like shiny, glittery rivers down the sides. Short stalactites jutted from the ceiling like sparkling shark's teeth, and they glinted in the light of her headlamp.

"Bruce, look at this," she said, stepping further into the narrow opening. She gave a little laugh. "It's almost like stepping inside a large crystal *Jaws* mouth."

He came up behind her, which was a little more difficult than it sounded, for the angular passageway had narrowed into a space less than three feet wide and growing tighter.

"It's really something," he said, edging in close behind and slightly to the side of her. Although she could move forward, the passage narrowed sharply, and they were in very close quarters as he looked over her shoulder. She could feel the warmth of his body along her left side and back—a contrast to the ever-present chill and damp of the air.

His helmet bumped against the ceiling and a small cascade of rubble fell from above, clattering over the tops of their helmets. "Sorry," he said, shifting aside and back with a little twist. "I— *Ugh!*"

She felt rather than saw him jolt then stagger a little behind her, his words cut off with a cry of surprise and pain.

"You okay?" She turned in the arrowhead-like space between him and the narrowing tunnel and found him half bent, wedged between an outcropping of rock against the wall. There was a little nook there that neither had noticed as they passed by because the opening faced ahead. But as he stepped back, he'd ducked into it and...

"My foot's caught. And twisted pretty bad. Damn. This is what I get," he said, his voice tight, "for criticizing Kylie."

Her gloved hand on the wall, Marina aimed her headlamp down and saw what he was talking about: his foot was definitely trapped—

wedged into a very narrow cleft in the ground inside the hidden alcove. He must have stepped in just precisely the wrong place at the wrong angle to not only go into the tiny space, but get his foot down into the hole on its floor.

"You couldn't have done that if you'd *tried*," she said grimly, looking at the situation.

She didn't want to ask the obvious—whether he could pull out his foot and how badly he was hurt—and so she merely leaned against him so he could use her for leverage as he tried to free himself. He was twisted to the side in the skinny opening because his shoulders were too broad for him to stand square, facing forward.

"I can't get my foot out," Bruce said. "Dammit. How the hell did I do that? I didn't see anything like a hole."

"Let me take a look." Marina slipped out from under the arm he'd put around her—probably less for stability than for comfort—and aimed her flashlight and headlamp beams down.

On the floor of the slender aperture where Bruce was wedged, his large boot was swallowed by a crevice that appeared to close around his ankle. She couldn't see how he'd even managed to get his foot down in there in the first place—toe first, maybe?—for the opening didn't look big enough for it to fit through.

But strange things happened in caves. Spaces that seemed too narrow were traversable; areas that seemed plenty big enough—like the hole Benny James had tried to explore—turned out to be far tighter than they appeared. Rocks and rubble moved unexpectedly, water burst in from nowhere—then disappeared into nowhere—and air currents swept up and blustered through passageways, then softened into nothing moments later.

It was a dark and dangerous world here in Gaia's womb.

"All right, let's see if we can get your boot off," she said. Because of how he was situated in the tight space, Bruce wouldn't be able to bend down far enough to work the laces loose on his own. "Then maybe you can pull free."

"My foot's throbbing like a bitch. I can tell it's already swelling," he said from between gritted teeth. "I don't think the boot's going to come off…or out very easily." He swore sharply and profusely under his breath.

"I'm taking off my helmet for a minute," she said. "The brim is in the way, so I can't get down close enough to see. Don't move, all right?" She didn't need any rocks falling on her bare head.

"I'm not going anywhere," he said.

Marina set aside her helmet so that its light beamed onto the ground where Bruce's foot was trapped. Then, flashlight in hand, she eased herself down to her knees on the cold, muddy floor.

Only the top inch of his boot was visible above the ground, which would make it difficult to unlace and remove it. She felt her way, probing with her fingers around his ankle to gauge any loose areas.

Her conclusion: the foot wasn't getting out without serious intervention—likely chipping away at the mud and stone around it.

And because of Bruce's position, she couldn't get past him to go for help. Adele, who'd slipped on ahead of Marina and now sat patiently while the humans discussed the situation, could probably squeeze past to go for help. Or they could radio to the outside.

In either case, they'd need help for the extraction—something Marina knew would make Bruce feel even more frustrated and annoyed with himself.

"Well?" he asked.

"You're right. You're not going anywhere," she said. "She's got one hell of a hold on you, Bruce."

She felt the tremor run through his leg and wondered whether it was a shiver of cold or a ripple of pain.

They had been in the cave for a while, and although Marina felt surprisingly comfortable temperature-wise because of her activity, she wasn't in pain or shock from an injury. Best to get him extracted as quickly as possible—especially if his ankle was swelling rapidly inside the boot.

She was just about to rise and make the radio call when her comment from a moment ago slid back into her thoughts.

*She's got one hell of a hold on you.*

She. Gaia.

It was a strange idea that settled in her mind at that moment, but before she could give it much thought, Marina stripped off her gloves.

"What are you—"

"Just give me a sec," she said. "I want to try something."

Another tremor, this one more violent, told her that Bruce's mood and opinion of the situation wasn't improving.

She ignored him for the moment, settling her bare hands on the muddy ground around his trapped ankle. She closed her eyes, wishing she could turn off the lights but knowing that would prompt comments and questions that she didn't want to address.

She felt the vibration of energy, of life, in her bare fingers and palms as she pressed gently into Gaia's grip. *Please release him... Please ease your hold and release him, Mother Gaia. Your daughter begs you to please loosen your grip and allow him to pull free.*

She thought those words as hard as she could, sending the message from her head and heart down along her arms, through her fingertips and palms, and into the muddy stone ground. She slipped her fingers down around the top edge of the hole and felt a shimmer of heat, a small, subtle zap of electricity, and something told her: *Now.*

"Pull," she said as she maneuvered his foot within the opening. She *felt movement*...the earth literally moved, shimmied, shivered, almost as if it were exhaling, loosening, and Bruce's foot moved, shifted... then—miraculously—slid free.

Marina kept the shocked gasp to herself and helped work Bruce's boot all the way out of the hole as he grunted with pain.

"Wow," he said when his foot was safely liberated. "How'd you do that?"

"Just moved it a little differently," she said. *Thank you, Gaia.* She placed her hands on the ground, curling her fingers into the opening in a reverent embrace and fiercely thought the words of gratitude.

Then she rose and began to help Bruce make his way out of the cave.

# FIFTEEN

When Marina finally stepped out of Turncoat Don for the last time, just behind a limping Bruce, she discovered that it was well into night. The sky was the darkest of blue, sprinkled with only a few visible stars. Others and the moon were obstructed by blanketing clouds. The air out here was much warmer than inside the cave. She unsnapped her helmet and removed it with a heartfelt groan of pleasure, running a hand through her matted hair and over her scalp.

Now that Benny James was safely extricated and on his way to the hospital for assessment, the rescue team had begun to disperse. Work tents billowed down into flat puddles, the spotlights that had been powered by generators popped off, and the table legs folded away. Equipment packed up and packed *in* vehicles—all of these the normal exercises after a SAR mission of any type.

"Thank you for that, Dr. Alexander," said the sheriff as he approached, offering her a bottle of water and a dish for Adele. "You and your talented dog."

"I'm happy that we were close enough to help," Marina replied, kneeling to pour water into the dish for Adele. When she stood, the sheriff handed her a second bottle for herself. "I'm relieved everything went so well."

"It would have taken us several hours to even assemble the team, let alone get inside the cave. So thank you again—from the James family and from my team."

Marina shook her head and was just about to reply again when she caught sight of a figure standing next to one of the vehicles, several yards away.

She froze as she met his gaze, and lowered the water as they stared silently at each other. From this distance and in the faulty light she couldn't see the color of his eyes, but she knew they were a brilliant, intense green.

For a minute, she considered turning around and walking away. Ignoring the man. Leaving and escaping from whatever threats, chaos, or temptation he brought with him.

"Ready to go?" Bruce's voice just behind her startled Marina, and the bottle of water jerked in her hand. "I can still drive even with my bum foot, so you can rest if you want."

"No," she said. "Not quite yet. Excuse me."

She didn't wait for their responses and started across the trampled grass.

"Long day?" said Varden when she and Adele got close enough. To her annoyance, he bent to greet Adele, and the dog—who'd not been instructed otherwise—eagerly went forward for a sniff and a pat. "Who's this?" He looked up at Marina with those penetrating green eyes.

"That's Adele. Boris is back home," she said before he could ask. He had met Boris when an injured Varden broke into Marina's house and insisted she stitch closed a severe laceration on the back of his head.

"From what I heard, she did her job well," Varden said, straightening back up. He glanced over her shoulder and his expression changed. "Looks like we've got a problem."

Marina didn't have the chance to turn before Bruce stepped into the small circle. "Hey," he said, bumping companionably—possessively—against her. "What's up?"

Before Varden could speak—and she could tell he was about to say something snarky or arrogant—Marina responded to Bruce. "I'll be ready to go in a minute. Would you please feed Adele while I take care of this here? I haven't had a chance to dig out her food, and I know she's hungry."

For a moment, she thought Bruce was going to make a big deal about her sending him away, but after an awkward pause, he said, "Okay," in a clipped voice.

"Adele, go with Bruce. You hungry? Go with Bruce."

"Looks like you've got your own watchdog," said Varden snidely as man and dog walked away.

"Looks like I've got two. Neither of whom I need or want," she replied with a pointed look at him. "What are you doing here?"

Though she'd had a moment of furious "how the hell did he find me" thoughts, Marina shook them off. Not worth spending energy on that question—Varden had proven time and again that he kept tabs on her in myriad ways.

It infuriated her, but there was little she could do about it other than revel in the fact that she traveled often. That meant his surveillance budget, if he kept up with her, must be through the roof.

The only other thing that made her feel slightly mollified was knowing that Varden kept an eye on her only because Lev asked it of him, and did so very grudgingly. He'd made that very clear in the past—along with what Marina considered his unearned antipathy toward her.

There were times when Varden's interference had actually saved her life, much as she hated to admit it. But that didn't mean she wanted or needed him around, keeping tabs on her.

"Hedron Burik has been banned from the compound," Varden told her.

It was not what Marina had expected to hear. "Hedron." That was the man—a Skaladeska—who'd tried to kill her and Eli Sanchez when they were in the Amazon. She recovered and regrouped quickly. "And where is the Skaladeska compound these days?"

His mouth moved in what might have been a quickly repressed smile. "You'd have to visit to find out."

She narrowed her eyes and looked up at him. "Are you offering to take me there?"

Now his expression became a definite grimace. "Only if you asked. Or if Lev ordered it. Fortunately, he's held back from doing that so far."

"And Roman?" Marina didn't know whether Varden was aware

that Roman was actually her father. In fact, she didn't know whether there was anyone besides herself and Roman who knew. Everyone believed he was her uncle.

"Yes, if Roman ordered it, I would take you there. They are both concerned for your safety."

"Hence, you—my unwanted bodyguard." She settled her hands on her hips. "Well, you can report back to them both that I'm alive and well and haven't been embroiled in any international intrigues or threats since I heard from them and their copper beetles. And I'd like to keep it that way."

"Understand that Hedron hasn't forgotten the way you outed him to Roman and the *Naslegi*."

Marina gave a short, sharp laugh. "I? Out *him*? No, he did that all himself—trying his damnedest to kill me and Eli Sanchez. Apparently Roman didn't fall for Hedron's pretend innocence."

"As I said, Hedron has been banned from the compound. Which is why I'm here, since you did ask."

"Better than you breaking into my house again," she murmured. "Or my hotel room."

Another twitch of his lips was quickly suppressed. "I prefer not to become predictable, Dr. Alexander. Besides, I'd wanted to see you in action for a while. This was the perfect opportunity. I was even able to assist...but I don't believe you noticed, distracted as you were by the big guy glowering over there. The EMT team was short a person, and as an off-duty ER doc, I offered my expertise."

That took her by surprise. "Are you saying you were in the cave?"

His expression became solemn; she fancied he looked almost reverent. "In the embrace of Gaia. Yes, I was there. She was reaching out to you. Could you feel it?" His voice was a low rumble.

Marina didn't reply. Her moments of commune with Gaia had been private and sacred, and the fact that Varden had felt the same... perhaps even was attuned to her personal, electric connection to Mother Earth...unsettled her.

He seemed to understand, and it disconcerted her even more when he said, "Much as I despise admitting it, Mariska Aleksandrov, you are instrumental to the Skaladeskas and their—our—connection to Gaia. To protecting her. You are the heir, after all."

His steady gaze caught and held her eyes, and for a moment, Marina felt the shimmer of connection with Varden. It was the same energy she felt when she was in Lev's presence, or when she was close to Gaia, recognizing Her power and life.

"Lev needs you to stay alive," Varden went on, his voice hardly more than a low rumble. "And you must understand that you're in danger. Not only from Hedron, but also from *him*." He flicked his eyes from hers to the space behind Marina.

"I'm not involved with Bruce," she snapped before she could stop the words, then felt a wave of fury toward herself for giving Varden exactly what he wanted: information. And the emotion behind it, dammit.

She knew that was why he was here—giving her soulful glances and probing looks, making ambiguous statements and threats, and then very nearly flirting with her. He was just skirting the edge of that type of banter.

Rue Varden wanted information; he wanted to unsettle her (and dammit, he had, simply by showing up here). He also wanted to remind her that despite how much Lev and Roman claimed they needed her, *he*—Varden—saw her only as a barrier to his own importance in their eyes.

"It doesn't appear that he's received the message," Varden replied. And this time instead of only a glance at Bruce, he kept his eyes fastened over Marina's shoulder for several seconds.

And then he stepped nearer to her, and, in one smooth movement, gathered her close by sliding two strong hands over her upper arms. She hadn't even registered this shocking action before he bent to cover her mouth with his.

Marina was so stunned that she was paralyzed at first, unable to react, or even think or breathe…but then she found herself responding to the warmth of Varden's lips on hers.

But it was only a matter of seconds before real sense took over and she realized what she was doing, and with whom, and *where*, and she turned her face away and started to pull back.

"Easy now," he said. He kept hold of her arms—not tightly enough to imprison her, but to keep her from making a sharp, rejecting movement. "Let's not ruin the effect, shall we? I'd hate to have to do that again."

He released her slowly, and Marina—whose head was spinning from shock and surprise and far too much heat—stepped back. "I suppose you think I ought to thank you," she said coolly, proud that her voice was steady. *What the hell was he thinking?*

"He's not the man for you," Varden said.

"As I said," she replied tightly, "it was never going to happen. Your little stunt was unnecessary."

"Lev will be relieved to hear that. And Roman too. Now, one last thing I must impress upon you, Marina… I urge you to heed me on this. It's Hedron. He's here in the States, and neither I nor Dannen Fridkov—nor any of us—know what he's doing or where he is, but we're concerned that you'll be his target. So please take care of yourself."

"You can tell my grandfather that I'll be careful," she said, and wondered where she'd found those placating words. The strange thing was that she meant them—both the sentiment and the promise.

"He will be grateful. Goodbye, Dr. Alexander." With one last caress—the stroke of a hand down her arm—he turned and walked away.

# SIXTEEN

*An undisclosed location*

Roman Aleksandrov strode down the narrow corridor, reminding himself that it was *he*, not his father, who was the *sama*.

He was the one who strategized and planned and coordinated. He was the one who'd lived in the Out-World and understood how it functioned, how everything was related to money and power.

He knew there was nothing that would change the minds of those oligarchs who controlled the world and its economy. They didn't care about Gaia. They hardly cared about threats or dangers to anything but their own loss of money or chinks in their power. More, more, more…

This was why he and his father couldn't agree. And this was why Lev insisted on trying to be involved in the tactics and plans of the Skaladeskas and why Roman was forced to prevaricate. Because his father was old and simply didn't understand how things *must be*. He couldn't.

The corridor ended at a passage that led to the outside—into the very Breath of Gaia, as Lev would say.

Roman paused before opening the door. He knew that what was beyond this exit from the compound was a different world. One layered with spirituality and vibration, energy and knowledge.

Elements he had barely begun to comprehend. Elements that his father had lived and breathed for over a century.

At last, gathering his thoughts and marshaling his strength, Roman placed his hands on the heavy wooden door. Between them, carved into the mahogany cupped beneath his fingers, was a prayer.

*O Mother Gaia, we work and live at your pleasure. We are one with you, and you are one with us, and we live only to serve you. All we do is for your sacred life, for your benefit, for your name.*

He said the prayer—even in a rush, even distracted, he would never fail to properly give praise and gratitude—then pushed open the door and stepped into the outside, into the world.

Earth. Mother Nature.

Gaia.

Thick green grass grew soft and velvety, pleasantly cool beneath his bare feet as he stepped from the man-made tile floor onto Gaia's carpet. Beneath the grass was earth and stone. Around him was green, flora, scent, sound, fluttering, scampering…shifting.

Above were clouds, the buffet of fresh air, the competing scents of myriad organisms—both living and decaying, as was the way.

A vast, unyielding, uncontained being surrounded him, enveloped him. He was a son of Gaia.

A flicker of emotion thumped his heart when he saw his father sitting there. Knobby knees, bare white feet, homespun hair like a tuft of dandelion on a pink scalp.

*So old, you are, Father. So frail and so withered and worn. And so powerful.*

Despite their differences, despite the dishonesty and secrets between them, Roman loved and respected his father even now…even as he saw how the elderly man had grown weak and how he waned.

Whether Lev had truly been born from Gaia—brought forth from Her, the Living Earth—during the events in Tunguska over a century ago, Roman couldn't know.

At the end of the day, it didn't matter whether that legend was true—or whether Lev had been born from some simple woman and as an infant, miraculously survived a horrific earthly event. It didn't matter…because in either case, it was clear to Roman and to those who were members of their people that Lev was sanctified and holy and that he was undeniably close to Gaia. That he was Gaia's chosen son—for if She hadn't birthed him, She'd at least somehow protected him as a defenseless infant.

Lev looked up as he approached, the peaceful calm and the startling clarity in his blue-gray eyes taking Roman by surprise, as it always did. The man's body might be failing him, but his mind and consciousness were as sharp and keen as ever.

"Sit, my son," said Lev. He himself was positioned in his favorite place: beneath the spread of the limbs of a great tree, nestled between rearing roots that formed a sort of moss-upholstered, grass-covered chair. This tree was a broad, leafy specimen, with smooth bark and gnarled roots embracing him.

Despite the different locations where the Skaladeskas had made their place over the years, there was always a tree waiting for Lev like this one: a shaman-like organism, centuries older than he, with knowledge and experience and a place for him to sit, meditate, and journey.

Roman marveled that his father always found a tree for himself near where they lived—especially in the years since their original Siberian hideaway had been discovered. Now, here in their current location, there was yet another holy tree—just far enough beyond the compound where they lived that Lev could have privacy to commune with Gaia, but near enough for his old bones to travel easily and on foot.

Lev looked up at him as Roman approached then lowered himself onto a gentle cupping of the grass just in front of Lev. The elderly man smiled gently. "It's not that the tree is found near our place, Roman… it's that our place is to be found near the tree."

Roman inclined his head, not at all taken aback that his father had somehow read his thoughts.

Of course he had.

Roman felt a bit foolish, which was a little infuriating. All these times that he and Nora and Varden had meticulously plotted and planned for the safety and secrecy of their hideaways, Roman believed he'd been the one in charge and in control, making the decisions, being the clever one. But in reality, it had been Lev—and Gaia Herself—that brought them from Siberia to the Amazon and to other safe places since.

"Of course, Father," he said. How was it that at nearly the age of seventy, he should feel like a boy of ten when faced with his father and his father's calm power?

Not because Lev was condescending or overbearing, but because Roman thought more of himself than he should. A lesson he learned many times over…and had done once again today. He was not, and never had been, truly in control of the Skaladeskas. Not really.

"Have you any news of Hedron?" asked Lev.

Roman shook his head. "There's been no communication for over a year."

"And how long has he been gone now…three years?" Lev's face had settled into graver, deeper lines.

"Yes. Since Marina—ah, Mariska—was here." And had nearly died at the hands of that bastard Hedron and his ham-handed son.

Lev didn't know the full story of what had happened back in the Amazon when Marina and the entomologist escaped. He didn't know that Hedron had been willing to allow Marina—the heir to the Skaladeskas—to die because of a personal grudge against Roman and Nora and the others of the *Naslegi*.

He didn't know that later, Roman had barred the compound against Hedron—the man who wanted to destroy Roman and his daughter, and anyone else who stood in the way of his gaining of power among the Skaladeskas.

And Roman certainly couldn't tell his father that the decision he'd made while enraged by Hedron's actions had endangered the Skaladeskas more than any other action he'd taken over the last five decades.

What Roman *had* to do instead was to find Hedron and silence him and his sons Brand and George permanently.

"What is it? There's something you aren't telling me." Lev tilted his head a bit like a scrawny, wizened owl as his gaze pierced that of his son's. Then the elderly man's expression tensed and his body seized and quivered. "No. It's not Mariska…"

"No. She's safe. And well." Roman knew this—he made certain he was kept informed of his daughter's activities. Despite the fact that she had rejected him as her parent, and the Skaladeska way as a whole, Roman would never leave her unprotected and ignored.

Someday, she'd return to them and she'd stay. They had so much for her here—so much that would make her happy. And they needed her.

"Very well. Is all else well, Roman?"

He inclined his head. "Yes. There is little to report otherwise, Father."

"Very well, then. I have something to tell you." Lev's expression was grave. "There is a danger coming. We are threatened."

Roman frowned. "Are we not always threatened?"

"This is a different sort of threat," replied his father. "A deeper one that strikes at the core of Gaia, and of the sacred."

"The sacred?"

"At one of Her centers," Lev said.

Roman wasn't certain he fully understood, but from the expression on his father's face, he knew it was a serious concern. "What must I do?"

"Find Hedron. I sense he is at the core of this threat."

Roman gritted his teeth and nodded. "I'll redouble our efforts." He wavered for a moment, wondering if he should tell his father what he knew. But before he could make the decision, Lev spoke.

"I wish you to journey with me."

Roman jolted, jerking his attention up to his father's face. A sudden, all-encompassing joy rushed through him. *Father.* Again, he felt like a ten-year-old boy, but this invitation was so unexpected... and so long desired.

The warmth that lit Lev's eyes was a balm to Roman. "I thank you for that, my son," he said, and Roman understood that his parent was just as touched about his response as he was about the invitation.

"I shall be ready whenever you say," Roman replied, and Lev nodded, still with that gentle, beatific smile.

"Soon. Very soon."

The gulf between father and son had narrowed some, and it was good.

# SEVENTEEN

B y eight a.m., Fil was exhausted and stressed—and still without caffeine.

He'd contacted all of the drivers to let them know what happened, though most of them had already heard through the radio network—which meant that he had to field a bunch of questions he didn't have answers to. He'd met with the safety enforcement people—from a variety of agencies, including law enforcement and FEMA—multiple times, as well as with his boss and his boss's boss. He'd contacted everyone who worked in the warehouse to let them know whether to come in or not—because they sure as hell weren't going to be accepting any loads today.

There were lawyers crawling all over the place, which Fil didn't really understand, since there was no way Cargath was responsible for whatever weird thing happened to the truck drivers. It'd be like Domino's Pizza taking the rap for a delivery guy's tire blowing—stupid. The drivers took care of their own tractors, period. They weren't even employees of Cargath—just contractors. Yeah, they'd been toting hazmat material, true, but that still didn't make Cargath liable. At least, not that he could figure.

"Hey, Fil."

He turned to find Sandy standing there in the middle of the empty dock area. She looked like she hadn't gotten much sleep either, but it sure as hell wasn't because someone called *her* out of the marital bed at freaking midnight.

Her pink hair spiked every which way except on one side, where it was smashed flat like she'd gone to bed with it wet, and she looked really different. Kinda sickly. It took him a moment to realize that was because she wasn't wearing makeup. Normally, she had bright blue or green or pink stuff above the eyes, real dark lashes and brows, and shiny, colorful lipstick. But today, her face was bare of paint and even looked like it was sagging a little bit.

"I can't believe all of this." She appeared bewildered and shocked.

"Tell me about it." Fil looked around blankly, then back at her. "I thought I left a message that you didn't have to come in. Didn't I? I meant to." Everything was a damned blur.

"You did. But I just couldn't stay away. I just had to do something. Poor guys," she said, her voice cracking. "I wonder if they—you know—knew…you know, what was happening."

Fil didn't want to think about it. He'd been thinking about it and talking about it enough today. He'd even seen a few photographs—not that he wanted to, but it had been impossible to avoid them. One thing was sure: those images were going to stick with him for a long while.

Man, he needed coffee. Or *something* to get rid of the incessant pounding deep inside his skull. Maybe a steel spike driven into his brain would help.

"What do they think happened?" asked Sandy. Without her colorful makeup, she seemed so much less vibrant and assured.

Fil could only shake his head and throw up his hands in a weak gesture. "Don't know. Have no idea. But since it wasn't one but *three* of them, I think they're trying to pin it on us somehow." That made his head thud harder, and his stomach pinch painfully.

"Us? Cargath? But how?" Sandy's outrage mollified him a little. "We don't even go near their tractors— I just— It doesn't make any sense."

"I know, I know. No one even goes out there in the yard except the drivers. For the most part, anyway. What do they think happened?"

He was mostly talking to himself, because he was running on two hours of sleep and a hell of a lot of stress.

"I know. It's— Wait..." Sandy suddenly looked at him with big eyes. "What about the guy cleaning the tractors yesterday?"

Fil was rubbing the bridge of his nose, pressing really hard in the hopes that it would somehow relieve the pounding inside his head. Or at least distract him from it.

He pulled his hand away and looked at her. "The guy cleaning the tractors." Suddenly, he felt ill and cold and hot all at once. Then he dismissed it. "I don't know who he was, but there's no way him cleaning the rigs caused anything."

But Sandy wasn't convinced. "What if he wasn't cleaning them? What if he was—I don't know, spraying them with some sort of acid or something? Something that made them malfunction?"

"They didn't malfunction," Fil replied, glancing over as he realized his boss was trying to get his attention. "They just sort of... Well, we don't know. But it wasn't the engine. It might have been the axles or something that just collapsed. No one's sure yet." He gave a brief wave to let Gallagher know he was coming. "I gotta go. Probably another meeting."

"But what if it was something that messed up the trucks?" Sandy asked, walking with him a few steps. "Somehow? I mean, *we* didn't send him out there, and you said Ritter didn't know what was going on...so who *did*?"

Fil shook his head again. "I don't know who sent him or what, but whatever he was spraying was harmless—I got it all over the front of me when I threw away the canister. It was just water. Thanks anyway, Sandy, but I gotta go," he said grimly. "So much for my hundred twenty-third day of safety."

# EIGHTEEN

*Champaign, Illinois*
*July 9, Wednesday morning*

E li was reasonably sure he hadn't been followed.

After the unsettling event at his hotel room, he'd arranged for an Uber to meet him outside the front lobby. The place was silent and empty, though well lit, as he walked through carrying the box of Patty's papers.

Whoever had tried to break into his room surely wasn't stupid enough to try again—at least right away. So Eli took up the box and slipped out of his room as soon as he gathered his thoughts. The hall was empty, and he waited inside the ice vending room for a few minutes to make sure no one was around. Then, feeling like Jason Bourne, he jogged down the three flights of stairs to the lobby, pausing on each floor to check the hallway.

It was three thirty in the morning. He encountered no one.

Once downstairs, he found a chair tucked in the far corner of the lobby and parked himself there in the shadows—watching, watching—until his Uber driver arrived.

This would be the test—either the intruder was waiting for him to leave and would follow him and the vehicle, or not.

Either way, Eli had a contingency plan.

While he waited, he dug out the business card of the police officer who'd interviewed him about Tina's death and the car bomb. Detective Perle. He didn't want to wait in town to talk to the man sometime tomorrow—or today. He had the need to get out of here, to get home, to figure out what the hell was going on with Patty's notes.

But he had to report the incident. Someone had—he was pretty damned sure—tried to break into his hotel room. With a syringe.

And now, with two of his students dead… He didn't *want* to get wrapped up in this any more than he'd already been, but it was out of his control.

So he left a voice mail for the detective and gave as much detail as possible. Then, having done his duty—and knowing full well he'd hear back from the cop—he set his phone aside and waited to see whether he'd be able to leave the hotel safely.

But when his Uber, a Corolla, pulled out of the hotel drop-off area with Eli in the back seat and eased out of the parking lot, there were no other vehicles nearby, no headlights in sight. It was almost four o'clock, and the night was just pushing up against dawn.

Nevertheless, Eli kept watching out the back of the Corolla. He must have made the driver nervous, for at last Chuck (that was his name) gave an uncomfortable laugh and said, "You running away from an angry husband or something?"

"No." Eli relaxed in his seat, holding the shipping box carefully. He was eager to dig around inside and see what the hell might have upset someone so much, and at the same time was certain there was nothing in there that could have done so.

Much as he loved his Coleopteroids and Apis and other insects, Eli knew they simply weren't that exciting to an average Joe. Or Jane.

So he was probably mistaken.

Still. The man had been trying to get into his room. While waiting for his driver, Eli had done a quick YouTube search for how to break into a hotel room and found several videos showing how easy it was to slide open a U-bolt using a standard hotel-issue Do Not Disturb sign.

Just went to show that maybe camping out under the stars in the Amazon jungle was less dangerous than staying in a supposedly secure hotel room in the suburbs.

Still channeling Jason Bourne—while picturing himself as Idris Elba, because why not?—Eli had his driver drop him off at an all-night grocery store, where he connected with a second ride—this time, a Lyft driver—and had *that* person take him to a twenty-four-hour breakfast place. He was getting a little hungry, and needed to bide time till he could get to the car rental place.

But all that clandestine activity was more than six hours ago, and now Eli was just about to exit I-74 at Urbana when he realized maybe he didn't want to go home just yet.

A little prickle of unease washed over him as he drove past his exit while considering the situation. He'd planned to drop off the rental car then have an Uber take him home, but was it safe to even go there?

Probably, because surely the man who'd tried to break into his hotel room hadn't seen him leave and was likely still in Cincinnati—or just on his way here. The idea that he was being followed was so crazy, yet possible, that Eli's stomach tightened painfully around the coffee he'd been swilling over the last two hundred miles.

In the end, he decided not to take any chances someone might be waiting at his apartment.

So he dropped the car at the rental place and had an Uber take him to campus. He had a change of clothes and toiletries in his office at the lab for when he worked out at the ARC, and he felt secure, since no one could get into the lab's elevators without an ID badge—which, fortunately, had been in his wallet and not in his computer case when the car blew sky high.

He huffed out a sad, heartfelt breath as he thought again of Tina Janeski. He'd have to send out a message to the entire department, and he'd call her parents with his condolences as soon as he got their contact info.

Once inside his office, Eli locked the door. He sank onto the chair and stared at the shipping box.

*Well, here goes nothing.*

He pushed back the flaps and began unloading Patty's effects.

The computer tablet, stamped with the school name, was on top in its rugged field case.

Books—some familiar texts and others he didn't recognize, like a tourist guide to India and Nepal and a memoir about Buddhism and beekeeping. He set the latter aside because it looked like something he'd want to read regardless of whether it was relevant.

A well-equipped toolkit for gathering specimens. This one, in a leather case, had Patty's monogram on it, and Eli felt a pang of grief. He recognized it, for it had been a gift from her parents. He was surprised they'd included it.

That was it, besides the half-empty bottle of tequila and the syringe he'd added to the box.

Eli reached for the tablet; it was the obvious answer to the question *what are they after?*—whoever they were.

But he was stymied again—the tablet was, of course, drained of battery. Muttering to himself, Eli scrabbled around in his office for a charging cord, since there wasn't one in the box, and realized he'd have to obtain Patty's login information before he could access it anyway.

As he plugged in the tablet, he thought about the syringe his would-be room invader had dropped, and picked up the phone to text his friend in the biochem lab over at Noyes. Maybe Milea could identify what the asshole had intended to use on him.

He sent a message for her to call him or let him know when he could meet up with her urgently, then decided to walk over to the ARC and clean himself up a bit in the shower.

After that…well, who knew?

He was just picking up his gym bag when the email dinged on his desktop. He'd bumped the mouse while unloading the box, waking up the computer, and now all of his emails had downloaded.

Probably a good thing, since his laptop was in ashes back in Cincinnati. He didn't have time to go through them all now. He skimmed the list. Many were condolences about Patty, and others were staff notices that he usually filed in the trash.

But then he remembered something, and began to scroll back up through his old emails until he found it.

Yes, it was the last email he'd received from Patty other than the excited text (which would have cost a fortune to send) two days later telling him she was going to change her thesis.

He clicked to open it.

*Eli:*
*Just a short note…I've gotten to know one of the local guys here in Thik-*

*sey, which is one of the little mountain towns in Ladakh. He took me out to see the dorsata hives and—you told me they were huge, but they're really huge! Totally covering the side of a small mountain. Wish I was going to be here during honey-hunting season—I'd love to see those guys knocking down the hives.*

*The most exciting thing is this guy, Manish, was telling me about a very rare bee. Its hive is tucked away in the mountains—his English isn't great, and my Pashto is even worse, so I think that's what he was saying. He showed me pix on his phone (everyone here has a phone—and solar chargers!—but they mostly use them for taking pictures). I wanted him to send me the pictures, but he refused.*

*Anyway, this bee is like nothing I've ever seen—I'm dying to know what you think. We couldn't figure out how to get the pix to my phone from his, so he's taking me up there to look at them—I think he likes me ;-)—but he says it's a couple hours' journey.*

*Eli, from the picture, this bee looks incredible. You wouldn't believe it. Tiny bees, gorgeous rose-gold in color, absolutely glorious colors all over— and the legs are really light. Almost golden yellow! I'm not sure whether to believe the colors in the photos are real, and I won't until I actually see them in person, but he swears (at least, as far as I can understand with our language barrier) that they're accurate.*

*As near as I can tell, they would be Apis melliflera, senso strictu, except: size and color. He also was trying to tell me they had more than one queen, but he must be talking about the splitting of the colony or something like that—like I said, we aren't communicating perfectly. At least, not verbally. ;-) Did I mention he likes blondes?*

Eli laughed at this. Tall, fair, and gorgeous Patty surely attracted a lot of attention from the dark-skinned, dark-haired people in India.

*Anyway, he's going to take me up there tomorrow, I think. If this turns out to be something exciting, you better believe I'm changing my thesis!*

*Hope you're well back in super-boring (but much cooler) Champaign and aren't being chased by too many wide-eyed undergrads (ha, ha!)—I'll write back and send pix (I hope!) as soon as possible. Thanks again for the satellite converter.*

*Can't wait to show you more. Miss you! Patty.*

Eli sighed as a renewed rush of grief swept over him. Hard to believe he'd never see the enthusiastic, smart-as-a-whip, and funny-as-hell Patricia Denke ever again. *What a loss.*

He decided to print the email so he'd have it, because if his suspicions were correct, this message had more information than he'd been able to get so far from her dead tablet. And now, he needed to get out of here and figure out what was going on. He glared at the tablet, which was still charging, and mentally ordered it to hurry.

Just then, there was another *ding* in his email box and he automatically glanced at the new message. The subject line snagged his attention: *Weird bee—can you help my colleague?*

He really didn't have time to mess around with stuff like this (he already knew it was going to be a Halictid, like these "weird" bees always were—their metallic green color really set people off) when someone was blowing up cars and breaking into hotel rooms with syringes, but being an entomologist first and a reluctant Jason Bourne second, Eli couldn't help but click on the email, which was from a friend currently at the University of Chicago.

The message was short and to the point, from Ghomie Prana: *A librarian archivist here found a strange bee packed up in a box sent from Paris in 1897! Weird. Can you take a look at it, see if there's anything special about it? Photo attached. Copying Jill Fetzer, the archivist, on this for your response.*

Eli absently clicked on the photo just as his cell phone rang. "Milea," he said as he answered. "Thanks for calling me."

"You said it was urgent, so here I am." Milea had a high-pitched, squeaky voice that made her sound as if she were a preteen, but in reality she was a forty-year-old biochemistry wiz.

"I've got something I need tested," he said, picking up the syringe, still with a tissue, just in case there were fingerprints. He hadn't returned Detective Perle's callback to his message yet. "As soon as you can. Do you have access to a database that would include the chemical makeup of drugs—or medications?"

"Drugs? What's going on, Sanchez?" Even with her squeaky voice,

Milea sounded no-nonsense. "You bring something illegal back from Brazil?"

He laughed wryly. "It's been a couple years since I've been there, so no. It'd be easier for me to explain in person. Can I meet you at your lab?"

Fortunately, her lab was only on the next block and not on the other side of Green Street—although that meant Milea worked in an older, less state-of-the-art facility. Only the "big bucks" majors—like engineering—with the fancy new buildings and state-of-the-art labs were north of Green. Every other discipline—like entomology and biochemistry—located south of the main drag was basically chopped liver. Nonetheless, Milea ran her older, draftier, less state-of-the art lab with precision and care, and Eli trusted she'd be able to help him determine what someone had tried to inject in him. He began shoving Patty's things into his gym bag, ending with the syringe, bundled in tissues.

"I'll meet you there in fifteen minutes." Milea still sounded suspicious, but friendship obviously won out. "I've got to teach a class at four."

Eli disconnected and was about to walk out of his office when he saw the tequila. After snatching it up—God knew he might need it later—he grabbed the box with Patty's things and rushed out without shutting down his computer.

# NINETEEN

J ill checked her email yet again and ground her teeth. This
Dr. Eli Sanchez *still* hadn't responded to Ghomie's message
on her behalf, asking about the bee. It had been over twenty-four hours, and Ghomie had said he knew the entomologist
was in town for the summer because he'd just seen him the week
before.

*It must not be anything special, then.*

Jill was disappointed. She had become strangely attached to the
small creature that had traveled so far—both in geographic distance,
and in decades. He—it—was so small, and it looked like no other
insect or bee she'd ever seen. The color was uniquely beautiful: a soft
pinkish metallic hue, like a rosy gold. One of the wings had been
dislodged, probably during the voyage; she'd found it tangled in the
cotton batting and saved it.

Jill had propped him back up on his little display cube via the pin
stuck through his abdomen, and he sat next to where she'd spread out
her work. She'd brought the package sent to Alexina Donovan back
to her townhouse so she could work on transcribing the letter in the
evenings after the train ride home from campus.

It was, technically, work because it was some sort of historical
find—but she felt a little guilty spending time on it when she was
in the middle of research for a book about how, at the turn of the
century, folk medicine had competed with the practices at Catho-

lic charity hospitals in Chicago. However, being on sabbatical this summer made it slightly easier to allot the time, and she didn't allow herself to work on it until after eight o'clock each night.

And this little mystery was so much more interesting. The ancient medicinal pot—which she hadn't attempted to break the seal on and open yet. The tiny bit of research she'd allowed herself during her lunch break today had Jill fairly certain the letters etched on the jar were Sanskrit, or some similar language, so now she needed to find an expert on that.

But first she needed to read the letter. The task was slow-going—deciphering the spiky, smudged, splattered, and slapdash penmanship of Nicolas Notovitch.

A warm breeze dampened by an early summer rain during her train ride home filtered through the open window. Jill turned her face toward it to catch the fresh air, and frowned when she heard thunder in the distance. She might have to close the windows—something she hated doing when the weather was so mild.

Turning back to her laptop, she clicked away from email and pulled up Google. Jill hadn't yet done the obvious—a basic online search—because she wanted to stick with the primary source to see what she could learn from it alone. But her eyes were tired and dry, and she was mildly annoyed with this supposedly brilliant Eli Sanchez and his silence.

She dove right in, typing in the search box: *Alexina Donovan Rand McNally*. And then stared at the results.

*Whoa.*

The very first thing that came up was a listing: The Secret Life of Jesus Christ *by Nicolas Notovitch. Translated by Alexina Loranger Donovan. Published by Rand McNally, 1894.*

Well, that was easy, she thought. And that answered several questions: what her great-grandmother had done for Rand McNally, and how she knew Notovitch. And possibly why he would have sent her something. Though a *bee*? Really?

Just as she was about to click on the link (the secret life of Jesus? Talk about provocative!), she heard something.

A rustling, just outside the window.

In her backyard. In the shiny, damp darkness.

Something about the noise made Jill's skin prickle. Her breath became a little shallow as she looked out into the damp night.

Not one to be easily spooked, Jill was nevertheless one to pay attention to instinct—something she hadn't done when she married Phil Traft, unfortunately—and she curled her fingers around her mobile phone, all the while still looking into the darkness.

Still alert. Still prickling.

*Why don't I have a dog?*

There was no good answer for that; she loved dogs—but now was not the time to bemoan the lack.

A shadow moved somewhere where no movement should have been—just beyond the small, postage-sized patio off her sliding door.

Which wasn't locked.

Or even closed.

Jill swallowed hard and refused to panic. She insisted that her mind remain clear and focused even as a cold sweat broke out over her skin.

Her front door was locked. At least he couldn't get in that way. Or through the garage.

She peered into the darkness without being obvious. The last thing she wanted to do was tip the guy off that she'd seen him.

If anyone was even there.

Maybe she hadn't seen anyone after all. Who would be lurking around behind a row of townhouses, anyway? It was only nine o'clock—people were still up. The only reason it was dark was because of the rain.

Her mouth dried.

*Maybe he's waiting till everyone on the block goes to bed.*

She felt sick. Then an idea came to her. Looking at her phone, she pretended to answer it.

In a clear voice that carried, she said, using the first name that popped into her head, "Nick! Where are you? Two minutes? Excellent. I'll open the wine. Oh, Brad's with you? Well, that should be fun. I've never played poker with a cop before!"

Even as she carried on this faux conversation, Jill wandered casually toward the sliding door. She watched the darkness without seeming to. Nothing moved. Nothing lurked there at the door.

But her hand was damp with sweat and her insides churned as she slammed the door shut. She finished the movement by snapping the lock into place immediately, still pretending she had no idea someone was out there.

But now she *knew* someone was—for when she got to the door, just before she shoved it closed, she'd clearly seen the silhouette standing there. Just beyond her patio table with the umbrella. *Right there in her backyard.*

Her heart was in her throat, and now she dialed 911, speaking quickly and calmly while she watched the patio from safely inside her house. Nothing moved. But she knew he was out there.

Just as Jill hung up the phone with the dispatch—who was sending someone out immediately—her email dinged from the laptop.

Though her mind was on other things, she automatically looked at her inbox.

*Eli Sanchez.*

Well, it was about time the entomologist got back to her.

It felt good to think about something else for a moment. Jill was shaking and clammy, and she felt like she was going to puke. But the police were on the way and her doors were locked, so she had time to read Dr. Sanchez's email. It would calm and distract her.

But the contents of his message left her even more shocked and startled:

*I need to see that bee in person, ASAP. Don't tell anyone about it. Text me ASAP a place to meet. Be careful!*

Be careful? What did that mean? Why had he said that?

Instinctively, she glanced out into the darkness. Nothing moved. Whoever had been there was gone. She swallowed, and her dry throat crackled.

*Please let him be gone.*

*Be careful?* What did Sanchez mean by that? Why had he said that?

Jill's hands were cold and damp and her stomach felt like the skin of a drum. Her attention rested on the bee.

*What the hell is so important about this little insect?*

# TWENTY

*Champaign, Illinois*
*University of Illinois at Urbana-Champaign*
*July 9, late evening*

"**D**ude, what the hell you got going on here?" Milea's squeaky voice had dropped several notches into tenor territory. "Why you carrying around a syringe with sufentanil in it?"

Eli winced and, despite the fact that no one was around the building at night, closed the door to his colleague's biochem lab as he considered how much to tell her. He'd dropped off the syringe earlier and then had to wait until now, when she finally got back to him with the results. He'd spent the day hiding out and making sure he wasn't followed or seen by anyone, wearing dark glasses and a ball cap for the Red Sox—the perfect disguise, since everyone knew he loathed the Boston team and wouldn't be caught dead wearing the big red B on his hat.

He was beginning to feel like a cross between Jason Bourne and *The Man Who Knew Too Much*—which reminded him of Marina Alexander and all of the vintage Hitchcock posters on her walls in Ann Arbor. The last time his life had been endangered like this, it had been the two of them escaping from the Amazon jungle in a little plane after being kidnapped from a hotel in Chicago. His hair still stood up all over his body whenever he remembered that harrowing adventure...what, three years ago? Four? The last time he'd seen Marina was a little weekend sojourn a little more than six months ago, when they were both in Mallorca for different conferences during the winter. He smiled a little at the memory of their own personal, very private happy hour.

Then his smile faded because he remembered the photograph of the "weird bee" that had been sent to him by Ghomie Prana. He hadn't had a chance to look at his email again until about an hour ago. That was when he actually looked at the photo of the bee for the first time, and his heart had stopped and very nearly didn't start again, because that bee had matched the description of the one Patty had emailed him about.

Eli had immediately emailed Jill Fetzer and asked her to text him ASAP, praying he wasn't too late. He hadn't heard back from her yet.

"I'm not sure what's going on." *Understatement of the year.*

Eli glanced at his smartphone again. No texts, and it was nearly nine p.m.

Maybe he should call Ghomie and see if he could give him the phone number for this Jill Fetzer. Chances were it had nothing to do with whatever was going on—what *was* going on?—but he tended to err on the side of caution. Last thing he wanted was another innocent person to get hurt because of…whatever it was that was going on.

In the end, he decided on the truth without details, mainly so that Milea would take the situation seriously. "Someone tried to break into my hotel room, and they dropped the syringe. I figured I'd better find out whether the asshole was trying to kill me, or just put me out for a while."

"Well, I've got good news, doc—he was trying to kill you. But at least it would have been quick and fairly painless," Milea said.

"How's that good news?"

"Means he wasn't going to work you over and then kill you; he was just going to kill you. It's an opioid that's about four times stronger than fentanyl. They mostly use it for large animals in veterinary practices. There's enough in here to put down an angry bull. Permanently." She shrugged, but her eyes were filled with worry. "What're you mixed up in, Eli?"

"Like I said, I have no clue. But I'd better get out of here before whoever came after me with that catches up to me here. I'm sorry to get you—" He paused when his phone dinged with a text message.

*Finally.* It was Jill Fetzer, the woman who wanted to know about the bee.

*Where do you want to meet? Someone tried to break into my place two hours ago. What is going on???? This is Jill Fetzer. Ghomie's friend.*

Crap. So much for keeping an innocent out of whatever mess this was.

"Sorry, Milea, I've got to run—I don't want you to get any more involved," he said. "Probably best if you haven't seen me, you know? And…just be careful, all right?" Eli gave her a quick, hard hug. Then he snatched up the syringe—which she'd put into a small box for safe-keeping—and slipped from the lab, leaving her staring after him with wide, round eyes and shaking head.

He prayed she'd be safe.

Instead of texting Jill Fetzer, Eli called the number as soon as he'd ducked into a silent, empty lab two floors below Milea's.

A woman answered right away. "Dr. Sanchez?"

"Yes—"

"Before we go any further, tell me what color Ghomie Prana's hair is right now."

Despite the gravity of the situation, Eli couldn't hold back a smile. "He doesn't have any hair. Bald as a baby's bottom. But he's got a tattoo on the back of the scalp that's the Chinese symbol for life. So—"

"And what's a-a Coleopteroid?" she demanded, a little breathlessly.

"My favorite insect—a beetle," Eli replied.

"Okay." Jill let out her breath in a long whoosh. "Okay. Sorry about that, Dr. Sanchez, but I'm a little freaked out."

"All right. Are you somewhere safe?"

"The police just left—left here, my house. Someone was out back, lurking around out there, and I called the police. And then I got your email, and it really freaked me out." She whooshed out another long breath. "Sorry I keep saying that, but I'm not— This isn't what I… I mean, I'm an archivist, not a—an entomologist. I work with old documents, not— Well, I had no idea the bug world was so cutthroat."

*Insect world.*

"Trust me, it's usually not," he said dryly. "All right, look, I don't know what's going on, but I need to see that bee you found. From the picture you sent, it looks like… Well, it doesn't matter. I need to see it, and I need you to be safe and careful about it. At least one person—maybe two—have already died, and I think it's because of that bee."

"Are you *kidding* me?" Her voice was taut and high. "A *bee*? What the hell does it do, spin golden honey?"

Eli bit his lip to keep from correcting her about how Apis bees made honey. "We need to meet up—or at least you need to get the bee to me."

It took another five minutes to make a plan because Jill was, understandably, *freaked. Out.* At least Eli had been in life-threatening situations before—both on entomology excursions in the Amazon jungle and elsewhere, and when he was entangled in the whole *cuprobeus* beetle and Skaladeska mess with Marina Alexander. The woman on the other end of the phone had clearly never been in anything more dangerous than a fender bender. And he intended to keep it that way.

Unfortunately, Fetzer was north of Chicago, and he was here in Champaign, which was almost a three-hour road trip.

And, even more unfortunately, it seemed that whoever was after the bee had already pinpointed Jill and her location. He didn't think for one minute that it was a coincidence that she'd had someone casing out her house half a day after she'd emailed him—but he didn't know how whoever it was had pinpointed her and her location so quickly.

Eli didn't want to upset Jill any further, but he had to impress upon her the severity of the situation. Together they came up with a plan that, he hoped, would keep her safe until they could meet and he could get the specimen from her.

"All right," he said, once they both felt comfortable with the plan. "I'll be there as soon as I can."

"I really need to get a dog," she said, then disconnected the call.

Eli left the biochem lab like a wraith, slipping into the corridor and listening carefully for any sign of life. If there were any custodians around, they gave no indication by making any noises. That made him a little nervous, because at least over in the entomology building, the crew was always bumping around at night, using the vacuum and other cleaning equipment.

The short hair beneath the ponytail at the nape of the neck prickled as he bounded down the stairwell, his footsteps only faint thuds on the metal steps. His gym bag, which held Patty Denke's tablet and papers, among other necessities, bumped gently against his hip.

He got to the ground floor and stepped out into the warm summer night. Because it was a college campus, there were floodlights everywhere that in different circumstances he'd consider severe light pollution offenders—but here the illumination was necessary to help keep the students safe. And Eli had never been so happy to have it. No one was around, and there was nowhere for anyone to lurk.

He'd had to leave his beloved but very recognizable Juanita parked in the garage at home, and had been using the campus bus system and Uber and Lyft all day to get around. Now he was going to have to chance getting Juanita out and onto the road for the drive to Libertyville.

Confident that he'd kept whoever had been after him in Cincinnati off his trail so far, Eli knew he just needed five minutes to get into the garage, get into the Jeep, and get on the highway without being noticed.

But as he started down the street on a fast walk to catch one of the campus buses at RAL, he caught movement from out of the corner of his eye. Across Mathews and from behind…someone was coming up fast and silent.

Swearing under his breath, Eli dug into the pocket of his gym bag, where he'd tucked the small knife he took with him to the jungle. Small but sharp as a wit, the blade would be no match for a firearm, but Eli was banking on the fact that whoever was following him would use a silent weapon rather than one that would draw attention.

Gripping the hilt in his left hand, he changed his mind about crossing Mathews—he'd head over to Wright and be more likely to catch the bus there. He increased his pace and darted across the quad. The light was lower here, which could allow him to blend into the shadows, and hopefully his pursuer wouldn't be able to see him as well. If he could reach the bus stop, he might be able to jump onto the bus before the asshole got to him, and then he'd be surrounded by witnesses. And he might be able to jump off at a stop before his pursuer could catch him.

Across the quad, he started down the wide cobblestone path that ran between the English Building and Lincoln Hall, keeping to the shadows as much as possible. The traffic on Wright was fairly steady, and there was no sign—or sound—of the bus yet.

Then he heard it—the distinct sound of the bus, squealing and farting from its exhaust pipe as it turned down Wright.

He ran over the uneven cobbles, the gym bag bumping against his hip—aware that footfalls behind him were coming louder and closer and faster.

Eli came out between Lincoln and the EB to where the bus pulled up to its stop in front of the bookstore. He cast a glance back to see how far away his pursuer was…and at the last second, Eli darted around in front of the bus instead of getting on it.

Using the beast-sized vehicle as cover to block him from the view of his pursuer, Eli ran up the middle of Wright. As he heard the bus pull out from the stop a half a block behind him, he bolted back across the street toward the quad, taking cover in the shadows on the north side of the EB.

Panting, he leaned against the smooth brick wall just behind a stately column and watched as the bus rolled away.

It was too dark for him to tell whether his pursuer had climbed into the bus—not that he'd gotten a good enough look at the guy to recognize him through a window anyway.

His only impression had been that of a hatless man wearing unrelieved black and moving with confidence and determination. He'd been too shadowed to tell what his skin color was, but his hair was dark and neither very short nor very long.

Eli watched the area for another few moments but saw no sign of the man who'd been chasing him among the few pedestrians who strolled past.

But he didn't wait too long, and when he left, he didn't go back out onto Wright. He went back toward the quad, staying in the shadows while moving briskly.

He'd have to get an Uber—that was the safest way to get himself back home, where he could sneak into the garage and retrieve Juanita and hopefully make his escape without anyone seeing him…then be on his way to Libertyville.

Which made him pause mentally, for if Jill Fetzer had someone lurking around her house—presumably after the bee—who the hell was chasing Eli here in Champaign?

Maybe whoever was scoping out Jill's house wasn't related to the bee situation after all. That realization made him feel a little less worried about her.

Because surely there weren't *two* people after the bee…?

He turned the corner sharply and nearly bumped into someone coming toward him—or waiting for him.

Eli had an instant of shock and realization, but that wasn't enough time to react. The man reached out, caught him by the throat with a bare hand, and pressed hard.

Eli's world shuttered black as his knees gave out.

# TWENTY-ONE

When Eli opened his eyes, the moon was blaring right into his gaze, blinding him. He blinked rapidly and looked away before he realized it wasn't the moon but a streetlight shining down on him in the quiet July night.

He was sitting half propped against some bushes that he recognized as being a hedge growing along the foundation of the English Building.

He felt achy and out of sorts, but there weren't any specific injuries on his body. He pulled himself easily to his feet. *Whoa.* The earth moved for a sec, then righted itself just as he remembered what happened: a man dressed in black reaching toward him with a brief, efficient move. And then nothing.

Immediately following that flashback was the stark realization that his gym bag—the bag with Patty's tablet in it—was gone.

Eli swore violently in Spanish and stamped his foot for emphasis. Just *great.*

He felt around his pockets and was relieved to discover that the assailant hadn't taken his mobile phone. When he checked it, he saw the time—*Madre*, he'd been out for at least fifteen minutes—then called Jill.

She answered immediately. "What's wrong? Where are you? Are you on your way?"

"Not yet. I got delayed. I just wanted to make sure everything was all right on your end." He thought it best not to fill in the details of his experience, for Jill was already freaked. Out.

Now that he knew she was safe and that whoever was after Patty's notes about the bee was here in Champaign, he felt more relaxed.

The asshole got what he wanted, and so he had no reason to bother Eli again. And although Eli had lost Patty's tablet, he knew he should be able to access her backup via the cloud with a little help from IT. In the meantime, he needed to meet Jill.

And, he supposed, starting off down the street at an easy jog, it was definitely time to return the call from Detective Perle from back in Cincinnati. Eli had a lot to tell him.

Twenty minutes later, Eli and Juanita were barreling up I-57 toward Chicago and her suburbs. He'd done a little what he thought of as Jason Bourne movements—doubling back and around—just to make sure no one was following him, but when Eli finally got onto the highway, the road behind him was dark and empty, and it stayed that way for a long time.

Juanita had just had an oil change, and she was running pretty smoothly for a fifteen-year-old Jeep with three hundred thousand miles, and whose rear bumper was attached by a trio of bungee cords. Eli's friends teased him that he obviously had no problems with commitment because he wouldn't even consider trading in his beloved for a newer, sexier model. Why should he, when she was all broken in and he knew every purr and growl and rumble she made? Plus, the seat was perfectly broken in to the shape of his butt.

While driving, he first made a call to the IT help department at UIUC. He needed to make sure someone grabbed Patty's data and notes off the cloud before the asshole who stole her tablet hacked into it. Because it was a university, where work and technological issues happened at all hours of the day, the call was immediately answered by a perky sounding young woman…

…who wasn't inclined to help Eli get into someone else's account on the basis of a simple phone call.

"I'm sorry, sir, I'm not able to do that," she said in a perky, rather tinny voice. "Every university account is confidential, and I'm not able to grant access to anyone without proof of identity."

"I can prove my identity—"

"But you're not the owner of the account," she replied in a very reasonable, still perky tone.

"I'm her graduate advisor," he said in his own reasonable tone. "And she—Patricia Denke—just *died* over in India, so she isn't going to care if I get access to her notes."

"I'm sorry, I can't just take your word for it, you know? We have security issues here, strict security rules, and—"

"Look, uh—what's your name again?" He usually tried to remember the names of any faceless person he spoke to for things like this, but his brain was a little fried at the moment.

"Rindy."

"Look, Rindy, I was assaulted earlier tonight and someone stole Patty Denke's tablet from me. I just want to make sure whoever stole it can't use it to get to her notes on the cloud and delete them."

"I'm *really* sorry, sir—"

"Doctor," he said, still keeping his voice smooth but deciding it was time to pull rank. This was, after all, a matter of life and death. "It's *Doctor* Eli Sanchez—"

He heard a shocked intake of breath. "Did you say Eli Sanchez?" The voice came out a little squeaky now.

"Yes, Eli Sanchez. I'm Patty Denke's advisor, and—"

"The beetle guy? Who worked with the FBI? You were on NatGeo, weren't you?"

Thank heaven for *National Geographic,* their interest in the copper beetles, and UIUC pride. "Yes, that's me."

"Oh, wow, I can't believe I'm talking to you! I just thought that was the coolest thing ever—the copper beetles that caused the big blackout? And a deadly disease? Who'd have thought it! And you got to work with the FBI? You helped avert a *terrorist attack.*"

"I did…and—can you keep a secret?"

"*Yes.*"

"I really, *really* need to secure Patty Denke's account and all of her notes, because it's—now please don't repeat this—very possibly a matter of national security." He lifted his eyes to heaven and added mentally, *Sorry.*

"Oh." She was quiet, and for a moment Eli thought he'd lost her. "Well…"

"Someone might try to hack in to get or destroy those notes, and we have to make certain they're copied—and protected. Even if you can't let *me* have them"—he could worry about getting access later—"we have to make sure they're copied and protected. Can you at least do that?"

"Hold on a minute."

He waited, holding his breath and praying as the trusty Juanita trundled along and Rindy clattered away on her end of the line. He tried not to get too anxious, thinking about the possibility of an unknown hacker deleting the files as he drove along, helpless to stop them because of a bunch of bureaucratic nonsense…

Finally—after three mile markers—Rindy came back on the line. "All right, Dr. Sanchez, I looked it up and it turns out you're an authorized user on Patricia Denke's account."

He was? Well, wasn't that convenient. Hmmm.

"So now what?"

"Now, if you like, I can transfer all of her files to your account—"

"That would be *amazing*. Because I'm driving right now, and it's kind of urgent."

"No problem, Dr. Sanchez. I'm doing it right now. If you can just verify your identity for me…"

So, still chafing with impatience, he went through the process of confirming he was who he said he was. Finally, twenty-seven minutes after he first made the call, Rindy (his new favorite person) confirmed that she'd transferred all of Patty's files to Eli's own account.

"I can't thank you enough for helping me out," he said.

"I'm really glad I was able to," she replied in such a way that confirmed his suspicions: he hadn't actually been an authorized user on Patty's account—at least until about fifteen minutes ago.

After he finally disconnected with Rindy, Eli made his overdue call to Detective Perle, who, unsurprisingly, didn't answer his phone at one o'clock in the morning (Eastern time). But Eli left a detailed message about what happened in his hotel room and how things had hardly gotten any better since he returned to Champaign.

He didn't mention the bee element (because even Eli hardly believed someone would kill over an Apis bee), but he figured he could fill in that information if he and the detective ever had an actual live conversation. He guessed if he left that information on the voice message, the detective would think he was a little paranoid.

As he disconnected the call, though, Eli realized that whatever was going on was now occurring in two different states—Ohio and Illinois—and that meant the Feds would need to be involved, not the local police.

And he happened to know a Fed…who just happened to be stationed in Chicago; at least, last he'd heard. Special Agent Helen Darrow was sharp, intelligent, calm, and utterly professional—for all he knew, she'd been promoted back to Quantico or somewhere. He'd gotten to know her during the copper beetle debacle (as Eli privately called it) that ended up with his and Marina's escape from the Amazon jungle hideaway of the Skaladeskas.

He'd call SA Darrow in the morning and let her know what was going on. At least she wouldn't think he was a crackpot.

Besides, he had proof that someone had definitely tried to kill him back in Cincinnati. And he was lucky he'd only been knocked out tonight instead of killed…

Eli frowned, squinting in the darkness—not in order to see better, but to think better.

The man who had been trying to break into his hotel room obviously intended to use the syringe, which was filled with enough sufentanil to murder a horse. But the man who'd accosted Eli tonight had merely (merely!) tweaked that certain spot in the neck, dropping him like a bag of rocks…and leaving him basically unharmed. Less a gym bag with some apparently sensitive data, but unharmed nonetheless.

Eli had assumed it was the same person…until now. Because if it was the same man, why so murderous the first time, and more lenient (for lack of a better term) on this second assault? If anything, one might think it'd be the other way around.

Eli stared at the never-ending ribbon of highway, dotted regularly and rhythmically with the pale orange glow from streetlights, and tried to remember everything he could from each incident. *Was* it the same man?

His first instinct was *no*.

No…when he closed his eyes (only briefly; he was, after all, driving) and tried to imagine each of his attackers in turn, the memory didn't feel the same. The first man seemed broader and maybe not as tall as Eli; the one tonight had given more of a long and lean impression.

Both had dark hair, and neither had skin of pale white, though it was hard to tell whether either had brown, tan, or olive skin…

A sharp image popped into Eli's mind just as he passed Kankakee. A gloved hand—the left hand—reaching toward his throat…the black sleeve above it, pulling back a little to reveal a swatch of bare skin on the attacker's wrist…a swatch of skin interrupted by a tattoo.

*Yes.* There'd been a tattoo. Eli was sure of it. Right on the back of the wrist. Letters or maybe numbers in a neat row. He tried to bring focus to the memory, to drill down to the screenshot in his mind and identify what was written in the ink…

Damn. Now his head hurt.

But at least he'd figured out something helpful. And when he thought about the man who'd been there at his hotel room door, Eli simply didn't have the same impression. Had that man even been wearing gloves?

He couldn't remember. Not for certain.

But now that Eli concluded he'd been attacked by two different men, his moment of relief for Jill's safety evaporated. There was no reason to think the two men were working together—or separately. It was simply impossible to know. But what he did know was that if the non-murderous one was in Champaign, where was the one who wanted to kill him?

Juanita swerved a little as he grabbed for his phone and fumbled to call Jill Fetzer.

He just needed to know…he needed to know she was all right.

But Jill didn't answer.

# TWENTY-TWO

*Libertyville, Illinois*
*July 10, just after midnight*

J ill wondered for the millionth time whether she'd been right
to trust this Eli Sanchez person.

She didn't have any reason *not* to trust him—after all, he was a
friend of Ghomie's, whom she not only trusted but had actually dated
for a short time (when she was twenty years younger and about the
same poundage lighter, pre-marriage and divorce)—but this whole
situation was so beyond her norm that she spent the entire time sec-
ond-guessing herself while she was waiting for the guy to show.

What else was she going to do while sitting in the well-lit all-night
diner she'd chosen for their meeting place? She'd done a search on
Dr. Eli Sanchez, who was apparently some seriously hotshot insect
professor from the University of Illinois who'd supposedly helped save
everyone from some deadly copper bugs a few years ago. Who could
have imagined a James Bond-type entomologist?

From the pics she found online, Jill had to admit he was attractive,
if you liked the long, lanky, and dreadlocked or ponytailed type. He
wasn't at all nerdy looking, like one would expect an entomologist to
be, and she figured if she was going to be going on the run with a guy,
it wouldn't hurt that he wasn't bad to look at.

The idea of actually *going on the run* made her stomach pitch and
drop a little. She didn't know what was going to happen, but she was
pretty sure she *didn't* want to go on the run—even with Eli Sanchez.

Once she'd exhausted the Google results about Sanchez, Jill found she couldn't focus on any of the games or apps on her phone. She didn't want to watch the news that blared from the single television screen—the current story was about some horrific, single-vehicle semitruck accident in Ohio. From what she could tell, the driver had basically been smeared all over the highway beneath the wheels of his rig.

Nor did she need any more coffee—she was wired so tight that when some jittery old guy down the way dropped a spoon onto his saucer, Jill nearly shot out of her seat.

What she really needed, she told herself, was to do a little bit of yoga stretching and maybe some meditation—both of which she'd been working on over the last few months as ways to control and ease her anxiety.

Her yoga teacher kept telling Jill to focus on her Third Chakra—apparently that was the center of energy located in her belly, and it was related to anxiety and stress—and hers was often blocked or wasn't spinning freely…whatever that meant.

There were, the yoga teacher had told Jill earnestly, seven main centers of energy in the human body—called chakras, a Sanskrit word—running all the way up the spine starting from the root of the spinal cord up to the crown of the head. Each one had its so-called specialties or focus on types of energy, and if one of them was clogged or blocked, it could cause an unbalanced feeling.

The Seventh Chakra, which was located at the very top and center of the head, was the one that fascinated Jill the most. It was the energy center that represented what her teacher called the Universal Consciousness—the fact that everyone through all times and spaces were somehow connected through their souls. She wasn't sure she actually believed it, but in a way, it made sense. She did believe in a higher connection, and in some sort of afterlife…so it could be true.

But Jill seemed to be stuck on getting her Third Chakra to spin properly; she was nowhere near ready to focus on that seventh and highest center of energy. And so she tried to do extra yoga poses and breathing exercises that focused on the solar plexus chakra, which apparently also responded to the color yellow. So she had a lot of lemon in her tea, and ate a lot of summer squash and yellow peppers.

She even bought a sunny goldenrod-colored candle and burned it in her office when she felt stressed.

But yoga stretching and meditation were not about to happen here at Pete's All-Niter. Jill's meeting place with Eli Sanchez was the epitome of classic diner environment: a long counter with round stools upholstered in worn black vinyl on thick columns of stainless steel. A revolving pie server, carefully protected by its plastic cover, offered six different flavors. The strong smells of coffee and fried foods, along with the lingering, permanent odor of now-banned cigarettes, filled the air. Handwritten specials menus with spelling errors and misplaced apostrophes hung on two different walls. Booths of worn crimson vinyl lined the windows. And there was a single, jaundiced (both literally and figuratively, for she had a yellowish cast to her well-lined skin that implied many decades of tobacco use) waitress who didn't bother to write down any orders and unceremoniously plopped the plates on the table in front of each respective diner. She never seemed to get anything wrong—or, at least, no one dared complain if she did.

The other occupants of Pete's were also of the type one would expect to find in such a place after midnight on a Wednesday two grizzled and ball-capped truckers who appeared to know each other, although they sat four stools apart at the counter while they discussed the semitruck accident in graphic detail. The old, disheveled man was stirring his coffee with a shaking hand that dropped the spoon and startled Jill. He was wearing a heavy plaid shirt, though it was July and seventy-nine degrees outside.

There was another man who looked altogether too disreputable and a little scary for Jill's taste, with his furtive, dark eyes that bounced around the restaurant. But he'd already been sitting there when she came in, so it was impossible for him to be the man who'd tried to break into her townhouse.

Unless he'd somehow overheard her conversation with Sanchez and managed to get her before her…but what was he going to do to her anyway, here under the bright, obnoxious lights of the diner? That was why she'd picked Pete's All-Niter: there were windows everywhere and it was well lit.

Besides, there were two cops sitting in a booth on the opposite side of the restaurant. One of them was facing her, so Jill felt quite safe.

The piece of cherry pie she'd ordered was long gone from the classic white diner plate and now churned unpleasantly in her stomach, along with the two scoops of ice cream she'd had with it. The swishing and twisting inside was getting so ugly that she thought she better go to the bathroom...just in case. Too much sugar, caffeine, and stress were not a good combination.

She rose, deciding to leave her coat draped over the booth in case Dr. Sanchez arrived while she was gone. She'd already told him she was wearing a bright yellow raincoat so he'd be able to identify her—though she hadn't expected to be the only woman in the place except the waitress and one of the cops.

Jill's phone was in her oversized purse, which she hugged close to her body as she slid from the booth. Her stomach felt like a clothes dryer, tumbling in an ugly, incessant circular motion that did not bode well. She had an iffy digestive system on a good day, and this was decidedly not a good day.

As she walked quickly to the short hallway where the restrooms were, Jill saw a pair of headlights pull into the parking lot as she passed the window and glanced out to see whether it was Dr. Sanchez.

The man who got out of the car was dark-haired like the professor, but she couldn't see his face to tell whether it was the insect guru. But Jill couldn't wait to find out—things were getting quite desperate in her nether regions, and she trotted quickly into the ladies' room.

It was a two-stall deal with a small sink area, which meant she didn't feel the need to hurry too much, since she wasn't hogging the whole bathroom. But, *oh,* she felt really sick, and she bolted into the nearest stall.

She made it just in time.

Ten minutes later—and feeling worlds better—she was just coming out of the stall when the door to the bathroom opened.

She saw the man coming in and had a moment of shock—had she run into the wrong bathroom? How mortifying!—then in an instant she realized there were no urinals, and just as she was about to inform him *he* was in the wrong place, he stepped deliberately toward her.

Jill managed a strangled scream a millisecond before his hand covered her mouth. Something sharp pricked her through her shirt, and all at once, she went woozy…then slack…then dark.

She didn't feel the cold, sticky floor when she landed on it, and she certainly didn't feel him yank the purse off her arm.

# TWENTY-THREE

Pam Budd had been working at Pete's All-Niter for over forty years. She'd even been married to Pete for ten of them before they decided they were better coworkers than spouses—although they did burn up the sheets pretty good back in the day.

They still did on occasion, because why not?

Pam generally knew every type of customer that came in on the overnight shift—which was the one she worked because she preferred it that way. It was just busy enough to keep her from getting bored, but not so busy she couldn't slip out back for a cigarette every fifteen minutes or so.

Damned antismoking laws had really put a cramp in her style, because until they came around, she could just keep the last booth on the opposite side from the johns for her "break" area and even let her ciggie sit there waiting in the ashtray for a quick puff between delivering orders. It used to be much more efficient, juggling food, customers, and her nicotine habit.

Now she had to go all the way outside to light up, and that was a real pain in the ass when it was zero degrees or storming out there.

Government interference in her personal life burned her butt.

Even though Pam was used to the types of customers who came in between midnight and four a.m., every now and again she was surprised by the unexpected.

Tonight was one of those nights, when the fortyish woman in a yellow raincoat came slinking in, looking like she was ready to bolt at the slightest provocation. She was hunched over all expectant-like, waiting for some hammer to come down on her head of mousy brown curls or something. She clutched a big purse to her side and carried a small cardboard box like it was filled with jewels or something equally valuable.

Now, Pam had seen women come in who were definitely on the run from someone—usually a husband—and waiting for the bus to pull into the station next door, and though this gal looked like she was pretty worked up, it just didn't feel like the same sort of anxiousness as someone trying to get away from an asshole husband. Plus, there was that little cardboard box she was clutching—not a suitcase, which was what most of them carried—but a scrappy little box. Couldn't even fit a loaf of bread in it.

Pam, who watched a lot of late-night movies and crime shows (hazard of the job), entertained herself with thoughts about what the box might contain. The most intriguing option was that it held a severed finger the woman was delivering to someone for some reason. She sniffed a little when she got close to take the woman's order, figuring if it was a severed finger, she'd smell blood or rotting flesh—or maybe formaldehyde.

But all she smelled was the woman's perfume, which wasn't unpleasant, but it was combined with a tinge of body odor—and the mixture was rolling from the woman's pores like steam.

The woman in the yellow raincoat was definitely worried about something—but she couldn't have been too worried when she ordered cherry pie and actually ate all of it, plus the ice cream (two scoops of strawberry), and drank two cups of coffee. Anyone that scared shouldn't have had such an appetite, so maybe she wasn't delivering a severed finger.

Maybe it was a drug deal—which Pam liked the idea of, because, after all, Officers Parente and Didik were sitting right in the booth over there, and it would be one hell of a ballsy move for this woman to pull off a drug deal right under their noses.

Pam was just refilling Officer Didik's coffee when she noticed the woman's face turning decidedly pale. Sickly pale. Pam Budd had been around long enough to recognize churning guts when she saw them.

"Better get the mop," she told herself, watching as the woman made a dash for the bathroom. "She might not make it."

Pam went outside for a smoke first, though (no reason to rush), and when she came back in, Biggie Jones called her over to the counter to refill his coffee, and they got to talking with Wayne Muir about the bad trucking accident that was all over the news.

"And there was another one real simular," said Biggie, "down'n Kentucky way. Man, that's some bad juju happening out there. Glad I'm not on the road right now."

"Tellin' me. I heard Bill Nodd on the radio talking about how it was a friend of his got smashed up 'ere down on I-71. They were s'posed to meet up tonight for dinner. Guy never made it cuz he's like butter on toast, spread all over the road," said Wayne, giving a little shudder. He prodded his empty coffee cup toward Pam. "Couldn't pay me to drive through Ohio."

"What's wrong with Ohio?" demanded Biggie. "They got the Buckeyes!"

"It's flat as a bra-less granny, and only fifty-five miles per hour's what's wrong with Ohio," said Wayne as Pam gave a gravelly chuckle.

Just then a man came in, looking around like he expected to see Santa Claus or someone exciting like that.

"Take a seat anywhere," Pam said, still leaning on the counter as she checked out the newcomer.

Looked to be under forty, and not a tragedy to look at. Brown skin (a little dark for Pam's personal taste), chocolate-brown hair pulled into a short ponytail that reminded her of that Antonio Banderas in one of those Mexican drug lord movies. He had a goatee that was getting a little gray at the corners of the mouth, but Pam acknowledged at least it was trimmed up nice. The guy wore a soft, clinging t-shirt of dark green with something on the front she couldn't identify—looked like a bug or something?—and nice, broken-in jeans.

He was still standing there, looking around anxiously. "Was there a woman here, with a yellow coat?" he asked, coming over to the counter.

Well, she hadn't expected *that*. *Those* two?

Gotta be a drug deal.

Or...maybe a custody switch? The kids were sleeping in the car and had to go with Dad (or Mom) for the weekend?

"Yeah, she's sitting right over there—where the yellow coat is— Oh, it's gone. She must have left." Pam hadn't noticed the woman come back after her dash to the restroom, but she had seen the yellow coat hanging over the booth when she was in the john.

So much for a custody switch.

Pam went back to the drug deal story because she liked it best. Maybe she oughta try writing one of them thriller books.

"Are you sure she's gone?" The guy was looking around, and now *he* looked anxious—but in a different way. Not scared like the lady with the coat, but concerned in a sort of protective way.

Maybe he was supposed to be the recipient of the severed finger, Pam chortled to herself. "Looks to me like she's gone now."

"Her car's still out there," said the guy, still looking around. His attention seemed to linger on the two officers as if he were considering involving them.

Now Pam had walked close enough that she could see what was on the front of his shirt, and she very nearly spat out a laugh. It was two cicadas humping each other, right there, plain as day on his shirt. Geez.

"Well, last I seen her, she was going to the bathroom. Guess I could check and make sure she's all right in there." Pam was really hoping the yellow raincoat lady was still in the john, because now she was dying to see what the heck was going on with these two mismatched people.

The guy with the bug porn on his shirt lingered there looking tense as Pam strode down the short hall. She pushed on the ladies' room door and it didn't open all the way.

It took her about two seconds to realize why: for the second time in forty years, there was a body on the floor of the john.

Oh, for Pete's sake. Why did this shit have to happen on her shift?

"You all right, miss?" Pam said, pushing a little harder. Maybe the lady was just feeling sick.

But all at once, the bug porn guy was right there just as she got the door open. He pushed his way past her right into the ladies' room and knelt beside the crumpled body. The interior of the bathroom smelled like crap, literally, and Pam was happy to keep the door open to air it out. Sheesh.

"She's dead," said Bug Porn Guy, looking up at Pam.

"Man, I thought she looked sick, but I didn't think she was *that* sick. Hey, Officer Parente! We got a problem back here!" Pam shouted.

She saw no reason to be circumspect; the three other people in the place were going to know about the body in ten seconds flat anyway.

The bug porn guy, who'd obviously been trying to meet up with the dead woman, crossed himself like he'd been praying, then rose to his feet as the officers slid out of their booth.

"Did she have a bag or anything?" the bug guy asked.

It was a damned good thing Pam was observant.

Hell, she could've given Columbo or Adrian Monk or freaking Sherlock Holmes a run for the money, with her powers of observation. Forty years waiting tables—you learned how to notice stuff, you know?

"She had a purse. And a small cardboard box." Pam was still hoping to find out what had been inside. "And I don't see her coat anywhere." She frowned. It had been draped over the booth—she definitely had seen it there when she noticed Dead Lady hoofing it to the john.

Bug Porn Guy swore under his breath. Sounded like a different language, too. He looked Mexican.

"What's the problem?" asked Officer Parente. Pam had called for her specifically because it was the ladies' john.

Pam explained then stepped aside so the police could do their thing. Didik was already calling it in on the radio.

"She didn't take the coat to the john with her," Pam said to the bug porn guy, walking back to the booth where Dead Lady had been sitting. "But it's gone now."

Wait a minute…

If she didn't take the coat with her and it was gone now, where was it? Had someone taken it? Who? Why?

Bug Porn Guy obviously had the same questions, and he seemed really stressed. He swore again and looked kind of nauseated himself. Pretty sure he hadn't somehow copped the coat.

"Okay, look, if she didn't take it with her to the john and she never left the john, that means someone else took it," Pam said. "And that means that someone must've known she died…" Or *helped* her die?

That was what Adrian Monk would say.

"And her purse, too, right?" Bug Porn Guy looked devastated. Then suddenly he swung his attention to her. "A cardboard box? You said she had a cardboard box too."

"She did. Looked like it was the freaking Holy Grail or something, the way she was carrying it."

"Did she take it to the bathroom with her? You said she left her coat…but that she took her purse. Did you notice if she took the box?"

"No," said Pam. "She was in a hurry, and she only had the purse. Like I said, she even left her coat."

"Where was she sitting?"

"That one." She would've gone over with him, but Parente was calling her back to the restroom hallway. She supposed she'd have to give them a statement now, wouldn't she? Not the first time; probably wouldn't be the last.

By the time she finished talking to the cops, Bug Porn Guy was gone. She frowned. He probably should have stuck around to give his statement too. Seemed like he knew the lady, after all.

Just then, the bell over the door jingled and she looked over, half expecting to see the bug guy coming back. But it was a freaking *priest* walking in the door.

His clothing was unrelieved black, and the collar of his shirt was unfastened with its white tab hanging loose. He was one of those Father What-a-Wastes—youngish, good-looking, broad-shouldered, and, for some archaic reason, required to be celibate. He looked foreign too, with olive skin and soft black curls that clustered tight to his head. It was like the freaking United Nations here tonight.

"Have a seat anywhere, father," Pam told him. She hadn't set foot inside a church for twenty years, but she still had a healthy respect for the clergy.

Then he spoke, confirming Pam's suspicion that he was foreign. There was a hint of an accent in his words; not that she could tell from where. But with him being a priest and all…maybe Italy. Or South America. "Is everything all right?" he asked.

There was something about the way he scanned the place, the way he held himself as if at attention—or ready to spring into action—as he looked around.

She narrowed her eyes speculatively.

What was he looking for? Some kid to baptize or something?

He just didn't *seem* like a priest.

"We just had a lady die back there," she replied, thumbing in the direction of the restrooms. "In the jo—in the bathroom."

"A woman died? How terrible. Is she still back there?" Father What-a-Waste turned smoothly and, to her surprise, began to fasten his white tab collar tightly around his throat.

"Yes, she's back there with the police. What are you doing?" she asked as he started toward the scene.

"I'm going to anoint her," he replied with a sad smile, and pulled a small brass container from his pocket. "Extreme Unction."

What?

That was when she noticed the bracelet-like tattoo across the back of his wrist, right where his hand met his arm. It was four letters with a small cross at the beginning and ending: **+ I E N S +**

What the heck sort of priest was this guy, with ink on his hand? Maybe he'd been in prison.

A felon-turned-priest.

Pam shook her head and went back to refill Biggie Jones's coffee.

She sure as hell saw it all, working midnights in a late-night diner.

# TWENTY-FOUR

*An undisclosed location*

Roman looked around the room at the members of the *Naslegi*—the governing body of the Skaladeskas.

They were seated around an elongated triangular table. At the point—the head—of the table sat the clear crystal globe containing the essence of Gaia. It was larger than a man's head. Inside the precious sphere, energy glowed, churned, and swirled in all shades of blue, green, purple, gold, and orange, reminding everyone in the chamber that Gaia lived and breathed among them at all times.

And that they were charged and obligated to protect her.

As Roman met the eyes of each one present, he was reminded of those who weren't present.

His father, of course, who'd long retired from the meetings and relied on Roman—as well as his own intuition and guidance from teachers, spirit animals, and guides—to be apprised of what was happening.

Rue Varden, who had been permanently in the Out-World for over ten years but was no less important a contributor to those who governed the decisions made in honor of Gaia and their responsibility to her. Although he rarely could attend council meetings, Varden was responsible for the single most important initiative of the Skaladeskas: keeping Marina Alexander safe. Included in that was reporting back on any relevant activities...including relationships that could result in a child.

Knowing of any offspring or progeny was of paramount importance to Roman and the rest of his people, since Marina carried the weight of their progeny on her slender shoulders. Roman had no other children, and Viktor, his brother—who everyone believed was Marina's father—had not procreated either.

The other most obvious missing attendee was Hedron Burik, Roman's personal nemesis and rival. It was the absence of Hedron— and a development related to it—that had prompted this meeting.

"Let us all remember our Mother before we begin," Roman said. He placed his hands over the smooth, warm globe and led the group in the words from the sacred writings.

Once the room subsided into silence, Roman immediately began to speak. "As you are all aware, a former member of the *Naslegi* continues to no longer be with us. I have word on the status of Hedron Burik, and it is worrisome.

"As some of you are aware, when Mariska came to us in the Amazon needing treatment for the *cuprobeous* virus, we treated her and her companion, the entomologist Eli Sanchez. During their time here, Hedron attempted to injure and even kill the Heir of Gaia: the daughter of my twin brother Viktor, the granddaughter of our esteemed Lev, Son of Gaia."

It was a constant source of pain to Roman that he could not, at least yet, publicly acknowledge Marina's true parentage. Someday, perhaps, once Lev had gone, he could do so. But until then, his father must remain ignorant of how he and Viktor had traded places during their time living in the Out-World.

Roman went on. "When confronted by me shortly after those events, Hedron attempted to explain away his actions as accidental. But there could have been no accident relative to the fact that he attempted to lock Mariska and the entomologist—while unprotected—in the chamber with the lethal copper beetles…and then, when they found their escape, he chased them down carrying firearms and attempted to assassinate them.

"You all are aware of my feelings related to firearms," he added, scanning the chamber with a serious look. "We are a peace-loving people and take up arms only in the name of Gaia: to defend and to protect Her." His expression turned grave. "And as Mariska Aleksandrov could never be a threat to our Mother, there would never be a need to harm her."

There were nods and rumbles of agreement from around the table. Several of the attendees displayed clear shock in their reactions. For many of the twelve-member council, this was the first time they were hearing about the truth of what happened during Marina's "escape" from the Skaladeska stronghold in the Amazon jungle—and Hedron's involvement in it.

"Additionally, I come before you today to advise you of even more troubling news that has come from the Out-World. As you are aware, we are continually developing and implementing tactics and offensives on those Out-Worlders who lack respect for our Mother, and who continue to rape and pillage Her. As you may know, we were in the process of testing the Volvoticus bacterium, which was discovered—regrettably—by a team of microbiologists whose liaison with the Skaladeskas was Hedron. Thus, he is fully aware of the capabilities of this particular bacterium, and we must assume he will employ its usefulness as he conducts his own sort of warfare in the Out-World."

"What is his intent, now that he lives in the Out-World?" asked Clarista.

Roman shook his head. "I cannot say for certain—which is the cause of my concern—but I suspect that he will at least attempt to finish what he started in the Amazon: to destroy Mariska Aleksandrov—and in doing so, to destroy us and our hereditary line to Gaia."

A sharp intake of breath from Clarista and more shocked, concerned expressions rippling around the table bolstered Roman's confidence.

"But to what end? Why would he harm Gaia in that way?" asked Ballio.

"Perhaps he intends to install his *own* family line in place, rather than that of Lev's, who we all know is Gaia's true son." Roman paused to allow those words to sit and settle over the group. Then, after feeling that his point had been made sufficiently, he went on.

"Today, I stand before you members of the *Naslegi*, prepared to take the full responsibility for this upon my shoulders. It was I who made the decision to cast out Hedron, along with his sister Nila—

who was also my life mate, as you are aware—and the small cadre of family members who supported him. In total, fewer than a dozen of our tribe has exiled with him. However, in so doing—by imposing such a sentence on Hedron Burik—I have irrevocably endangered us and our objectives. For he took with him not only knowledge of the bacterium but possibly a sample of it as well, along with many of our future initiatives. Additionally, he seems to have removed several pieces of literature from Ivan's library."

More exclamations and wide eyes—as was to be expected. Protecting and keeping the Lost Library of Ivan the Terrible, as it was known in the Out-World to the few who were aware of its existence, was the other sacred duty of the Skaladeskas.

It was also the lure by which Roman intended to bring Mariska fully into the fold of their tribe—to her vocation and calling.

"What pieces have gone?" asked Ballio.

"An Atlantean piece, a selection of Buddhist writings in Sanskrit, and original maps from Marco Polo—these are the pieces that have been identified as missing. There may be more," Roman confessed. "As you are all aware, the cataloguing of the library has been a painstaking and incomplete process over the centuries, considering the lack of expertise in our fold."

This was true—the fundamental responsibility that had been placed on the Skaladeskas was to protect the library, not necessarily to study or catalogue it. When the library was brought by Leonid Aleksandrov to the desolate mountains of Taymyria where the small tribe lived, more than four hundred and sixty years ago, Leonid had begun the process of organizing it. But over the centuries, there were few members of the Skaladeskas who had the ability to read, study, and translate the wildly varied collection of documents, and the cataloguing process had slowed considerably.

"Why did he take those particular pieces?" asked Yumeva.

"We can only conjecture on Hedron's intentions. It may have been simply that he took what was easiest to remove, protect, and carry. Dannen Fridkov has been charged with the responsibility of tracking down Hedron and relieving him of the documents as expediently as possible."

"Do we know where Hedron is?"

"At last report from Fridkov, Hedron was located in the Midwest United States." Roman looked around at the members of his trusted council. "Once again, we can only conjecture what he is doing in that area—since Mariska lives in the American state of Michigan, which is considered part of that region." He spread his hands and shook his head, fear stabbing his belly. "We can only hope that Mariska will remain safe from Hedron Burik and his determination for revenge."

# TWENTY-FIVE

Villiani's mobile rang. When he saw the number, he snatched for the phone so quickly that he fumbled it off his desk. He scrambled for the device as it fell in his lap then careened to the floor…and he finally snatched it up, answering the call just before the buzzing stopped.

"Rastinoff. What have you to report?" he said, trying not to sound desperate or breathless. He'd hardly slept since he learned of the situation, spending an inordinate amount of time on his knees in the chapel. "Have you been able to contain the problem?"

"Yes, Your Eminence. But there have been some unexpected developments."

"Tell me. I want all of the specifics." Villiani picked up the crucifix from his desk and curled his fingers around it like a lifeline. *The secret was still safe.*

"All data from Ladakh—from the location in question—has been removed and deleted from the girl's system, and the hardware was blown up with a car bomb."

"Any casualties?" Villiani whispered, gripping the crucifix tighter.

"A girl. But the contact who most worries me has thus far evaded us. Name of Elijah Sanchez. He's the mentor of the girl who was in Ladakh, and she sent her notes and other communications to him. We intercepted it, but he is still at large. We've lost track of him—only temporarily."

"Find him."

"Of course. During our work, we've learned that another entity has knowledge of the—matter. And possesses a specimen. Unrelated to the girl who was in India."

"What? What are you talking about?" A cold sweat broke out over Villiani, instantly soaking his shirt beneath the armpits and at the small of his back. "Someone else knows? Someone else has a specimen? Who?"

"An old package found in an attic included some information from the last century—it was only by chance that we discovered about it when we gained access to Sanchez's computer. No one would have thought anything of it if we hadn't already been working to contain it."

Villiani licked his dry lips. "But *we* drew attention to this—this attic package?" He closed his eyes. *God help me.* "And now?"

"That avenue has been—shall we say—dead-ended. Permanently. Only Sanchez remains, and he is on the run. We'll find him."

"And silence him. And you must destroy any evidence."

"Of course." Rastinoff stopped suddenly, as if catching himself before continuing, then went on. "It appears, Your Eminence, that you are not the only one eager to quash all evidence of the—matter at hand."

"What is this?" Villiani straightened up in his seat. His stomach pitched violently. *No.* "What do you mean?"

"Evidently, we are not the only party interested in obliterating this matter. We've nearly crossed paths with another individual who seems to have the same goal in kind—but without the same permanence. If you understand what I mean to say."

Villiani nodded, though the other man couldn't see the affirmation. "Someone else. What do you know about this other party?" His insides recoiled, turning cold and icy.

If someone else at the Holy See knew about this…if the others knew that he, Villiani, had made his own arrangements to shut it down…

Then he could be ruined.

"What do you know about this other party?" he said more urgently.

But his bowels were shifting horrifically and his stomach churned with violence.

He already knew the answer.

*Leo Colón.*

They'd sent Leo Colón.

And if the Holy See found out Villiani had superseded them—had kept them in the dark and sent Rastinoff…

*Dear God.*

# TWENTY-SIX

*Chicago, Illinois*
*July 10, before dawn*

**A**t last.

Eli had to create a makeshift ento lab, but he wasn't going to wait a minute longer to get a good, close look at this beautiful little Apis bee.

"Let's see just what we have here," he murmured as he gently unrolled her onto a clean white paper.

He was in his hotel room just outside of Chicago, only minutes from the FBI Field Office, where he was going directly tomorrow morning—or rather, later this morning, for it was nearly two o'clock by now.

He paused once again to send up a heartfelt prayer for Jill Fetzer's soul. There was no doubt in his mind that someone had killed her and stolen the purse that he or she believed contained the bee.

Whoever it was must have arrived shortly after Jill was seated, maybe observing her for a time. Then they took the opportunity to attack and kill her in the restroom. Based on his own experience, Eli guessed that it was a man and that he'd used a syringe of sufentanil… while the man who'd most recently attacked Eli—and didn't kill him—was still back in Champaign. Jill's killer must have been the one lurking about her townhouse. He might have overheard her, or even followed her to the diner.

Thank God for the gravelly-voiced waitress, who clearly noticed everything—or just about everything—that went on in her diner.

If she hadn't mentioned the cardboard box, Eli would have assumed Jill had the bee in her purse or coat, and that it was lost to him. But the cardboard box had been on the floor under the table—possibly knocked off when the murderer snatched Jill's coat and took off. Eli wished he'd had the opportunity to ask any of the other diners whether they saw someone come in and then leave quickly, but the police were already involved and Eli wanted to get the hell out of there before he got caught up in the investigation and delayed.

Or, worse, lost possession of the small cardboard box.

He justified this decision in two ways: first, he needed to get the bee to safety and to find out what was so special about it, and second, he was going to tell Agent Darrow everything as soon as he could talk to her. Hopefully tomorrow morning.

He hadn't wanted to take the risk of the authorities relieving him of possession of the bee as evidence in a murder investigation.

Not after all of this.

Not when he'd caught just a glimpse of the little beauty in her tiny glass case, right before he floored Juanita and zoomed out of the parking lot. He'd had to open it, had to look inside just to make sure she was there. And what he glimpsed in that all-too-brief moment had been enough to set his heart racing. The Apis had been small, unusually small, and her coloring…bands of dark, chocolate brown, and pinkish-gold! He'd never seen anything like it.

He made certain no one was following him—but who would be now? His assailant was back in Champaign, and Eli was confident he had not been followed—besides, the attacker had already retrieved what he wanted: Eli's gym bag with Patty's data in it. And Jill's killer had already absconded with what he believed was his loot.

With this in mind, Eli had made a quick stop at a Walmart to get a few things for his makeshift lab: a stack of plain printer paper, a ruler and measuring tape, two flashlights, and some tweezers that would have to double as forceps. A tiny, sharp pair of scissors he found in the housewares section would also be useful, as well as a cheap headlamp that would leave his hands free—*and* he'd snagged a magnifying glass from the craft section. But best of all, in the toy department, he found a pretty decent kid's microscope that would at least give him a start on the exam.

Now, he spread everything out on the table in his hotel kitchenette and began to work. The headlamp was surprisingly bright and sturdy, and when he brought over the desk lamp to the table and turned on the two flashlights, he had more than sufficient illumination.

He started by simply examining the Apis with a magnifying glass. He couldn't believe she hadn't been destroyed by dermestid beetles—which could eat through cork and loved to dine on other insects. She was completely intact.

"She's rather small for a honeybee—which I guess isn't too surprising, her existing at a high elevation. I would guess she uses pollen for nutrition as much as honey, as food sources would be limited in the mountains," he murmured to himself…then stopped, took up his mobile phone, and opened the voice memo app. He could dictate and write up the notes later. He repeated his initial thoughts than went on.

"Such an unusual coloring." He was simply delighted with the gorgeousness of the dainty insect. "All right, let's look at specs." He used the ruler and began to dictate into the phone.

"A. patricia is small for a bee—six millimeters in length. The abdomen is banded with shiny pinkish-red gold at the base of each segment. It shades to a darker color—possibly varying with age; to be determined—at the apical portion of the segment.

"The abdominal hairs are light, golden to rose-gold in color. Suspect that if they break and shear off, the apical portions of the segment would present darker over time or with age."

He was smiling with pleasure and excitement as he spoke, and yet he was conscious of a heavy weight, like a smothering blanket, hanging over this beauteous discovery. Patty should be here; they should be discussing this together, trading theories and enthusiasm.

Why had she needed to die? What was it about this bee?

He returned to his examination, aware that he had to blink rapidly in order to alleviate the sudden damp in his eyes.

"The abdomen hairs are sparse for an Apis bee. All the legs are a light golden yellow," he said, his voice rising with surprise. "Very unusual for them to be so light in color—and there is reddish shading at the ends of the segments as well. The rest of the thorax is obscured by the characteristic branched body hairs typical of an Apis bee."

Gently, he used the makeshift forceps to lift one of the creature's wings. "The wings are more opaque than transparent—this being unusual, but we can see the veins in the wings, which are…" He squinted through the magnifying glass, but this was a situation where he needed the microscope to see the colors of the wing veins.

He didn't want to dissect this single specimen, and so he carefully used the tweezers to lift the wing away from the body enough that he could get a glimpse under the microscope. "The veins in the wings appear to be that same rosy-gold color instead of the dark one would normally expect."

Removing her from the microscope tray, he resumed his examination with the magnifying glass. "The head is typical Apis in shape, with typical hair distribution except with three large seta at the meeting point of every facet of the compound eye!" His voice rose a little even though he was trying to keep the dictation professional and factual. "These setae are vibrantly metallic, rose-gold. There are three ocelli, located in standard arrangement. The ocelli are also this same rose-gold, while the mandibles…" He fumbled for the microscope again, because what he was seeing in the magnifying glass simply wasn't enough.

He was able to align the specimen on the scope so he could zero in on the head. "The mandibles are deep crimson at the tip, shading to hot pink and then the now-typical rose-gold at their base. The labrum is dark—burgundy—while the maxillae are nearly translucent crimson. Very unusual," he muttered.

He went on, describing the details of the thorax, coxa, femur, tibia, and tarsus—which was typical Apis.

And it wasn't until he was nearly finished with his recitation that Eli realized something astonishing about this bee.

It had no stinger.

This bee was unable to sting.

# TWENTY-SEVEN

*Chicago, Illinois*
*July 10, midmorning*

Special Agent Helen Darrow breezed into the small meeting room carrying a tablet, smartphone, and cup of coffee. Her dark blue mug had the FBI seal on it.

She was an attractive woman in her thirties, probably just past the middle of the decade, Eli figured. She was a balanced mix of cool professionalism, intelligence, and snark. Today she wore a charcoal-gray suit and, beneath it, a silky patterned blouse with pink, blue, and yellow flowers. The neckline showed not even one millimeter of cleavage—but it wasn't all up-to-the-chin Victorian, either. Her shiny honey-blond hair was twisted into a bun sort of thing at the back of her neck, and the only jewelry she wore was a wide gold band on her thumb and two sparkling stud earrings that might have been real diamonds, but considering what Eli knew about the Feds' pay scale, he thought not.

"Good morning, Dr. Sanchez," she said, placing onto the table one by one the items she carried: coffee, tablet, phone. She lined them up next to the pad of paper and holder of FBI-logoed pens that were staples of this and every other meeting room in the office—at least, from what Eli had experienced. "It's nice to see you again. It's been, what...three years? Four?"

"Nearly four. Thank you for seeing me on such short notice," he replied. He was fully aware that his attire was far less professional than hers—cargo shorts, a CARPE INSECTVM tee, and the most comfortable footwear in the world: his well-worn Birkenstocks.

"Considering how you kept our collective asses from being in a sling over the *cuprobeus* beetle virus back then, I figured not only did I owe you, but that you wouldn't ask for a meeting unless it was important."

He nodded and smiled. "Exactly. So let me tell you why I'm here."

She sat her tablet up on the table in its stand, revealing a small keyboard attached to it. "I'm going to take notes, but I'm also going to record if you're agreeable."

"Definitely. So, here's the story: I'll give you the high level first and you can ask questions to fill in the details you need. One of my doctoral students was in India studying Apis bees and mad honey, and while she was there, she messaged me saying she wanted to change her thesis to studying a novel Apis bee that she'd found while there."

"Mad honey? Is that the honey that causes hallucinations?" she asked, surprising him with her knowledge. "It's Turkish, right?"

"That's the most well-known location of what people call mad honey—or *deli bal*—but there are other areas it can be found, such as northern India and Nepal. It comes from honey made from rhododendrons that have grayanotoxin in their nectars—of which there are very few in the world. A taste of *deli bal* can give you a wonderful high, but also hallucinations and other unpleasant reactions. The Turks and others who harvest it locally use it for medicinal purposes, but also for the euphoric feelings it can give you." Eli felt himself go into professorial lecture mode, but he didn't feel the need to hold back. Helen Darrow was an intelligent woman and seemed interested in what he had to say.

"Have you tried it?" she asked with a sly smile.

"You bet," he replied. "It went right to my head, but it wasn't an unpleasant experience. You only take a little of it, often mixed with milk. When you hear about poisoning from *deli bal*, it's usually because some yahoo wanted to trip out and had too much of it. In fact, you can build up a sort of immunity to its effect if you take it regularly—which is why it doesn't affect the locals in the way it might affect someone who's never tried it before. There's a legend that when the Romans invaded the Black Sea area to oust King Mithridates in, oh, about the late sixties BCE, some of the king's men seeded their path with pieces of honeycomb made with *deli bal*. The Roman soldiers supposedly ate too much of it—fresh honeycomb is really an incredible treat—and they got so intoxicated and high that they were easily defeated." He took a sip of water. "Incidentally, the makeup of any honey can be very different depending which flowers are used to make it. You can analyze a sample of honey and tell not only where it was made—what region—but also the types of flowers and nectar that were used to make it."

"That's fascinating. Really," Helen replied. "I can tell you love your profession. But I'm not exactly sure what all of this has to do with why you're here. Your graduate student who was in India contacted you about changing her dissertation, and…?"

"Right. And I had no problem with her changing her dissertation if she wanted to—especially if she was studying an unknown species, which was what she was proposing. But that was the last I heard from her before I learned she'd died in an accident in Ladakh."

"Ladakh?"

"It's a region in Northeast India near Nepal and Tibet—in fact, they call it Little Tibet. Very mountainous and isolated. That's where she was. I attended her funeral in Cincinnati—was it only two days ago? *Damn*—and when I was there, her parents gave me all of the university property that had been sent back to them from India— mainly, her tablet and some notes. When we walked out of the funeral home with me carrying those items to put in the car to go back to Champaign, the car—which was being driven by another student in the entomology department—exploded from a car bomb. A young woman named Tina Janeski died in her own vehicle when she turned the ignition. In the parking lot of a Methodist church."

"In Cincinnati." Darrow arched her brow, and he could already see the wheels turning. But it was a credit to her trust in Eli that she didn't question him yet.

"Not really something you'd expect, right? Once I got past the shock and horror, it occurred to me that it was a strange place for that to happen—but I was mostly devastated that Tina had just been blown to bits. And there was nothing that could have been done about it."

"If you had been in the car with her, you'd have been blown up as well," said Darrow.

"That's beside the point—which is that hers was a senseless death because she simply wanted to drive with me to the funeral.

"It was horrific and awful and I couldn't believe it, but I didn't think she—or I—were actually targeted for death until that night at my hotel in Cincinnati. Someone—a man, not white, with dark hair and of indeterminate age—tried to break into my room. He dropped a syringe when I took him by surprise, and he fled because I know how to defend myself. I subsequently had a friend at UIUC test the contents of the syringe, and she informed me there was enough sufentanil in it to kill a horse."

Darrow's fingers flew over the keys even as she kept her eyes on him.

"After I calmed down," he said dryly, "and thought about things, I came to the conclusion that someone wanted Patty's information—specifically her notes that had come back from India. Because," he added when Darrow looked like she was going to speak, "I also learned that her parents' house had been broken into the night before the funeral—the night before the car bomb.

"The only reason the perp didn't get the information they wanted was because her parents had taken it all to the funeral home and left it there, not knowing which day of the visitations I would be there to retrieve it. I realized that was the only thing that made sense for all three events, because they—whoever blew it up—must have assumed I'd be in the car with the notes when the car bomb went off. And I would have been if Tina hadn't insisted on pulling the car up to pick me up at the entrance to the church. What other reason would there be to explode the car of a second-year entomology student who didn't know anyone in Cincinnati?"

"Right. Could they be interested in the mad honey?" Helen asked. "Maybe it's being used for a newfangled drug. Drug lords are always coming up with new takes on ways to get high and escape."

Eli shook his head. "I don't think so, because Patty wanted to change her dissertation from the topic of *deli bal* to the study of a unique species of bee she learned about while there. So I don't think it's related to the mad honey, and anyway, there's already too much information about *deli bal* out there."

"All right, go on," she replied. Not exactly skeptically, but with reserve in her tone. Yet she waited, obviously trusting that there was more.

"So I got back to UIUC midmorning yesterday— Oh, by the way, I did call and report the attempted break-in to my hotel room to the detective working on the car bomb, but I haven't actually talked to him. We've been playing phone tag. I'm guessing you'll want to talk to him after this.

"Anyway, I got back to Champaign and went into my office, and while I was there I checked my email—out of habit, but I was still really out of sorts because of Tina, and I guess I needed some normalcy. There was an email from the friend of a friend of mine here at U of C asking me about an unusual bee. I took one look at the photo she sent and realized it's *the same bee* that Patty found—in India.

"And that's where I really, *really* effed up," he said, feeling miserable and horrifically guilty. Not only was Tina Janeski's death on his hands, but he believed Jill Fetzer's was as well. "I didn't shut down my computer because I got the call from my friend in the lab that she could help with the testing of the syringe—I didn't know at that point whether the person breaking into my hotel was trying to kill me or just trying to hurt me. But either way, I was certain by then that their purpose was to obtain Patty's notes. There was simply no other reason for someone to try to break into my room at the freaking Holiday Inn in Cincinnati. Anyway, I left in a hurry without logging out."

"So someone must have seen the email on your computer," Darrow said. "And knew someone else had information about this bee. The *same* bee? That's a little bit of a coincidence. And whoever it was got the name and location of the person at U of Chicago."

"They must have walked into my office and seen it—I mean, I never lock my door. Why would I? I'm an entomologist, for God's sake. Not like I deal with IT trade secrets or weapons of mass destruction." His voice was grim with irony, because they both knew that the *cuprobeus* beetle had, in fact, been a weapon of mass destruction.

"Or they hacked into your email themselves and got the information that way," she said. "Not necessarily anything you could have done about it."

He shrugged, not quite willing to let himself off the hook. "So I got in contact with the woman at U of C who has a specimen of this bee. It is a coincidence, I guess, but it seems to be the same bee based on Patty's—that's my grad student—notes. Our mutual friend said it was shipped by someone in Paris a hundred years ago; but that simply doesn't make sense.

"Anyway, she was very upset because someone had been lurking outside her house as if prepared to break in. They must have been after the bee—and this was an actual specimen of the Apis, not just a photo." He couldn't help that his voice got a little high with excitement.

Now Darrow lifted a brow. "Timing's off on that, Dr. Sanchez. How could someone have looked at your email or hacked in and suddenly gone from Champaign—where they had presumably followed you, if your theory is correct—and then showed up near the University of Chicago, more than three hours away, so quickly?"

"Because there was an over six-hour time lag between when I opened the email and when I had the chance to contact her. I didn't actually look at the photo till late afternoon. But it was on my computer as of the morning." He grimaced.

The special agent nodded in acknowledgment and waited for him to continue.

"Her name is—was—Jill Fetzer," he said, and noticed that Darrow's mouth tightened when he corrected the tense. "Yeah. She's— Well, let me finish. So we made arrangements to meet at a twenty-four-hour diner just outside Libertyville, where she lived and where the man was presumably trying to break in—she reported it, by the way, and I happened to call her when she'd just finished contacting the local police. So I'm on my way back to my house to get Juanita—"

"Your...dog?" she ventured.

"My Jeep. And on the way, I notice I'm being followed. So I did a little Jason Bourne thing and lost the guy—or so I think—then I come around the corner and nearly run into him. Before I could react, he grabbed me by the neck and did that tactical move, you know, right there at the pressure point on the neck? Dropped me to the ground. When I came to, my bag—with Patty's stuff in it *and* an excellent bottle of tequila—was gone. And I'm almost positive it was a different guy than the one who'd attacked me in the hotel."

"All right. That explains why you're talking to me and not the local cops."

"Right. I called Jill Fetzer to make sure she was all right, and she was still fine and ready to meet me, but obviously tense and anxious. Then I hightailed it up to Pete's All-Niter—you'll want to make a note of that, because I'm pretty sure someone killed Jill Fetzer in the ladies' room there last night."

"Before or after you got there?"

"Before. *But,*" he said, aware that his eyes were shining with excitement, "whoever it was grabbed her purse and her coat but did *not* know to take—or to look for—the small cardboard box that holds the Apis bee that everyone seems to be interested in."

"So you have this bee that potentially three people have died over, and one other—you—has been assaulted. If I were anyone else, I'd probably never believe people could kill over an insect...but I clearly know otherwise." Her smile was wry and cool. "So what's so special about it?"

"I don't know yet," he confessed. "I mean, I took a really close look at her last night. I grabbed a few things from Walmart, and, well, essentially, she's atypical of the species in many ways—including that she has no stinger. I would agree with Patty's assessment that she's a novel Apis—and that's just with a cursory physical exam, not even investigating her society and habits. I haven't gotten her into a full-blown lab because I don't know if someone's going to ambush me and run off with or destroy her. Oh, by the way, I should mention—she's not a living specimen."

"The one in the cardboard box."

"Correct."

Darrow eased back into her chair and folded her arms over her middle, looking at him speculatively. "So we have explosives, three murders, assault, two states, and potentially a second nation—India—involved in this morass. Over a *bee*."

"That would be correct."

"How soon will you be able to tell whether—and why—this bee is so special?"

"I don't know. I'm wondering if I might have to go to Ladakh so I can see her in her habitat. Do you want to see her?" He mainly asked because he simply couldn't wait to show someone else the gorgeousness of this delicate and petite Apis bee—and also so he would have an excuse to look at her again. In honor of Tina, Patty, and Jill, he knew he had to notify the authorities first before locking himself away in a lab, or—better yet—heading to Ladakh to see the sweetie live and in person. And then he could take his time with the beauty.

"Sure. I should take a picture for the report anyway," she said.

"There are a few other items in the box as well—which, if you notice, was mailed from Paris to someone here in Chicago over a hundred years ago," Eli said, carefully setting the container on the table.

"With the bee in it?" Darrow lifted her brow once more. "A hundred years ago?"

"Yes. As far as I can tell, anyway. There are a few other things in the box that might explain why." He'd barely looked at them because he only had eyes for the lovely little Apis.

With reverence and care, he opened the shipping box and flipped up the lid of the smaller, more decorative container. It looked like a vintage French cigar or cigarette box.

From that box, he removed the small drinking glass he'd borrowed from his hotel room. It contained—protected—the wadded-up mass of cotton and tissue he'd used to wrap up what he'd begun to think of as the Apis patricia. Carefully he unrolled the packet until he revealed the specimen and let her tumble onto the pad of white paper—the better to show off her colors and the delicate formation of her wings.

To his delight, Darrow took a really good look at the beauty, turning the paper around so she could view A. patricia from all angles, even carefully lifting it to bring it closer to her eyes.

"It's small. But look at the colors!" Darrow lifted her eyes to meet Eli's. "The stripes are like a Montana rose-gold."

"I *know*," he said, delighted that she'd noticed the unusual coloring. "Chocolate mocha and rose-gold. I don't know of any other Apis bee that has that pinkish-magenta-gold coloring. And yes, she's small for an Apis—which isn't surprising if she comes from northern India or Nepal. It's colder there, and they have limited resources."

"You keep calling it a she…how can you tell it's female? Don't bees just have one queen?" Darrow scrutinized him with her dark hazel eyes.

Eli's cheeks heated a little. "Oh, all insects are 'she' to me, just naturally—like all ships are female?—until or unless I determine their sex. And although there's only one queen per hive, all of the worker bees are female. The males—the drones—just sit around eating and waiting to get laid. And then they die."

"Well, at least they die happy—presumably." Darrow set the bee back onto her nest of cotton wadding after giving the insect far less attention than she warranted. "What else is in the box? And what did you say about it coming from India or Nepal? Why would a bee be inside a box shipped from Paris a hundred years ago?"

"From what I've been able to gather—without actually looking at Patty's notes—my doctoral student came upon this same novel Apis species in Ladakh. She was pretty excited about it and mentioned its unusual coloring in the note to me about changing her thesis. I believe—because there's simply no way there are two *different* Apis bees, especially with that coloring, that are causing all of this havoc and…and espionage, sneaking around and killing people—I believe it has to be the same bee."

"But I don't understand how it could have become trapped in this box from Paris."

"She wasn't alive when she was packed up and sent overseas. Look—there's a pin and the small block of wood on which she was mounted, so that indicates she must have been put in the box purposely. I can only surmise that this particular specimen somehow made its way from India or Nepal to Paris, where this Nicolas Notovitch packaged it up with the other things in that box and shipped them here to someone named Alexina Donovan—and I suspect that Jill Fetzer obtained it through some family connection."

Darrow nodded. "All right. What else is in the box that can help explain why people are—apparently—willing to kill for this bee?" She lifted her gaze suddenly. "For a *dead* bee. Why do they care about a bee that's been dead for a century? This is bizarre."

Eli shook his head. "I don't have the answer to that—yet. But once I get a chance to fully examine her, I might have a better idea."

"While I'm fully aware of the problems with honeybees in our country, and elsewhere around the world, that they're dying out for no apparent reason—"

"Well, there *are* reasons. Most honeybee species have been brought over here from Europe and are what we call managed colonies—basically, honeybee farms. Often they're mobile—the colonies are moved from place to place depending on season and crop to do the pollinating. We do know some things about what causes CCD—er, colony collapse disorder—which is when all the bees in a colony are dead except the queen and some immature bees, so therefore it can't function and dies out. There's no single cause of CCD, but in recent years we have seen a decrease in incidents. But more concerning to me is that there's been a nearly fifty percent decrease in the habitat of bumblebees here in North America, which means even bees in the wild—those who are native here—are having a difficult time existing." As Helen's eyes were beginning to look a little hazy, he decided to stop there, though of course he could have gone on for hours.

She gave him a weak smile. "My point is: in light of the problems with hive collapse and the rest of it—the endangerment of bees and so on…could that be a reason someone wants this particular bee? Some ecoterror—" She stopped suddenly, sharply, and their eyes met.

"Ecoterrorist," Eli finished for her.

Neither of them needed to say what they were both clearly thinking, since it had been the Skaladeskas—the most dangerous of all ecoterrorists—that had brought them together on the *cuprobeus* beetle threat.

She released a long, slow breath. "It's all speculation at this point—

at least until you finish your examination and assessment of the bee. You said you need a lab?"

He nodded. "I was going to ask Jill Fetzer to get me into a lab here at U of C, but under the circumstances…" He grimaced.

"I can get you into a lab here," she said. "But it might not be set up for what you need. We don't generally dissect or examine bugs—insects, I mean." Her lips twitched in a smile; clearly she remembered their previous conversations.

"I appreciate that, but I think I'm going to see if Dr. Alexander can get me access to an entomology lab in Ann Arbor. She's on staff at Michigan, as you probably remember. She might be able to help with other things as well."

Darrow nodded, but her expression was grim. She understood exactly what he wasn't saying for the benefit of the recording she was making—and to her credit, she didn't push him to verbalize the fact that Marina was a direct connection to the Skaladeskas.

If they were somehow involved, she'd either know or be able to find out more.

"All right. What else is in here?" Agent Darrow turned her attention to Jill Fetzer's box. When she looked in the package and saw the smaller box inside it, her eyes grew wide. "Oh my God…is this an original Mucha cigarette box?"

Eli looked up from gazing in adoration on his new entomological love. "Whatever it is, it sounds important."

"Not important so much as beautiful—and probably worth a tidy sum of money. It's in perfect condition. Look at those colors."

While Eli couldn't deny that the image printed on the box was lovely—a woman dressed in flowing clothing, with all of its sinuous curves and feminine and floral details—his attention kept returning to the patricia.

Darrow carefully removed one item after the other from inside the cigarette box: a thick sheaf of papers, tied together with an old string. A small clay pot that appeared to have been sealed a long time ago. And a single sheet of paper that was the cover letter.

"I don't read French," said Eli, gesturing to the latter. "So I didn't get very far with that."

"I do," replied Darrow as she scrutinized the enclosure. "But this is old and very difficult to read. Still, I can make out a few words here and there... Mind if I make a copy of this—all of this?"

"Sure," Eli replied.

The special agent picked up the phone on the table and called for an admin to make the copies. Then she turned her attention to the petite clay pot.

It was about the size of a small jar of fancy, expensive French mustard—maybe six or eight ounces. It was formed from clay in an unpainted dung color. The top of the pot had a crude handle made from a small chopstick-thick stick about two inches long. It had been stuck through two nubs of clay. Darrow pulled gingerly on the handle, but it didn't open the jar.

"I don't want to break it," she said, lifting the pot to eye level. She turned it around in her hands, examining it from all sides. "It's sealed pretty tightly—with wax or maybe some sort of adhesive. But it looks really old. Much older than 1897. And there's marking engraved on it—I think it might be writing rather than decorative markings."

"Agreed. That's why I wanted to contact Dr. Alexander. She's an historian with an expertise in epigraphy—old texts," he said. "Kill two birds with one stone, if you will."

Darrow nodded, then lifted the pot near her ear and shook it gently. "Nothing moving inside; no rattling." She sniffed the clay. "It smells old and earthy." Then she looked at Eli. "You'll let me know what Dr. Alexander says."

He nodded. "Of course. I'm not a fan of nearly being killed, you know." Then he frowned. "From a law enforcement perspective, do you think there's any chance there are two different people—entities—after this bee?"

Her eyes narrowed. "What are you thinking?"

"Clearly the man who broke into my hotel room intended to kill me. And Jill Fetzer is dead—*I* can't get the police report details to find out how, but you can," he said slyly. "What if she was killed by an injection of sufentanil? That would be the same MO as the guy who tried to off me. But—"

"But last night, the man who assaulted you on campus at UIUC only incapacitated you for a few minutes," she said, nodding.

"He could easily have stuck me with a syringe and I wouldn't be sitting here now," he said, still disgusted by his own stupidity—literally walking into the man.

"Well, there are definitely two different people involved. The timing and the distance between you and Jill Fetzer makes that clear."

"Right," he said. "And one attack was lethal and one wasn't. Which could imply two different, I don't know, parties involved."

"Or simply that one of the team members prefers deadly force while the other does not."

"True. I'd rather it only be one party rather than two that I have to watch my back on," Eli said with a wry laugh.

There was a knock on the door, and the admin came in with the copies. He gave Eli a casual, lingering glance. "Can I get you some coffee, Dr. Sanchez?"

Eli smiled back, but not too warmly. "No thanks. I've been living on caffeine for thirty-six hours now. Maybe some water, though?"

The admin disappeared to comply, and Eli looked back at Darrow. "Well? What now?"

"I'm looking at this letter. The gist of it seems to be that the sender—Nicolas Notovitch—wants Alexina Donovan to keep and protect his notes. He uses the word *prueve*…which means evidence."

"Evidence…of what?"

Darrow was shuffling through the thick sheaf of papers, which had been unfastened for copying. "It's all in French. It looks like a— Wait. There are photographs too. Some of these are photographs of written pages. Not French, but some other…" She picked up the little clay pot. "Yes, see, Dr. Sanchez—it's the same writing as on here. I think it might be Sanskrit."

"Sanskrit." Eli nodded. "They've certainly been writing in Sanskrit in India and elsewhere in the East for centuries. And that's where Patty was."

He stood. "Now I really want to get a good look at this. I'm taking it to Dr. Alexander—and the pot, too."

Darrow stood, and for a moment he thought she was going to try to keep him from taking the box and its contents with him. He picked it up and held it firmly. Law enforcement or not, it wasn't evidence of any crime that anyone could prove—yet—and he wasn't about to lose possession. She had her copies of the paperwork.

Darrow must have read the intent in his expression, and that, as well as their shared history, had her standing down—so to speak. "Very well. I'm not sure I should allow you to keep the box, but I don't really have a valid reason for retaining it. At this time. And presumably you'll report back to me anything of interest?"

"I will. And I'd sure as hell like to know what you find out about Jill Fetzer's death."

Darrow seemed to understand the quid pro quo, but she gave him a cool look nonetheless. "On a need-to-know basis, Dr. Sanchez."

"Well, I think I *need to know* if someone's still trying to kill me," he said just as coolly. "Goodbye, Agent Darrow. I'm sure we'll be in touch."

He left the room just as the admin arrived with his water. "Thanks," Eli said, accepting the plastic bottle even as he felt the ever-present pang of guilt over the sheer non-ecological atrocity of paying for plastic-encased water.

"I'll be in touch," said Helen.

Though he knew there was no requirement for her to do so, he believed her when she said she would.

Now…off to Ann Arbor. And Marina.

# TWENTY-EIGHT

*Cleveland, Ohio*
*July 10*

Sandy just couldn't wrap her head around it all. Those poor guys.

It sounded like from what she'd heard that whatever caused those rigs to crash had been weird—as if the bottom fell out of them and everything just sort of collapsed while going sixty-five miles an hour on the highway.

But for three of them to have the same things happen... No matter what Fil Strung said, Sandy couldn't shake the feeling that it had something to do with that weird cleaner guy.

After all, it was *that very same day* the trucks crashed. And no one had ordered in anyone to clean or spray down the trucks. Who would've done that?

She wanted to push Fil over that, but he looked so tired and stressed that she just couldn't add to that unhappy light in his eyes. He was a good guy—if a little narrow-minded and a *tad* sexist—and she knew he really cared about the safety of everyone working there.

So instead of pushing him, she decided to do a little poking around instead.

"Hey, Jim," she said, walking up to the docks supervisor. He wore the same shell-shocked expression as Fil Strung had. "Did you send anyone out to hose down the tractors yesterday? Out in the yard?"

"Hose 'em down? No," he replied, holding a McDonald's hot cup. "What'd you mean?"

"Some guy was out there spraying down Randy Ritter's rig, and he was bitching about it," Sandy replied. "Just before he left."

"I didn't see anyone out there." He shrugged and grimaced like his stomach hurt. "Can't even believe it. Just can't believe it." He shook his head.

"I know. It's awful." Sandy wandered off, looking for someone else to talk to about the cleaning guy. She was pretty sure she'd seen him, whoever he was—but she hadn't paid much attention until Fil started complaining about him leaving the canister out.

*The canister.*

He'd thrown it in the garbage, hadn't he? She spun on her heel and rushed over to the trash can she'd seen him pitch it into late yesterday.

There it was, still inside there. She heaved a sigh of relief, then bent over to fish it out of the depths of the garbage.

It was a simple opaque white canister made from plastic, with a black sprayer hose attached. There was no label on the canister, and she realized too late that if there were any fingerprints on it (wow, she was really starting to think like the team on *CSI*—albeit a little too late), she'd probably smudged them when she dragged it out. Or Fil had when he picked it up and threw it away.

Still, at least she had the canister. It just didn't make sense that someone no one knew about was out there washing down the trucks. Sandy just *knew* in her gut that that guy and this canister had something to do with whatever happened yesterday…but now she wasn't sure how to proceed.

She hefted the canister—it wasn't heavy and was nearly empty, but something sloshed around inside. Should she tell Fil about it, press him to do something? Or should she just give it to one of the investigators?

No, she couldn't do that. Fil would be really *pissed* if she went around him. He was a nice guy, but that just wouldn't be cool, and she couldn't blame him. It might put him in a bad light with the investigators and the big bosses.

What should she do? Sandy fumbled with the spray hose and wondered if she should just spray it somewhere to see what happened… after all, if it was just water or cleaner, like he said, it would be harmless. But if it wasn't, then she could say, "Look at this!" and have a good reason to do so.

But what if it was hazardous? She couldn't just go around spraying shit on things—but didn't Fil say he'd sprayed himself yesterday? Accidentally? And he didn't seem to have a rash or any problems today.

She frowned, undecided, and kept looking at the canister, rolling it around in her hands (remembering again, belatedly, that she was probably destroying any fingerprints. Crap!). That was when she noticed the mark on the bottom of it. It looked like someone had drawn a sort of symbol on the bottom in black marker. It wasn't a name...maybe it was a company logo or something. But it didn't look familiar to her.

"What're you doing?" Fil's tense voice had her starting so that she nearly dropped the plastic container.

"I—I just found this in the garbage can," she said. "Don't you think it's worth looking into, just in case?"

"What do you mean looking into?" He seemed to be in a much worse mood now than he had been fifteen minutes ago. Maybe someone had just reamed his butt in a meeting.

Whatever had happened to the trucks, it wasn't Fil Strung's fault. She knew that. It couldn't even be negligence, because the dockyard wasn't locked or anything—anyone could drive around or walk around in there during the day—although maybe that *could* be considered negligence?

But it just didn't make sense to lock up the yard during the day when they were getting ready for a load—because how else were the truckers supposed to get their rigs back there? Ring a damned bell every time they needed in? Stupid. They'd be running to the gate every five minutes.

"Look, Fil, a weird thing happened yesterday with the guy

spray-cleaning the rigs…and then a few hours later, three of them crash. It's got to be more than a coincidence, don't you think?"

He was still looking at her with those hard eyes and pinched face, but it didn't offend Sandy. They were all stressed and the company was in deep trouble and three men were *dead*—everyone was allowed to be a little tense. "I don't know—maybe." He heaved a sigh. "But honestly, what the hell would that even do? It's just water and maybe some cleaning solution. How's that gonna cause a problem?"

"I don't know," she said, shaking her head. "I don't know. Maybe it's something else that's, you know, colorless and odorless—like, uh, carbon monoxide? Or something like that? But it does something to metal?" She shook her head sharply; it didn't even make sense to her ears. "I know it sounds weird. But I think you should at least mention it to the safety people. Just in case."

Fil heaved a sigh. "Maybe. I don't know. It just sounds so far-fetched. Remember—I even got some on myself, and nothing happened. I didn't get sick or anything."

"Well, what if it doesn't do anything to humans? What if it—I don't know—eats away at metal or rubber or something?" Sandy knew she was just throwing out crazy ideas, but there just didn't seem to be any other answer. "Look at it this way—no one has ever had anyone hosing down the trucks before, and we do yesterday—right before it *rains*? Who does that?—and then they crash. I mean…it really could be related. Maybe there was some sort of, I dunno, *acid* in that canister."

Fil's face was losing some of its tension, and that was being replaced by comprehension. "Holy crap. *Holy crap.*" His eyes bugged wide. He actually seemed to go pale right in front of her—which was significant, since his skin was already pretty colorless.

"What?"

"My belt buckle," he said in a sort of whispery voice. "My boots…"

She waited as he struggled with the words.

Then, all at once, his expression changed into determination. He yanked the canister from her hand. "I've got to get this to someone."

And without an explanation—or even a thank you—he took off across the warehouse at a very unsafe-workplace run.

Helen Darrow sat back in her chair and looked at the computer screen. She'd just plugged Nicolas Notovitch into Google, and what popped up there was absolutely not what she'd expected.

"So you wrote a book called *The Secret Life of Jesus Christ*. And you sent your notes about it to someone here in Chicago— Oh, wait," she said. "Alexina Donovan was the translator of your book from French—your name's not French, though—to English."

She had a lot of other work on her desk—including her review of anything her analysts had put together from their daily screens on the Chicago area and Midwest threats, as well as what she considered her own personal wheelhouse of the Skaladeska tribe and potential threat. There were only a small number of people in the Bureau who knew much about the ecoterrorist group, and she was one of the elite team that worked with similar counterparts in the CIA...which included her old flame Gabe MacNeil. Unfortunately.

But despite the daily report that sat there on its yellow paper waiting for her to review, Helen found herself unable to put aside the bee mystery that Dr. Sanchez had dumped into her thoughts. Maybe because the secret life of Jesus Christ—whatever it was—and the pretty pink-gold bee was a hell of a lot more intriguing than reading a bunch of analytics.

*The Secret Life of Jesus Christ* turned out *not* to be, as Helen had expected, a blasphemous, *Da Vinci Code* sort of work of fiction, but a kind of messianic exposé. The book was purportedly a nonfiction account of... Her eyes bulged and her brows rose as she looked at the Wikipedia entry.

*Well, that's interesting.*

Apparently, in the late 1880s, one Nicolas Notovitch—a Russian Jew living in Paris writing about Jesus; go figure that one—had traveled to the mountains of northern India and Nepal. He stayed in a Buddhist monastery while recovering from a broken leg, and while there learned from the monks some bombshell information: that Jesus Christ had *traveled throughout India.*

"Well, if that idea—true or not—doesn't send tremors through the Christian world, I don't know what will," she said, still looking at the computer screen. "No wonder Notovitch sent his 'proof'—if that's what it is—here to the U.S."

She had just clicked "Buy Now" to order a copy of the book—at this point, she had to know more—when her mobile phone rang. "Darrow speaking," she said, scrolling through more information from the Google search. *Lots* of entries debunking the Notovitch book over the last hundred years. So whether his contentions were true or not remained to be seen.

"We've just got a hit on the Skaladeskas," said Cody, one of her analysts. "You'd better take a look."

Helen agreed and disconnected the call. The Skaladeskas had been quiet for the last two or three years. Which meant she hadn't had any reason to be in touch with Gabe.

But it looked like that was about to change, and that meant she'd be bringing in her colleagues from the CIA.

Helen wasn't certain whether she was more anxious about dealing with the ecoterrorists or her former lover.

# TWENTY-NINE

Marina was in the most beautiful place she'd ever imagined. Lush greenery glittered with diamond dew. Silky grasses swayed and flowering bushes shimmered in a subtle breeze. The loamy scent of rich earth mingled with sweet nectar and pungent pine. Crystal-studded water danced over the stony creek bed, twining through the forest like a silvery ribbon.

It was Gaia at her best, showing off her wares.

Marina wandered through the growth, her fingertips brushing over feathery grass heads, satiny blossom petals, rough bark. Her bare feet trod upon cool grass, smooth pebbles, and dark earth in turn. She heard birds singing and calling, the rush of water, the gentle clatter of branches against each other, the happy buzz of insects.

It was a strange location…not rainforest nor deep woods nor mountain region nor meadow nor desert…and yet wherever she was, there were elements of all those environs. Cacti and pines, wildflowers and liana, maples and birds of paradise, orange blossoms, scrubby boulders, edelweiss, and tulips.

She walked, breathing in the beauty of her Mother Gaia, listening for her heartbeat, admiring the array of life that surrounded her.

And then she came to the tree.

It was a massive specimen, reminding her of a tropical banyan. This tree had a trunk ten feet in diameter, and its bark appeared smooth and silky, and of a rich cocoa hue. Its broad network of branches boasted a deep and wide canopy of green, gold, crimson, orange, even purple and blue leaves. Powerful roots surged from the earth like limbs caught in the act of erupting from the dirt.

Beneath the tree, in the embrace of two such undulating roots that formed a natural throne, sat an old man.

*Grandfather.*

Lev watched her, welcoming her with fathomless blue eyes as she moved toward him, her heartbeat pounding throughout her body as if to remind her that she was, in fact, alive, awake, and real.

And so was this.

*Mariska.* His lips didn't move, yet she heard her name as if he'd spoken aloud. *At last you've come.*

*Where are we?* She meant to speak, but her mouth didn't move.

*We are in the Lower World. I've been waiting for you to join me here for far too long.*

Somehow she knew where to sit: facing him, yet slightly to the left. There was a protruding root that curled and created a moss-upholstered seat. As she settled into the place waiting for her, Marina realized she had somehow come to be wearing a long, loose robe of some light, natural material with a sheen. It slid pleasingly over her skin.

*Did you bring me here?* she asked.

*I've made the invitation often. This is the first time you've chosen to accept it. To travel here. Something has happened.*

Although she was surrounded by a stunning wilderness, with its brightest, deepest, truest colors, scents, sounds, and textures, Marina also felt as if she were underwater...or in some sort of strange airless environment in which she could, nevertheless, breathe.

And although what she could see and feel—the emerald moss, springy and velvety beneath her palm, the stunning scarlet flowers bursting from a vine crawling up the banyan, the perfect lavender bird watching her from a slender twig next to Lev—just beyond her near surroundings, everything was muted and blurry and soft.

*What happened, Mariska?*

She didn't think she knew what he meant, but somehow she responded. *In the cave...I spoke to Gaia. She heard me, and She helped me.*

Lev nodded. Something gleamed in his eyes as he watched her steadily.

*Why am I here?* Marina thought-asked.

*You're here because you've at last acknowledged your deep connection to Gaia and have experienced it. Now you recognize who you are and what you are capable of. Tell me what happened in the cave.*

*I think you already know, Grandfather.*

His mouth moved slightly, just a brief uptick at the corner, indicating acknowledgment and humor.

*I can't come to you, Grandfather.* She wanted to speak those words, moving her mouth, to make certain he heard and understood how strong they were—how deeply she believed and knew them—but still the statement came only from her mind to his. *I won't join a movement of death and destruction.*

*As you say now. Despite my sadness and disappointment at your stubbornness, I know that too will change. Because you are who you are. You are a Daughter of Gaia, and you must not forget that. You cannot deny your calling, no matter how much you try. You already know it. I am patient—for all must make the journey in their own time, in their own way…but I don't know how much longer Gaia will allow me to be here on this Earth.*

Those words of finality acted like a sharp thorn in her belly. Was Lev dying? Was he already dead? Had she missed her opportunity to know him?

*Roman.* The single word escaped her mind and shot between them. Then more: *My father.*

Lev looked at her, his eyes suddenly spearing her. *So it is true.*

They looked at each other there in the shadow of a tree in a place on—in—*below?*—the earth that didn't exist. She reached out to him. *You didn't know.*

*I suspected.*

*I won't be part of what he does, Grandfather. What he and Nora and Hedron and Varden do is murderous.*

Lev shook his head. *It is the way of nature, the way of the world, the Way of Gaia. If one species threatens that of the whole, it shall be expelled. For the good of all.*

She curled her fingers, felt moss and dirt and bark beneath them. *Killing people is not the way.*

*It is no different than the wars you Out-Worlders fight, than the choices your governments make, the way men spend their capital: some will always die in the pursuits of freedom, safety, protection. Some will always die in poverty and from illness because only a few hold power and money.*

*Does not the safety and saving of all—of our very* world—*justify the destruction of some few? That is the way of Nature, Mariska. The way of Gaia. You cannot deny it. Life and death is the cycle. To protect oneself is only natural.*

She tried to stand, ready to leave, but her legs wouldn't move. *Now you would hold me here?*

He shook his head so slightly that it was nearly unnoticeable. Marina more felt the shift in the air than actually saw him move. *We need you. Gaia needs you. You can help protect all of us—everyone—even those who threaten the sacred being. They threaten me as well.*

*I can't—*

*You must speak to Varden. Work with him.*

Her response was short and powerful: *No.*

Lev looked at her, his thoughts silent, his eyes probing. Marina felt the earth around her shiver and shift and vibrate oh so gently—as if to remind her who she was, whom she was with. In whose arms she rested.

A soft buzz caught her attention, and she turned to see a small insect hovering next to her. It was a bee, and it suddenly dove, burrowing into a large white flower that had not been present a moment ago. Somehow, light filtered through the forest—or jungle, or wherever she was—and illuminated the busy insect, setting her awash in pink and gold and magenta. She was beautiful. Stunning. Delicate. Powerful.

*Sacred.* The word settled in her mind, and she wasn't certain who'd put it there—Lev, herself, or Gaia.

When Marina looked up, Lev was gone. The tree was gone—even the roots that had made her own chair.

Now she sat in the sun. Just…in the sun. Nothing below her, above her, around her…only warm light.

The bee was still there. It swept up from the white flower, hovering for a moment in front of her eyes, then flitted away, her translucent wings glittering pale rose in the light.

The next thing Marina knew, she felt something cold touching her hand.

She was in her chair, and Adele's damp nose was nudging the back of her hand. She gave a quiet whine, like an *Are you here?*

Marina looked around. Yes, she was here, in her own house in Ann Arbor, and both of her dogs sat there looking expectantly at her.

She blinked and came back to herself fully.

"Need to go out, huh?" She pulled to her feet, still trying to shake off the...whatever it had been. Not a dream, she didn't think. She wasn't groggy as if she'd been sleeping.

It was more like a journey. Out-of-body travel. What had Lev said? The Lower World.

She had been in the Lower World.

A shiver skittered across her shoulders. She'd heard of the Lower World—and the Upper World and the Middle World. Those places belonged to shamanic traditions. They were places one traveled on shamanic journeys.

Marina opened the front door, and her two dogs bounded outside, eager to do their business—and to sniff around and chase squirrels and scratch in the sun.

As she stood there, watching Boris and Adele examine and then secure their domain, Marina dug the phone out of her pocket.

Several messages had come in while she was doing...whatever she'd been doing. One from Bruce, asking if she wanted to grab dinner and talk about the rescue at Turncoat Don. *No thank you,* she thought, and decided not to answer right away. She was going to need to have a conversation with Bruce, but not via text and not today.

There was also a message from *Eli Sanchez*, of all people! That gave her a burst of pleasure, and she smiled, hoping she'd have the chance to see him soon. The third text was from a number she didn't recognize. It had just been delivered. Within the last minute.

Something made her insides feel funny, and she clicked on that third message before she checked Eli's text.

*We need to talk.*

That was the message from the number she didn't recognize. As she stared at it, a strange frisson of knowing settled over her—and she immediately dismissed it. But whoever had sent the message—and dammit, she suspected she knew who it was—was now typing something else.

*Lev's request. Not mine.*

Marina went cold and then hot as she stared at the phone. It *was* Varden.

And she certainly wasn't going to meet up with him.

So Marina, still feeling a little unsteady, tapped Eli's message.

*Incoming. You around?* This was followed by a sly smiling emoji.

Her mood lifted again. *Yes. ETA?*

His response came immediately: *Ten minutes?*

Marina's brows rose. Well, that was fast. Good thing she'd showered this morning. She responded with her own sly smiling emoji, and, as she tucked the phone back in her pocket, leaving both Bruce's and Varden's messages unanswered, she looked around covertly.

Was Rue Varden watching her even now?

She lived in the Burns Park area of Ann Arbor, where a good number of university faculty, like herself, resided. It was a neighborhood of many mature, leafy trees, curving residential streets, and single-family homes built in the forties and fifties. Her home was one of the smaller ones in the neighborhood—a little brick bungalow on one of the quiet, winding streets shaded by many tall, broad oaks, maples, and elms. She'd made use of one of those large trees several years ago, climbing from the window of her upstairs bathroom onto one of the limbs to escape from Dannen Fridkov—one of Roman Aleksandrov's operatives. He'd had a gun, and intended to kidnap or kill her. She'd never actually learned which.

Marina had used the cover of the tall, leafy, expansive trees, climbing and jumping from limb to limb and tree to tree above the ground to make her way from her yard to a neighbor's, then down and away, eventually meeting up on the ground with CIA operative Gabe MacNeil, who'd previously warned her about the dangers of the Skaladeskas.

Since then, Marina had considered but not yet succumbed to the idea of buying her own firearm. And every day when she came out to her yard, she thanked all of the trees for being there to help her escape.

And they whispered back in response.

Shaking off this strange melancholia, Marina looked up just as a vehicle came around the curve of the street. She recognized it right away: Juanita, the battered, worn, trusty Jeep that had loyally carried Eli all the way from Champaign, Illinois. She wondered what had brought him to Ann Arbor or its environs.

Boris and Adele alerted as the truck slowed and turned into her driveway, but they were trained well enough to wait for her command.

"It's okay," she told them once the Jeep had safely come to a halt. "That's Eli. Friend. Say hi."

Thus given permission, the two dogs bounded joyously forward, barking their greeting, tails beating the air as if it were a soufflé. Eli, who'd slung a gym bag over his shoulder, bent to respond to each in turn. He looked up at Marina even as he continued to pet the younger dog. "This must be Adele. She looks very capable. And you—Marina, you look *good.*"

So did Eli. He was wearing a white t-shirt emblazoned with the words SEX, BUGS, AND ROCK & ROLL, along with his normal garb of well-worn, slung-at-the-hips cargo shorts. He was missing his lab coat, but was wearing his favorite footwear: dark brown Birkenstocks.

Marina stepped into a more-than-just-friends embrace against his hard, lanky body, and smiled when he pulled back to kiss her on the mouth with a prickle of his mustache. She liked the way he tasted.

"Nice to see you, Dr. Sanchez," she said after a moment of enjoying him. "What brings you to my neck of the woods?"

"Did someone say necking?" he teased, then drew her back close for another kiss, and a quick, enticing nibble on the side of her neck.

Chuckling, she extricated herself, then slid her hand down to hold his. There was still a lot of boyishness left inside Dr. Eli Sanchez. That was one of the things she liked about him. "Come on inside and we'll talk." She gave him a promising look that had him grinning in return.

She called the dogs, and they were just about to follow her inside when a car cruised down the street. Always on alert, Boris and Adele stopped to watch as the dark blue Focus eased closer, then meandered past.

Marina brought the dogs inside, and when she turned back to Eli, she saw that he was watching after the sedan with an arrested expression.

"Everything all right?" she asked.

"Probably. For now, anyway." He followed her inside, setting his bag down in the living room.

"It's so…I don't know, synchronistic that you're in town today," she said, walking into the kitchen. "I had the weirdest sort of dream about a bee just before I got your text—maybe my subconscious knew my insect guy was in the vicinity."

"*Your* insect guy?" He leaned his elbow comfortably on the bar counter that opened from the living room into the small kitchen and gave her a smoldering look. "Hmm. Not sure how I feel about being a possession. We might have to negotiate terms."

She laughed, leaning in on the counter across from him. She'd missed his easy sense of humor, intelligence…and other attributes as well. "I have beer, iced tea, an open bottle of Chardonnay, water, and coffee. What's your pleasure, insect guy?"

The smolder got a little warmer, then faded away as he gave a sort of grimace. "Probably just water for now. Best to keep heads clear. I've got something I need your help with."

"All right. Let's sit in there."

Eli looked around the small, cozy living room, which boasted a real wood-burning fireplace and worn oak flooring. There were two dog beds and several rope and chew toys in one corner, and a four-shelf unit filled with books. As he watched, Adele picked up one of the ropes and settled in her bed to gnaw on it. Boris, who was a little more suspicious, curled up in his bed and watched over his mistress and her guest.

On the white plastered walls were a collection of framed vintage Hitchcock movie posters—*The Man Who Knew Too Much* and *Rope* were two of his favorites (gotta love Jimmy Stewart). Two shadow boxes hung on the wall displaying artifacts: a fragment of woven material that looked really old and was probably Asian, and a piece of parchment that was likely Middle Eastern or maybe Asian too—Eli really had no idea.

A dark red throw rug that looked Nepalese delineated a conversation area in front of the fireplace with a sofa and two chairs. The glass-topped table in the center reminded him of a low museum case, displaying other interesting objects Marina had obviously found on some of her travels. A squat, cracked vase that had once been blue and he guessed was Pan-American, another piece of parchment (this time with a different kind of marking on it that might have been Thai), a bowl holding a collection of rough stones that glittered blue, black, and violet, and—to his delight—a familiar mounted and framed Coleop.

"Nice," he said, gesturing to the insect, which was a perfect specimen of the coppery *cuprobeus* beetle. He'd written and published several papers on that deadly little beast, and done many more media interviews.

They had settled on opposite ends of the broken-in leather sofa, facing each other companionably. When Marina curled up her bare feet onto the sofa, Eli saw the tattooed mark of the Skaladeskas on the heel of her foot. Few people were aware of her undeniable connection to the mysterious tribe.

"I thought it was the perfect memento of everything," she replied with a smile that reminded him of the dinner—and afterglow—they'd shared in a small town in Ecuador after their harrowing airborne escape from the jungle.

He smiled back, wishing he had no ulterior motive for being here other than wanting to see Marina. The blue Focus that had cruised down the street a moment ago looked a lot like one he'd seen on the highway during his journey here.

But then again…there were a lot of blue Focuses. And there was no way anyone could have followed him here. He'd been very careful, and had told his plan to come here to no one except Helen Darrow. He hadn't even been in contact with Marina until fifteen minutes ago. He forced himself to relax. "Yeah. So…you had a dream about a bee?"

Her smile faded. "Not really a dream. I don't think. It was…" She lifted her hands in a "whatever" gesture. "I was with my grandfather."

Eli nodded, and for the moment put aside his own agenda. He'd briefly met Lev, the elderly shaman of the Skaladeskas. There was something about that man—hell, there'd been something about that entire experience—that made him look at things differently. "Go on."

But Marina shook her head. "That's all right. I think I need to just sit with it for a while first." She smiled warmly. "Tell me what brings you to Ann Arbor."

"What…you being here isn't enough of a reason?"

"Considering the fact that you didn't text me until you were already here, Dr. Sanchez, I'm fairly confident it wasn't my sparkling personality and rapier wit—not to mention the fact that I have several pizzas in the freezer—that brought you here."

He smiled, then allowed the levity to fade away. "A bee brought me here."

Her easy expression faltered, then cleared again. "Shocking that an entomologist should be in pursuit of a bee. Tell me more."

"Believe it or not, someone seems to be trying to kill me—and has already killed others—over a bee."

"Okay. Wow." She squeezed her eyes closed, clasped her hands together, then looked at him with an odd expression. She heaved a breath. "The bee…it's not pinkish-goldish-magenta is it?"

"Got it in one. Mine has chocolate stripes along with the pink-gold."

She swore under her breath and shook her head.

"So, I'm guessing the bee in your dream with Lev is an unusual rosy gold."

She nodded then narrowed her eyes. "What made you come here? To me?"

"I'm not trying to get you killed, Marina," he said quickly, suddenly horrified at the unintended implication. "I wasn't—"

"Considering the fact that I nearly got *you* killed back in the Amazon, I'm not one to point any fingers. I've gotten used to dodging murderers," she said dryly. "That's not at all what I meant by the question. What I should have said is, how can I help you?"

"I came here because I need access to a lab where I can examine the specimen in detail, and UIUC and U of C aren't safe. Plus there was the added benefit of your frozen pizzas. *And*," he added as she began to chuckle while shaking her head in exasperation, "I need your expertise in looking at some markings—writing, I think—on a small clay pot."

She nodded. "All right. Pizza now or later?"

"I could eat—then I hope you can get me to a lab. I'm dying to get my hands on this specimen under a real microscope. Why don't you put a pizza in the oven and I'll tell you what's been going on? Or... we could order in from that local place with the really good crust." He waggled his eyebrows. He had fond memories about eating that particular pizza—laden with pepperoni and feta cheese—in Marina's bed one evening after a particularly energetic afternoon. "It's almost as good as Chicago style."

"Cottage Inn? I won't argue with that. I've only got Red Baron in the freezer."

"Now you're talking." His voice was easy and so was his smile, but inside, Eli was struggling. He had, after all, brought his own problem and danger directly to Marina's doorstep.

The last thing he wanted to do was endanger her.

# THIRTY

H elen rose as Gabe MacNeil strode into the conference room. He looked pretty much the same as he had the last time she'd seen him, although there was a little more threading of gray beginning at the temples in his dark brown hair.

At thirty-seven, the CIA agent was about six feet tall, with an average build and blue eyes. He was clean-shaven and clean-cut, with charming crinkles at the corners of his eyes and a square chin, and was the kind of man that got appreciative looks from straight women whenever he walked into the room. And when he spoke, his voice was flavored with just a sugary hint of West Virginia—which sent many of the straight women into even deeper mental swoons. As one would expect, he wore a dark suit and tie and carried a leather briefcase.

But he wasn't alone. Helen hadn't expected him to be accompanied by his boss, Colin Bergstrom.

Helen and Gabe had been identified by their respective agencies as lead liaisons on anything related to the Skaladeskas, and the two of them created a sort of special task force team for any intelligence about the ecoterrorist group. Bergstrom had not been identified as being a member of the special task force, but as Gabe's superior, he certainly could include himself in any meeting he chose.

She greeted them both familiarly, but flashed a meaningful look at Gabe behind his boss's head. Her former lover grimaced slightly, but smoothed out his features as soon as the trio settled around the small table.

"It's nice to see you again as well, Agent Darrow," said Bergstrom. He was a man well past sixty, probably even over seventy by now. His comfortable little paunch had decreased a little since Helen had seen him last, but the thick eyeglasses he wore still sat heavily on his soft cheeks, making shallow indentations on them. Nonetheless, his eyes remained sharp and careful as he swept the small room with his gaze. "Not bad for a smaller field office."

"Please call me Helen, as before. And—I wanted to meet here in Cleveland so we could be near the site in question," she replied. "So let me fill you in on what we know."

"Mind if I get some coffee first?" Bergstrom asked. "Been up since four and still need the fuel. I'm not as young as I was."

"Oh, I'm sorry—of course. I can have some brought in—"

"No, no, I saw the breakroom. I'll get it myself. I see you're all set, Helen, but Gabe, do you want anything?" Bergstrom paused with his hand on the doorknob.

"I'm fine, thanks, Colin." The minute the door closed behind his boss, Gabe said in a low voice, "Sorry. He insisted on coming."

"Does he know you know?" she replied.

"I've not said anything to him. I hoped he'd retire before anything else came up with the Skalas. I thought he was going to go last year, but not yet."

Helen eased back in her seat and looked at him as she toyed with the stylus from her tablet. "Maybe we should tell him that we know. Or—*I* could tell him."

"That might just upset the balance even more." He sighed, rubbing the space between his brows with a thumb and forefinger. "I like and respect Colin very much. He's a good man, an excellent mentor, and he's been fair and supportive of me for my entire career—"

"So you'd want to protect him from doing anything that might upset his *own* career. Especially if he's near retirement."

The door opened and Bergstrom strode in, tie fluttering and two cups of coffee in his hands. "They were small cups," he said with a fleeting smile. "Sorry about the delay. What's wrong?" His attention sharpened as he set the coffee on the table. "How bad is it?"

Helen didn't look at Gabe. She didn't want to take any chances that Bergstrom—who hadn't had a distinguished career in counterintelligence because he was a fool—might read between the lines. "It's not great, Colin. I'll be honest with you. But before we get started, I feel the need to be up front with you about a piece of intelligence relative to your ex-wife." She met his eyes calmly. "If you'd like to ask Gabe to leave, I'd understand."

The older man's expression gave no indication of surprise or fear. Instead, he gave a small, contrite smile. "No, that's not necessary. If Gabe isn't already aware—and I'd be surprised if he weren't—he should be advised as well."

Helen felt a shudder of relief deep inside, but she didn't even flicker a glance at Gabe. "All right, then, Colin—clearly, you aren't going to deny or try to subvert the fact that your ex-wife Nora is the— uh—partner of Roman Aleksandrov, who is the de facto leader of the Skaladeskas."

"To my knowledge, that's correct," Bergstrom replied. "Since I haven't had any communication with Nora since our divorce, I can only surmise based on intelligence and incident reports. But since she left me for Roman," he said, his voice going cold, "and since she's still with the Skaladeskas, that would be my assumption as well."

Silence hung in the small room for a moment and was only broken when Gabe shifted in his seat and said, "I suspected there was a personal connection when you first put me on to the Skaladeskas, Colin. But I didn't confirm my suspicions until a few years ago."

"That's why you're one of my best people," Bergstrom replied. "I would have expected nothing less."

"I could ask you to recuse yourself from this investigation," Helen went on. "However, at this time I'll refrain from doing that—with the understanding that both Gabe and I reserve the right to make that decision if at any time your personal connection appears to conflict with our investigation."

Bergstrom pursed his lips and nodded once. "I wouldn't expect anything different from you. I can assure you, I won't—as I've not in the past—interfere. I simply want—*need*—to…know." His voice was a little unsteady at the end, and Helen felt a tiny stab of sympathy for the man.

"All right," she said briskly. "Let me tell you what we know. You've probably heard about the three trucking accidents that occurred two days ago. All single-vehicle incidents, all the same sort of event. All of them, as it turns out, were rigs that came from Cargath Steel here in Cleveland."

"Yes, I heard about them. They were horrific from what I know. It sounded as if the bottom dropped out of the driver's seats," Colin said.

"That seems to be exactly what happened. And because each of the rigs—or tractors, as I understand they call the parts that tow the semi-trailers—were independently owned and operated, there didn't seem to be any sort of safety issue with the logistics company.

"Until the safety manager—one Filbert Strung—brought to the attention of the investigating authorities that he noticed someone cleaning the trucks just before they left. It happened to be raining, and one of the drivers who died—Randy Ritter—was complaining about why someone would be out hosing down the trucks when it was pouring rain.

"Mr. Strung realized belatedly that perhaps whatever was being sprayed on the trucks as a cleaning agent had something to do with the accidents, and so he—or rather, one of his associates—dug out the canister that the cleaning agent had been using. What was in the canister wasn't a cleaning solution. It wasn't even water—or only water. What it appears to be is some sort of— Let me get the actual scientific description." She flipped through her notes and grimaced. "I can't find the science-y words right now, but basically the cause of these accidents was a bacteria that feeds on metal."

"A metal-eating bacteria?" said Gabe, looking as skeptical as she'd been when the news hit her desk. "Is there such a thing?"

"Apparently there is—I've done a little research to corroborate the findings. Back in 2019, a pair of microbiologists at Caltech accidentally discovered a bacteria that uses manganese for resources—basically, as its food. There's a whole article in *Nature* about it from 2020, but I didn't read anything other than the abstract to get the gist. They named the bacteria, uh…let's see if I can get this right…*Candidatus Manganitrophus* noduliformans." She looked up at Gabe. "To be clear, the bacteria we're concerned about is not this particular one. I only cited it as proof that such a thing exists."

"And so it seems we have something like that here?" said Bergstrom. "How do we know the Skaladeskas are involved? Presumably that's where you're headed with this."

"Mr. Strung claims that when he first found the canister, which the perp—we can call him that at this point—carelessly left sitting in the middle of the warehouse dock, he accidentally sprayed some of its contents on his person. Later that evening, his large metal belt buckle and the metal grommets on his shoes—both of which would have been sprayed by the contents of the canister—were gone. As if they'd disintegrated." She looked at the two men across from her. "He hasn't been able to find the metal belt buckle or the grommets anywhere. It's like they literally disappeared."

Gabe was staring at her, and she saw the spike of anxiety in his eyes. "A metal-eating bacteria that works *that quickly?*"

"It appears to be. We've got microbiologists working on the analysis, of course, but at first blush, it seems that the bacteria is inert until it's exposed to its, uh"—she glanced at her notes to find the term—"necessary resources. No, actually, it's inert until it's exposed to oxygen, so if it's kept in, say, water, it would be harmless until exposed to the air."

"There's oxygen in water," Gabe pointed out.

Helen shrugged, scanning her notes again. "I'm not a chemist or a microbiologist. I'm delivering the facts as they're presented to me, and based on what they took out of the canister, that's their postulation. So the form of oxygen is apparently relevant—liquid versus gaseous."

"Right, of course. Just thinking out loud," he said.

She nodded. "What I'm getting from the report is that manganese or some sort of metal is the resource that *activates* the bacteria—that makes it grow or spread or multiply. The microbes might just exist in a sort of limbo in water or wherever, but once they get the right conditions—uh, resources—meaning their food, the right atmosphere, and so on, that's when they explode and take over."

"How do we know the Skalas are involved—I'm guessing they left some sort of message, as they usually do?" Gabe asked.

"Their mark was on the bottom of the canister, which Mr. Strung had thrown away. That's how we got looped in. It's also important to note that the canister, and all parts of it, are made from plastic, which apparently is *not* a resource for this bacteria."

Bergstrom had finished his first small Styrofoam cup of coffee, and now he lifted the second one. "And so the Skaladeskas have a fast-working bacteria that eats—or destroys—manganese. Metal. All sorts of metal. Steel. Iron. Everything. And you're saying that over the course of several hours, this bacteria ate through enough of the bottom of a semitruck that the whole thing collapsed?"

Helen nodded. She already knew what horrors were going through the minds of the men across from her.

Trains. Planes. Ships. Bridges. Buildings.

All were made from metal.

# THIRTY-ONE

While they waited for the pizza to be delivered, Marina listened intently—and with growing concern—while Eli filled her in on what had happened since his graduate student Patty died.

"So three people are dead—and you aren't, but you nearly *were,* twice—because of this bee?" she said when he finished.

Eli nodded, his expression sober. "Possibly even four. I'm pretty sure Patty was the first victim, and that her death in Ladakh wasn't just a random accident."

"So what about this bee could be cause for such violence? Do you have any ideas? It must be some sort of rare specimen...but what would make it so important?"

He nodded, still holding his glass of water. "Not only rare. I've never seen or heard of anything like her. She's an unusual color, and fairly small as far as Apis bees go. I haven't seen any pictures from Patty's notes—I haven't taken the time to log in and look because I haven't been on a secure network—but it has to be the same bee that came in the package from Paris over a hundred years ago."

"That's pretty random," Marina said with a frown. "Your grad student comes across a unique and rare bee, and at the same time, someone discovers it packed away in an attic from a hundred years ago."

He nodded. "Like you said earlier—it's synchronicity. And you just had a dream about the same kind of bee. Not a coincidence. Something's going on...something that has the whole universe involved."

*Or Gaia.* She exhaled, nodding. She couldn't argue with that, considering her recent dream—or journey—with Lev. "I'll tell you about my dream—and I want you to show me this bee—but let me take out the dogs and feed them. The pizza should be here any minute now."

"Mind if I freshen up a little? I've sort of been on the run for the last two days." He grimaced. "I feel like Jack Ryan."

"Of course. You know where everything is," she said. "Use the upstairs bathroom."

Boris and Adele did their business in the side yard, then, just as Marina was taking them back in, a car with a Cottage Inn sign on it appeared up the street.

She went to grab her wallet, and when she came back out to greet the pizza delivery person, she found him talking to a man in the driveway behind Eli's Jeep.

"That's for me, I think," she said to the delivery man with a smile.

The other man turned to her, and she saw that he was a priest. "Oh, hello," he said. "I was just telling this man here that I was considering how to convince him to let me take that off his hands." He gestured to the pizza with an engaging smile. "We don't have deliveries like that where I come from."

Marina smiled in return and guessed from his accent, blue-black hair, and olive skin that he might be from Italy or somewhere in the Mediterranean. "Cottage Inn is an Ann Arbor staple," she said, paying the driver and taking the pizza. Since she didn't see a car on the street and didn't recognize the priest as a neighbor, she said, "Are you visiting for long?"

The delivery man was already in his car pulling out of the driveway when the priest replied. "For a short while. Are those your dogs?" He looked toward the house where Adele and Boris were barking, noses pressed to the glass sidelight on one side of the door. They did *not* like it when their mistress was with strange people and they weren't there to protect her.

"Yes," she said, and decided it was time to end the conversation— after all, she had a hot pizza in her possession, and she was getting a too-interested, nosy vibe from the priest. "Enjoy your walk," she added as she turned to go up the sidewalk.

"It's a beautiful neighborhood," he replied, gesturing with his hand. "Birds singing everywhere, flowers in bloom, bees buzzing around."

Marina didn't stop, but something about his words stuck with her as she let herself into the house, maneuvering around the dogs—who'd lost interest in the visitor outside in favor of investigating the smells coming from the flat box she carried.

Eli bounded down from upstairs just then. His chin-length hair was damp from a shower, hanging loose and dripping on his SEX, BUGS, AND ROCK & ROLL shirt. "The pizza delivery guy was a priest?"

Marina chuckled. "No, just someone taking a walk at the same time."

"That smells really good, so I'm going to eat while you tell me about your bee dream." He grinned.

"I'm not sure it was actually a dream," she said once they settled back on the sofa with their plates of pizza. "I think it might have been a—a journey. Lev said I was in the Lower World."

"Lower World…are you talking about a shamanic-type of journey?" he asked, then started on his pizza.

Marina was relieved that Eli seemed to have at least a basic understanding of shamanic traditions. And that he wasn't looking at her as if she were losing her mind. "It's never happened before, but I don't have any other explanation. I wasn't sleeping. I was just sitting in my chair and thinking about things, and then…well, I was gone. Somewhere. Lev was there, and there was a bee. I assumed it was that unusual pinkish color because it was in the Lower World—in the journey— but it seems as if a bee like that really exists."

"Did Lev speak to you in the—during the journey?"

She nodded. "We spoke. He made his case again for why the Skalas do what they do." She couldn't tell Eli that every time she spoke to her grandfather, heard his arguments and listened to his emotional pleas, her determination to stay away—to reject the Skaladeskas—wavered a little more. Lev's words were compelling, and now, after directly experiencing her connection to Gaia while in the Turncoat Don cave, she felt the personal connection even more deeply.

"What is it, Marina?" Eli watched her intently. He even put down the pizza he was holding.

She couldn't tell even Eli about what happened when Gaia released Bruce's foot. Could she?

"The bee was the last thing I saw in the journey—even after Lev was gone. And I heard the word 'sacred' in my head. I think…I think that bee is—is sacred or holy or something special."

He nodded, frowning as if in deep thought. "I don't know if this has anything to do with it, but the specimen came from the man who wrote a book called *The Secret Life of Jesus Christ*. We've got a holy—so to speak—connection there, nebulous as it seems."

She was enjoying her pizza, but not enough to keep from asking, "*The Secret Life of Jesus Christ*? What's that all about?"

Eli shrugged. "Don't know. I haven't really delved into that part of the mystery. Admittedly, I've been more focused on the Apis. But there was a letter in the same box, and Helen Darrow was able to translate a little bit of it. Something about proof—it seems that the box contained Nicolas Notovitch's 'proof'—presumably related to the book and whatever Jesus's secret life was. Or is alleged to be. I haven't gotten around to Googling it because—"

"Because you've been distracted by your bee. Of course." She smiled. "So a letter and a bee were mailed from Paris? Anything else?"

"Other documents were in there as well—in French and Russian and, I think, Sanskrit." Reaching for the gym bag on the floor next to the couch, he withdrew a sheaf of old, yellowed papers and plopped them onto the table with a little less care than Marina would have liked. They were, after all, at least a hundred years old.

Many were handwritten in ink, and there were the splotches and blots that came from dipped-fountain-pen writing. Marina wiped off her hands well and looked through them briefly. She saw diagrams, sketches, photos—and yes, some Sanskrit as well as Russian and French. She paused at a grainy black-and-white photo of two Buddhist monks that had obviously been taken more than a century ago. They appeared to be standing in front of a rocky aperture.

Eli fished out a glass jar from the bag. It was filled with wadded-up cotton bandaging. "And here she is. The star of our show."

He removed the jar's lid, then carefully unrolled the delicate cotton weave to reveal the bee.

The hair all over Marina's body prickled when she saw it. "It looks like the one from my journey," she said, aware that her physical response to this little being was surprisingly intense. "I've never seen any insect with that sort of coloring—and definitely not a bee."

Eli was gazing upon her—the bee, not Marina—with adoring eyes, and it took a moment before he seemed to hear her. Despite the gravity of the situation, Marina couldn't control an affectionate smile. The man and his insects.

When he finally looked up, he saw her smirk and grinned back. "It's not often that a guy gets to discover a new species—although I'm not the one *discovering* it," he added quickly. "Neither did Patty. Someone—maybe even a group of people—has known about and have maybe even protected these Apis for who knows how long. So it's not a matter of discovery. But I certainly hope to *study* her."

"Protected." Marina nodded thoughtfully. "This bee's been protected. Yes, that's the right word, isn't it, considering that at least one entity—probably two—are trying to destroy the information you have so that…what? No one knows about the bee? Or are they trying to destroy the bee itself?"

He was nodding. "Exactly. Are they trying to keep her—the bee—a secret, and thus protected and unnoticed, or are they simply trying to destroy her so no one has her? The answer is: I don't know. We don't know."

"Did you look at Patty's notes that the tech person transferred to your account? Nice going on that, by the way. No one here at Michigan would have agreed to do that without written authorization." She gave him a wry smile as she slid another piece of pizza onto her plate.

"I haven't looked yet. I want to be on a secure network before I access my files—including the ones from Patty," he told her. "And the only reason Rindy—that was her name, the person in IT—gave me access is because apparently she saw me on NatGeo." He gave a bashful smile and began to devour another piece of pizza. "Celebrity does have its perks, I guess."

"I bet it helps with grants," she said with a knowing smile. Adele came over and gave her a nudge with her cool, damp nose. *I need to go out,* said the nudge.

"Doesn't hurt, that's for sure. And Patty—she was a real asset to the department. She was very articulate and interesting—not to mention smart as a whip—and funny in a self-deprecating way. It didn't hurt that she was tall, blond, and not too hard on the eyes." He shrugged. "It sounds mercenary—yeah, totally sexist—but Patty often said the same thing herself. You know how it works. Unfortunately."

"I certainly do," she replied. She knew how much funding she could get if even *one* of the documents in Tsar Ivan's library came into her possession.

But that wasn't an option.

"But there's still no obvious reason why this little bee is important enough to kill," she said, looking at the delicate, fuzzy thing while she absently scratched the patient Adele between the ears. The specimen was surprisingly intact for being an unprotected century-old. "But it's got to have something to do with the book written by Nicolas Notovitch, don't you think?"

He nodded. "There was something else in the box, too, that I wanted you, in particular, to see."

"All right—I'll let these two out in the back so they can chase squirrels and leaves, and then you can show me." As soon as she stood, Adele and Boris crowded her, looking up with anticipatory eyes, shifting and dancing with excitement. Then Adele perked up and ran to the back door, barking. Boris clattered after her, barking just as loudly. "Must be a squirrel out there," she told Eli with an apologetic grin.

She released the still-barking dogs out the back door into the fenced-in yard. It was just turning to twilight and shadows were growing long, but that didn't matter, because the two shepherds could see a leaf blowing across the yard at midnight.

Just as Marina stepped back through the entrance, someone knocked at the front door. She caught sight of the figure in the sidelight as she walked toward it and recognized the priest she'd spoken to earlier.

Maybe he was lost.

Nonetheless, Marina opened the door cautiously. "Hi."

"Pardon me, ma'am…so sorry to bother you," he said. "But I dropped my phone and now it's not working—I need to call for my friend to pick me up." He showed her the very damaged mobile phone. "Perhaps I could use yours? Or you could call for me? I think I know the number. It was a very nice walk, but I'm ready to leave now and I don't have a car here, you see." He smiled, and his brown eyes glinted with humor.

"Yes, of course," Marina said. "Let me just get my phone."

She stepped back from the door just as Eli called, "Who's here? Everything all right?"

"Yes, I'm just—" She stopped, the words dying in her throat when she saw that the man had pushed through the front door and was now standing in the foyer.

The priest had a gun pointed at her.

# THIRTY-TWO

"It's good your dogs are safely outside," said the man with the gun. He was dressed in black with a distinctive white-tab collar, but Marina strongly doubted he was actually a priest. "I wouldn't want them to get hurt. Now let's just move easily to join your friend, yes? Into the other room."

Eli had risen, obviously hearing Marina's stifled cry of alarm. He was standing, frozen, as they came into the living room, with Marina moving slowly, since the gun was trained on her.

"Sit here, if you please," the man said, using the gun to point to the place she'd recently vacated on the sofa. "Dr. Sanchez, you will move to that chair, slowly and carefully, and keep your hands where I can see them." Eli, after a brief exchange of glances with Marina, complied. The priest stood above and behind the sofa close enough to Marina to hold the gun on her.

"How did you find me here?" Eli demanded as soon as he was seated. "It was you, wasn't it? You knocked me out and stole my bag, back in Champaign. How did you get *here*?"

The man shrugged. "It's of no concern now, is it? I'm already here. And I don't anticipate this taking very long. Where is the bee?"

But before either Marina or Eli could speak, the man's attention fell on the specimen, which sat precisely where they'd left it. He nodded.

"Ah, good, there it is. Now, if you could wrap it back up— I see you have a container for it, Dr. Sanchez, excellent. Just put it back in the jar and set it right on the table here for me." He didn't need to warn Eli not to make any sudden moves; the unwavering barrel of the firearm was far too close to Marina for anyone to take any chances.

"What's so important about the bee?" Marina asked as Eli complied with their captor's demands. "Why are so many people after it?"

The priest's mouth tightened, turning white at the corners. "Indeed, it's true—I'm not the only one you've encountered in this competition of sorts, am I, Dr. Sanchez? Unfortunately, I arrived at your meeting place with the Fetzer woman too late."

"She was murdered over this bee," Eli said, his mouth so tight the words sounded chopped off. "She and Tina Janeski and Patricia Denke. And I nearly was as well. I deserve to know why." He slammed down the jar with its burden, making a hard thunk on the edge of the table. Marina was relieved he hadn't broken the display glass.

Still keeping the gun directed at her, the intruder reached for the jar with his free hand and slipped it into his pocket. The barrel of the weapon didn't so much as jiggle as he did so. "What do you think it's all about, Dr. Sanchez? Surely you have some idea. Dr.—Aleksandrov, is it? Your theory?"

"Are you really a priest?" she countered. He inclined his head, and she scoffed. "A priest who brandishes a gun and uses it to steal what he wants?"

"*In eius nomine sanctum*," he replied.

She knew Latin well enough to get the gist of what he said, but before she could pursue that, the priest said, "And what is that?" He was looking at the stack of old, brittle papers that had come in the package from Paris. They were sitting on the table next to Eli.

Eli glanced at Marina, but kept his mouth closed. That didn't deter the man with the gun, however, for he gave a sharp gesture with his free hand. "I'll take those as well. They appear to be important. Put them on the table there, Dr. Sanchez, and remember that I've got your colleague under my bead. And I have perfect aim. Especially at close quarters."

Eli did as ordered while the man kept his firearm steadily trained on Marina. "Thank you. Now." He eased closer to Marina, grasping her by the arm to pull her to her feet. She saw the bracelet-like tattoo on the back of his wrist and the letters lined up there—**I E N S**—as he directed her to stand. "Now, Dr. Sanchez, in order to keep everyone safe, you'll want to remain seated. Dr. Aleksandrov, you'll retrieve those papers there, moving very slowly and carefully as you do so. You'll put them in that satchel on the floor there."

Her heart thudded hard as she did as directed, gathering up the papers with surprisingly steady hands and shoving them into Eli's bag. From the back of the house, she could hear Boris and Adele barking. Those were not "I see a squirrel" barks…they were agitated and warning barks.

They knew something was wrong.

If only Marina had installed a doggie door that would allow them to gain access to the house. But she never had, and it was just as well. The intruder had a gun, and he surely wouldn't hesitate to use it. She couldn't bear for anything to happen to her pets.

"Now hand me the bag. And then we will walk to the front door, Dr. Aleksandrov. Very slowly."

She did as instructed, and just as she took her second step out of the living room, she felt a flutter in the air behind her—a swift movement—followed by the sound of a gunshot…and then the sound of something tumbling heavily to the floor.

*Eli.*

"Keep moving," said the priest in a steely voice.

"Why are you doing—"

"*In eius nomine sanctum,*" he murmured near her ear. It sounded like a soft-breathed prayer.

"In whose name?" she demanded, turning to look at him—to face the gun bearing down on her. "In whose name are you doing these things?"

"In Her name," he replied. His dark eyes were steady and calm, without the slightest bit of frenzy or madness in them.

Before she could respond, he pulled the trigger. A sharp pain tore through her shoulder and everything went black.

# THIRTY-THREE

Eli opened his eyes slowly. His head felt as if it weighed a hundred pounds, while his limbs felt weightless.

He was aware of an incessant pounding from somewhere distant… and something that sounded like barking.

*Barking.*

His eyes jolted wide, and he realized he was on the floor in Marina's living room. The barking was coming from the back of the house, and it was frantic.

"Marina!" he called, dragging himself to his feet even as he took inventory of his body.

The bastard had shot him—point-blank—but there was no blood. No blood anywhere that he could see. And he was standing up—albeit a little dizzily, and the room spun like he was in a top—but there was no blood.

But he knew he'd been shot.

"Marina?" he shouted again, stumbling a little as he felt himself up and down over his torso… *Ouch.* There was something very painful right in his chest, just above the ribcage.

"Marin—"

"Here." Her voice was weak, and he could hear the sounds of her movements in the foyer. By the time he took the five steps that got him past the sofa and into the front hall, she was upright. "You're not dead," she said, moving past him with the help of the wall as she made her way to the back door, where the dogs continued to bark.

"Neither are you," he said, still marveling at the fact. "But I think he got me with some sort of dart." Assured that she was as unharmed as he seemed to be, he took the time to pull up his t-shirt and examine the tender area on his chest.

It was about the size of a quarter, and in the center was a needle-thin puncture wound. It reminded him, fittingly, of a bee sting, but it was a hell of a lot more painful. And swollen.

"What the hell," he muttered, and went back to the living room to look around for the bullet—or whatever had come out of the gun and lodged in the center of one of his pecs. Whatever it was, it had worked almost instantly to knock him out.

Thank God that was all it had done. Knock him out...

Just like had been done in Champaign that night when he encountered the same man.

*How the hell did he find me here?*

Eli didn't understand it; maybe when his brain wasn't as fogged-over and his head wasn't as heavy, he'd be able to figure it out.

He felt around the wound on his chest again and winced. There was something still there...probably the tip of the dart. He was going to have to dig it out. Or ask Marina to do it. Even in the moment, he couldn't contain a smile. He liked having her hands on him.

The sounds of wildly happy and relieved whining, along with the excited patter and clatter of dog feet on the tile, indicated that Adele and Boris were not only unharmed but happily reunited with their mistress.

Convenient that the dogs had gone outside just before the priest had knocked on the front door...

But Marina had let them out because they were barking at something in the backyard. Eli's mouth twisted wryly as he made his way into the kitchen—his mouth was parched—and met Marina in there.

"He said he'd broken his cell phone and wanted me to help him call for a ride. He showed me the phone," she said as if reading Eli's mind. "I had no reason to distrust him."

"The priest clothes certainly helped," he said, filling a glass with water from a filtered tap. Even in that moment, he had an instant of appreciation that she didn't use bottled water. Stepping out of the way so she could fill her own glass, he gulped down half his drink in one long swig. "The dogs started barking pretty hard before you let them out."

She was nodding behind her glass. When she pulled it away, she said, "Yes. He drew them into the backyard—probably was right there on the outside of the fence when I let them out—so they'd be confined and not a threat. Then he came around to the front."

"He took the bee and the papers," said Eli with disgust, still fiddling with the painful welt and its tiny needle. "I've still got something in my skin. Probably needs to be dug out in case it's still oozing whatever it was. Do you?"

Marina nodded. "Yes, I can feel it."

She retrieved a pair of tweezers and rubbing alcohol. It took only a few moments to pull out the dart needle. It was about two inches long, and Eli felt a little sick when he thought about it shooting into his body. Nonetheless, the effects of the drug seemed to be waning.

"Best keep that for evidence," he said, and she nodded.

"Eli, he took the bee and the papers, true, but he didn't get this." She pushed past him to go back into the living room. "I kicked it under the couch when he made me sit down."

He watched from the kitchen on the opposite side of the open counter as she crouched by the sofa. Moments later, she produced the small earthen jar that had been in Nicolas Notovitch's package.

The last vestige of his grogginess evaporated as Eli laughed with delight. "Brilliant, Marina! Good thinking."

"Better that we have it than him—whoever he was."

"He was a real priest. I'd bet my life on it," said Eli, refilling his glass once more. Whatever had been used to drug them, it felt as if it had sucked every last bit of moisture from his body.

"Why do you say that?"

"*In eius nomine sanctum.* That's what he said, right? I translate that as 'in her holy name.' Her would be the church—the Catholic Church, of course."

She tilted her head, smiling. "You know your Latin."

"Eight years of Catholic school," he replied. "And before you ask, no, the nuns weren't as bad as you might have heard, yes, it was an all-boys' school, and no, we didn't have any pedophile priests there. My school was run by the Jesuits, by the way, which are—if you'll excuse the expression—the more liberal representation of the church."

"I see." She was looking at him quizzically, and it made Eli feel a little self-conscious. "You're certain 'her' refers to the church and not, say, Gaia? After all, he did refer to me as Dr. Aleksandrov—which only the Skalas would think of me as."

He lifted his brows. "Pretty sure. Did you notice the tattoo on his wrist? It had those letters on it, I E N S; *in eius nomine sanctum*, and the rest of the design—it looked like a bracelet, right? It was actually a decade of the rosary. Ten beads, equidistant, and then another bead further away."

"All right, then, I'll bow to your Catholic expertise—"

"Besides, it makes sense when you think about it. Those papers from Nicolas Notovitch about *The Secret Life of Jesus Christ*?"

"What about them?"

"That has to be the reason," Eli said. "I'm not sure of the bee connection, but we've got a mercenary priest showing up and making off with those papers. I get the sneaking suspicion that the church is involved in covering up whatever Jesus Christ's secret life was. And the bee must somehow be related to it."

Marina had picked up her laptop, and even as he spoke, she was typing "The Secret Life of Jesus Christ book" into the search bar. It only took her a few moments of skimming to get the information.

"According to this, a man named Nicolas Notovitch—that's the guy who sent the letter and package, isn't it?—wrote a book claiming that Jesus Christ lived in India." She frowned, clicking on another link, then another. "I don't see anything about bees, though."

"So we've got India—where in India?" asked Eli. "And a bee that seems to be from the same general region. We've got a priest showing up to relieve us of everything in the box Notovitch sent here to the U.S.—and I'm going to go out on a limb and suggest he sent it for safekeeping."

When Marina lifted a sardonic brow, he went on. "Look, there's no way the church would want there to be any hint about Jesus Christ that doesn't fit with its—*her*—narrative. Her being the church, right? If Jesus lived in India—and more importantly, if there was irrefutable proof that he did—that brings a whole bunch of questions to the forefront, and maybe some of those answers don't fit with Catholicism and even Christianity as a whole. So they want to snuff out anything that might come to light."

"It says here that, according to the book, Jesus traveled throughout India, probably on the Silk Road, during the fifteen or so years after he was bar mitzvahed back in Israel until he began his public preaching career at age thirty, back in Jerusalem. Or so the story goes." Marina was still skimming articles, reviews, debunkings, and counterarguments as she and Eli spoke.

"That would make sense, as we have no writings about what Jesus did during that time period—at least, no writings officially condoned by the church," Eli said. "If during his formative years, he traveled through India and Pakistan and maybe even Tibet and China, that would definitely be disturbing to the powers that be of the Catholic Church."

"Why do you think that?"

"Because, and I'm being only a little sarcastic here, if there was anything that didn't fit with the Judeo-Christian narrative, and was—well, let's use the word *contaminated*—by Eastern philosophy or religion, that could upset the Vatican's applecart, so to speak. And I don't think the evangelical Christians would be pleased to know that their savior hung out with Buddhists or Hindus or Zoroastrians or whatever. It just doesn't fit with their belief system…all that yoga and meditation and stuff." His voice was dry with sarcasm.

"So apparently in India, Jesus was known by the name Saint Issa," Marina told him. She was now twelve pages in on the search results, looking for new information instead of the same articles regurgitated on different sites. "According to Notovitch. And apparently he stayed at a monastery in Hemis, which is where he supposedly saw Buddhist writings that talked about Saint Issa and that he was Jesus of Nazareth. Eli, Hemis—that's in Ladakh," she said, looking up and meeting his eyes.

"*Boom.*" He sat up straight, suddenly excited and animated. "There it is. There's the connection. Ladakh, India, where Jesus was known to have stayed, is where Patty found this bee—this bee that seems to have been protected and kept secret for centuries. She was in a little place called... I can't remember. Thick-something. But that's got to be it. I've *got* to go to Ladakh!"

"Oh...boy. Oh...*wow*," Marina said, staring at a new article that had come up on the screen. "Eli, there's more. According to this—the source isn't Notovitch, but some old writings by Buddhist monks... This is a centuries-old document someone's translated from the Sanskrit..." She frowned, reading the words and looking at the translation. "This is buried way deep in my search results—I only got here because I added 'Sanskrit' to the search string because of the little pot there," she said absently, still looking at the document—which she was able to access via a private online library because of her academic credentials. "Whoa. Okay. Now it makes sense why the church sent someone after you." She shoved the laptop away a little and looked at Eli. She pursed her lips. "You're not going to like this, Catholic boy."

"What is it?"

"According to these writings, Saint Issa traveled throughout India during what we would call 15 through 30, Common Era—which used to be called AD, or *Anno Domini,* for you old-school people," she said with a wry grin as he rolled his eyes. She knew very well he knew what she was talking about. "Issa was known as a very spiritual man and a healer. *But*, and here's the part that I had to dig way down to find...apparently he was traveling in India *after* 33 CE."

It took Eli only a fraction of a second to follow, and then his eyes goggled. "Are you saying...Jesus was seen in India *after* he resurrected from the dead?"

"That's what these Buddhist writings are saying," Marina replied. She wasn't attached to the Christian religion at all, but she was well versed in its belief system—as she was with most other world religions. It went part and parcel with her work. "That Saint Issa—who is apparently Jesus of Nazareth—was seen in India at that time. So if there's *proof* that Jesus was alive and in India *after* he was crucified, then that means—"

"He didn't ascend to heaven as is taught—"

"Or that he never actually died and rose from the dead at all."

Eli swallowed audibly. "Holy shit...no pun intended." He gave a pained laugh. "That would do it. There's no doubt in my mind that the church would do whatever it takes to make sure that information didn't come out. *Whatever* it takes."

# THIRTY-FOUR

As Eli's words hung there between them, filled with worry and shock, Marina picked up the small earthenware pot.

"So how is this connected?" she mused. "I suspect the papers our friendly priest just stole include proof of Notovitch's allegations, but why did he send this?"

She turned the small object around in her hands. It was very old, and she knew it had already been around for centuries when Notovitch packed it up in Paris and sent it to Alexina Donovan.

There was Sanskrit writing on it, which was ostensibly why Eli had brought it to her—so she could look at it and possibly translate. She felt his eyes on her as she picked up a piece of paper and began to write down all of the markings.

"There's Aramaic etched on here too," she said, looking up at him suddenly. "It's not only Sanskrit."

"Jesus," he said, his eyes widening. "Aramaic was Jesus's native language."

She quirked a smile. "I'm aware of that. My ancient Aramaic isn't great, but since the Sanskrit looks like it says Issa, I'm going to guess once I get it translated that the Aramaic says—"

"Jesus of Nazareth." Eli let out a long breath, his dark eyes so wide she could see the full circles of his irises. "Holy shit, are you saying Jesus made that pot?"

"I'm not saying anything, but if his name is marked on it in two different languages, it's not much of a leap to assume he was at least in possession of it." She shined the flashlight from her phone on it and scrabbled for the small magnifying glass she kept in the drawer next to the sofa. "Hazard of the trade," she said with a grin when Eli raised his brows at its convenient appearance.

"All right, Sherlock, what do you see?" he asked as she handed him the phone for its flashlight.

"There's a marking on the bottom of the jar. Hard to make it out, but I think it looks like some sort of bird. There are wings. Or maybe it's an insect. Take a look for yourself, doc." She handed him the jar and the magnifier.

"Insect," he said after only a moment of examination. "I think it's an insect."

"You sure you're not just prejudiced?" she teased.

"Can't guarantee it, but look—it's got more than two legs. So not a bird. Hard to see because the etching is worn away, but I think I'm making out at least five legs… What if it's a bee?" He looked up. "What if it's *the* bee?"

"All things considered, that could make a lot of sense," Marina replied. She reached over absently to pat Boris on the head, then Adele nosed her way in for attention too. "I want to open it, but I don't know if we—"

"Yes!" He pulled the little jar close to his chest as if to embrace it, then winced. "Ouch. Still hurts where our friendly priest *darted* me." He rubbed the spot just below his clavicle. "I was hoping you'd say that. This sort of thing—artifacts—isn't my wheelhouse, so I didn't want to suggest it, but you'd know how to do it safely."

She frowned. "It's so old, we really should do it in a lab with the proper tools—"

"Don't tell me you don't have the proper tools here," he said, giving her a look. "Marina, this could be one of the most amazing discoveries of our time—"

"Which means it really should be done in a lab with a lot of preparation and safety precautions," she replied coolly. But she felt the spike of excitement that was blazing in his eyes inside herself. There was something about that little jar—when she'd held it in her hands, she *felt* something.

Something real and strong. Energy. Warmth.

Something that almost felt as if it were *living*.

Was that just because it had been made from earth—from Gaia? And that Marina was becoming highly sensitive to her energy?

Eli was still looking at the jar, holding it up in front of his eyes, turning it around and around. He tugged gently on the little stick that made the top's handle, and it broke, then disintegrated under his touch. "Oops," he said, looking flustered. "I really didn't mean to do that. I just— Marina, the top moved. Just now. I think the seal might be broken."

She couldn't contain a smile. The guy looked like a little boy on Christmas begging to open a package. "Could be because it's been exposed to the air and been jostled around since Jill Fetzer opened the package—what, two, three days ago?"

"Right." He looked wistfully at it. "It's not going to damage anything if we just take the top off, since it's already loose, right?"

Marina sighed, but she couldn't deny her own thrill of excitement. And after all, it wasn't as if she were an archaeologist who had found the object and needed to preserve its location—the jar had long been removed from its origination. She knew how to handle delicate artifacts, however, and it was better her than Eli, she decided.

"All right. Let's see how loose it is and then decide. I have tools in my office."

Moments later, she'd spread a lint-free white cloth down over the kitchen table, which had a good light over it. She'd donned gloves (although it was a little late now, since the jar had been handled and rolled over the floor when she nudged it under the sofa) and laid out a row of tools. Hardly able to contain his excitement, Eli hopped impatiently from one foot to the other as he watched her.

"It's not like we're going to find a new specimen of insect in here," she said with a laugh as she picked up a small scalpel.

"Well, you don't know that...but it's very possible *Jesus of Nazareth* held that pot! What if there's some sort of jewelry in there, or—or something else that belonged to him?"

"Well, we'll soon find out—you're right, the top is loose. Whether it was from natural exposure or a little contemporary assistance, we'll never know," she added, giving him a wry look.

She carefully slid the scalpel along the seam between top and bottom, slowly, painstakingly working the tip of it around the joint. Her phone gave a quiet ding from where it sat safely on the kitchen counter—a text message alert—and she said, "Can you check that, Eli?"

Anything to get him from breathing down her neck and jockeying around for a minute. Good grief—she didn't remember the guy being like this in his own lab.

"It's from Gabe MacNeil. He says, 'Need to speak to you ASAP.' Oh, now he's calling."

"Just let it go. I'll call him back in a sec— Ah, here we go."

"You got it?" Eli dropped her phone onto the counter and swiftly came back. His long fingers gripped the edge of the table as if to keep himself from grabbing at the pot.

"Yes...all right..." Holding the jar steady with a gloved hand, she used the scalpel to slightly lift the top, then let go of the jar to grasp the broken part of the top's handle and gently pulled it away.

They nearly bumped heads looking down into the little jar, and Marina eased back with a little laugh. She'd had a glimpse of what was inside: some thick, dark substance. Not oil, but—

"It's *honey*," Eli said, shock and awe in his voice. "It's *freaking honey*." He looked at Marina. "What do you want to bet it's from that rosy-gold bee?"

"I wouldn't be surprised if it were, but would we be able to tell?"

"Maybe...if we got to the bee's habitat. That settles it—I'm going to Ladakh, and I'm going to find the place where Patty heard about the bee. You want to come?"

Marina felt a jolt of excitement at the idea. But before she could respond, her phone rang again. "It's probably Gabe. When he says ASAP, that usually means he's just around the corner," she said dryly. "Like someone else I know."

Eli gave her a little smile, then returned his attention to the pot of honey as Marina picked up her phone. Yep—it was Gabe.

"Hey," he said. "We've got a problem. Are you in Ann Arbor?"

She gave Eli a look, then raised her eyebrows when she saw that he'd dipped a tiny spoon into the honey. "Yes, at the moment. But I'll be leaving for Ladakh in the next day or two. What's going on?"

"Ladakh? Where's that?"

"Northeast India—mountainous region on the border near Tibet," she replied, watching as Eli examined the little spoonful of honey. He'd flashed a broad smile when he heard Marina announce her intention to go with him. "What's going on?"

"Did you hear about those weird truck accidents—there was one in Ohio, one in West Virginia, and a third in Kentucky."

"The single-vehicle accidents where the truck kind of collapsed? Yes, I was actually in Ohio when the roads were blocked off from it. Why?"

"We—Helen, Colin, and I—are pretty sure your people are involved."

"They're not my people," Marina replied flatly. "And if I recall correctly, there was a lot of hazardous material lost because of those trucks going down. That's not typical of the Skaladeskas. They wouldn't hurt Gaia by spreading dangerous environmental waste."

"Marina," he said just as calmly and evenly, "Helen and Colin and I think you should know about what's going on because the Skalas *are* connected. Maybe there's something you can do to help—"

"I haven't talked to any of them"—oh, shit, except for Varden—"for years." Technically, that was true—she hadn't talked to them. She had received random messages from Roman via email or even in the regular mail over the last three years. But nothing substantive—only nudges to remind her that they still existed.

Still wanted something from her.

Not something, but *everything*.

"Marina, can we meet?" Gabe said again in that deep, steady voice. "We need to talk to you about this."

"Yes, of course," she replied reluctantly. It was merely a request now, but it was possible it would become an edict later—as she had learned previously when dealing with Colin Bergstrom. That was the bad part about being related to an ecoterrorist group. "But I'm leaving for Ladakh as soon as I can. I suppose you should just come here—I'm assuming you're in town or can get here. Can you tell me more about what's going on before?"

She listened as he filled her in on the three accidents and how Helen Darrow's people made the connection to the Skaladeskas based on a tip from the foreman at the trucking company. Just as he was finishing the explanation, Marina suddenly remembered that not only had *she* been in Central Ohio when she heard about the trucking accident—that was why there hadn't been enough emergency staff to help at the Turncoat Don cave incident—but that Rue Varden had been there as well.

Surely that wasn't a coincidence.

They agreed that the team—Gabe, Helen, and Colin—would be at her house in a few hours. Just then, another text message came on her phone. Marina didn't even have to pull the phone away to look. She already knew who it was from.

She just *knew*.

She ended the call with Gabe and looked at the text from the random number she knew was Varden.

*Need to talk to you.*

Yeah? Well, she needed to talk to him too.

"You put centuries-old honey on your skin?" Marina glanced at Eli as she settled on the couch. "Isn't that a little…risky?"

He settled back in the sofa and grinned as he scratched Adele between the ears. They were waiting for Gabe and the others to arrive—which would be any minute now. "Not at all. Honey never spoils. It doesn't go rancid. As long as it's not contaminated with water or anything, it's as edible as it was the day it was scooped out of the hive. There have been urns of honey found in the Egyptian tombs that were completely fine, millennia after being sealed up."

"You didn't eat it," she said. "Tell me you didn't eat any of it."

"Of course I ate some of it. Just a little taste. It's Jesus's honey!" His eyes were dancing, and she couldn't tell whether it was from mischief or excitement. "And yes, I also smeared some—just a tiny bit—over the dart mark our priest friend gave me."

"Why?" Marina couldn't contain a smile of her own—he looked so happy and self-satisfied. Nonetheless, she had a lot of unpleasant thoughts she hadn't shared with him.

According to Gabe, the Skaladeskas were responsible for the three truck accidents. She didn't understand how that would be possible, knowing those trucks carried hazardous material. Dumping—or allowing a spill of dangerous waste—went against their very purpose of saving and protecting Gaia. Surely they weren't involved.

But why was Varden in Ohio if the Skaladeskas weren't involved? *Because he was following you.*

Yes, that was very possible. Coincidental. She did need to talk to him, but she didn't want to do so when Eli was around, and she certainly didn't want Varden showing up here when Gabe and Helen were around.

So she'd responded to Varden's text with a terse *Soon.*

"Honey has antiseptic and healing properties," Eli said. "Put it on a cut and it'll help it to heal. I figured if this was Jesus's honey, its healing power might be even more potent. Can't hurt to try." He was still grinning. "I can't believe it. We might have found Jesus's honey. Can you imagine what this would mean to the world?"

Marina could, in a way. It would be an earth-shattering discovery for many reasons—whether or not this honey had any special properties. But she couldn't dismiss that the idea was intriguing and exciting. She didn't follow any organized religion, but there was no denying that Jesus of Nazareth had been a historical person of great interest. Any find related to him would have stunning worldwide effect.

"It would turn things upside down," she said.

"Exactly. And that's why our priest friend has been on top of this from the beginning," Eli replied.

"But he's not working alone," Marina said. "He confirmed it, didn't he? When he said he arrived at the meeting with Jill Fetzer too late."

"I caught that too. Someone else killed Jill. The question is whether Father Dart Gun knows him or not. I'm going to ask Helen Darrow what she knows about that."

"Speaking of Helen Darrow, she just texted that they're on their way from the Ann Arbor airport," Marina said as she looked at her phone. "ETA ten minutes."

"Okay. That gives me time to check and see if that dart wound is looking any better." Eli began pulling up his shirt to reveal a lean brown torso.

Marina watched in amusement and admiration. Other than the clinical work of digging out the remainder of the dart, it had been a while since she'd had her hands on that torso, and she was looking forward to the possibility of doing so again soon.

"It's *gone*," he said, his voice cracking with shock. "Holy shit. The puncture wound is completely *gone*, Marina. Look!"

She stared. He was correct. There was no sign of any wound on his skin where she knew he'd been shot. The only evidence that something had been there was a small shiny patch that was probably the remnants of the honey. "That's…impossible," she said, even as she knew it obviously wasn't.

"Show me yours," he said. "Let's compare. We got shot within minutes of each other."

Marina unbuttoned the front of her shirt and opened it to reveal the place she'd been injured. The puncture wound was still there—a small, angry red dot in the center of a crimson wheal that was painful to the touch.

They looked at each other, the only sound in the room their ragged, shocked breaths.

Then Eli said, "We found Jesus's honey."

# THIRTY-FIVE

"Well isn't this a little bit *déjà vu*," said Helen Darrow as she walked into Marina's home. During the copper beetle situation, they'd met here as well, so she was familiar with the place. "Dr. Alexander, I'd say it's nice to see you again, but under the circumstances, we can probably both agree maybe not so much."

Marina gave her a wry smile. "Likewise. Nothing personal, Agent Darrow, but my life is a lot less frantic when you're not involved in it."

They both chuckled, at ease with each other and their respective positions within the dynamics of the ad hoc team. As Helen greeted the two dogs, she noticed that Marina had grown her dark brown hair out a little longer since they'd last worked together, but it was still layered and choppy on the ends. She had intelligent hazel eyes that were devoid of mascara or eyeliner; in fact, the only makeup she wore was a swipe of lip gloss that might just as easily have been tinted SPF lip balm. Marina Alexander's style was casual and low maintenance—bordering on earth mother. Which, Helen thought, was rather appropriate, all things considered.

"Have a seat. I've got coffee and tea for anyone, and, yes, some Cottage Inn pizza," Marina added with a nod at Gabe. She told the dogs to lie down, and they went to two different floor cushions and began to gnaw on their respective treats.

"Dr. Sanchez." Helen nodded at him as she settled into the comfortable chair her hostess had indicated. The seat seemed to have been positioned as the focal point in the room, and Marina was clearly giving her the lead. "I didn't expect to see you here." She lifted a brow and considered whether she should insist he leave. After all, this was a confidential meeting.

Still, he'd been involved and instrumental in the previous debacle with the copper beetle, and Helen doubted very much that Marina Alexander would have brought him along if his presence wasn't relevant—although how, she couldn't imagine.

"Why, Agent Darrow—you haven't changed a bit since I last saw you several hours and a time zone ago," said Eli with a smile. He was wearing the same uniform as he had been every time she'd seen him: an entomology-themed t-shirt and shorts with Birkenstocks. The only variety she'd ever noticed was that sometimes in deference to weather, a button-down shirt or lab coat flapped open over his tee, and he wore chinos instead of shorts. "Sorry to crash the party, but I was here with Marina when MacNeil contacted her, and I've got some information for you relative to our meeting—which was, I can hardly believe, only this morning. Both Marina and I have. And it might even be related to why you're here."

There was an extra sparkle in his eyes that hadn't been there when they met earlier, along with an underlying thrum of excitement that made Helen curious. He seemed ready to burst.

But she had a meeting to run, and the topic was serious and urgent. There would be time for questions later.

Marina and Eli greeted Gabe and Colin, and Helen noticed without even a blip of pique that Marina and Gabe exchanged warm embraces and quick kisses on the mouth. Their vibe was low-key. Whatever romance that had been between the two of them years ago had cooled into something like easy, casual friendship and mutual respect.

As for Helen and Gabe's relationship—such as it was—well, they lived too far apart and were too busy in their current jobs for it to be anything other than casual friendship and mutual respect as well.

Once everyone was seated with their choices of beverage and, in Gabe and Eli's case, slices of thick-crust pizza, Helen began the meeting without any preamble. She filled in Marina and Eli about the truck accidents and the cause of them.

"So you're saying the Skaladeskas have a bacteria that feeds on manganese, which can destroy anything metal in—in hours?" Eli said when she was finished. "That's not good."

Helen almost laughed at the understatement. Instead, she nodded, then looked at Gabe and Colin. "Since we met yesterday, my team has collected and analyzed more information about this bacteria. It appears that this particular bacteria—and forgive me for the simplicity of what I'm about to say, because I'm not a bacteriologist and I'm reporting on how it was described to me as a layperson. But know that as simple as what I'm about to say might sound, my team has the science to back it up. Should any of you want to delve into it." She gave Gabe a wry look.

"No, no, layperson info is enough for me at this point," he replied with a laugh as he wrapped a long string of mozzarella around his fork.

Helen nodded. "As I mentioned previously, this seems to be a novel bacteria, but it actually is not. Apparently, there's an academic paper that was published seven or eight years ago discussing this particular bacteria that feeds on manganese." She glanced at Gabe and Colin. "Not the one that was discovered by the people at Caltech. I'm talking about the particular bacteria that caused these trucking accidents. It was discovered by a group of scientists in a variety of disciplines who were studying the Tazhnev Glacier in northern India, near the Chinese border.

"Apparently, traces of this bacteria attached itself to some of their gear and anything that was stainless steel or other metal disappeared— or, more accurately, was used for resources to help the bacteria grow and spread. As the paper told it, the crew had no idea about it until a ring of keys to one of their UNICAT Volvos disappeared."

"Ouch," said Eli.

Helen couldn't control a smile. "Exactly. I don't think they enjoyed the situation at all. But it certainly awakened their curiosity. Subsequently, they released a paper about what happened, in which they discussed the characteristics and makeup of the traces of the bacteria that they were able to find on their belongings. But afterward, they couldn't isolate the bacteria again—they weren't certain where it had originated."

"The glaciers are melting more rapidly now due to climate change,"

Marina said. "And that speedier melt is exposing amazing archaeological finds as well as other novel bacteria, and even some flora and fauna that would otherwise never be discovered. There's an entire wealth of information locked up in those chunks of ice."

"Right. But with what's happened in the last few days, it seems the Skaladeskas have gotten their hands on this metal-eating bacteria—which, by the way, was named with some long, Latin name ending in Volvoticus for obvious reasons by the glacier explorers who authored the paper," Helen told them.

"But as I said to Gabe when we spoke earlier," Marina said, "it simply doesn't make sense for Roman and the others to plan for accidents that cause harm to the Earth. It's the precise opposite of their mission."

"Indeed...their modus operandi has always been to harm the *humans* who are threats to Gaia, not Gaia herself," Colin said flatly. "Regardless of whether it makes sense, Dr. Alexander, the Skalas are involved. The container—I believe it was, of necessity, made from plastic, no, Agent Darrow?—had the mark of the Skaladeskas on it. It was a message left where anyone could find it—just as they've done in the past. Like any other terrorist organization, they want us to know what they've done."

Marina's expression was set into stubborn lines, and Helen—who'd spent her career analyzing data in order to come to logical conclusions—couldn't help but sympathize. In some ways, it *didn't* make sense...and that was why she and Gabe had decided to bring the professor here. If anyone could help ferret out the truth, it would be Marina.

"Maybe it was accidental that the trucks were carrying hazardous materials," Eli suggested.

Marina and Helen shook their heads in tandem. "No," said Helen, then went silent in order to give Marina the floor.

Everything Marina said was relevant to the Skaladeskas, even if it didn't seem to be. Helen was fully aware that the other woman wasn't completely forthcoming about her ecoterrorist family, but she didn't fear her loyalties. She knew—because of her own assessment and Gabe's as well—that Dr. Alexander was not about to risk people's lives to make her own life easier.

"That's not the sort of mistake Roman would make," Marina said. "From everything I've seen and experienced, what they do is deliberate and well planned. What exactly was the source of the hazardous material that the trucks were carrying?"

"Waste from a water-bottling company," Helen replied. "Plastic and chemical waste. EcoDraft is the name. They're headquartered in Pittsburgh but have a bottling location in Cleveland."

Marina grimaced and fell silent. Helen thought she knew what Marina was thinking—that plastic was the bane of the Earth because it didn't decompose, and bottled water was anti-environmentally friendly as well.

"So were they targeting the water-bottling plant too?" said Eli. "Not that I blame them," he added, holding up his insulated, reusable water bottle. "It's a two-hundred-billion-dollar industry that rapes the Earth and diverts water from places that need it. I wouldn't care if every designer bottled-water company went bankrupt."

"Those are questions that we're hoping Dr. Alexander will help us to answer," Helen said. "If she's willing."

"That assumes I have the means to contact them," Marina replied coolly.

Helen hid a smile. Dr. Alexander was a smart cookie.

"You must have some way to get in touch with them," Gabe said. "After last time, when you needed to get treatment for Dr. Sanchez because of the copper beetle poison, you were able to make a connection."

"That was nearly five years ago," replied Marina, still holding her cards close to her vest. "I'll admit, I've received occasional letters from Roman over the last years—which I'm certain you're aware of—and an email or two—again, which I'm certain you already know—but there's no two-way conversation going on between me and my father or grandfather. Which you *also* already know."

"Nonetheless," Helen said, "I'm certain you could contrive the means to contact them if you wanted to." She'd been watching Marina carefully, and as a trained observer, she'd noticed a subtle flicker in

Marina's eyes during her last speech. "Perhaps Dr. Varden would be your easiest point of contact."

*Aha.* Helen suppressed a smile and kept her expression bland, but she'd seen the slight tightening at the corners of Marina's mouth.

To give her credit, Marina didn't attempt to prevaricate or evade. "Very well. I'll attempt to make contact and find out what I can."

Colin opened his mouth, but before he could speak, Helen's phone chimed. She looked down at it and said to the others, "I need to take this. Will you grab me a piece of that pizza while you're up, Gabe? Hello, Wei," she said into the phone. "What do you have for me?"

She listened with growing concern as one of her analysts back in Chicago filled her in on the reason for his contact. When she ended the call, she saw that everyone had gone silent.

Apparently, they'd read her expression.

"Not good news, I take it," Gabe said.

"Not very." Helen gathered her thoughts then said, "It appears that the bacteria Volvoticus is on the market."

Gabe swore under his breath and Colin sat up straighter. "Good heavens," he said, adjusting his glasses.

"They're trying to sell the bacteria?" said Marina. Helen could see the wheels turning in her mind. "That doesn't seem right."

"It's certainly a departure from the Skaladeskas' activities in the past," Helen replied. "But I suppose they have to generate revenue somehow. Those fancy hideaways in Siberia, the Amazon, and who knows where else aren't cheap."

Marina's mouth tightened a little, but Helen didn't regret the sharpness of her dig. Marina surely knew it wasn't directed at her, but at her family—who were known terrorists. And according to Marina, she wanted nothing to do with her father and grandfather.

But whether she felt the same way about Rue Varden was another question. Helen was aware that Marina and Dr. Varden had interacted over the years, and any vociferous denials Marina had made about the Skaladeskas never specified him.

Helen had encountered Varden herself during the copper beetle threat. He'd given her antidotes for the poison and walked away scot-free, to her fury and dismay. But Helen knew she wasn't the only one who'd apprehended Varden, only to be manipulated out of the situation by the man himself. Gabe had had a similar experience.

Helen wondered if Marina had as well.

"So they're planning to sell the Volvoticus bacteria to the highest bidder?" said Eli. "How do we know this?"

"They're not being coy," Helen replied. "We received a message from Cargath Steel, the trucking company in Cleveland that was the source of the three accidents. The owners of the bacteria are about to demonstrate its efficacy on a larger scale...apparently in order to justify its price of five point three *trillion* dollars. That's the starting point for what seems clear will be a bidding war."

"And presumably the bidders will include not only certain government or military entities, but also corporations as well," added Gabe. He looked as ill as Helen felt.

Everyone in the room did. Even the dogs seemed to understand that something was wrong, for Boris and Adele rose from their beds and came over to butt against Marina with soft, inquiring whines.

"So, this demonstration..." said Marina after a moment. "We have to assume it will be something larger and more terrifying than three semitrucks splattering over the highway—not that that wasn't horrifying enough on its own."

Helen nodded; she couldn't bring herself to speak. The implications were astounding and horrifying. Not only was there an imminent terrorist attack that could cost unknown lives, but there was the very real possibility that this terrifying bacteria could fall into the hands of any number of nefarious groups.

Marina rose sharply. "I'm taking the dogs for a walk. I need to think." Gabe made as if to rise as well, but Marina stopped him. "By myself."

Helen's suspicions were confirmed. Yes, Marina Alexander definitely had a way to contact the Skaladeskas.

She wavered for a moment, wondering if she should insist that Gabe or even herself follow Marina, but squashed that thought. Dr. Alexander was far too intelligent to be used in that way.

Helen only hoped Marina could get the information they needed in time.

# THIRTY-SIX

Marina took her dogs through the side yard of one of her neighbors, putting a tall hedge of arborvitae between her and her house and going at a quick jog as she cut through a few yards to get a few blocks away.

She wasn't a fool. She knew Helen wondered about her relationship with the Skalas, and she wouldn't put it past the federal agent to follow or watch her...or have someone else do it.

She also knew that Helen was fully aware of the reason she'd decided to take Boris and Adele for a walk at that moment.

But Marina didn't care.

She brought the dogs to a nearby park and released them from their leashes to explore while she contacted Varden.

*How soon can we talk?* she texted.

Then waited.

And waited.

No response.

Frustrated and annoyed with herself for expecting him to be watching with bated breath for her to contact him, she rose and threw one of the tennis balls she always carried. Boris and Adele raced for it, with the younger one leaping to snatch it out of midair while the slower and older one was still yards away.

"Come on, Boris," she called, and tossed a second ball to him. Poor boy. He was definitely slowing down, partly due to hip dysplasia, which was common in older German Shepherd Dogs.

Marina retrieved the ball from Adele when the dog returned grinning happily around her prize, then fired it across the park just as she felt someone come up next to her.

"Took you long enough," she replied, even though her heart did a little jump of surprise. She hadn't exactly expected Varden to show up unannounced, but she wasn't all that unsettled he'd opted for in-person instead of responding to her text.

It was safer that way.

"That's one official-looking car in your driveway," he replied mildly. "Darrow or MacNeil?"

"Both," she replied, looking up at him. His jade eyes were cool and steady as they scored over her.

"We shouldn't talk here," he said. "My car is over there."

She hesitated, then replied, "Boris and Adele ride too."

Varden inclined his head. "They won't be pleased their playtime is cut short."

"They're more disciplined than that," she replied, calling the two dogs to her with hand signals.

Whatever she'd expected, it wasn't for Varden to drive them five minutes to downtown and park in one of the surface lots, then suggest they get a table outside at one of the many restaurants that lined Main Street and its perpendiculars.

"This isn't a date," she snapped.

He gave her an arrogant look. "The very last thing on my mind. But the dogs need water, and you can't leave them in the car in this heat—and besides, where's the best place to remain unnoticed but in the middle of a crowd?"

She couldn't be wary when he suggested being in such a public place, so she agreed. Maybe he was afraid his car was bugged or being tracked.

Maybe her phone was being tracked...by someone other than Varden himself.

The thought soured her even more.

"This is serious and urgent," she said tightly.

He looked at her when they paused at a crosswalk. "You wouldn't have contacted me otherwise. Here." He gestured to a table at The Black Pearl away from others that were full, and near the street where they would be less likely to be overheard by passersby. The hum of regular traffic would also act as a distorting background for any conversation.

At her command, the dogs lay down under the table, panting lightly, with their heads lifted to watch the activity. Marina would ask for some water when the server came out.

"The truck accidents," she said without preamble. "Why is Roman doing that? They spilled waste all over."

"Truck accidents?" Varden shook his head. "It's not Roman. Why would you think that?"

Marina studied him for a moment, trying to read the truth in his eyes. He met her gaze steadily, and for a moment, she felt a little wobbly. There was something about him…and, damn, there'd been that weird kiss too. Not that it had actually *been* weird. It had been anything but weird.

She steadied her thoughts and concluded that Varden was telling her the truth—at least as far as he knew. "A container was found on the site with the Skaladeska mark on it."

That was obviously news to him. He muttered something in Russian, then met her eyes again. "It's not Roman. It's Hedron." He swore again. "What do you know about it? Tell me everything, Marina."

She didn't respond because a server had appeared. Varden ordered a glass of wine and looked at her. Feeling very strange about the situation, Marina nonetheless ordered the same. The last thing she wanted was to draw attention to them. The server pointed them to a dish of water for the dogs, which was nearby. As the server walked away, Marina considered her options.

Surprisingly, she believed Varden about Roman not being involved. So, with only a pang of guilt about sharing potentially classified information, she told him what she knew about the metal-eating bacteria.

As she described what Helen had told them, Varden's expression turned harder and more forbidding. "I'm familiar with that bacteria," he said after a moment. "They call it Volvoticus. Nora was studying it in the lab. Hedron must have taken it or somehow found a source, but that's unlikely, because they've never been able to locate an origin—a source—for it. Hedron must have stolen what was in Nora's lab, but

Roman didn't tell me if he did." His handsome face looked like stone. "Roman might not realize it."

"Whoever's doing this—as you suspect, Hedron—has since issued a statement…and has put the bacteria for sale on the black market." She watched him closely, still trying to determine whether he was telling the truth. "There's to be a second demonstration to display the scope of its abilities. Surely it'll be more destructive than the three truck accidents. Do you have any idea what Hedron would have in mind?"

"No." His response was so hard and sharp that Boris lumbered to his feet and looked at them.

The server arrived with their wine, and she brought two dog biscuits as well. Marina thanked her and gave her permission to offer them to Boris and Adele. When the server walked off, Marina took a sip of the wine and looked at Varden.

"My question is, is Hedron doing this to point a finger at the Skaladeskas—to put them at risk somehow? To put them under scrutiny so he can go about doing whatever it is he wants? Or is he doing it for some other purpose?"

"Money, obviously, if he's going to sell it," Varden replied. "Which I believe he would, without hesitation. And, just as likely, a side benefit would be pointing at Roman and Lev."

"Would he really sell it?" Marina asked. "Or would he reserve some for himself?"

Varden shrugged, then tasted his wine and lifted his brows. "That's good. How's yours?"

"Not a date," she reminded him. "Why did *you* need to talk to me?"

"The bee."

How the hell did he know about that? "Which bee?"

Was he talking about the bee she'd seen in her journey with Lev, or the bee Eli had been trying to protect?

Were they the same bee?

He eyed her over the rim of his glass. "Tell me what you know, Marina. Was that why you had a visit from the priest?"

So he did know.

It was so damned annoying that he was always a step or two ahead of her.

"If you would open yourself up to what Lev and Roman have to offer you through Gaia, you wouldn't feel so out of touch and confused, Marina," he said. "I know because I'm open to it. I'm part of it."

"Yes," she replied, toasting him with her glass. "You're part of a murderous terrorist organization. So much for 'first do no harm,' hmm, Doctor?"

Something flashed in his eyes. Fury. But his expression remained cool. "We've had this conversation before. It's tiresome. There are times," he said, leaning forward a little—causing the dogs to bolt to their feet and eye him warily, "when one can do only so much to mitigate damage. And no one—no one—is lily white. Ask your friend Colin Bergstrom about that. And Gabe MacNeil."

She studied him again, thinking about what he'd said as she took another sip of the wine. It *was* good, but she wasn't about to tell him that. He'd chosen it, after all.

Instead, she opened her mouth to retort that Gabe and Colin had never purposely killed anyone—except perhaps in self-defense—then she decided better of it. After all, both men were CIA. Who knew what they had been required to do in their careers?

Which was, she realized, exactly Varden's point. And so was the idea of self-defense.

Gaia's self-defense against Her destruction by humanity logically included loss of life, and was understandable to Marina. It was the fact that the Skaladeskas helped Gaia—and always by using Her own tools—that kept Marina from embracing their objective.

"We're at war," Varden said quietly, as if reading her mind. "Gaia is at war to defend Herself. But even Roman isn't about wanton destruction…he's about *mitigating* the damage."

"With plenty of *collateral* damage," she replied. Still. "Since we're never going to agree on that, let's get back to the matter at hand—what's the deal with the bee?"

"Surely by now you've realized it's special," he replied.

"Yes, but I'm not sure what's special about it. Even Eli isn't certain. But…" She hesitated, hating that she wanted to tell him about her journey with Lev, but if she was ever going to find answers, it was probably through Varden. "I met Lev in a journey to the Lower World," she said in a rush, still uncomfortable with the idea of putting the experience into words. "And when he was there—actually, when he left—there was a bee. It looks very much like the one the priest was after. A bee that seems to be from India. I'm sure that's no coincidence. They're the same bee."

Varden was watching her so steadily that Marina felt as if she were under a microscope. After a moment, he nodded. "The bee, like Lev, is special. Sacred, if you'll excuse the term. I'm not surprised he showed it to you." He drew in his breath as if to speak, then fell silent.

"What is it?" she asked when he remained quiet.

He gave a short laugh and shook his head, then took a sip of wine, looking off contemplatively. It was the first time she'd ever seen Varden seem so introspective. She waited, reaching over to pat the top of Adele's head.

At last Varden looked at her, still with that pensive expression. "I've only journeyed with Lev once. It was to the Lower World, and it was…exquisite. Everything was incredibly beautiful and vibrant."

"It was," she replied, surprised by the emotion in his voice. She suddenly wanted to tell him about what happened in Turncoat Don when Gaia released Bruce's foot, but held back. That was far too personal, and Varden was not someone with whom she could get personal.

"And so there is a sacred bee," she said. "But I don't know what to do about it."

And then suddenly she remembered what Lev had said to her. His words reverberated in her mind as if he were speaking them to her once again: *You can help protect all of us—everyone—even those who threaten the sacred beings. They threaten me as well.*

"The bee is in danger," she said, suddenly understanding. "And because the bee is in danger, so is Lev." She frowned. "I don't understand that."

Just then, her mobile phone vibrated in her pocket.

Varden glanced meaningfully at her when she didn't move to answer it. "They've run out of patience. Best answer that."

Since she agreed with his assessment, Marina dug out her phone and saw that she had several unread texts from Gabe and now a missed call from him.

"Tell them you're going to India," Varden said.

"I *am* going to India," she replied, pausing from the response she'd been texting. "How did you—"

"I know you are," he said grimly, "because you're going with me."

# THIRTY-SEVEN

While Marina was taking her dogs for a walk, Eli told Helen what they'd learned about Nicolas Notovitch's book and the shocking assertions that Jesus had lived in India after his resurrection. The only thing he didn't tell them was what happened when he put some of the honey on his dart wound. He was keeping that to himself for a while because…major implications.

"You're saying a priest broke in here?" said Gabe. "Are you sure it was a priest?"

Eli was certain, and he explained why, but as he finished, he noticed Helen's expression.

"There was a priest who showed up at Pete's All-Niter," she said. "Apparently after you'd left—rather sneakily, Dr. Sanchez, before the authorities could interview you about Ms. Fetzer."

"I knew I was going to see you the next day," he said, giving her an affable smile. But his smile faded. "A priest showed up at the diner? Jill Fetzer was already dead—"

"Apparently he gave her last rites," said Helen. "And the waitress noticed a tattoo on his wrist—so it must be the same man. And no, he didn't kill her. But someone did. Fetzer was injected with a lethal dose of sufentanil in the ladies' room. Whoever it was took her purse and coat."

"That only strengthens your belief that there are two different parties at work here," Colin said, speaking for the first time since arriving. He'd been sipping coffee from a metal travel cup and nibbling on a piece of pizza.

"The priest confirmed that too, when he was here. He expressed regret that he hadn't gotten to the diner in time," Eli said. "Whether he meant in time to save Jill's life or to obtain the box—which he stole from us—I'm not certain."

"So you think this bee—and the honey—is somehow related to Jesus, and that's why there's a priest trying to shut it down," Gabe mused, nodding. "I can actually see it. It's not like *The Da Vinci Code* was that far off with its portrayal of the Catholic Church and what it will do to keep its secrets. Think about what would happen if the church and even the Christian religion as a whole was upended by this sort of historical information—and proof."

Colin was nodding. "International implications on a societal as well as economic basis. I'm not exaggerating," he said when Helen scoffed. "Not only is the Holy See extremely powerful in Vatican City and has wide-ranging resources we can only guess at, but think about how many governments and businesses are built on the Christian belief system."

Eli agreed with everything Colin was saying. He turned to Helen. "Did the waitress have a description of whoever killed Jill? I could tell she was the kind of person to always have a hawk's eye on everyone who comes in and out of the place."

"Medium brown hair, medium brown skin, not very tall, but bulky with muscle. We've got her working with a sketch artist, and I will do you the courtesy of sending the image once we have one."

"Thanks," Eli said with only a modicum of sarcasm. "It'll be nice to be able to keep an eye out for a guy who's trying to kill me."

"More importantly, we're hoping you can tell us if he was the man who tried to break into your hotel room," she replied.

"It's got to be the same person, otherwise we've got *three* entities trying to squash this poor little Apis bee," he said. He felt a very strong pang that the long-dead specimen was now out of his hands and in the possession of someone who might not care about her. "But more concerningly, I still have no idea how Father Dart Gun managed to find me here, and so quickly."

"He's tracking you somehow," Helen said dismissively. "Most likely via your phone."

"Marina's been gone on an awfully long walk," Gabe said suddenly. "It's been over an hour." He'd been looking at his phone, and now he pushed a button to make a call, lifting it to his ear. "I've sent her a few messages and no answer."

Helen muttered something and looked at Gabe. "What's she going to do? Run or help?"

He frowned at her. "I trust her. I know you don't, but—"

"She's obviously been in touch with them," Helen snapped. "It was patently obvious."

"Then she's probably trying to get as much information as possible," Gabe replied steadily. "She's not answering her phone."

"Dammit," Helen said, rising abruptly. She turned to Eli. "What do you know about this?"

"Not a thing," he replied pleasantly, just as he felt his phone vibrate gently. "We've only talked about the bee, not the Skalas."

She gave him a shrewd look but turned away and began to type on the computer tablet she always carried. "We need to find out what this demonstration is—and we need to stop it from happening. If Dr. Alexander isn't going to meet us halfway—"

"Agent Darrow," said Colin. "We are all on the same page here about finding out what the next phase is going to be. It's urgent, and while we have a resource in Marina Alexander, we can't rely only on her—for a number of reasons. But at the same time, she has helped us in the past, and so there's no reason to think she won't in this case."

Helen's lips firmed, but she nodded. "I know. But there is something else going on with her, and I don't know whether this is a priority."

"It's a priority, Helen. Saving lives is always a priority with Marina," said Gabe gently. "She just may not go about it in the same way you or I would want her to."

Eli felt his phone vibrate again, and he had a feeling he knew who it was. But how to check it without all of these people breathing down his neck…

He stood, and they all swiveled to look at him. "Uh…bio break okay?" he said with more than a little irony.

He didn't wait for replies; he simply walked out of the room. As soon as he shut the door to the bathroom behind him, he looked at his phone.

*Meet me in Ladakh.*

Holy crap.

# THIRTY-EIGHT

*New Delhi, India*
*July 13*

When a man tried to kill you, his face was forever imprinted in your mind. Even though years had passed and appearances had changed, you still recognized the man.

Which was why when Eli saw *him* in the crowded airport in New Delhi, he knew that, random and coincidental as it was, the Skaladeska named Hedron was here.

Although maybe it wasn't quite as coincidental as one might think, considering that there had to be some connection between the Skaladeskas and his gorgeous, elegant Apis patricia…otherwise, why had Marina been shown the bee in her journey with Lev?

Another shocking thing about seeing Hedron was that the man was with—of all people—the passenger Eli had sat next to on the flight from Paris to New Delhi. But if Eli hadn't been looking for the man—whose name was Allen Schlueter—to see if he wanted to share a cab, he might not have even noticed Hedron among the scads of people.

Eli considered it one of those blessed life-saving instants that he'd seen Hedron before walking up to Allen, who was managing his own bags to the door outside the terminal.

Keeping a comfortable distance between himself and the two men, Eli took a moment to buy a hat from one of the wallahs—which he'd learned was a general term that meant any sort of worker—inside the airport. With his brown skin and dark hair, he could easily blend in with the Indians, and a hat and sunglasses would help disguise him. He didn't want either of the men to see him.

The moment he stepped outside of the airport, Eli was assaulted by noise, smell, and oppressive heat. And people. *So many people.*

Beggars pushed toward him, holding out their hands and calling, shouting, babbling for attention. Hustlers shoved in closer too, trying to sell him whatever they had—sunglasses, bottles of water, scarves, wallets, bracelets, flowers, and more, with a constant patter of "wanna buy, wanna buy, wanna buy?" There were others going about their business, walking past the beggars and hustlers—travelers coming or going from the airport, greeters, drivers, and more.

People were everywhere, moving about, standing there shouting, pushing through the crowds. The men were usually dressed in chinos or khakis with short-sleeved shirts, while the women all wore loose, colorful saris that Eli immediately envied, for he was in his cargo pants, tee, open button-down shirt, and Birkenstocks. At least his feet could breathe.

The air was clogged with exhaust from waiting buses and cabs, and he felt as if he were walking through fog, it was so thick and heavy. And smelly. Body odor, the smells of human waste, cigarette smoke, and more filled the air.

As he watched Allen and Hedron push past the aggressive beggars and shouting sellers, making their way toward a battered car that might have been a cab but didn't have a sign on it, Eli decided he had to follow them. There was no way he was going to let them slip away without finding out something about why a murderous Skaladeska was with a man whose business was selling bottled water.

The fact that he'd sat next to the man from Paris to New Delhi—nearly nine hours—who ran a company that conducted a business that, in Eli's opinion, was one of the worst insults to the environment and climate was ironic. What was even more ironic was that Eli would have to partake of that product the entire time he was here. He'd been warned not to drink any water in India that wasn't bottled and sealed by a reputable source, and therefore he would have avail himself of a product he usually avoided at all costs.

Eli battled his way through the throngs of people, confident that neither Allen nor Hedron would recognize him even if they looked back. He hated to ignore the beggars, because they looked so pathetic and worn, but he knew from experience that once you showed kindness to any one of them, the others would swarm, knowing you were an easy mark. Not only could it be dangerous to be jostled and surrounded by desperate people, but Eli knew he would lose his chance to follow Allen and Hedron.

So he steeled himself and ignored the beggars and sellers, pushing past them as he searched for a ride that was near enough to Allen's that the driver could follow him. That meant ignoring the hundreds (or so it seemed) of other drivers who called at him, reached for him, waved, shouted and coaxed, as he marched past with his duffel and backpack. Eli was almost afraid to breathe the gray, disgusting air.

It was monsoon season, so everything was wet and humid along with being sweltering. Eli wasn't certain whether he should be grateful it wasn't raining at the moment, since the downpour could last for hours at a time, yet offer some relief from the oppressive heat.

He maneuvered his way near Allen and Hedron's vehicle and then picked a car that looked relatively safe and kind of reminded him of Juanita. Only one bumper was sagging, and rust hadn't yet eaten away the entire door. Without waiting for the driver to help load his bags, he dove inside. "I need you to follow that blue Opel," he said to the driver, pointing at the other car.

Eli had no idea how impossible a task he'd given the man until the car tried to inch out into the never-ending, nose-to-butt line of vehicles trying to leave the airport. He consoled himself with the fact that Allen's ride couldn't go any faster than his own.

Inch by inch, they made their way into the river of vehicles, and Eli stripped off his outer shirt then dug out his mobile. He'd traveled to out-of-the-way places often enough that he had a satellite sleeve for his phone, although he didn't think he'd need it here in New Delhi.

He wanted to send Marina a message that he was in India and, more importantly, that he'd seen Hedron. He was also hoping she would have contacted him, but so far no other messages other than her original "Meet me in Ladakh." Which was a pretty tall order, considering how big the region of Ladakh was—and how difficult it would be to get around. The area was all mountains and curving, rocky roads. At least it would be a lot cooler up there in the north.

As they inched their way closer to Old Delhi, Eli found himself overwhelmed by the magnitude of everything: vehicles, people, noise, smells. The sharp, pungent smell of petroleum had not abated in the least, and now the stench was accompanied by that of a variety of organic waste. There was a cacophony of noise—mostly car horns, honking incessantly.

It seemed as if every driver of every single car was constantly *toot-tooting*, including his own. There was no escaping any of it, as all the windows were down on the car, of course, because air conditioning was rarer than the Apis patricia. Eli wasn't certain whether it would actually be more comfortable with the windows rolled up—hotter, yes, but perhaps quieter and less smelly.

There were not only cars, buses, and trucks on the streets, but they mingled with every other kind of vehicle one could imagine: scooters, motorized jitneys, man-pulled jitneys, bicycles, and wagons pulled by goats.

The actual navigation and driving was worse than anything he'd experienced, even in Rome. They'd gone less than a meter and Eli had seen his life flash before his eyes at least five times already. His fingers were aching from gripping the granny stick, and he considered whether he should just close his eyes.

But he couldn't; there was just too much to see and experience.

There seemed to be nothing resembling lanes in the five-lane road, and definitely nothing like turn signals or driver courtesy. Traffic lights hardly existed, and when they did, they were blatantly ignored. Cars, buses, bikes, and carts simply went wherever they wanted with no regard to any other vehicle or direction. Lots of horn honking, though. All the time. Eli's ears were ringing because his driver not only kept *toot-tooting*, but he had jaunty Indian music playing at a high volume, and people were shouting and whistling out on the streets as well.

Eli gaped in astonishment when he saw a man riding a bicycle down the street among the cars with two large wooden planks protruding from each side. It made the bicycle look like a biplane, but even more shocking was that there were people—presumably the man's family—sitting on the "wings." Eli counted eight people of various ages perched on that bicycle, not counting the rider.

He couldn't take his eyes from the sight—hoping and praying none of the little children or the elderly woman would fall off and into the street…that was, until he saw an actual *elephant* ahead, joining the flow of traffic—if one could call it a flow. More like countless bottlenecks on steroids.

The elephant, which was being used as transportation for three people who rode atop it, plodded along on its wrinkly gray-brown legs, looming over the cars and other vehicles around it. And, Eli realized, probably dropping a healthy load of waste at any given moment.

Aside from the elephant, there were also cows everywhere. Simply wandering around, also dropping their dung wherever they pleased. In the ratty, grassy, treeless barrier between the two sides of what would be called a boulevard in any other city, Eli saw people camping, cooking, and squatting. No one sat on the ground, he noticed. Everyone squatted all the time, which he guessed he understood, since the ground was filthy. Even from the car, he could see the trash and waste that was everywhere.

"You want out here?" said the driver, pointing with a jerky hand motion as he swerved into a sort of parking place near one of the hotels. The front nose of the car narrowly missed a jitney, which was being pulled by a skinny Indian man and carried a woman and her child.

Eli saw that the Opel with Allen and Hedron had pulled into the driveway of what looked like a very expensive hotel, and, after a brief hesitation, he said yes. Thanking the driver, Eli paid him with a healthy tip. Then he grabbed his duffel and backpack and bolted from the car. His quarries were extricating themselves from their own vehicle with the help of a bellman at the hotel entrance.

This gave Eli a moment to edge closer while doing his best to avoid cow shit and one of the skinny, rat-like dogs that darted forward to snatch up a bit of food-covered trash. It also offered him a bit of information—that Hedron seemed to have luggage of his own. Until now,

Eli hadn't been certain whether Hedron was in the airport meeting Allen Schleuter or if he had flown in as well.

Maybe the two men didn't really know each other, and they were simply sharing a cab like Eli had thought to do. Either way, Eli decided he was going to book a room at the same hotel.

Since his trip had been so last-minute and he wasn't exactly sure where he was supposed to meet Marina, he hadn't made any specific arrangements. He'd just gotten himself to India, and soon he'd be getting himself to Leh—which was the capital city in Ladakh and had the best airport in the area. Whether or not he actually met up with Marina was one thing—although he certainly intended to—but his main purpose was to find the "guy" named Manish who'd told Patty Denke about the bee.

If he hadn't seen Hedron, Eli would have already booked his flight to Leh. But he couldn't leave New Delhi without at least trying to find out what the man was doing here.

Once again leaving a healthy distance between himself and his quarries, Eli wove through the throngs of people and followed them into the hotel. As he did so, he reflected on just how he was going to go about learning what Hedron was up to. The best option would be to try to "run into" Allen when he was alone and pump the guy for information.

But first he was going to check in and find something cooler to wear. And he was wildly hungry. The smell of food cooking outside had been enticing even with the underlying eau de shit and petroleum; now that he was walking up to the hotel (which was already slightly cooler thanks to the many ceiling fans on the roof of the exterior colonnade), he could smell their kitchens, and his stomach gurgled expectantly.

Eli's plan took a nosedive when he actually walked into the lobby of the hotel and saw the place. It was opulent and gorgeous, with four-story ceilings in the lobby, gilt and mahogany furnishings he would be afraid to touch let alone sit on, and boat-sized fresh flower arrangements everywhere. Stunning crystal chandeliers hung from the ceiling all along the front of the desk, and huge potted citrus trees were incorporated into every chair and table arrangement. There was a massive glass Buddha in the middle of the room with its own dome upholstered in red and gold brocade hanging from the ceiling above him. The statue's base was clear and contained a light that sent a glow up into the figure.

There was *no way* Eli could afford to stay here. But he walked up to the counter anyway, figuring he might overhear something from his quarries while he bullshitted his way through a conversation with the clerk.

But to his surprise, the cost for a room at the place was only a few dollars more than he'd spent at the hotel in Cincinnati. Figuring he might as well live in style at least one night while he was here—since if he went to Ladakh he'd be pretty close to roughing it—Eli whipped out his credit card.

He kept his eyes on Allen and Hedron the whole time he continued the check-in process, trying to see what information he could glean from hand gestures as they checked in a few stations away from his. Since the two men were waited on by different clerks, Eli concluded they were getting separate rooms and were not on the same bill.

They all finished their business around the same time, and Eli hung back as the two men started for the elevators, then eased closer in an effort to pick up their conversation. He kept his head down, pretending to look at his phone as he followed them, and caught just enough of a conversation to hear "Leh."

Holy crap. This could not be a coincidence.

Eli pretended not to notice when the elevator arrived and the two men stepped on...but then at the last moment, he dove inside and turned so he faced the front of the elevator, still seemingly intent on his phone.

His heart pounded violently as he stared at the closed elevator doors. He was, after all, in a closed space with a man who'd tried to kill him. The hair on the back of his neck prickled as he realized he couldn't see what was going on behind him, but the two men were talking as if nothing was out of order. Allen would be more likely to recognize him, since they'd sat next to each other on the plane, but, Eli realized with a modicum of relief, he'd taken off his overshirt and added a hat to his attire, so he didn't look the same at first glance.

Hopefully Allen wouldn't recognize his ratty feet bared by the Birkenstocks.

Eli remembered belatedly to touch the number for his floor, but it was already lit. Two numbers were lit…which meant he was going to be on the same floor as Allen or Hedron.

*Madre de Dios*, as his mother would have said.

"…tomorrow morning," said Hedron in excellent English accented with Russian. "The flight to Leh is just ninety minutes, and then we travel by car to the meeting place—an hour or so. The water minister will meet us there with the contracts you've already reviewed."

Allen replied, "I have the contracts with me. I'll be signing those. I don't trust them to have the most updated version."

"As you like," Hedron replied. "Ah, eleven. This is my floor."

Eli felt a wave of relief that it wasn't the fourteenth floor, where he was staying.

"I'm going to settle in and then get something to eat," said Allen as the elevator lurched to a halt. "At the bar downstairs. Join me?"

"No, thank you. I've got some work to finish up," Hedron replied as the doors slid open.

Eli scooted to the side to let him pass, then returned his attention to the screen of his mobile phone. He wasn't ready for Allen to recognize him yet.

Two floors later, the elevator stopped on fourteen and Eli fairly bolted through the doors as soon as they opened. He strode down the hall, leaving Allen in his wake, then turned at the first corner and listened to see if he could hear where the other man was going.

Footsteps came closer, ceased, and then Eli heard the click of a lock and the sound of a door opening. He peeked around the corner and pinned the location of Allen's room with his eyes so he could get the number later.

Then, having finished playing James Bond, he went about finding his own room. It wasn't until he slipped inside that he realized his knees were a little wobbly.

What the hell were the chances?

And what did all of this mean?

# THIRTY-NINE

Eli was sitting in the hotel bar for only ten minutes before Allen Schleuter meandered in.

He'd chosen a table with a view of the entire room as well as a scope of the broad, tall gallery that connected the hotel lobby to the bar. Though Hedron had indicated he would stay in his room, Eli was taking no chances on a surprise appearance.

"Allen? Is that you?" he called out. "What are the chances?" he added, giving a little laugh as the older man looked toward him.

Allen smiled and gave a friendly wave. He was carrying a slender briefcase. "Mind if I join you? It's nice to see a familiar face. I was going to do some work, but it can wait." Allen took a seat across from Eli and set his briefcase on the empty chair next to him.

"I looked for you in the terminal after customs, but I didn't see you," Eli lied as the wallah came over to take Allen's order. Eli already had a plate loaded with a variety of chaat topped with every imaginable delicacy—shrimp salad, steak tartare, lobster bits, savory dal, spicy tofu, creamy vegetables, and more—along with an array of chutneys. He'd been enjoying every bite. The spicy coconut mint on the steak tartare was his favorite combination so far. "If I had known, we could have shared a cab."

"I'm here with a business associate," Allen told him after ordering a gin and tonic and being assured that the ice cubes were made from "triple-boiled water." "We're heading to a place in the middle of nowhere tomorrow—Ladakh. Way up in the mountains right by the Himalayas. Nothing up there but mountains and goats. Figured I better enjoy my creature comforts while I can," he added with a laugh. "Get out of the monsoons up there too—or so they say."

Eli hesitated, then plunged onward. Best to have established his presence now than have Allen wonder about it. "That's a hell of a coincidence, because I'm flying to Leh tomorrow—that's up that way too." Too late, he realized he might have set himself up for a problem if Allen suggested he and his business partner might meet up with Eli during travel or while there. *Damn.* He wasn't all that good at this espionage stuff, was he?

Allen was surprised. "What are you going to be doing up there?" A hint of suspicion lit his eyes, and Eli realized he had to backtrack, and quickly.

"Oh, a graduate student of mine has been working on a project up there—her thesis is about"—*oh, shit, oh, shit, what would make sense?*—"a, uh, Coleopteroid—I mean, a beetle—that lives at high altitudes." Eli realized too late that he dared not mention a bee, but he also had to keep to something he could talk about comfortably. Stick as close to the truth as possible, right? "This species is very unusual due to the number of ocelli—it has *three*, if you can believe it. And its elytra—the hard covering, which is like an outer wing that protects the under, or hindwing—is quite distinct in that it contains elements of copper." He purposely rambled on with boring, specific details about the insect—which happened to be the deadly copper beetle he'd gotten to know so intimately in the Amazon—so that Allen's eyes would glaze over.

Before that actually happened, the wallah appeared with Allen's drink and some chakri—which were like flat, savory spiral cookies—thus interrupting Eli's lecture and allowing him to change the topic. "What are you doing up in Leh?" he asked.

"Business," replied Allen, then took a big drink of the gin and tonic. He smiled and sighed with gusto. "Ah, I needed that."

Eli lifted an eyebrow. "What sort of business is there for a water-bottling company— Oh, let me guess... Fresh Himalayan water springs, right?" He grinned, and was surprised when Allen gave him a direct look. It was not a pleasant one.

"Who told you that?" Allen put down his drink and pinned Eli with a hard gaze.

Shocked by such an overreaction, Eli shrugged and said, "It was just an educated guess—and mostly a joke. What else would interest a bottled-water company CEO in the mountains?" He chuckled.

Allen seemed to relax a little, but Eli definitely felt suspicion continuing to emanate from him as the food arrived.

"It's confidential," Allen said after the wallah left.

"Oh, sorry," Eli said. "Corporate secrets and all that? I guess I never imagined bottled-water companies would have such big secrets to protect." He laughed and took a drink of the ice-cold beer, bottled, not draft, that he'd been enjoying.

"You'd be surprised," Allen replied with a wry smile.

Eli shrugged and decided it was best to leave the topic…but at the same time, he was even more curious. What on earth would be so proprietary about bottled water? Something so confidential could only be the source of said water, but water was water, wasn't it?

Mountain springs and so on…what was the big deal?

He turned the topic to the food in front of them, and they raved about the variety, the presentation, and, of course, the taste of their respective meals. Allen ordered a second G&T, and Eli wondered how many of them—along with certain jet lag—would make the man's tongue loose enough to spill a few more secrets. The water CEO had downed the first one pretty quickly.

Eli decided to hang tight and try to find out, but he kept his eyes on the entrance to the bar to make certain Hedron didn't come wandering in.

He kept the conversation on other things—their respective flights from the United States (it seemed Allen had come in from Pittsburgh on his way to Paris), the crazy drive from the airport, and the comforts of the hotel.

"There was a bumper sticker on one of the trucks," Eli said. "It said 'Tootle Your Horn, Yes Please!' I guess everyone was listening, because no one ever stopped honking their horns." He chuckled, thinking about the cacophony.

"Did you see the sign posted—I don't remember where it was; on one of the streets here in Delhi—that read 'Do Not Urinate Here,'" Allen said. His eyes were a little glassy, and Eli had counted four gin and tonics, with a fifth having just been placed in front of him. "It was just right there on the street! And there was a guy who whipped it out right next to the sign and was peeing right there in front of everyone. It would have been a great photo—the guy peeing right there in the middle of the street, next to the sign that says not to pee there." He gave a wheezy laugh and took another big gulp of gin and tonic. "I sure hope they weren't lying about the ice cubes being triple-boiled water," he said, looking at the glass. "Because otherwise I'm fucked."

"I'm sure the ice and water are both safe, being served in a place like this," Eli said, then he winked. "But I really think if your company doesn't have the contract to supply water here, they should get working on it."

Allen laughed and pointed his finger at Eli. "You're damned right! I need to speak to a manager!" he said. "There might be a better opportunity in the near future, you know," he said in a lower voice, waving off the bar wallah who'd looked over at them in question when Allen had raised his voice. "Once these contracts are signed." He patted the briefcase on the seat next to him.

"I wouldn't be surprised," replied Eli, suddenly very interested in the contents of that briefcase. How the hell was he going to get a look at them? "Another round?" he asked, gesturing to the wallah.

"Sure, why not? I'm on vacation!" said Allen expansively. "At least until tomorrow, when I have to play the cutthroat CEO. I'm gonna sleep like a baby tonight, let me tell you…"

Six gin and tonics over less than ninety minutes had Allen's words slurring quite a bit by now, but even though Eli tried to gently introduce the topic of business, Allen continued to evade it.

At last, Allen decided he was done and called for the wallah to bring their tabs. He rose a little unsteadily after signing off on his room bill. "Nice seeing you again—what was your name?"

"Eli. Good luck with your—uh—business. Maybe I'll see you in the airport in Leh." *I'll make sure of it—and that you don't see me.*

"Right," said Allen, patting his suit coat pocket as if to ensure he had his wallet and room key. "Don't forget not to urinate there!" he added with a chortle, and then he toddled off.

Leaving his briefcase forgotten on the chair.

# FORTY

Eli hesitated only for a moment. He'd been creeping a look at the bar bill so he could get Allen's room number.

He'd actually been entertaining the idea of breaking into the room while the CEO was snoring his brains out after the drinks and jet lag—it wasn't that difficult, as Eli had cause to know from his research online about breaking into hotel rooms after the incident in Cincinnati.

But this plan was much, much better and less likely to get him arrested.

Eli swiftly snatched up the briefcase and hurried from the bar. If anyone saw him, they could attest to the fact that he was on his way to hail Allen and return the briefcase.

But once he got outside the restaurant, he ducked behind a huge column and turned to opening the briefcase, praying it wasn't locked.

It wasn't.

He didn't have time to look at everything now—surely it wouldn't take Allen long before he realized he'd left it.

Eli looked in the direction of the elevators, but Allen wasn't in sight. Hopefully he was already on his way up to the fourteenth floor, which gave Eli some time. Then he looked around more and saw the sign: Business Center. *Perfect.*

He hurried over to the glass-doored suite and went inside. The copy machines were right there, self-serve with a credit card, thank goodness.

Quickly, he opened the briefcase on a worktable next to the machines and thumbed through its contents. Travel docs, itineraries—

that was good; he tossed that onto the machine and hit copy—and then a manila file folder. It was labeled *CONFIDENTIAL.*

This had to be it. He opened the folder to find contracts. *Yes.*

Removing the staple while eyeing the lobby through the glass doors, Eli felt his pulse shoot to high speed when he saw Allen step out of the elevator.

*Shit.*

He shoved the contracts onto the copy machine and pressed go. *Hurry, hurry, hurry…*

The machine was as fast as the hotel was luxurious, and he had the copies in seconds. He watched Allen as he toddled away from the elevators, and Eli realized he was going in the wrong direction for the bar. Not a surprise—the hotel was huge and Allen was impaired.

Still, Eli didn't waste time as he stapled the original contract back together then replaced it in its folder with the original travel itinerary on top. His heart was still pounding wildly as he hurried out of the business center and back into the lobby, folding his copies in half and then in half again before shoving them into the cargo pants pocket low on the side of his thigh.

"Allen!" he called when he saw the CEO in the lobby. He had obviously realized he was going in the wrong direction and was now heading toward the bar. Allen turned and looked at him owlishly. "There you are!" Eli said as he rushed toward him, brandishing the briefcase. "You left this behind."

"I came back to get it," replied Allen, taking it from Eli. "Can't believe I forgot it."

"I didn't notice until I got up to leave," said Eli. "It was hidden by the tablecloth. I came back to the lobby but I didn't see you, so I was going to ask the bartender if he could ring your room—but here you are."

"Thank you, young man," replied Allen. "Appreciate it." Then he squinted a little lopsidedly. "You didn't look inside there, did you, now? Corporate secrets and all." He laughed.

Eli laughed in return. "Didn't have a chance—I went running out after you right when I found it. Have a safe flight tomorrow, and good luck." Before Allen could press the topic, Eli walked off. He couldn't wait to get back to his room and look at those contracts.

# FORTY-ONE

*Ladakh region, India*
*July 14*

Marina opened her eyes.

She was in a small room with simple furnishings: a narrow bed blanketed by a brightly colored, woven coverlet, a water-filled pitcher and small basin atop a small bureau, and a surprisingly comfortable rag rug, also very colorful. It was just dawning, and the single window offered a view of the rugged countryside, with its scrubby trees, rough, stony land, and austere snow-capped mountains in the distance.

A cot had been set up across the small room, and the unmoving lump under its bright red, pink, green, and blue blanket indicated that Varden was still sleeping.

She could still hardly believe that only days ago she'd been in Ann Arbor, Michigan, and since then had traveled by air through Amsterdam to Delhi and then from Delhi to Leh, the largest city in the Ladakh region.

Now, she and Varden were in Hemis, a village about an hour's drive on the bumpy, narrow, winding roads from Leh. They'd arrived last night and shared a meal with the others at the guesthouse, then, exhausted from nonstop travel, had stumbled to the room they had no choice but to share.

It was pure luck that they were able to obtain even a single room at this small but clean guesthouse, nestled against the side of a small mountain. Made from whitewashed brick with three floors stacked like haphazard cake tiers, the inn had a flat roof made from battered aluminum painted brown.

Upon their arrival in Hemis, they'd learned that this morning began the first of a two-day religious festival that brought travelers not only from the nearby countryside, but from other areas as well. As there were only a few options for lodging in the area, they'd been fortunate to find even a single room. It didn't bother Marina to share the space with Varden; she was used to rough conditions and a lack of privacy on search-and-rescue missions.

She slipped very quietly from the bed and gathered up her backpack. She needed some time to think… Some time alone.

There was only one bathroom in the guesthouse, which offered eight rooms, and Marina was relieved that it was currently available. More importantly, it was clean and there was an actual toilet, unlike many places in India—although there were two brick outhouses on the guesthouse property as well. She washed up, then slipped from the lavatory and out of the guesthouse.

The sun was just visible from between the mountains, and golden light streamed through in concentrated beams. Marina's breath came out in soft white puffs, and she was glad she'd tucked her jacket in the backpack. She needed it now, though it would get warmer later in the day.

Marina drew in a deep breath of the crisp mountain air and held it in her lungs for a moment, savoring the purity of it. Then she began to walk away from the guesthouse and away from the small village.

The ground was uneven and rocky. What little vegetation there was reminded her of what she'd seen in Siberia—but without the snow. She saw scrubby bushes like juniper, spindly trees, and patches of growth that included some wildflowers such as penny-sized daisies, columbine, and yellow moss rose. Marina paused to admire a cluster of furry-leafed green plants growing among craggy rocks. The soft-looking crinkle-edged plant was interspersed with puffy flowerheads of gray leaves that looked like tiny, cottony sagebrush. She wondered what it was called.

Marina walked on, grateful for her sturdy hiking boots and insulating jacket, happy to put space between herself and people. After spending the last five days surrounded by electronics and steel vehicles, flying and riding and moving about, Marina needed to feel Gaia again. She needed to remind herself of the beauty and strength of Mother Earth.

This was also the first chance she'd really had to consider what they needed to do now that they'd arrived in India. While she agreed with Varden that they'd had to be here, and they must find the bee, she still wasn't certain what they were supposed to do once they did.

They'd come to Hemis because that was the location of the Buddhist monastery Nicolas Notovitch had mentioned in his book—the monastery that allegedly was the source of the information where Notovitch learned about Jesus having traveled through the area.

But what about it? Why was Marina involved at all? Why had Lev shown her the bee and brought her into this?

When she saw the large tree with its broad trunk and wide, welcoming branches, Marina knew what she had to do. She settled beneath it, resting her back against the solid, rough trunk. Putting her backpack aside, she took off her shoes and socks, because something told her to get as close to Gaia as she could.

If she wanted answers, she needed no barriers.

Here, in this desolately beautiful place, with little in the way of man-made electronics, structures, and sounds, there was nothing to interrupt her connection with Gaia. Her bare feet and hands pressing into the prickly grass and cool soil steadied her, and she felt the thrumming of the Earth's energy. It shimmered through her, vibrating gently and sweetly through her limbs and into her center.

Even when she'd been inside Turncoat Don, silent and dark within Gaia's womb, Marina hadn't felt her energy so strongly.

She tipped her head back against the tree trunk. The bark caught her hair, and she thanked Gaia for her loving touch. Marina felt something crawl over her toe and opened her eyes to see a small insect she couldn't identify traversing her olive-skinned foot, and she thanked Gaia for sending part of herself as greeting.

A golden eagle flew overhead with its broad wingspan, circling elegantly then flying off, and a shy rabbit darted from behind a boulder and bounded away. Marina once again acknowledged that there were countless parts of the great, complicated, awesome organism that was the Earth…all of which worked together in a give-and-take, push-and-pull, cyclical entity.

She closed her eyes and relaxed, spreading her fingers wide over the rocky, grassy ground and pressing her feet flat into the same.

The world was silent but for the gentle rustle of breeze through the leaves and the distant call of a bird.

When Marina opened her eyes, she wasn't alone.

*Grandfather.*

Lev sat beneath his tree with its broad spread of branches and glossy green, blue, purple, red, and orange leaves.

*Mariska. You've come.*

*I've come, but I don't know why I'm here.*

She felt the rough, rocky soil beneath her feet and hands, and the thrum of Gaia's heartbeat. Silky green grass surrounded Lev, and the moment she had the thought, the ground beneath her was lush with green velvet and studded with sweet flowers of every color. Tall, fuzzy-tipped grasses swayed gently around her and her grandfather, who was about three meters away. Pink and orange blossoms danced above and among the tips. A purple butterfly darted about, followed by one of butter yellow and another of scarlet.

Birds sang joyfully, launching themselves off tiny, delicate feet from branch to branch, gliding up and around through the air. She saw an antelope bound off in the distance, and the grasses shivered as some other unseen creatures made their way through. A vine laden with bright berries of crimson, yellow, and purple grew, twining itself around the tree branch above Lev as she watched. Spontaneous buds appeared, bursting into colorful blooms with long stamen and velvety petals.

*Here is the sacred. It is a source of great energy and sacredness. It is one of the centers of Gaia's life…an area that feeds Her even when She is battered and assaulted. It must be protected. In protecting Her here, you also protect me…and more.*

Marina nodded, and the bark behind her head was softer this time. *I understand. What of the bee?*

*The bee is part of the sacred. In protecting Her, you protect all that is sacred and holy. And you protect this center of Gaia.*

*Yes, Grandfather. But how? What is the threat?*

He looked off into the distance, and the mountains suddenly came to them. Tall, rugged, forbidding boulder-scapes reared next to their respective trees, as if someone had zoomed in on a photograph. She felt the sudden wet chill of snow beneath her hands and feet and realized she was there, somehow, atop one of the craggy places. Her tree was now a tall, sprawling juniper with prickling needles and fragrant berries larger than pearls. A bee—*the* bee—flitted into view, her golden-rose coloring glinting in the sunlight.

Marina looked at Lev and saw that although he sat against the mountains, his tree remained the same.

*Mariska.* There was deep emotion in the voice she heard, and it reverberated within her heart. *You are part of me and you are part of Her. You are* Her *progeny. Never forget that. What hurts me hurts you. What destroys Her destroys you. What threatens Her threatens you. We are all connected.*

She felt his words so deeply that she shuddered inside. *My father. Roman?*

Lev tilted his head and closed his eyes. When he opened them, he said: *Roman is not you.*

The mountains surged away, back to the distance. Their snowcaps glittered gold and pink in the sun, and the ground around her became velvety and green once again.

Marina felt movement behind her, and she turned her head. The movement felt as though she were underwater, slow and hampered… yet there was no distortion or murkiness to her vision.

*Varden.*

She tensed when he came nearer, feeling as if his presence somehow sullied the moment.

He seemed more confident and powerful than before, striding over the grass in long, bare feet. When Varden looked at her, his eyes greener than bright moss, she felt a jolt of something deep inside. She pushed it away. She didn't want that feeling. Not with him.

*Lev.* Varden was speaking in her head as well, and all of his attention moved from Marina to her grandfather. He bowed. *Thank you. I am honored to be here.*

Lev nodded and looked up at him. *She cannot do this alone.*

*She won't,* Varden replied.

Why could Varden express himself but she couldn't? Marina tried to speak again, tried to rise, to go to her grandfather, but found she couldn't move. Her thoughts were muted until Lev turned his attention to her. She felt the force of his gaze like a blow—something she'd never experienced before.

Marina wanted to speak, to defend herself, but the words wouldn't come. Nor would the thoughts that she wanted to hurl at her grandfather and at the man standing there next to them.

*You will trust him,* Lev told her.

*Grandfather…I don't understand. He—we—*

Even in her mind, her thoughts were a stammering muddle, and she spared Varden a look to see if he could hear them. He gave no indication that she was even present.

*I do not ask you to understand. You must do. And you will trust him. You must. All is at stake.*

Once more she tried to move, to reach toward Lev, but her limbs would not cooperate.

*Protect us, Mariska.*

*Protect Gaia. Protect the sacred.*

Lev and his tree faded away. Varden was gone.

She was alone.

But she felt the weight of something watching her.

Marina looked up and her heart lurched.

The great cat stood on a nearby rocky outcropping, perhaps twenty meters away, looking down at her.

A snow leopard, majestic and attentive, with small, delicate ears and a beautiful coat of gray-white splotches. He looked at her with blue-gray eyes as her heart pounded. She knew snow leopards were endangered…and that they didn't attack humans.

And she knew that he belonged to Gaia just as she did.

Marina looked back at him, and their eyes met. He saw her, recognized her, lifted his chin in acknowledgement.

Then he turned and padded silently away.

With a little gasp, Marina opened her eyes.

She hadn't even realized she'd closed them, but somehow she had… and somehow she was sitting back beneath the same scrubby tree with her backpack next to her, bare feet on the spare, rocky ground, shoes and socks set neatly aside.

As she shifted, straightening her legs and pointing her toes up and back in a good stretch, Marina heard the sound of footsteps approaching, knocking small rocks aside and grinding on the rough terrain.

She sat upright against the tree as a young man made his way toward her. From his coloring, she knew he was Ladakhi, although he was dressed in Western clothing, like most Indian men. He looked as if he were in his early twenties, with a sparse beard and smooth skin.

When he drew near, coming up a small incline in front of her, she saw that his attention was fixed on her bare feet. Surely he was looking at the Skaladeska symbol tattooed on the bottom of her heel. Her skin prickled. She resisted the urge to move, instead waiting to see what would happen next as he stared at the ink on her skin.

At last, he looked at her and their eyes met. "I am Manish," he said, finishing the mild climb to come nearer.

"Marina."

"Why are you here?" He squatted next to her, his butt just above the ground, feet flat, knees fully bent.

Her skin prickled again. "I'm looking for a bee."

His eyelids fluttered and he nodded. "There was another who was interested in bees. She came earlier this summer. And now she's dead."

"Her name was Patty," Marina replied. It was difficult to tell whether his pronouncement was a warning or simply a fact.

Manish looked at her, and despite his youth, she saw acceptance and wisdom in his eyes. "You knew her."

"I did not. But a friend of mine knew her well. He is grieving her death."

"Who are you?"

"I am Lev's granddaughter." Marina had no idea why those words came from her mouth. But there was more. "And Gaia's daughter as well."

His eyes flared a little. Then his mouth twisted in a grimace. "There is no bee," he said, looking at her steadily.

Marina returned the gaze and gave a little shake of her head. But she said nothing. Waited.

Manish's attention returned to her foot, but to her surprise, he said nothing. Instead, he rose easily from the squat.

"There is no bee," he said again, then walked off.

# FORTY-TWO

B y the time Marina returned to the guesthouse, the sun was higher between the valleys of the mountain peaks. The pale gray cast to the early-dawn world had given over to full color, such as it was in these rugged, desolate environs.

She found Varden in the dining room with the other guests and realized how hungry she was. He gave her a glance, then indicated a seat next to him on the low bench.

Here, like most everywhere in India, people sat on benches just inches above the ground. The long seats were covered with fat, colorful cushions in pink, orange, green, blue, and yellow, and embellished with intricate embroidery, sequins, and tiny mirrors. The Indians definitely did not shy away from the colorful and ornate. The single table in the dining room was long and low to the ground as well. It was crowded with platters of flat bread, chutneys, and momos—boiled dumplings containing a variety of fillings.

Marina accepted a cup of *gur gur cha*—a pink-hued tea that she'd first sampled last night. It was a kind of chai made from green tea and had originated with the monks here in Ladakh. This was a traditional drink to which they added salt, which helped prevent dehydration at the high altitudes, and baking soda—which was the chemical reaction that gave it the rosy pink color. The monks also added yak butter to their tea, as well as spices like star anise, cardamom, and cinnamon. A sprinkling of crushed pistachios decorated the top.

Marina, always adventurous, happily drank the savory tea with all of its traditional ingredients—including the yak butter. She'd brought high-altitude medication with her and dosed herself accordingly, so she was feeling fairly normal.

"How is it?" asked Varden, nodding toward her cup. He appeared to have a simple black tea in his own mug.

"It's an acquired taste, I think," she replied. "Salty. But it's beautiful to look at."

She hated that she felt a little strange sitting next to him after seeing him during her journey with Lev. She wasn't certain whether Varden had actually been there—and whether he'd have a memory of it—or not.

They didn't talk about anything of consequence during the breakfast, considering they shared a table and seating with the other guests and the guesthouse's host. Instead, there was a lot of enthusiastic conversation about the religious festival that was starting within the hour.

Phyang Tsedup was a festival celebrating the triumph of good over evil. It honored Skyabje Jigten Gombo, the saint and founder of the monastery, and would last for two days. The monks at the nearby Phyang Gompa—the monastery—would wear colorful costumes and dance in the streets. At the zenith of the revelry, the monks would bring out the *thankga* of the saint—which was an old silken tapestry that was kept locked away and protected except on special occasions. The centuries-old *thangka* was as large as a movie theater screen and usually depicted an important personage in bold, vibrant color and intricate design.

Marina knew she would enjoy watching the high-energy celebration, but it was unlikely she and Varden could take the time to attend.

Still, since everyone for miles around had traveled here and would be distracted by the festival, she wondered if it would be easier or more difficult to find out about the bee during the celebration.

One thing was sure: she wanted to find Manish again if she could. Surely he would be at the festivities.

"Let's go," Varden said when he noticed her cup was empty.

She nodded. They had things to talk about.

Instead of returning to their room, Varden gestured to the door, and soon the two of them were far enough away from the guesthouse and partway up a small mountain so they wouldn't be heard. He sank down onto a large gray boulder that offered a view of the village of Phyang below. People were moving en masse along the roads up to the monastery, mostly on foot, but there were a few dilapidated cars and some goat-drawn wagons. The monastery was set atop a small, gravelly hill and had outbuildings that cascaded down the incline and looked like tumbling blocks. Like all of the other buildings, it had a flat roof, and the main buildings were constructed of brick and mud that had been whitewashed.

Inside, the building would be filled with bright colors—every inch painted and decorated with red, gold, and blue designs, intricate and bright. It would take forever to look at every detail inside the holy place, with its totem-like columns and inset ceilings that would give the Sistine Chapel and St. Peter's in Rome competition for the most beautiful and complicated.

Varden looked at her as she took a seat on another boulder, and she got the impression he was struggling for something to say.

His hesitance answered the question that had been nagging her. "You were there," she said. "This morning."

He nodded. "It wasn't my intention, Marina. I'm sorry. Lev pulled me in."

She nodded back, more surprised than she cared to admit that he'd apologized. She'd expected him to adopt the arrogant attitude that he usually had—that it was his right to know everything going on with her because Lev had given him the responsibility to watch over her.

But the realization that he'd been there, melded within the deepest part of her consciousness, made her feel strangely intimate with him. It was a feeling she wasn't certain how to handle. And although it made her uncomfortable, it also settled some of her mistrust of him. Surely Lev wouldn't allow Varden to become that intrinsically connected with either of them if he didn't trust him, and Marina sensed that Lev could see far more and far deeply into a man's soul than she could.

"Did you see Snow Leopard?" she asked.

"No." There was quiet awe in Varden's voice. "But I saw the bee. It…she…was magnificent. Everything was magnificent."

"Yes."

He looked at her, his gaze sharpening as if her words had penetrated after a delay. "Snow Leopard was there? Did you speak to him?"

"He didn't speak to me, so I'm not certain whether he is one of my spirit animals or not. Perhaps he was only there because we are here, where he lives. This is his natural habitat, as I'm sure you know. And he's endangered. I think he is guiding me—us—for, right after I opened my eyes from seeing him, there was a Ladakhi man there." She told Varden about Manish and how he'd seemed fixated on her Skaladeska mark.

"He told you there was no bee? You didn't believe him."

"No, and he knew I didn't. I think he was warning me that it was dangerous." She sighed and pulled out her mobile phone. Thanks to a satellite adaptor, she should have service up here in the mountains. She just needed to turn it on and connect, for she'd mostly kept her phone off to conserve data and battery. "I need to check in with Eli. He texted that he arrived in Delhi yesterday. I need to find out if he knows who Patty Denke spoke to about the bee when she was here."

Varden said nothing as she connected, and then a string of text messages downloaded to her device in a chorus of quiet dings.

She skimmed through them, finding several from Gabe—who hadn't been too pleased when he learned she'd taken off for Ladakh so unexpectedly three days ago.

But Varden had convinced her that it was best to leave right away before she was stopped from traveling out of the country. And since Colin Bergstrom had threatened to keep her from doing just that the first time she met him, Marina had agreed. Fortunately, she had a go-bag at the Ann Arbor Airport—where she parked her small plane—and she'd taken to carrying her passport with her all the time. She'd learned the hard way that dropping everything for sudden travel—whether it be related to search-and-rescue missions, her work, or the Skaladeskas—had become part of her life. She and Varden had dropped the dogs off at Adele and Boris's dog-sitter—who was also accustomed to Marina's last-minute trips—and headed to Detroit Metro to catch a flight to Amsterdam. From there, they'd flown to Delhi. All without returning to her bungalow in Ann Arbor, where Helen, Gabe, and Colin had been waiting.

Marina sent a quick text to Gabe to let him know she had arrived safely in Ladakh—she'd kept him basically apprised of her plans so he didn't worry—then went on to the string of texts from Eli. Her eyes widened in disbelief as she read through them, then she looked up at Varden.

"You won't believe who's in India and is also headed to Ladakh," she said, sending a brief response to Eli letting him know they were in Phyang, which was less than an hour from Leh's airport. When Varden responded in the negative, she replied, "Hedron."

He swore, his expression a mask of shock. "How? What the hell is he doing here?"

But they both knew. It had to have something to do with the bee.

"Eli saw him in Delhi, and they're both flying in to Leh this morning. So far Hedron hasn't seen Eli, but I'm not sure how he's going to manage being on the same plane and not noticed." Though, Marina thought, if anyone could manage it, she trusted Eli could.

She scrolled through more texts—Eli had been busy! "There's more... Apparently, Hedron is involved in some sort of arrangement with a bottled-water corporation for them to divert runoff from a particular glacier to be bottled exclusively by the water company. The contracts are supposed to be signed here, somewhere near Leh, today or tomorrow. He—Eli—isn't sure about the timing."

Varden was frowning. "Glacier runoff... The Volvoticus bacteria was found in a particular glacier. Could that be the connection?"

"It's got to be." Marina looked out over the countryside. She'd been here in Ladakh for less than twenty-four hours, but she already knew how important the runoff water from the Tazhnev Glacier was to the ecosystem and lifestyle for the Ladakhis.

From her vantage point on this small mountain rise, she could see the Phyang Gompa—the Buddhist monastery hosting the festival—as well as the local village, which consisted of no more than a small street marketplace and a smattering of mud-brick homes dotting the rugged mountains to the south and east.

But several miles to the north, she could see a great spill of water, frozen into a massive, thirty-foot glacial tower. The blue-white ice rose in what had become famously known as an "ice stupa," which was a man-made reserve of water from the winter melt that came down the mountains from the glaciers.

For millennia, the spring ice melt had created rivers and streams that fed the dry, scrubby area, and Marina knew that the flow of water—and its timing—was essential to the livelihood of all those who lived in the villages of Phyang, Hemis, Thiksey, and, indeed, everywhere else in the Ladakh region. But with climate change, what had once been regular flows marked by the seasons had changed radically over the last decades. Now, the melt was happening much faster and too early—during the winter months instead of later in the season. The rapidly melting glaciers now caused floods during the winter and drought during the summer, because the water evaporated too soon in the higher temperatures.

To combat this dangerous change to the ecosystem, a Kashmiri engineer named Sonam Wangchuk had conceived of a way to store the water that flowed too much and too fast in the winter. He used the pressure of the water from the mountains and the force of gravity to channel the flow into a hose attached to a twenty-foot—or taller—pole. The water spilled out and down, creating a frozen tower from the ice melt that was situated in the shadow of the mountains—which would help shield it from the spring and summer sun. The tall, man-made glacier would slowly melt during the agricultural months and provide a more regulated water supply throughout the growing season.

As she looked out over the terrain and contemplated the stark blue-white ice tower, standing out so starkly against the dark brown-gray of the mountains around it, Marina felt a little prickle run over her shoulders. A prickle of *something*…something she was missing, something important.

*Here is the sacred.* The words of her grandfather echoed in her mind. *It is a source of great energy and sacredness. It is one of the centers of Gaia's life…an area that feeds Her even when She is battered and assaulted. It must be protected.*

The vibration of energy, of awareness, shuttled through her more strongly. Her palm, resting on the boulder next to her, tingled as the warmth and life of Gaia pumped through the living rock and into her skin.

*Protect us, Mariska.*

*Protect Gaia. Protect the sacred.*

She looked up and found Varden watching her.

"Now I think I understand," she said quietly, and she felt Gaia shudder beneath her fingers.

"It's this place," he said, lifting his own hand to look at it, as if he too had felt Gaia's tremor. "It's special. It's…"

"It's sacred." She gave a little laugh as she looked around. "Not what one would picture when they think of a sacred or beautiful place—it's so desolate and rugged and cold."

"There are centers of energy in every being," he said, the corners of his eyes crinkling as he squinted against the sun and looked out over the land. "In Gaia too. Some talk about the crossing of ley lines, energy vortexes…the Hindus call them chakras."

"Yes," she said, nodding, understanding where he was headed. Then her eyes bolted wider. "I once saw a map of Earth's chakras— Her main energy centers." She scrambled to her feet, knocking stones and gravel in a little cascade down the side of the incline. "I'm certain there was one here, or near here…in the Himalayas. I don't remember which one—which chakra it was, though." She dragged the phone out of her pocket again. "I don't know if it matters which one, but—"

"The Seventh Chakra," Varden said, still looking out over the land. "If I had to guess, it would be the Crown Chakra, the center of spirituality and enlightenment. Pure energy. The ultimate in universal consciousness."

Marina lowered her phone, the hair all over her body standing on end. "You're right." She looked around, and that prickling over her body became even stronger. "This is a special place. There's a lot going on here, geographically and spiritually, I think," she said slowly. "I'm not sure I understand all of it, but I can *feel* it."

"And our task—your task, and mine by association—is to protect it somehow." Varden shook his head slowly, his expression projecting uncertainty.

Her phone vibrated at that moment, and she looked down. "Eli's on the ground in Leh. He's coming here—it should take him less than an hour."

Varden nodded. "Let's go."

When he reached for her hand, she allowed him to clasp it, and they went down the hill together.

# FORTY-THREE

The single street of Phyang was filled with pedestrians making their way up the hill to the monastery, or *gompa*. Marina was surprised by the number of people who'd come for the festival.

Several hundred by her estimation, and probably others had arrived previously.

And a new influx of arrivals had obviously just come in on the plane in Leh, because there were buses and a few cars arriving—all of which were crammed with people.

She found Eli, noting that he was wearing sunglasses and a battered brown linen fedora pulled down low over his forehead. Trying to blend in and remain unnoticed by Hedron—whom she hadn't yet seen—she assumed. Eli was carrying his backpack along with a duffel bag and was, of course, wearing his Birks. But the rest of his attire was casual—a plain red tee (shockingly without an insect reference) and khaki shorts with lots of pockets.

Eli greeted her with an affectionate hug and full-on-the-mouth kiss, then stepped back and gave her companion a curious look. "Dr. Varden. I'm not sure whether I should be glad to see you again or not."

"Likewise, Dr. Sanchez," Varden replied. His eyes were also hidden by sunglasses, but the rest of his expression was bland. "Yet here we are."

"Yes," Eli replied. "And I have a lot to tell you both. Too complicated by text…and besides, Helen Darrow assumes Father Dart Gun has been tracking me by my phone—that's how he found me in Ann Arbor. Which is why I've had it turned off most of the time. Plus it's damned expensive running on satellite."

"Same here," Marina replied as they eased out of the throngs of people heading up the hill and into the marketplace area—which was filled with wallahs selling food, drink, and other goods to the tourists. She was still scanning the crowd. "Where's Hedron? Did he see you?"

"I made certain he didn't—I sat in the back of the plane and boarded after him. Kept my head down. I'm pretty certain neither he nor Allen Schlueter—he's the water CEO—saw me on the plane or in Leh. I don't know where either of them are now, but I am pretty certain I know where they're going to be."

"And where's that?" Varden asked as they stopped between two vendor stalls.

"Thiksey—a village just a little north of here. There's a dam just outside it."

The wooden poles that created the vendor stalls—tree trunks that had been de-barked—were painted the same rainbow of colors and design that seemed to decorate every surface in India. Tarps made from canvas or plastic covered the tops of each stall and shuddered gently in the breeze. The early dawn chill had long worn off and Marina no longer needed her jacket, but the temperature was by no means hot.

Their position between the two stalls kept them mostly out of sight from the tourists, although Marina noticed that Varden situated himself so that he could keep an eye on the throughway of the marketplace.

"All right, Eli. Let's hear it," she said.

Marina and Varden listened as Eli described how he'd met Allen Schlueter on the plane and then followed him and Hedron—whose appearance was obviously a shock—and booked into the same hotel. "I'm having PTSD from experiencing the traffic in Delhi," he said dryly, then went on to explain how he'd obtained copies of the papers in Schlueter's briefcase.

"Based on the itinerary, the contracts, and some other notes in there, I think I've figured out what's going on," he said. "They're going to execute these contracts that give Allen's company—EcoDraft; remind me never to buy another bottle of water from them again even if I'm here and it's the only kind available—the exclusive rights to divert and bottle the water that's coming from the Tazhnev Glacier.

Apparently, this whole deal is confidential and proprietary and no one knows about this arrangement except the government official—I'm not sure if he's a mayor or some other regional leader or what—who's signing it here."

Marina shook her head. "So they're going to steal the water these people here need to live? Their livelihoods and livestock and the environment? Why would Hedron do this?"

"I think we've already seen Hedron's lack of conscience when it comes to Gaia and human life," said Varden. "More to the point, why would any government official in Ladakh agree to it? It would destroy the ecosystem here."

"Absolutely," replied Eli. "That's why it's all hush-hush—"

"But I don't even see how that could happen," Marina said. "Surely once everyone realizes this company has been diverting the water—and how the hell would they do it in secret anyway?—there's going to be a big problem."

Eli nodded. "Exactly the thoughts that I slept on last night and mulled during the ride to the airport in Delhi—I figured out that closing my eyes made it a little less harrowing. But the nonstop horn tooting was pretty intense. Anyway, the best I can come up with is this, and feel free to poke holes: we're basically in the middle of nowhere here. There's probably numerous passages in or through the mountains, and the rivers and streams from the glaciers are long and winding…no one can monitor *all* of them, *all* the time.

"Maybe they're just going to build this water diversion system—or maybe they already have done—far enough upstream or in some hidden location that it wouldn't be easily found or accessed. I mean, they just need a big pipe, and it uses the gravity from the mountains like when they made the ice stupas, right? And so the people who live here would just write it all off to climate change and the glaciers melting more quickly, so the water flow is interrupted?" He shook his head. "I know this theory barely holds water—ha!—and I'm not sure how all the glacier melt water flow works, but it's the only explanation I can come up with. The Chinese are already doing something of the same nature—not secretly so much as just *doing* it by force: diverting water on land they don't own here in these mountains. It's a big problem."

"Maybe they'll try to blame it on the Chinese or the Pakistanis," Marina said. "I read somewhere that the Chinese—not sure if it's government or industry—are building dams in an effort to contain and divert some of the water running down from the mountains—"

"There's a dam," Varden said suddenly. "We drove past it—did you see it, Marina?"

She remembered it now. "Yes. It was just to the northeast of Leh. But I don't..." A sudden rush of prickling energy blasted over her. "Wait. Wait a minute...there was a news report not very long ago..." The vibration of energy was growing stronger, lifting the hair all over her body. She closed her eyes, appreciating that neither Eli nor Varden interrupted or distracted her as she tried to discern what her subconscious was telling her.

When she opened her eyes, she felt clarity. "There was a news report about a dam breaking in Uttarakhand—somewhere in the Himalayas, so it has to be in this general region. The dam was broken when a large piece of glacier detached and flowed downriver, causing a huge flood and crashing into the dam. The flood covered an entire village, destroying it and trapping people inside tunnels. It was a disaster of broad proportions, and it will be a long time—years, because of its remote location—before the area is cleaned up and restored."

Varden was looking at her; she could almost see the intensity of his jade eyes behind his shades. "The dam here...is it made from metal?"

She was nodding as he spoke. "I don't know, but there would have to be steel or iron parts to it, right? Bolts or retaining rods, or even the walls of the dam itself... Am I crazy?" She looked at both of them—though it was difficult to read their expressions with their eyes hidden by sunglasses. Eli was muttering something in Spanish. "I'm not crazy, am I? We know Hedron has the Volvoticus bacteria. Could this be his next demonstration?"

Varden's expression was stark. "If something were to happen to the dam here—"

"This whole freaking place would be destroyed," Eli said. "And if it happened, say, today or tomorrow, with all of these people here for the festival—"

"A disaster," Varden finished. "Utter disaster."

"And no one would be paying any attention to what was going on up in the mountains…for a long, long time," Marina said quietly. "Any change of water flow could be attributed to the disaster of the flood, climate change, and whatever other fairy tale they want to sell the people."

"But a disaster like that would bring responses from all over—you know, disaster responses," Eli said. "People like Marina, and medics, and all of that. Lots of people here to see what's going on."

"What better way to camouflage the labor needed to create or implement the water diversion?" Marina said.

She was calm, because now she knew. It was the only thing that made sense.

"And, oh, Eli…" She grabbed his arm because now she understood even more. "If the ecosystem here were to be destroyed, or even significantly disrupted…what would happen to the bee?"

He swore again in Spanish and yanked off his glasses. "She couldn't survive," he said. "If her habitat is destroyed—and there are so many flora and fauna specific to this region—it would directly impact the Apis patricia."

"Not to mention the snow leopard," Varden said, looking at Marina from behind his dark lenses. "And the entire energy vortex that's centered here in the region. It's only as strong as its ecosystem."

She shivered again, and the image of Snow Leopard, the same one who'd appeared to her in the Lower World, flashed through her mind.

"Right," she said quietly. "So how do we stop this?"

# FORTY-FOUR

"Surely they wouldn't actually be signing the contracts at the dam itself," Varden said.

"Why not? What better way to make sure everyone holds up their ends of the bargain?" said Eli. "Sign the contract, apply the bacteria to some vulnerable part of the dam—"

"And then get caught up in the ensuing flood?" Varden retorted.

"They've got to have a way to get out of there quickly," Marina said. "A vehicle or small plane? But it would be nearly impossible to land or take off in a plane around here."

"Probably an ATV of some sort," Varden said. "And we're going to need some way to get to the dam ourselves if you really think that's where it's going to happen." He frowned at Eli.

"Have you seen the vehicles they have here?" Eli replied, apparently dismissing Varden's skepticism. "Deathtraps. We might have to go back to Leh to find something that'll make it on these roads."

"If it's not a dam, what else could it be? There aren't any bridges around here," Marina said thoughtfully. "Or highways with lots of vehicles."

"No, but there are things like that," Varden said, pointing.

They all looked over, down the road a bit. Marina saw exactly what he meant: there was a heavy metal grid that reminded her of the type of scaffolding one might see against a large building. In this case, the metal framework was rusted and old, and it covered the entire face of a mud-and-brick building from ground to four stories high. She wasn't certain what its purpose was, this metal grid, but it was a large and heavy structure. She couldn't tell whether it actually held the building upright, and it couldn't be security type of grid—the spaces were larger than a picture window and wouldn't keep anyone from climbing inside.

Whatever its purpose, the rusted metal grid was heavy and dangerous, and if Hedron decided to use his bacteria on something like that, the demolition would surely cause injury and death…especially with so many people out on the street.

"The roof of the *gompa*—the monastery—also has metal pipes and structure," Varden said. "But most other construction here is that mud and brick, and wood."

Marina was just about to reply when she caught sight of a familiar face in the crowded marketplace.

She might not have recognized or even noticed Manish if he hadn't been staring right at her. "I'll be right back," she said, darting off into the throng of people.

Manish was slick and fast as an eel, and Marina dodged and ducked through rivers of people in order to keep him in sight. He knew he was being followed; he'd seen her. In fact, she was certain he'd *wanted* her to see him…and to follow him.

She thought she heard someone calling her name, but she wasn't about to stop for Eli or Varden. This was too important.

"Manish," she called when he left the crowded area of the small village and started off the road and onto the rocky, rugged countryside that led up the side of the small mountain. "Please wait! I need to speak to you!"

Not only did she want to ask him about the bee, but she felt that someone who lived here—who would be affected directly—needed to know what Allen Schleuter and Hedron had planned.

She hurried after Manish, rushing over rubble and grinding over gritty soil as he strode on what passed for a trail, winding along the side of the rough mountain.

At last, she came around an outcropping of boulder and found a small cluster of growth on a compact piece of flatland. The now-familiar patches of scrubby grass grew among gray rocks, along with bright pink flowers and the miniature sagebrush-like plants she'd noticed earlier.

Manish had stopped. He was not alone. An elderly man sat there beneath the single tree that grew on the tiny mesa—a juniper whose branches were laden with berries.

For a moment, Marina was struck by the similarity of this elderly man, folded into a seated position beneath the protection of a tree, to that of Lev the last few times she'd seen him. Journeyed with him.

But it wasn't her grandfather who sat there. The old man was obviously native to the region, with weather-beaten skin brown-red and a broad forehead. His sparse hair was still mostly dark, but was threaded with gray. Marina couldn't begin to guess his age—anywhere from sixty to a hundred—but his hands were knobby and arthritic, and his legs, covered by loose cotton trousers, appeared slender and fragile as sticks. He wore a matching tunic, its edges embroidered beautifully. His very presence gave her the impression that he was some sort of elder or tribal leader. Perhaps a shaman.

"Hello," she said, approaching slowly. "I'm Marin—Mariska Aleksandrov."

She didn't know why she gave her birth name instead of the name she'd used for over thirty years, but it seemed the right thing to do.

Manish glanced at the elderly man, who spoke to him in a language Marina didn't understand. Then he translated for her. "This is Gulam. He says, 'Show me your foot, Mariska Aleksandrov.'"

She understood that he was asking to see the Skaladeska mark on her heel, and she sat on a boulder in order to comply by removing her shoe and sock.

When she thrust her heel toward Gulam, he merely nodded, then looked at Manish once more.

Although Gulam didn't speak, the younger man—his grandson? great-grandson?—seemed to know what to say.

"I have been punished by my people for showing the blond woman about the bee," said Manish in good English. "When Snow Leopard led me to you and I saw your marking, I thought you were meant to know, but I dared not make the same mistake a second time. I thought the other woman was the one foretold..." He trailed off when Gulam said something sharply. Manish nodded, his head hanging a little, and

Marina took it to understand he'd been reprimanded again for his error once more.

And apparently the elderly man understood some English.

"I'm not here to harm the bee," she said, speaking to Manish but looking at Gulam. She pointed to the mark on the bottom of her heel. "I am the Daughter of Gaia. I'm here to protect Her, and the bee… and this place. I also bring an urgent warning."

She waited while Manish translated for Gulam. In the distance, she could hear the sounds of the festival beginning in the village below—the drumming and jangle of music, rhythmic singing, shouting, clapping.

She thought she heard her name being called, faintly in the distance—somewhere below—but chose not to respond. The arrival of Eli or Varden could disrupt this uneasy moment.

Gulam spoke, and Manish translated once more. "Speak this warning."

She told them, quickly and as simply as possible, about their fears related to the dam. She ended by saying, "This man, Hedron Burik, wears the same marking." She gestured to her foot. "But he is not a Son of Gaia, and he is not to be trusted. He has betrayed Gaia and my people…and he intends to betray Gaia here, in this most sacred place, with one of your own people."

When Manish finished translating her long explanation, Gulam rose to his feet and, on stick legs, walked to her. She rose from her perch on the boulder and realized she was several inches taller than the wizened old man.

"Do you know who this person is?" asked Gulam in English. "The one of our people who would do this?"

"There is a contract…I heard the name…" Marina tried to remember what Eli had said. "Lobzang. It was Lobzang…something."

The expression on Gulam's wrinkled countenance turned fierce and furious. Marina felt more than a flicker of fear as she saw the way his eyes lit and burned. His anger rolled off him, and she sensed the strength and power Gulam wielded.

When he lifted slender, wiry arms to place his hands on her shoulders, Marina felt a different sort of sizzle of awareness and energy rush through her. Her knees trembled, then gave out as everything went black.

# FORTY-FIVE

"**M**arina can take care of herself," said Eli.

He'd previously met Varden only once, briefly, and had thus reserved judgment on the man. And because Marina didn't talk about Varden—who was apparently an emergency room physician when he wasn't promoting ecoterrorism—Eli wasn't certain what *their* relationship was. Antagonistic for sure, but there was definitely something else there. Some sort of connection. Perhaps even grudging respect.

"It's my job to look after her," muttered Varden, still looking out over the crowd where Marina had disappeared. "What the hell was she thinking, going off like that?"

"Marina can take care of herself," Eli repeated, needing to remind himself of the same thing. After all, Hedron Burik was in the vicinity, and he wanted nothing more than to get rid of Marina. Eli understood that, at least, was due to a rivalry among the Skaladeskas.

Eli was just about to say something else when he caught sight of a head with short, dark curls making its way among the throng of people. He froze, then immediately started pushing his way through the crowd after the tall man.

No way. There was *no way* Father Dart Gun had found his way here…was there?

*He's probably tracking your phone's location.* That was what Helen Darrow had said, back in Ann Arbor. But Eli had kept his phone off as much as possible during his travels and even while he was here. There was no way the priest had tracked him here to Ladakh so quickly.

Unless he just assumed Eli was coming to where the bee was,

which, if that was the case, was a good confirmation that he was in the right place.

Or did the priest have another reason for being here?

If indeed it had been him.

"Did you see her?" Varden was right on his heels.

"No, but I think I might have seen the priest," Eli said over his shoulder, still making his way through the people. Who'd have thought there'd be such a crowd here in the middle of nowhere? Although he guessed maybe the people who lived here didn't have all that much to do besides celebrate the triumph of good over evil. And there were definitely a good number of tourists as well. It was the biggest festival in the area. Apparently, people really came from miles around.

"The priest who attacked you?" Varden said.

"Yes. And now he's gone—or whoever I saw is gone. It might not have been him. But it sure looked like him from behind," Eli muttered. "But there's no way he could have tracked me here this fast."

"Unless he's hacking your email for your travel plans," Varden commented.

"Nope," replied Eli. "I didn't send anything to my email. And I bought my ticket to Leh right at the airport in New Delhi. So I don't see how it could be him." He edged away from the crowd. "Now what do we do? Wait here for Marina to return, or try to find out what's going on at the dam—and stop them from destroying it and killing all these people?"

Whatever Varden's response would have been was drowned out by a sudden cheer from the people in the marketplace and along the small road that led up to the monastery. The sounds of drumming and other percussion filtered down to them, and people began to sing and chant and whistle as the performers began to parade their way down the hill.

The Tsedup festival had begun, and Varden and Eli were caught right in the middle of it.

The performers—the monks of Phyang—were dressed in long, loose tunics of every color imaginable. Their costumes were decorated with detailed embroidery, and each of the dancers wore a mask with a large white face and an elaborate headdress. They carried drums and instruments that reminded Eli of maracas, and the place was filled with activity: dancing, singing, rattling, shaking sounds, the dull thudding of drums that he felt deep in his chest.

Even the spectators got into the mood, chanting and shouting, swaying and whistling.

It was like being in the middle of a parade-like rock concert, Eli thought, but with brighter colors. And a lot more energy. It was a *pure* sort of energy, a clean, simple, primitive feeling that surrounded him as the people here participated in a centuries-old rite in gratitude for good conquering evil.

Varden nudged him. "He's here. I can feel him."

"Who? The priest?"

"Hedron," Varden said, already on the move. Instead of plunging into the crowd, or heading in the direction of the parade that was making its way down the side of the mountain, Varden went off, away from the people.

Eli didn't hesitate, although he realized that if they left the marketplace where Marina had last seen them, she wouldn't be able to find them easily when she returned.

Unless Hedron already had her.

He hoofed it faster, keeping Varden's dark blond head in sight and ignoring the tiny stones that got kicked up and caught in his Birks.

And what did Varden mean by he "felt" him? Had he not even seen Hedron but somehow sensed he was here? Sure, Eli had felt the intense energy of this place the minute he stepped on the ground in Leh. There was something very special about this rocky, desolate area—there *had* to be if Jesus had lived here and kept bees.

Which was, Eli reminded himself with a thrill of excitement, part of the reason he was here. He *needed* to see that bee, her habitat, her hive. He wanted to prove to himself that his theory was correct. He wanted to let those fuzzy little lovelies creep all over his arm and buzz around his face.

And then there was the honey, which had healed his dart wound so rapidly. It was miraculous! He wondered what else it could do. It could change medical history, such a treatment.

He patted his pocket, making sure the small pot was still there.

There'd been no way he was keeping it anywhere but on him at all times. Even on the plane, he'd carried it on—thankful that he'd thought to cool the honey so that it was solid and not a liquid that would cause the TSA to confiscate it before he boarded.

They'd been making their way from the center of the small village where all the celebratory activity was, leaving the noise and revelry behind them, when suddenly the sounds of the festivities changed.

There were shouts—angry, urgent ones—and the music and drumming ceased. Eli stopped in spite of himself and turned to look; something was wrong.

Still on the same level as the village, he didn't have a good view, but he could hear. It sounded as if the festival had been interrupted, and that someone was speaking…and everyone was listening.

He couldn't hear what was being said, but there was something in the timbre of the speaker's voice that made the hair on his body stand on end. Whoever was talking, whoever had the wherewithal and influence to interrupt the great festival, was important and powerful. People were listening. Eli wanted to listen—he was drawn into the speech and began to edge back toward the crowd.

Whatever was happening was important. Vital. Urgent.

And then, all at once, a great shout—a roar—rose from the crowd. It was the sound of fury and outrage, no longer one of revelry and celebration.

"What's happening?" Varden said.

"I don't know, but they're angry…and I don't think they're angry at him," Eli said, having just now spotted an old, wizened man who seemed to be the one who'd been speaking. He was standing on the shoulders of two tall, much younger men, held in place by a strong grip as he delivered his fiery, furious speech to the crowd around him.

The elderly man couldn't have weighed more than ninety pounds dripping wet, but he had somehow interrupted the celebration and was pointing into the distance…and then back to the people surrounding him.

Suddenly, a cry rose from the crowd.

"What are they saying?" Varden asked.

Eli listened; it was difficult to make out the syllables, and he wasn't even certain if it was English. But the crowd had now started to move. En masse, the people—including the monks, still dressed in their festival finery—began to follow the two young men who held the old man on their shoulders.

"It sounds like… Wait!" Eli's eyes widened. "They're saying something about Lobzang. Lobzang Nomgyal was the name of the local government official cited in the contracts I copied! They're calling for him—and they don't sound happy." He looked at Varden. "They must have found out what he was going to do. That he was going to sell them out and allow their village to be destroyed—and their people killed."

"Marina," said Varden, stopping. "She told them. She must have told them somehow."

"And now Hedron's plans are going to be ruined," said Eli. For the first time, he saw Rue Varden smile.

"Yes. He'll be fortunate to leave this place alive. They're angry, and that is a powerful shaman who leads them."

Eli shivered a little. But he had no real sympathy for the water CEO and his henchman.

You mess with Gaia, you get your ass handed to you by her and her people.

Because Eli knew for a fact that these people, these mountain-dwelling people whose ancestors had lived here for millennia, understood and respected the Earth and her power.

# FORTY-SIX

When Marina opened her eyes, she found herself slumped on the boulder where she'd sat to remove her shoes for Gulam. She was alone, and there was nothing to indicate that he or Manish had been there. Even the tree under which the elderly man had been seated now appeared smaller than before.

She pulled herself to her feet and looked around, wondering how long she'd been out—and what exactly had happened. She felt a little achy, probably from collapsing unexpectedly onto the rock, but had no other residual symptoms.

But she didn't hesitate very long. Eli and Varden would surely be looking for her—in fact, she pulled out her mobile phone to check for communication.

Lots of missed messages and calls from both of them.

She messaged them both back at the same time to let them know she was all right and would head back to the marketplace right away, then stuck the phone back in her pocket. She was just about to begin the rough walk down the side of the mountain when she felt something.

Someone was watching her.

The skin at the back of her neck prickled and she looked up. Her breath caught.

Snow Leopard was there, standing several feet above her on a rocky ledge. He looked down at her with steady blue-gray eyes.

Marina met his eyes with hers and felt her heart trip as their gazes connected. He was a magnificent creature. Lean and muscular—she swore she could see the vibrations of his barely leashed energy, trembling beneath his fur. She'd never seen anything as beautiful as his coat, with the splotches of shades of gray and black over white, and more shades of gray. His small ears were upright, and as she looked up at him, he made a sound.

A meow.

Marina smiled, for that sound was so unexpected, coming from such a large and ferocious-looking creature. But ferocious though he might appear, she felt no fear. He was close enough to easily launch himself down upon her, but he seemed to have no intention of doing so.

After a moment, he turned and began to walk away. He'd taken no more than two or three steps when he paused and looked over his shoulder.

She heard the voice in her head: *Are you coming?*

And so she followed.

The path wasn't easy, but Marina was not about to lose sight of the large cat. It was half climbing and half walking along rocky ledges and hairpin turns—a journey that could never be taken by any vehicle.

She felt the energy of the Earth even more strongly as she followed the cat into a thick mountainside forest where the trees grew perpendicular to the slanted ground and fought for the meager sunlight.

There were eagles and hawks, goats and hares, and sparse growth that included spindly bushes, short, sharp-bladed grass, and a few flowers of pink, yellow, or blue.

By the time she'd followed the cat for nearly an hour, Marina was out of breath and feeling lightheaded. She'd taken her dose of altitude sickness medication, but even that couldn't alleviate every symptom. The cat didn't seem to notice or care that Marina wasn't four-footed with large, stable paws—he kept walking.

The forest gave way to another mountainside, and when Snow Leopard headed toward the nearest rocky outcropping, Marina sighed but kept going.

She had to be several miles from the village—from any sort of civilization. She'd seen nothing to indicate that any creature other than the four-legged or winged ones had been this way, other than the very crude, barely discernible path on which the great cat walked so nimbly.

A few yards later, her guide stopped to drink from a small stream tumbling down the mountainside. Marina took the opportunity to sit on the nearest boulder and drink from her own water bottle, which was carabined to her belt loop.

Snow Leopard didn't seem to mind that she was taking a break, and so Marina pulled out her phone. She realized she hadn't updated her companions on this new development—and sure enough, there were more messages and missed calls.

She sent a brief text explaining what she could, then looked up to see Snow Leopard watching her.

He was definitely eyeing her mobile phone, and there was a distinct sneer in his expression—the sort only felines could pull off.

*No phones, huh?* Her mouth didn't move, but she heard the words as if she'd spoken them aloud.

*No.*

She hesitated, then powered down her phone. All at once, she felt different. Lighter. Her head was clearer.

There was no longer any sort of impure vibration or energy emitting from the electronic device in her pocket.

*Yes.* The cat gave her what could only be described as a smile. And then he began to walk on.

Marina smothered a groan, but she followed him. She was in excellent shape, but this was beyond challenging even for her—especially since she didn't have any equipment to help with the climbing walk.

But her footsteps were definitely lighter, and she became even more aware of the world around her. There was more color, more sound, more texture…the scents of flowers and water and loam…

And suddenly there was Lev.

*Grandfather.*

*Mariska. You've come.*

He was, as always, sitting beneath a tree, cupped by large roots that created the arms of a chair for him, and a moss-covered mound beneath. The leaves of this tree were nothing like the other trees she'd seen on the mountainside; these were all the colors of the rainbow, and they danced in a pleasant breeze.

Snow Leopard had gone; Marina understood he had merely been her guide. Though the cat had disappeared, she thanked him as she walked closer to her grandfather.

And that was when she realized Lev was not alone.

Three other people sat there as well, each beneath their own tree. There shouldn't have been room for all of those massive trees so close together, but somehow, like the pieces of a kaleidoscope picture, they merged and connected together while remaining distinct.

Marina felt the energy of them all as if it were a blow to her body: solid, strong, vibrational, pure.

Having never found reason to praise or worship any entity—other than Gaia, and even what she felt for Mother Earth wasn't what she would call worship—Marina felt her knees wobble. She understood here, now, how people felt when they were in the presence of those known as Enlightened Ones.

And without being told, she knew all of those who sat with her grandfather.

Jesus of Nazareth.

Siddhartha Gautama, the Buddha.

Mohammed.

She recognized them all, knew their names without being told. Each of them, with their dark skin and dark hair, each of different age, shimmered with light. And then she saw others, countless others, in the background, hovering near and above and around this quartet, extending to infinity, each with their own tree—each with their connection to Gaia and to each other through their sacredness.

No one spoke, but the four of them—the ones she thought of as the Great Ones—looked at her with kind, knowing eyes. She felt the force of their combined energy and…the only word that made sense was *holiness.*

*Sacredness.*

She stood there, simply absorbing, and understood somehow that she'd done what she was meant to do…and that they, these four powerful, sacred beings—and the other, less distinct ones—were acknowledging that.

Her vision wavered and the lights around them began to fade, and they, too, began to fade. Marina felt a whisper of movement behind her, and she turned, expecting to see Snow Leopard to lead her back, but it was Varden.

He wasn't looking beyond her, at Lev and the others...he was looking only at her as he emerged from the forest that had somehow sprung up around them.

*Mariska.*

# FORTY-SEVEN

M arina opened her eyes.

She was back where she'd started, back where she'd met Gulam and where Snow Leopard had led her away—on a small ledge not far above the village.

Varden and Eli were there. Sitting, as if they'd been waiting.

"She's returned," said Varden as Marina blinked to clear the last of her vision.

"He said not to speak to you or touch you, not to pull you out of the journey," Eli said, coming over to her, kneeling in front of where she still sat on that same boulder. He put gentle hands on one of her knees. "That coming out too fast can leave part of your soul there—Marina, are you all right?"

She nodded. She was. She was more than all right.

She glanced up at Varden. He was looking at her, and once again she wondered how long he'd been in her journey and what he'd seen.

This time, she didn't feel as awkward and violated. But the intimacy still felt strange.

"Did you see them?" she asked Varden, even as she closed her hands over Eli's.

"Who?" asked Eli as Varden shook his head.

"I saw no one but you," he replied.

She drew in a shuddering breath, but before she could explain, Gulam appeared.

He didn't suddenly appear as if by magic; he walked from around the tree where he'd been sitting earlier. He might have been approaching from another direction, unseen, or he might have materialized from nowhere. She didn't know, and it didn't matter.

Manish was with him, but it was the elderly man who drew her attention. His eyes were lit with what could only be described as fire—power, determination—and she felt the vibration of energy rolling from his slender, fragile body.

"I will take you to the bee," he said. Marina realized that he spoke to her in Skaladeska—a language she never remembered learning, but one that had somehow been implanted in her mind.

"Thank you," she replied in the same language, realizing also that this was a show of gratitude from Gulam and his people.

Gulam looked at Varden and Eli, and Marina understood he was asking whether they were to accompany them. Or perhaps he was indicating that they were not invited.

But Marina couldn't do that to Eli—or to Varden. "They are my trusted friends, and I would not have known what was happening to your land and your people without them."

Gulam closed his eyes for a moment. When he opened them, he gave her a single nod.

She turned to Varden and Eli, who'd watched silently. Varden would have understood the conversation in Skaladeska, of course, but Eli would not.

"He will take us to the bee," she said, and was rewarded by the blast of excitement in Eli's expression.

He gave a reverent bow to the shaman and thanked him in English.

"Tomorrow. Today, we celebrate," Gulam said, gesturing off to the village and *gompa*.

The sounds of drumming and chanting had already begun once more.

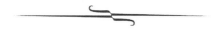

Despite the Tsedup festival being interrupted by Gulam and his call to action—which had obviously put an end to Allen Schleuter's intent to sign contracts with Lobzang Nomgyal and divert the glacier

ice melt—the attendees and performers seemed to have had no problem picking up where they'd left off.

In fact, Eli thought, it appeared as if the revelers would have an
even stronger reason for celebrating now that good had conquered evil
once more on this very day.

He and Marina stood off to the side with the festival-goers and
watched the dancing and drumming. Varden had gone off somewhere, which was fine with Eli. The man was pretty intense.

But a little while after he disappeared, Varden was back. "The water
CEO is gone," he told them. "I talked to Manish. Schlueter took off
when everything went bad and hired someone to drive him back to
Leh."

Marina nodded and frowned. "But Hedron is still here. I'm sure he
is." She shrugged when Eli looked at her. "It's just a feeling I have. And
he still has the Volvoticus bacteria…as far as we know."

"I think you're right. He could still try to destroy the dam." Varden looked up and around. "Or something else around here—just to
make a statement."

"He wants to damage—even destroy—the ecosystem of this
region," Marina said. "It's a unique, powerful center of energy. By
disrupting or destroying the area or those who live here, he hurts
Gaia—and Lev as well, because he's connected here. Everything is
tied together…just as we all are. From the beginning, Lev told me to
protect the bee. Protect the sacred. This place—this entire place—is a
center of sacredness."

"We'll have to keep watch for him," Eli said, scanning the crowd.

"Unless he finds us first," replied Varden.

And, Eli realized suddenly, if Hedron learned that Marina had been
the one to spoil his plans by telling the shaman, he would definitely be
looking for Marina—and for revenge. Eli edged a little closer to her.

His attention remained divided between the wildly garbed dancers
and watching the crowd for signs of Hedron as the people pressed into
each other along the edges of the street.

The costumes worn by the monks were large and complicated—
some as wide as they were tall, and some with extra height so that the
masks hovered and danced ten feet above the crowd. Lots of flow-

ing sleeves, tunics, and headdresses. Lots of color and a whirlwind of activity.

Lots of noise: drumming, chanting, singing, shouting.

It was a crazy and wonderful experience—far better than the wild, energetic Mardi Gras parade Eli had once attended, or any concert-palooza he could imagine.

Maybe it was because he couldn't understand anything they were singing or chanting. Maybe it was the way the beat of the drums reverberated through his center, as if he were part of the rhythmic music. Maybe it was the place—being here, in this sacred, special area, with a people who lived close to the ruggedness of the earth and celebrated the simple things.

He didn't know; he just understood that he'd become part of the festival in some primitive way.

Eli didn't know how long he'd been standing there, engrossed in the festivities, when Marina suddenly tensed next to him.

"Hedron," she said, gripping his arm. "There."

She didn't point, obviously not wanting to make a scene, but both Varden and Eli heard her and began to follow her as she slipped through the crowd.

It was slow going, pushing through the throng of people. Marina led the way, but she soon lost sight of Hedron.

Still, she kept going until they were free of the pack, and on a slightly higher elevation. Just a short way up the side of a small, rocky hill, which gave a good view of the colorful dancers and those gathered to watch and participate.

Varden came to close to her, his attention sharp as he scanned the area. "Lost him, have we?"

She nodded, but the back of her neck prickled. He was nearby; she could feel the animosity, the intensity of Hedron's attention on her. Directed at her. The fact that they were both Skaladeska made it easier for her to sense the loathing and hatred he felt for her.

A rock skittered from somewhere above, landing on the ground next to her. They all looked up to see Hedron, who stood several yards above. He was watching them, hands on his hips, fury in his eyes.

Wordlessly, Marina took off after him. Varden shouted something—he wanted her to stop, to wait—but she didn't listen. Hedron was not going to get away from her now. Not today.

She scrambled up the side of the mountain, following the rough, patchy barely-a-path as it twisted and turned around and up.

Varden and Eli were behind her, the former right on her tail.

She caught sight of Hedron up another ten yards, heading around a large outcropping of rock, climbing ever higher. What was he doing? There was nowhere to go but up. What was he going to do?

And then she saw it, as she came around a curve to yet another rise in the path: a large *iron* grid that had been built into the side of the mountain to keep the unstable, rocky wall from tumbling down.

"No," she shouted, scrambling faster, looking behind to see whether Varden and Eli had noticed it too. "Stop!"

Once Hedron applied the Volvoticus bacteria to the grid—even a small area of it—the cause would be lost. The grid would disintegrate and the mountain wall would collapse, crashing down onto the celebrating people below.

Hedron stood on the ledge, watching her as she and her companions struggled to make their way to his level before it was too late…

With a sly smile, he unslung from his shoulders the backpack he'd been wearing. From her angle below, she couldn't see exactly what he was doing as he let the bag settle on the ground, but she had a feeling she knew.

She already knew.

"Hedron, no!" she cried. "Don't do it! It will solve nothing!"

But he rose from a crouch and brandished a plastic spray bottle.

From behind, Varden swore and pushed past Marina as she stumbled on a pile of stones. She caught herself on the side of the mountain as Eli grabbed her elbow from behind.

"He's got the bacteria," she said, out of breath, then dodged a rock that tumbled down from beneath Varden's agile feet as he hoofed his way up.

"Damned sandals not so good for climbing," Eli muttered, but he kept going as she clambered on.

Varden and Hedron were both out of sight, but when she got to a short, relatively flat stretch and ran, she saw Hedron.

He stood there proudly, holding up the bottle. And then, keeping eye contact with Marina, he knelt and, with a flourish, sprayed the piece of iron nearest him.

He managed one or two squirts before Varden appeared from nowhere, launching himself at Hedron. As the two men tumbled to the ground, dislodging rocks and stones to rain down the side of the mountain, Marina began to run.

She could hear the sounds of their struggle as she drew nearer—this last bit was rough going but a direct path to where Hedron had been standing. She couldn't see them, for she was almost directly below, and she had to use handholds to help pull herself up the steep incline. More rocks and stones pattered down, rolling over the edge from where the men fought and down to where Eli was making his way up a little more slowly.

When Marina got to the top, barely able to see over the ledge, it was just in time to see Hedron's arm swing out in a wide arc, then shoot toward Varden. The long, shiny blade Hedron held plunged into Varden's side, and her friend jolted, freezing in shock as he fell to the ground.

Hedron stumbled backward, a dark grin on his face, the knife still in his hand, poised to plunge again, when he saw Marina.

With a cry of rage and desperation, she launched herself up and onto the ground and stood facing him. She had nothing to fight him with. Nothing to protect herself from the knife, now dripping with Varden's blood…nothing to keep Hedron from spraying more of the bacteria on the protective metal grid.

She felt the ground move beneath her feet, and the rage rushed up from the earth inside of her. "How dare you," she cried—and realized she was screaming in Skaladeska. "How dare you defile Gaia!"

She saw the large branch on the ground, lunged to seize it, thanking Gaia for putting it there within reach, and began to stalk Hedron.

Varden wasn't moving, but his eyes were open. Blood drenched his shirt, spilling over his hand, pooling on the dusty, stony ground. Glazed with shock and pain, his eyes found hers and held. When they connected, Marina felt a jolt of power, and she swung the branch as she lunged toward Hedron.

He sprang nimbly to the side, and the solid branch whuffed harmlessly through the air. Marina steadied herself, refusing to look at Varden, focused only on Hedron.

*Gaia, help me.*

She thrust out with the branch as if she were fencing, causing Hedron to dance out of reach. He still held the bloody knife, but it could do her no harm at this distance.

"Waste your time all you like," Hedron told her. "It's too late. Soon, this very ground on which you stand will tumble below." He gestured to the metal framework, old, rusted, but still very efficient… except when infected by the bacteria. "I can see that it's already eating away at it…and even as the bacteria does its job, and your friend's blood seeps into the ground, you stand here, helpless to do nothing."

The truth of his taunts enraged her, galvanized her, and Marina lifted the branch once more and steadied it—this time like a baseball bat. She lunged and swung at the same time, shouting something in Skaladeska that even she didn't understand—

And when she connected with Hedron, she felt the shock of the branch slamming into his arm, she lost her breath for a moment.

And then, as if in slow motion, she watched as he staggered, caught himself…and then the very bit of earth on which he stood *shifted…* right before her eyes.

The ground erupted, upending him, just enough…

And he went over the edge, tumbling out of sight with a loud scream.

# FORTY-EIGHT

Marina ran to Varden first, but even as she crouched next to him, she could look over the edge.

Hedron had fallen, not very far, but he must have hit some rocky outcropping on his way down, because he lay still. His head was bent at a strange angle, but more horrifically, blood streamed from his ears and nose.

"Rue," she said, frantically pulling away Varden's shirt to see the wound.

It was bad. So bad.

She already knew, from his labored breathing, the color of his pallor, that there was little hope. His belly shivered, his torso bare now as she tore away the thin shirt and saw the ragged, ugly, gaping laceration. It wasn't merely a clean slice—Hedron had shoved, twisted, jerked, cutting deeply into Varden.

She pressed Varden's shirt against the wound as hard as she could, pressuring it to stop the bleeding even though she knew inside the damage was worse.

"Mariska," he managed. "The...grid."

"It's too late," she said. "The bacteria—" But she scrambled to her feet, hating to leave his side but she wanted to look. Maybe it wasn't working. Maybe—

But it was. She could see the difference already; if it hadn't been such a dire moment, she would have been fascinated by the sight of the metal corroding, disappearing *before her eyes.*

Only moments ago—maybe five, seven, eight minutes—Hedron had sprayed onto one of the metal posts that jutted up a foot above the rocky edge. Now the upright part of the post had gone, and the metal rod was disappearing below the edge.

It was only a matter of time before the rest of it was eaten away, disappeared…and the side of the mountain collapsed in a deadly avalanche.

"It's too late," she said, scrambling back to Varden. His color was bad, his breathing unsteady. She could almost see his blood pressure dropping. How was she ever going to get him off this mountain? Get him help?

"Warn," he gasped. His lids fluttered over those green eyes, still intense even now as he swam with pain and semiconsciousness.

"Marina!"

She turned to see Eli, tottering into sight from below.

He was at her side in a moment, and she didn't need to give him any information other than: "Varden needs help. And we need to warn the others."

But there was no way to get the information down to the Tsedup revelers; she and Eli were too far away, too high up, and the sounds of the festivities would drown out any warnings they might make.

All at once, Eli's eyes widened. He pulled to his feet, digging in the pocket of his cargo shorts.

Marina felt a prickling over her shoulders, over her entire body, as he pulled the ancient clay pot from his pants and her eyes fastened on it.

Was it possible?

His fingers shook a little as he opened it, offered it to her, and Marina didn't wait. She thrust her fingers down into the honey, scooping a good portion of it into the cup of her fingers.

Immediately, she felt a shimmering sort of warmth from the substance, which was sticky and oozing just like any other honey. But it smelled different—it smelled like something undefinable. Pleasant, beautiful, pure. Certainly not old and musty, aged and useless…

She pulled the shirt away from Varden's wound, then hesitated. Putting honey—millennia-old honey—into an open wound… Was she crazy? Was that EMT malpractice?

"Do it," Varden whispered. His eyes met hers, the haze evaporating for an instant. "*Mariska.*"

She drew in a shuddering breath, then, without thinking on it any further, offered up a prayer to Gaia, and to any powerful being who might care to listen, and began to slather the honey over the pulsing wound. She dipped her fingers inside the opening, pushing the warm, shimmery honey into him, hoping and praying she wasn't killing Varden even faster.

It wasn't until she looked over toward Eli, to scoop her fingers through the pot once more, that she realized he'd moved. He was at the edge of the mountain, by the grid.

"Eli?" she cried, a little desperate. "What—" And then, with a sudden rush of understanding, she knew.

He crouched near the edge, right where Hedron had sprayed the bacteria onto the rusty metal. And when Eli looked over at her, his eyes were bright. The tip of his nose was a little red.

"It worked," he said. His voice was rusty. "It's working."

He pulled himself to his feet and came back to Marina and Varden, kneeling next to them. "I didn't know—but I put the honey on the metal where it was being eaten away…and I watched. And it stopped. *It stopped it.* I—I think the honey s-smothered the bacteria."

He'd offered her the clay pot as he spoke. She looked down into it—there was only a small amount left.

"Use it," Eli said, nodding at Varden.

She took the last bit, smeared it over Varden's laceration once more, then sat back. Her eyes were wet, her fingers trembled, and her breathing was unsteady and harsh.

"I don't know if it's working," she said, looking down at Varden. He seemed to have settled a little—his breathing was smoother and those wild green eyes were closed. She reached for his hand, clasped her fingers around it, and settled her other hand onto the surface of the earth.

She closed her eyes and drew energy from Gaia into her fingers and palm, up through her wrist and arm and into her entire being, and asked it to rush through her to help Gaia's son. The vibration, the heat, the healing, trundled through her…and when she opened her eyes some time later—she didn't know how long—she found Eli watching her.

His dark eyes were still wet, and he sat cross-legged, still, reverent. "It's miraculous," he said, holding up the small clay pot. "It's a miracle. She's a miracle."

She looked down and saw that the blood was no longer pumping from Varden's side. His color was better.

That didn't mean that he was healing on the inside, she told herself. It didn't mean he was going to be all right.

But when he opened his eyes and they found hers immediately, she felt the jolt when they connected. Powerful and real.

"Thank you," he said. His voice was stronger. "And thank Gaia."

# FORTY-NINE

They made it back down the mountain about two hours later. Varden was weak and slow, but they were going down instead of up, and Marina was relieved that his breathing was steady and his color was normal.

Eli had retrieved the spray bottle with what was left of the Volvoticus bacteria and poured it out onto the ground, allowing Gaia to absorb it.

"We don't know if there's any more of it anywhere," said Varden in a voice low with fatigue, "but there was never much of it to begin with. Hedron is gone, and I believe that with him died the secret. There's no reason to believe he had more of it anywhere—and the origin of the bacteria was never found."

Once they got back to the guesthouse, Marina was able to find a local doctor to check over Varden—against the patient's wishes. He claimed he felt fine, that he was healing thanks to the honey and Gaia, but Marina prevailed. But as the nearest place with serious medical capability was Leh, there was little the doctor could do but check vitals and provide some antibiotic.

She was about to insist on taking a car to Leh when the guesthouse owner came to the room she shared with Varden, and with him was Gulam.

Marina said nothing as the elderly man—who looked at her intently for a long moment before turning to Varden—approached the patient.

He laid his hands on Varden and began to chant as he closed his eyes.

Eli, who'd been offered a tiny room at a nearby guesthouse, looked at Marina but remained silent.

When Gulam was finished, he opened his eyes and looked at Varden. Then he turned to Marina and Eli. The dark, intense gaze seemed to delve deep inside her as the old man spoke. "You did right. He will heal." Then he touched Marina ever so gently on the hand as he passed by to leave. "Tomorrow, Daughter of Gaia," he said.

Despite the shaman's prognosis, Marina stayed with Varden for the rest of the evening, other than to eat dinner in the dining room. She sent brief updates to Gabe and Helen back in the US and let them know the imminent threat was contained. She'd fill them in with more details when she was Stateside.

Eli left for his own guesthouse shortly after the evening meal—which was late and crowded due to the festival.

When Marina returned to her room, she found Varden awake and aware.

"Eli?" he asked, his voice still rough.

"Gone to his room," she told him. "Tomorrow Gulam will take us to the bee."

Varden nodded, and she wondered whether he would be able to join them.

"Thank you," he said as she pulled up a chair next to him.

Marina nodded, and before she knew what she was doing, she brushed the short hair back from his forehead. He reached up, closing his fingers around her wrist...then brought her palm to rest on his chest.

She felt the thumping of his heart—steady, strong—and the rush of awareness she'd been fighting since the first time they met.

When she looked up, she found he was watching her.

The animosity she was used to seeing in those hard, brilliant eyes was gone. Instead, there was something else. Something that made her belly quiver.

"Mariska," he whispered, and she felt the sound of her name—her *real* name—settle deep inside her.

Wordlessly, she smoothed her hand over his chest—warm, taut, muscular—and when he gently pulled on her wrist, drawing her closer, she met him halfway.

When Marina woke the next morning, Varden was gone. She was alone, in the rumpled single bed they'd shared. The realization and memory of the night past shocked her, but she had no regrets. None at all.

She was shocked, however, to learn that he was actually gone. That Varden had left without a word, without a farewell.

He was simply *gone*.

Perhaps it was best, she realized. They'd had a connection here in this special place, during this desperate time…but that was over, and nothing changed the fact that he resented her for any number of reasons.

And she resented him for his interference in her life.

When Eli arrived at the guesthouse, he seemed only mildly surprised that Varden had left.

"You scared him off," he said with a quirky smile that made her give a husky laugh.

Eli might be right. Last night had been pretty amazing.

"Are you ready to meet your bee?" she asked, tucking her hand into the crook of his arm.

"Let's go," he said.

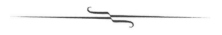

Marina wondered whether their travel to the bee was going to be a shamanic journey or one on foot, and her question was answered immediately as Gulam began to walk.

She and Eli followed him for a long time, with Manish bringing up the rear. There was no pathway to speak of; Gulam simply knew where to go, walking rapidly along the rocky ground away from the village and up. He climbed over boulders with surprising agility and skirted the rough, narrow ledges that jutted from the unforgiving side of the mountain.

After a time, they reached a sort of valley—though valley was a strange word, for this dip between mountain peaks was high above the ground level of the village. But the place was a small glen, protected on all sides by sheer rocky walls. A few trees grew in the rugged, stony ground, and flowers bloomed among the patches of grass. Marina spotted a golden eagle circling above.

But it was Eli who saw the bee.

He gave a soft, adorable sort of gasp and froze. His eyes were trained on a flower in front of him, and he slowly lowered himself as if to keep from frightening the insect.

"Hello, you," he said quietly. "You're just as beautiful as I'd imagined."

Smiling, Marina watched him. The boyish affection was there, mingling with the scientist who was carefully examining every detail of the rose-gold bee.

When she looked up, she was surprised to see that Gulam and Manish were gone. How strange that they should bring them up here to this secret place and then leave.

She felt a pang of regret that Varden wasn't there, then pushed it away. He had his reasons for what he did and didn't do, where he went and didn't go.

Marina shrugged, then stepped closer to Eli so she could see the bee. By now, he was sitting among the flowers and grasses and there was one bee crawling delicately along his finger, while another one bopped from bloom to bloom.

"I need to see the hive," he said, glancing up with glowing eyes. "I have to observe their communal and societal habits. And I really want to see the queen." He rose slowly, careful not to disrupt the bee that still sat on his finger. "Look at her—she's just sitting here, like she's surveying her domain. And no stinger, so no chance of being injured."

"If you ask her, she'll take you to the hive," Marina said, somehow knowing this was true.

"I'm asking," Eli murmured, still looking at his little lovely. "May I see your hive?"

Bee left his finger gracefully and began to dart through the air. Eli trampled after her, with Marina in his wake.

Although she knew this was no shamanic journey, Marina nevertheless still felt the intensity of the place, of the specialness of the place. She absorbed every detail, every texture, every scent, every sound as she and Eli followed the bee.

It wasn't a difficult climb, along the side of the rugged mountain. But it was a hidden one, an obscure one.

And when they came to a jagged, narrow opening in the side of the rocky wall, Eli paused to look back at her. "This is it," he said. His eyes danced; his entire body danced. And then he stepped back and gestured for her to precede him.

# FIFTY

The cave opening was narrow and rough, but Marina didn't hesitate. She slipped through the slender aperture and waited to turn on any illumination. She didn't want to upset the bees.

Eli was right behind her—she could have let him go first, since he was straining at the bit to see his "lovelies." But she was the caver, and she was Gaia's daughter. And he had gestured for her to precede him.

She led the way into the depths of the mountain.

The gentle buzz from the bees surrounded her, and as she eased in further, Marina felt the warmth and comfort of Gaia's embrace. Here, deep in the mountainside, well into Her womb, there was something like magic. It smelled damp and cool, yet not too cold—surprisingly.

Eli's breathing was quiet, but she could hear the excitement in it and smiled to herself. For him, this was like the first time she'd seen the Lost Library of Tsar Ivan. They were wonders that were unknown and kept secret from not only the world at large, but also scholars who would study and appreciate them.

A soft light came on—from his mobile phone—but he kept it trained onto the ground rather than blasting it over the bees. The moment reminded her of their experience with the copper beetles in the Amazon—how any sort of light sent them into a frenzy.

Obviously, the Apis patricia—as he'd been calling it—was used to the light. And indeed, rather than shunning it, these rosy-gold insects flocked to it in gentle clouds, as if they were curious about this new development.

She heard the quiet, choking gasp of delight from her companion as he stood unmoving for a moment, enjoying the swarm of the harmless and fragile creatures.

The beam of illumination revealed that the cave had opened from a two-foot-wide passage into one about five feet wide and seven feet tall. The rough, rocky walls were damp, with shiny rivulets trickling to the uneven floor. Following Eli's lead, Marina turned on the light from her own phone and carefully scanned the area.

With a jolt of excitement, she saw that there were markings—carvings—on one of the walls. Sanskrit for certain, and—*whoa*—was that Aramaic? Shock rippled through her. Aramaic in a Himalayan cave? That would be…unbelievable. Her chest felt tight as she stared at the letters…and read them.

"There it is," Eli said in a hushed voice that nonetheless was filled with excitement. "*There it is.*"

Marina knew he was speaking of the hive, but when she looked where he'd aimed the light, it didn't look anything like what she'd imagined.

A small clay urn sat on the cave floor, nestled against the wall. It looked similar to the pot that had been in Jill Fetzer's box—same color and type of mud. This urn was perhaps three feet tall and less than a foot wide.

And there were bees, flying into and out of it and around it.

And above and around the small urn, the hive clung to the wall. It was as if the hive had grown from its original moorings—the urn, or had the hive merely been built around it?—and expanded over the years.

Centuries.

*Millennia.*

Marina was aware, fully aware, of how shocking and radical this discovery was. It was mind-blowing on so many fronts.

She swiftly, mentally, corrected herself. It wasn't a discovery. It was a *secret*. Something that had been kept so for all this time. Gulam and his people knew about it, and had known about it, protected it—probably since the beginning.

Since this urn was brought here by Jesus of Nazareth. Saint Issa—

whose name was etched in Sanskrit on the wall, just as it had been on the small clay pot, and could very well also be on the urn.

"It was a traveling beehive," Eli said, his voice still low with reverence. "I'm sure of it—they—*he*—would have carried it on his back and traveled around. He probably healed people...visited them and healed them, taking the bees with him... Dear God... I could never have imagined something like this..."

Nor could Marina.

"They're so social," he said, crouching in front of the hive. His light didn't bother the bees. "I need to see the queen... I have to—"

There was a shift in the air, the softest of sounds behind them—maybe not even a sound. Just a presence. Marina spun as Eli tumbled onto his butt, his phone clattering to the ground.

The man standing there was familiar to both of them. Tall, muscular, dark of hair, olive of skin, wearing black from head to toe. The beam of her light landed on his wrist, revealing the tattoo with the letters IEMS.

The priest.

# FIFTY-ONE

"How did you find us?" Marina said, uttering the first words that came to mind. There were many more questions, but that one came out first.

The priest glanced at Eli. "He wears those sandals everywhere, doesn't he? Even mountain climbing. Still," he said, looking back at Marina, "I didn't need a tracker to come here."

"You know—knew—about this place," she said as Eli pulled himself to his feet.

"Of course." He shined the light in the space, slowing its movement over the urn hive and then settling on the Aramaic on the wall. "This is the closest one can come to Him, to being where He once was. To feeling it…" The priest's voice was quiet, hardly above a whisper.

Eli nodded next to her; she felt the same reverence and awe emanating from both of these men.

"And it's a secret," she replied.

"As it must remain," said the priest. "Surely you understand that."

"But why?" Eli burst out—still keeping his voice low. "It's a discovery that should be shared instead of kept to itself. It's—it's *amazing*. It's earth-shattering. It's—it's beyond anything I could ever have imagined—the connection of Jesus to the Buddhists, to Asia, the Silk Road—and the *bee*. She's unique and she should be studied—"

"*To what end?*" The priest's voice was cold and hard, and Marina felt a quiver of nerves. He hadn't killed them back in Ann Arbor, but that didn't mean he wouldn't now.

After all, someone had killed Patty Denke to keep this secret. And Jill Fetzer, and Tina Janeski…and who knew who else?

And she understood why.

Eli didn't respond. Marina felt the tension in his body and wasn't certain whether it was from anger or simply strong emotion.

"It cannot happen," replied the priest. "This can never be made known for many reasons I'm certain you understand. The least of which is—what would happen to this most holy and sacred of places? People would come here, droves of them, pilgrims, and then tourists, and then the big corporations—and the governments would get involved and they would fight over this land. So much of this area is already in dispute between the Chinese and the Tibetans, the Indians and the Pakistanis. We cannot draw attention to it. All of that—and it wouldn't be long before the place was destroyed. The habitat of these precious creatures would be dismantled. Surely you understand that, Dr. Sanchez." He turned his attention to Marina. "As I know you do, Dr. Aleksandrov."

She nodded. Everything he said was true. She understood it. She knew it. She *agreed* with it…and yet the scholar in her fought against it.

But her heart, her head, her *soul* understood.

"Your own grandfather sent you here, did he not?" the priest went on. "Because he wanted you to see the connection—to understand it—between that which is sacred, that which is holy…how it is all connected, all the same, all from the One."

Marina's heart was thudding so fast and so hard that she was certain the noise was echoing off the sides of the cave. The sound filled her ears like a drumbeat…a shamanic drumbeat.

"But the honey," Eli said desperately. "It's—"

"Miraculous," supplied the priest. "Yes. Of course it is. Everything here is miraculous. And that is why it cannot be revealed. Think what would happen, Dr. Sanchez. You know the faults of man. You know the greed of humans. You *know* what would happen. You know."

Silence fell among the three of them. The only noise was the gentle, incessant buzzing from the bees as they went about their business.

"Are you going to kill us?" Eli asked as he idly watched one of the bees trotting along his hand. "To keep the secret?"

"Do I need to?" replied the priest. "I truly despise confessing mortal sins."

Marina nearly laughed at the unexpected wit, and she saw the flicker of a reactive smile from the priest.

"The penance would be brutal," Eli replied.

The priest didn't respond, leaving Marina to wonder whether he knew about such penance from firsthand experience.

As the silence stretched, Marina caught a movement from the corner of her eye. She looked over toward the hive.

Gulam was there. He hadn't come from the entrance of the cave. He stood silently, unmoving. There was a faint glow around him…or maybe she was imagining it.

Marina glanced at the priest and found him watching the old man—the shaman.

Her heart pounded harder inside, thudding strongly, reminding her again of the beat of a drum. She touched the nearest wall of the cave and felt Gaia's presence as the drumbeat of her heart grew ever stronger and more powerful.

When Eli collapsed without warning, slumping to the ground, she gave a cry…but found she couldn't move to see to her companion. She looked at the priest, but he watched the shaman. The old man's eyes were wide and unseeing. His toothpick arms had moved slightly away from his body and his fingers were splayed, outstretched, in front of him.

The walls of the cave closed in around her—cold, hard, strong… alive. The buzz of the bees filled her ears, the drumbeat pounded inside her, and the mountain embraced her.

And she slipped away.

# FIFTY-TWO

When Marina opened her eyes, she was sitting on the same boulder on the same ledge where she'd met Gulam for the first time, and where she'd returned from her journey to seeing Lev and the other holy ones.

Eli was lying on the ground next to her, looking decidedly uncomfortable with the way he'd landed—or whatever the term was for how they'd traveled back to this location.

Marina knew they hadn't been on a shamanic journey to the hive. She knew they'd really walked there themselves, really found the place, really seen the markings on the wall, read the Sanskrit and Aramaic that were truly real…spoken with the priest.

But somehow, they'd returned here—to where she considered the starting point of her connection with Gulam.

It didn't matter how they got here; the message was clear.

Marina not only understood it, but accepted it as truth. The bee and the hive would continue to be a well-kept, sacred secret.

Whether Eli would come to the same conclusion remained to be seen, but Marina suspected that even if he didn't or couldn't acknowledge it, he wouldn't be able to find his way there again.

Not without Marina.

At that moment, Eli groaned and his eyes fluttered open. He pulled himself to a sitting position on the ground, wincing as his palm settled on a sharp rock.

"What the hell was that?" he muttered.

"That, I believe, was your first experience with shamanism," Marina replied with a smile.

His face fell. "Do you mean that was a journey? It wasn't real?"

She wasn't going to lie to him—it *had* been real—although allow-ing him to believe otherwise would be the simplest way to ensure he didn't divulge the secret. But Marina had far more respect and affec-tion for Eli than that.

"It was real," she replied.

He began to push to his feet and then stilled. Gingerly he settled back onto the ground while staring at the top of his hand.

She saw it then too: the small, rosy-gold bee, picking its way over the ridge of tendon on the back of his hand.

Eli drew in a low breath and carefully shifted to a comfortable position, staring down at the bee. "She's so beautiful," he murmured, moving a finger next to the roving insect so she'd crawl onto it. "So unique. Sacred."

He watched the Apis patricia for a long while, and then looked up at Marina. There was sadness in his eyes. "She has to be protected."

Marina nodded. There was a lump in her throat and she swallowed it back. There was something about this place that heightened every one of her emotions and awareness. And now she understood its power and sacredness.

It was the Seventh Chakra of Gaia.

# EPILOGUE

*Vatican City*

Theodore Villiani jolted in his chair as the door to his office opened unexpectedly.

He looked over, furious, prepared to berate whoever had the gall to invade his privacy so appallingly...but the words died in his throat. His entire body went numb, then flushed hot, then turned cold.

Very, very cold.

The man who'd stepped through the door closed it behind him, and Villiani heard the distinct *snick* of the lock being turned. The intruder, who was dressed all in black except for the neat white tab of his collar, strode silently across the plush rug to stand in front of Villiani's desk.

"Who are you?" Villiani demanded, although he had a horrible suspicion that he already knew the identity of the interloper. He'd never met him, but he knew of him. Who here in the upper echelons of the Holy See, privy to all the secrets of the Vatican, did not? "Wh-what are you doing here?"

"I come with a message, Your Eminence," said the priest. His tone was properly deferent, his demeanor calm. But Villiani's bowels were churning, and he could hardly think over the roaring in his ears. The look in this man's eyes...

*Dear God, Heavenly Father, please...please spare me...*

Nonetheless, Villiani must at least attempt to remain in control. Surely the man wouldn't kill him in his own office. "H-how did you get past...?"

The man gave him a patronizing smile. "I have a wide range of resources and talents, Your Eminence, all made available to me by His Holiness. As you surely are aware. Which is why I was startled—to be clear, startled in an unpleasant way—to learn that someone had contacted Ludo Rastinoff about a particular matter involving a bee."

A trickle of icy sweat ran down Villiani's spine, and from his armpits on both sides. He'd hoped no one would find out—he'd prayed and fasted and begged…but God had not listened.

And now Villiani's mistake was about to catch up with him.

"I-I trust the matter has been taken care of," replied Villiani in a voice that squeaked only a little.

"It has," replied the priest. "But not without some interference and some unnecessary unpleasantries." He placed both hands on the desk and leaned over it toward Villiani.

Terrified, Villiani tried to keep breathing and to keep his bowels from releasing at the same time. He bounced his eyes around wildly, fearful of meeting those of the man in front of him, and finally his attention landed on the priest's wrist. He saw the markings there, the large dots representing the decade of a rosary circling the dark wrist, and the band of letters—IENS—that connected them.

There was no question of the man's identity. Not any longer.

Dear God, it *was* him.

It was Leo Colón.

Villiani struggled to swallow. He truly thought he was about to faint. His shirt was soaked. He knew the stories about this man. What he was capable of.

"Three people died," Colón went on evenly, starkly. "Unnecessarily. Because of that clumsy, inelegant dolt. You'll confess those lost lives as sins, Your Eminence."

"Yes," Villiani whispered, his throat squeaking as he swallowed.

"You'll do penance," Colón continued. "And you will never contact Ludo Rastinoff or his like again. For any reason."

Villiani could only nod.

Did this mean he might live after all?

Colón eased back. A small smile played on his handsome face, reminding Villiani of a cat toying with a trapped mouse. "Because if you do, I will know." That was a definite promise. A cold one.

Villiani nodded again, swallowing hard.

Colón pulled a folded purple stole from his pocket, kissed it most reverently, and draped it over his shoulders. He sat in the chair that faced the desk and turned those dark, intense, all-knowing eyes to Villiani.

With shaking hands and trembling knees, Villiani rose from his desk and came around toward him. He knelt at the priest's feet.

With a quavering voice, he began, "Bless me, Father, for I have sinned…"

# A Note from the Author

Thank you so much for reading the latest Marina Alexander adventure. It took me far longer than I ever anticipated to pull this story together, but I hope you enjoyed reading it as much as I did writing it—at least, once I got near the end and could see how everything fit together.

If you enjoyed the book, I would greatly appreciate it if you would spread the word about the book. Word of mouth is the first and best way to ensure and promote the success of a series, and the more readers of the series, the more books that will be written. I also appreciate reviews of any length posted on Amazon, Goodreads, or anywhere else.

I always like to take a few moments at the end of the Marina books to let you know which parts are true and which parts are, shall we say, scientifically possible but not necessarily *probable*. (That's the phrase I use when talking to my "experts" when doing research on these books, and the "what ifs" that I posit.)

The first thing you should know is that Nicolas Notovitch absolutely did exist, he lived in Paris, had traveled to Tibet, and he did write the book called *The Secret Life of Jesus Christ* (which really was translated into English by Alexina Donovan for Rand McNally in Chicago). The book is still available (I've read it), and although the titillating idea that Jesus of Nazareth lived in India has been debunked by many people over the years…I'm not necessarily convinced it's not true.

I have close friends who've studied with the scholar, philosopher, and Jain leader Chitrabanhu, who claimed that it's quite well-known in India that St. Issa was Jesus of Nazareth, and that he did live there both during the "lost years"—between the age of twelve and thirty—and possibly even after his death by crucifixion. I also believe what Eli said when confronted with the idea: that the Catholic Church and other Christian leaders would be very determined to keep such information under wraps, for any number of reasons.

So I leave that with you: whether Jesus lived and traveled throughout India remains to be proven, but I believe it's likely—at least during his younger years. Because where did he go during that time? His life was in danger, and to stay in Israel would have been a death sentence.

What is completely fictional, however, is the idea of Jesus traveling about with a bee hive. There certainly could have been mobile bee hives as described—we transport honeybees today in order to make certain crops are pollinated—but I have no reason to believe Jesus, or St. Issa, had one of his own.

However, all of the Apis bee facts that Eli shares throughout the story are accurate, including that honey never spoils and that it has healing properties. The germ of the idea for this book actually came when I read about jars of honey being found in Egyptian tombs, and that the honey was unspoiled in unopened vessels.

Dr. Patricia Denke—the real person, not the fictional one—helped me to create the Apis patricia with which Eli becomes enamored. Therefore, the description and characteristics of the bee are right from the mind and heart of an entomologist.

Most of the information about glacier melt and its environmental effects is true—including the "ice stupas"—the huge frozen fountains—that were created in Ladakh in order to preserve the quickly-melting glacier water. The special colloidal "fountain of youth" water that Allen Schleuter is so excited about is a product of my imagination, but what he says about unknown bacteria being uncovered by melting glaciers, and the idea of special colloids in the water, are accurate.

The Volvoticus bacteria is also my own creation, however there was a team of scientists at CalTech (as described in the book) that accidentally discovered a metal-eating bacteria. My bacteria is simply a derivation of that one—but much faster and more powerful.

The descriptions of New Delhi are are based on the personal travel experiences of friends. The descriptions of Ladakh, the Tse-dup festival, the Buddhist gompa, the guest houses, and the flora and fauna, are all from my research—so any errors or inconsistencies are my own.

Additionally, the cave rescue that Marina Alexander, Adele, and poor lovelorn Bruce undertake is based on the similar, but with a far more tragic end, search and rescue operation known as the Nutty Putty Cave incident near Salt Lake City in 2009. I'm relieved that my fictional team had more success than the rescuers in real life.

In closing, I'd like to acknowledge that this book took a definite turn toward the metaphysical. But for me, it was the natural progression of Marina's character development. As I am a firm believer in the concept of Universal Consciousness, it makes so much sense to me that Marina, the daughter of Gaia, would feel a connection to Her, especially when in the area of the world near the Himalayan mountains. When I began writing and researching the book, I didn't realize that geographical area is considered by many to be the Seventh Chakra of the Earth—but it certainly made sense to me the more I researched the region, as well as how my characters and story worked out.

Thank you once again for reading *Sanskrit Cipher*. I would love to hear from you if you have thoughts or questions—I can be reached via my website (colleengleason.com) or email books@colleengleason. com.

—C. M. Gleason
June 2021

# Acknowledgments

I have many people to thank for helping me with this book. It took nearly five years to write, and it was one of those projects that I nearly gave up on multiple times. If it hadn't been for many of these people, I would not have a finished manuscript today.

First, Patricia Denke was instrumental in helping me with all of the entomological facts and practices in this (and the previous) book.

Gary March, my on-call medical expert and jack of all trades when it comes to knowing about random facts, poked, prodded, and pushed me over the last years to get this book finished. As well, his wife Darlene Domanik, and my other friends Erin Wolfe, MaryAlice and Dennis Galloway, as well as my husband, listened to me talk about this book *ad nauseam* over the last several years—and all of them had ideas and thoughts that helped push me to find the ending. Darlene in particular helped me with the Nicolas Notovitch angle as well as shared her personal travel experiences in India.

Big thanks to Marion Graham for checking me on the microbiology and bacteriology front—she was the one who said, yes, it's possible (but not necessarily probable)!

Myah Price was my go-to person about the campus of University of Illinois at Champaign-Urbana, and the neat map she marked up really helped me negotiate Eli's escape route.

And big thanks to Tammy Kearly for doing an early read of the pieces of this book so that I could ramble on about how to make everything work. Thank you for being my figurative shoulder to cry on!

And finally, thanks to Diane Davidson and Joyce Doele for giving it their eagle eyes for a final read.

Once again, I'm beyond grateful to all of you for your support—both emotional and literary—over the years. I wonder how long it'll take me to write the next one!

—C.M. Gleason
June 2021

**C.M. Gleason** is the pen name of the award-winning, *New York Times* and *USA Today* best-selling author Colleen Gleason, who has written more than thirty novels in a variety of genres. Her international bestselling series, the Gardella Vampire Hunters, is an historical urban fantasy about a female vampire hunter who lives during the time of Jane Austen.

Most recently, her Stoker & Holmes series for teens and adults has received wide acclaim from *The New York Times, Library Journal,* and is a YALSA (Young Adult Library Services Association) pick.

She has published more than thirty novels with New American Library, MIRA Books, Chronicle Books, and HarperCollins.

Her books have been translated into more than seven languages and are available worldwide.

## *Visit Colleen at:*
**colleengleason.com**
**facebook.com/colleen.gleason.author**
Or sign up for new book release information from
**Colleen Gleason at colleengleason.com/contact/**

Made in the USA
Columbia, SC
18 June 2021

40596511R00185